High
Potential

BER CARROLL

POOLBEG

Published 2007
by Poolbeg Press Ltd
123 Grange Hill, Baldoyle
Dublin 13, Ireland
E-mail: poolbeg@poolbeg.com

© Ber Carroll 2007

The moral right of the author has been asserted.

Typesetting, layout, design © Poolbeg Press Ltd.

1 3 5 7 9 10 8 6 4 2

A catalogue record for this book is available from the British Library.

ISBN 978-184223-225-5

Typeset by Type Design in Garamond 12/15
Printed by
Litografia Rosés S.A., Spain

www.poolbeg.com

About the Author

Ber Carroll was born in Blarney, County Cork, and moved to Australia in 1995. She worked as a finance director in the information technology industry until the release of her first novel, *Executive Affair*. She now lives in the Northern Beaches of Sydney with her husband and two children. Her second novel *Just Business* was also published by Poolbeg.

Acknowledgements

Thanks, as always, to the whole team at Poolbeg, especially Paula Campbell and Gaye Shortland.

Thanks to Brian Cook, my literary agent plus much more.

Thanks to Anna Kassulke and Amanda Longmore for your perceptive comments and wise recommendations.

For matters of law, medicine, geography, technology and history: a special thanks to Siobhan Lyndon, Anita Kanetkar, Harry Carroll, Rowena Tunks, Carol Long (Associate Producer of TV show *RPA*), Eric Carroll, Dee Woodward, Denis O'Mahony, Luke Wegener, Mark Worley, Martina Crowley, Sister Sarto and June Goulding (author of *The Light in the Window*).

Rob, your critical eye and unwavering support is evidenced in every page of this book.

Finally, a heartfelt thank-you to my family, friends, and all those who have read *Executive Affair* and *Just Business*. I hope you enjoy this one!

For Nellie

Chapter 1

"Sounds like a good party going on in there," the taxi driver commented.

Kylie Horgan nodded as she rummaged through her large black holdall. "It's my mum's birthday."

She found her wallet and handed the driver a crinkled twenty-dollar note.

"Keep the change," she said and got out.

"Thanks," he replied through the open window. He bared his pearly white teeth in a lopsided grin as he added, "The Irish sure know how to party."

She was about to ask how he knew their nationality when she registered the telltale music belting from the house.

She laughed. "Oh, the music! It's a good thing all the neighbours are at the party and aren't likely to complain about the noise."

He gave her a funny look. "Actually, it wasn't the music. It was you — those blue eyes had to be Irish."

Kylie did a second take, not sure if he was making an innocent observation or coming on to her. From the suggestion in his dark eyes, it appeared to be the latter.

"Call me if you would like to go out some time." He held out his business card. "Irish girls are good fun."

"Thanks, but no thanks."

"Got a boyfriend?"

"That's none of your business."

"Sorry, no offence intended. Enjoy your party."

He drove off, wheels spinning. Kylie laughed; she had never been propositioned right outside her parents' house before. Stephen, her brother, would find it hilarious too, but her mum and dad would be less amused. Better not say anything when she went inside.

Kylie walked up the short drive to the modest red-brick house. The door was unlocked and she let herself in. The hall ended in a homely kitchen with a latticed window and pretty hand-made curtains.

Food cluttered the countertop in varied states of preparation, and three of her mother's friends jostled for space as they prepared to feed the hordes. They greeted her with family-like familiarity.

"Kylie – you look tired – working too hard, I suppose."

"Kylie – you're late – your mother's out on the deck."

"Here, Kylie, can you carry this salad out with you?"

Kylie fondly returned their greetings and took the bowl outside, where the party was in full swing. Frankie and Rose Horgan were the centre of attention as they waltzed around the deck to "Sweet Sixteen".

"Kylie," Frankie called out when he saw his only daughter come through the French doors, "did you know your mother was just sweet sixteen when I first met her?"

"Yes, I did know, Dad."

Kylie shared a smile with Stephen. Frankie had told them a hundred times, if not more.

"And she's as beautiful today as she was back then," was his next predictable statement.

Rose shook her head in affectionate exasperation. "And you talk as much rubbish today as you did back then!"

She didn't look the sixty years she was celebrating, her hair more blonde than grey and her figure trim. Even her voice sounded girlish with its soft Irish lilt.

They finished the dance to a round of applause and Frankie went back to his post at the barbecue. His rough builder's hands were clumsy as they manoeuvred the tongs around the meat. He was still ill at ease with the art of barbecuing, despite the fact that he had lived in Australia for forty-three years.

"I'm an Irishman, not an Aussie," he would say later in self-defence when his guests would josh him about the blackened meat.

But for now, at least, the guests were enjoying a glass of wine and not paying too much attention to the warning signs of carnage on the barbeque grill. The last rays of sun warmed the wooden beams under their sandalled feet. *Happy Birthday, Rose*, stretched in a banner over their heads and flapped with the tail end of a breeze that gusted in from Botany Bay.

"You look tired, love," Rose said to Kylie.

"So I've already been told," she replied wryly. "Work has been busy. In fact, I had to go in to the office this morning."

"On a Sunday?"

Rose's disapproving tone seemed to bring a lull to the various conversations that were going on around them.

"Yeah," Kylie answered, keeping her voice low so it could be heard only by her parents. "I'll be away the week after next so I'm trying to get ahead."

Stephen lumbered over, beer in hand. "Did I just hear that you're going away?" he asked in his booming voice, thwarting Kylie's attempt to keep the conversation private. "Anywhere exotic?"

Stephen worked as an engineer in the family business, and due to all the time he spent on noisy construction sites, he was totally oblivious to the volume of his voice.

"It's a residential course at the Hunter Valley."

"What's the course on?"

Five years her senior, he took a keen interest in Kylie's career. Well aware that he was under-utilising his own talents, he seemed to need occasional reassurance that his sister was taking advantage of every opportunity that came her way.

"It's a High Potential programme," Kylie told him. "Six senior associates have been selected from the Sydney practice – they put us through training and three of us will be offered a partnership at the end of the year."

Her mother looked dubious. "It sounds like some kind of competition."

Rose had a knack for hitting the nail right on the

head and Kylie laughed. "You know what, Mum? That's exactly what it is when you cut it down to its most basic level."

"The others won't stand a chance against our Kyls," said Stephen, only half joking. "They should give you one of the partnerships straight up and fight amongst themselves for the other two places."

Kylie smiled. "Thanks for the vote of confidence but it will be a very even field."

"You mean the others are as determined and competitive as you?" he asked, cocking one bushy eyebrow.

"I don't know who they are yet, but I can assure you that they're *worse* than me. They'll be seeing dollar signs and won't care who they trample on to win."

"You know, kiddo, you're improving my impression of lawyers by the minute," he declared, ruffling his fair hair as if perplexed by the ruthlessness of it all.

They all laughed except Rose. "Does this programme mean that you'll have to travel?" she asked, her face telling that she would much rather see her daughter settled down than jet-setting around the world.

"Yes, possibly," Kylie replied when the truth was "Yes, definitely". The programme incorporated a compulsory four-month overseas assignment. However, she didn't want to divulge that news on her mother's birthday.

"No chance of getting back with Geoff, then?" asked Jean, their next-door neighbour, plump, kindly and totally tactless. It seemed that the conversation was now a free-for-all.

"No." Kylie felt herself tensing. Considering everybody there regarded themselves as pseudo aunts and uncles with the accompanying concern about her welfare, it wasn't surprising that they felt compelled to ask about her broken engagement. But the fact it was expected didn't necessarily mean it was any easier to talk about.

"Geoff couldn't keep up with our Kylie," said Alexander, a big, meaty Russian who had met Frankie Horgan on a construction site long before Kylie was born. "You're a career girl – eh, Kylie?"

All eyes on her now, Kylie mustered a smile, as if Alexander was right on the mark.

If only the situation with Geoff was as simple as me putting my career first, she thought.

However, she acknowledged that Alexander had seen her graduate through nappies, braces and sullen teenage rebellion before finding herself at university. Maybe he knew her better than she knew herself.

"Career won't buy you love –" Jean started to say.

"Where's Annie?" Kylie asked, changing the subject abruptly. "She told me she was coming."

Annie, Jean's daughter, was her closest friend. With only six months between them, they had been inseparable from toddlers to teenagers. Kylie had been maid of honour when Annie got married last year and she was godmother to her six-month-old baby boy, Zack.

Jean tutted with disapproval. "Zack is acting up again. I told Annie that being a mother was much harder work than a high-flying career — but she didn't listen. You young girls —"

Jean stopped in her tracks when angry amber flames whooshed from the barbecue. The burning fat sizzled and hissed as Frankie madly swatted the fire with his spatula. By the time it was under control, Jean forgot the advice she had been about to impart and the conversation moved on. Kylie breathed a sigh of relief and hoped that was the last she would hear of Geoff for the night.

*   *   *

The party didn't wind up until the early hours of the morning. Kylie walked Jean, who was more than a little tipsy, next door and then joined the rest of the family on the deck. The night possessed the chill of a looming winter and they had traded in short sleeves for fleece sweaters many hours before.

"Comfortable?" Stephen enquired as she stretched her denim-clad legs along the cane lounge.

"Not yet," she replied and propped some cushions behind her back. "Now I'd be entirely comfortable if you would pour me a glass of wine."

"Bloody hell – if you become a partner you'll want me to drop grapes in your mouth as well," he complained as he reached for the bottle of Chardonnay.

She smiled while thinking that nobody would be happier than Stephen if she got the partnership. They were very close and she was as ambitious for him as he was for her. He deserved the best, in his personal life as well as his career. Yet he was the first to admit that he was thirty-six and failing in both departments.

With the cool oak taste in her mouth, Kylie sank deeper into the weathered cushions of the lounge. She loved it out here on the deck. Frankie had built it when she was in her mid-teens. Right from the start, their whole family life revolved around the new deck, the perfect place to read, eat, socialise and relax. Potted plants, crowded along the base of the pale green fencing, added their scent to the sun-baked wooden beams and burned barbecue coals. Kylie took a deep breath in, storing up the calmness, creating a reserve to get her through the hectic week ahead.

The minutes ticked comfortably by until Rose broke the silence.

"I told people they needn't bring anything," she said, shaking her head at the table full of gifts and cards. Charmingly unpretentious, she never expected others to make a fuss of her.

Kylie came out of her reverie. "They only want to mark the occasion, Mum. There are some beautiful things here." She swung her legs down and reached for one of the cards.

Keep true to the dreams of your youth, Rose, and have a wonderful birthday,

From your dear friends,

Alice and Tom

Frankie and Rose's friends were akin to family; they replaced the people they had left behind in Ireland. Forty years' worth had gathered in the small house with the large deck to cheer Rose on as she entered a new decade of her life.

"I just wanted everybody to have a good time," said Rose. "Not to waste money –" She broke off as tears welled up in her eyes.

"Ah, come on now, Rose," said Frankie, drawing her to him in a gruff hug. "You're only a bit overwhelmed, that's all."

She sniffed and nodded simultaneously. "I know – I'm being silly – must be too much wine."

"Yeah, that second glass must have been your undoing," said Stephen flippantly. Rose rarely indulged in more than one alcoholic beverage.

"If only *you* stopped at two," she retorted, regaining her composure somewhat. "You'll have a fine head on you in the morning!"

Rose caught Kylie smirking into her glass of wine. "I don't know what you're laughing at – you're as bad as him – smoking yourself to death as well – thinking that I don't know what you do behind my back."

Kylie shrugged good-naturedly. "I know that you know – but I don't smoke in front of you out of respect."

Rose threw her eyes to heaven. Her motherly chiding was always underscored by a loving concern and her ability to laugh at all their foibles.

"Oh well, I'd better redeem myself and give you your birthday present." Kylie gave an exaggerated sigh as she put her glass down.

"I hope you haven't gone over the top!" said Rose.

"It's nothing that you don't deserve," Kylie replied. "Can you pass my bag, please, Stephen?"

He handed it over, grimacing at the weight of it. "Jesus! What do you keep in there?"

The bag's more sizeable contents included a

make-up pouch, an electronic diary and a bestselling novel. Smaller items, like old shopping lists, crumpled receipts and loose change, had gravitated to the bottom. Extremely ordered and tidy when it came to her work, Kylie was much less particular with her personal life. Chaos prevailed in both her handbag and her apartment.

The envelope for her mother came out looking a little tattered around the edges. Kylie leaned across to kiss Rose's cheek.

"Happy birthday, Mum!"

Rose tore cautiously along the envelope's seal. She slowly pulled out the contents and took a moment to read them.

"Tickets," her voice was faint, "to Ireland."

"To Ireland?" Frankie repeated incredulously.

They both stared down at the tickets in her quivering hand.

Kylie rushed in to fill the awkward silence. "You'll need to go for a few months – forty years is a lot to catch up on . . ." Her voice trailed away when it became evident that they didn't share her enthusiasm. "Sorry, Mum. Have I overwhelmed you again?"

Still no response. Kylie started to get a bad feeling. She shot a look at Stephen. He seemed to find their reaction as puzzling as she.

"Mum? Dad?" she prompted.

Only Frankie met her eyes. She instantly realised that he wasn't overwhelmed. He was utterly dismayed.

Chapter 2

"Mum, why are you crying?"

"I'm not crying."

"Yes, you are – I saw you."

"It's something in my eye."

"What is it? Let me look."

"Only a piece of dirt, I imagine."

"Your tissue is wet."

"I've been dabbing my eye."

"Are you sure you're not sad?"

"I'm fine, Kylie. Just fine. Now go and do your homework."

Kylie dragged her school satchel out to the deck. She laid

her books on the wooden table and decided to do her maths first. She carefully wrote the date on the top of the page: 11 June, 1984.

After dinner, Rose popped next door and Stephen went out on the street to have a kick around with his friends. Kylie had Frankie all to herself.

"Mum was crying today," she told him.

She saw him stiffen but he didn't deny it.

She continued to watch him very carefully. "Why was she crying, Dad?"

"Today is a sad day for her."

From the sound of his voice and the expression on his face, it seemed that it was a sad day for him too. She was about to ask why when they heard the all-too-familiar sound of smashing glass from the street.

"Don't tell me Stephen's put that ball through another window!" sighed Frankie.

He had, and with all the commotion that followed, both Kylie and her dad forgot all about the sad day.

Chapter 3

Kylie's computer screen danced in front of her eyes, the black print blurring into the white background. She blinked away the urge to sleep. The clock at the bottom of her screen indicated that she had only one hour to complete the draft contract for Citibank. Then Pete Wilde, the bank's legal counsel, would arrive at her office expecting a smiling lawyer, a near-perfect draft and a top-notch lunch. Yet again, she lamented that she hadn't left her parents' house earlier the night before. But she had been hanging out to give the tickets to her mother. What a let-down it had been in the end!

"Kylie!"

She jerked up her head when she heard the familiar no-nonsense voice. Claudine, the legal secretary she shared with three other senior associates, was standing at her door. Her auburn hair, cut in a brisk bob, framed a face that was prematurely furrowed with frown lines.

"You've been out all night!" she stated accusingly as her button-like eyes took in Kylie's exhausted face.

"It was my mum's birthday."

"Too much wine, too little sleep?"

"Precisely."

Claudine dealt with the demands and egos of her four bosses with steel-like efficiency. Kylie liked her and she was sure that beneath Claudine's brusqueness the feeling was reciprocated. The secretary's plain-speaking manner was a lifeline in what was sometimes a political snake-pit. Some days, without being aware of it, she helped Kylie keep her sanity.

"Then you won't be pleased that the launch of the High Potential programme has been moved," said Claudine.

"Don't tell me it's on tonight," Kylie groaned.

"Brent Lavell can't make Thursday and, as you are aware, *everything must revolve around Brent.*"

Brent Lavell was the Managing Partner of Morley

Ferguson James. He was an old-style leader who used a mix of bullying, fear and coercion to get results from the forty-odd partners and six hundred staff. Claudine's dislike of him was merited as he was particularly abominable to the legal secretaries.

"Don't say things like that too loud," Kylie cautioned her.

"It's not anything I wouldn't say to his face," she declared and huffed her way back to her desk.

I don't know what she's so put out about, Kylie thought with a weary sigh. *It's not as if she has to go to the launch.*

Her eyes returned to the text on her screen and she scrolled down as she scanned through the clauses. Tired as she was, she loved her job. She got great personal satisfaction from the attention to detail that was required to do it well. The underlying structure and justice to the law appealed to her own sense of order and fairness. Over the last year she had started to spend more face-to-face time with her clients, an aspect that she enjoyed enormously.

The midday sun filtered through the beige blinds and warmed her back as she worked. Small and functional, her office had pastel blue walls. A few bland prints hung here and there. The only hint of the personal was a framed family photograph on her desk. The offices of MFJ were places for work, not comfort, but Kylie didn't mind.

Her phone rang and she absently picked it up.

"Can you talk?"

It was Stephen.

"Only quickly. I have a contract for an overpaid executive that I need to finish."

"What did you make of last night?" he asked.

Kylie was sardonic. "You'd swear it was a five-thousand-dollar invoice I had given them and not a gift worth that amount."

"I've been thinking about it," he said in his slow, careful way. "Maybe they don't want to go back. After all, it's been forty years."

"How could you not want to go back to the country where you were born?" Kylie protested. "Where your brothers and sisters still live?"

"I don't know. Maybe something happened there . . ."

Kylie didn't have time to dwell on this for another familiar figure had appeared at her door: Neil Gatwood, her boss.

"I have to go, Stephen. I'll talk to you soon, OK?"

Neil leaned on the doorframe, hands in his pockets. Excessively thin and bespectacled, he was a nerd of a man. Nevertheless, he was Kylie's champion: the one who had pushed through her promotions, increased her visibility to the other partners and given her enough leeway to prove herself. She owed him a lot. Sometimes the debt was overwhelming.

"You didn't have to hang up on my account," he said, pushing his glasses higher up his nose, a constantly necessary action as they were far too big for him.

She shrugged. "It's not just you – I'm under pressure to get this contract done – Pete Wilde will be here soon."

"I won't delay you, then. I just wanted to check that you've heard about tonight."

"Yes, Claudine told me."

"Good. See you there."

There was little else to say. She and Neil had talked about the partnership many, many times. Now the time for talking was over. They both knew it was mostly up to her from here on in.

* * *

At 6 p.m. Kylie closed the door on the minimalist décor of her office. She yawned; it was eleven hours since she had started her work day, and a mere three hours' sleep was not enough fuel for her body to go the distance. Outside in the twilight, streams of people were making their way home and she wished she was one of them. She cursed Brent Lavell and his last-minute change of plans.

The restaurant was situated down in Darling Harbour, a twenty-minute walk from Park Street and a welcome chance to clear her head. She lit a cigarette and smoked as she walked. Her knee-high boots scrunched over dead leaves as she wondered who the other contenders were. There were ninety senior associates in all and an average of three a year got promoted to partner. It was a highly political process that, until now, had been conducted behind closed doors. Specialist knowledge, fee-earning history and client development were the criteria examined by the selection committee. If all else was equal, it came down to prejudice in terms of high school, golfing prowess and gender.

Kylie was under no illusion that Brent's greed was the primary motivator behind the High Potential programme. He was undoubtedly giving himself a pat on the back for a winning formula: allow six people to think they were in with a chance, reap the benefits while they work themselves to the bone and have no obligation to the three unlucky ones other than a "maybe next time".

Nevertheless, Kylie was excited about the opportunity. Even as far back as high school she had aspired to be a partner, and having an open competition somehow made the race fairer than it might otherwise have been. Kylie was well aware that she had two things working against her in MFJ: her gender and her early education. She possessed neither the testosterone nor the old schoolboy camaraderie to ingratiate herself with the senior partners. That left her with her fee-earnings, her experience and her clientele, all very commendable and hopefully enough to get her over the line in the two-to-one odds of the programme.

Heavy drops of rain started to fall as Kylie descended the steps to Cockle Bay and the tourists dived under the canopied shelter of the bars and restaurants. With no particular agenda, they could afford an impromptu drink while they waited for the rain to pass. Kylie was already a few minutes late and hurried on, intermittently looking up to check the neon-lighted name of each establishment. The rain quickly soaked into her hair and jacket. By the time she reached the end of the wharf, she was thoroughly wet and found temporary shelter while she called up Claudine's number on her mobile phone.

"I'm at the end of the wharf. I can't find the place."

"Go back towards the bridge and take the escalator to the second level," Claudine instructed, the sound of a TV in the background.

"Damn. I never thought of looking up there."

Kylie retraced her steps, her boots splashing through the fresh puddles of rainwater. The pouring rain was illuminated by the spectrum of lights that reflected off the dark waters of the harbour. She found the escalator and the restaurant was facing her when she reached the top. She was ten minutes late when she walked into the reserved function room at the back of the premises.

As soon as Kylie opened the door, she realised that she had underestimated what the launch of the programme entailed. Forty dark-suited champagne-drinking partners filled the room. Brent Lavell, with his silver hair and sallow skin, was up on the podium and the five other contenders formed a perfect line to his right. A few things struck Kylie in those first few moments. First: wet, bedraggled and looking her absolute worst, she would have to join the line of contenders. Second: Carole Matthews and Isobel Romero were there. With herself included, that made three women in total and an incredibly equal ratio of women to men. Third: behind the contenders, a large drop-down screen flashed the word *Congratulations!* and from what Brent was saying, it seemed that it was the catchphrase of the evening.

"And *congratulations* to Carole for boosting our cross-border business and qualifying for the programme!"

Carole smiled, elegant, poised, not a strand of smooth blonde hair out of place. Kylie didn't know her very well but the word around the corridors was that she was a Trojan worker, a talented lawyer and took no shit.

Brent spotted Kylie by the door.

"Kylie – you've arrived – nasty weather out there. Come and join us." With Kylie obediently in transit, he addressed the wider audience once more. "Last, but far from least, we have Kylie Horgan from Employee Law and Industrial Relations. Over the last two years, Kylie has made a name for MFJ in the financial-services industry and has been one of our top fee-earners. *Congratulations* on qualifying for the programme, Kylie!"

Isobel shot Kylie a sympathetic smile as she stepped onto the platform. Kylie, feeling like a drowned rat, grimaced in return. She turned to face the audience, a statuesque figure alongside the other two women. Isobel was the shortest, her dark hair level with Kylie's shoulder. Born and educated in Colombia, Isobel was very highly regarded by her clients and colleagues alike. She worked in the corporate division of MFJ and often put jobs Kylie's way. Kylie tried to return the compliment when she could. She was glad to see Isobel in the line-up; there was nobody more deserving of a partnership.

Brent moved on. "I am most proud of the fact that we have an equal representation of females and males in this programme because I am personally very committed to affirmative action . . ."

Somehow Kylie kept a straight face. The fact that just two of the forty existing partners were female spoke for itself. Brent's bias towards the men was even evident in the order he apparently had called the contenders to the podium: the men first, the women a lame afterthought.

". . . and I have no doubt but that they'll give the male contenders a run for their money."

Kylie knew the male contenders to varying degrees. David Smythe was the first in line. Sandy-haired and podgy, his appearance was rather like that of an overgrown schoolboy. David had been a senior associate for more than ten years and made it known to all that he considered a partnership his due. He specialised in taxation law and, on the occasions that Kylie had to consult with him, she found him self-satisfied, arrogant and totally humourless.

Jim Donnelly was next. Tall with rich brown hair and a strong lean face, he was physically as different to David as you could get. Jim had been seconded from the Dublin office a few years back. After contributing to some ground-breaking precedents on

Australian soil, rumour was that Brent had begged him to stay permanently. Now Jim travelled extensively around the state resolving disputes and, when settlement couldn't be reached, instructing barristers. As he was rarely in the Sydney office, Kylie only knew him well enough to exchange the most fleeting hello on the rare occasions that their paths crossed.

Oliver Thame was the third male contender and Kylie knew him the best. In fact, Oliver was good friends with Geoff and up to a few months previously they had socialised in the same circles. When the split became public, Oliver had approached Kylie to say how sorry he was and that he hoped they would still be friends. Kylie had been touched by his sincerity. At work Oliver was quiet, diligent and very suited to his specialisation in the government arena. On a social level he was less reserved and often had a naughty sense of humour.

As soon as she saw the other contenders, Kylie realised that the odds were not as good as she had initially thought. Jim and Isobel had a strong lead. That left Kylie, Carole, David and Oliver to fight for the third partnership. It would be a fierce and dirty fight. One that she wasn't at all sure she could win.

Brent was still talking and she tried to concentrate on what he was saying.

"This programme is an intensive training camp for the future partners of our business. Firstly, there will be a one-week residential course where you will learn the theory of leadership and explore your own leadership style. You will have a few weeks to put the leadership theory into practice here in Sydney before you depart on a four-month overseas assignment. Later in the year there will be a second residential where you will have the opportunity to share your overseas experience with your colleagues. Your performance at both residentials will be independently assessed by the facilitators and the feedback will form an important part of our decision. Your billable hours will be tracked while you are overseas and you will be expected to meet your annual target. Similarly, there will be no adjustment for the time spent away on the residential courses. It's tough at the top, guys!"

He laughed and there was a corresponding titter from the audience of champagne-drinking partners. But not one of the aspiring partners smiled. As it was they were expected to bill seven hours a day to clients. With emails and general admin often not billable, the only way to meet such a target was to work an inordinate amount of overtime. It would be nigh on impossible to rack up enough billable hours to offset the time they were away at the courses.

Brent was still smirking as he delivered his final words. "Due to the last-minute change in plans, we won't be having a sit-down meal tonight. Finger food will be served while we mingle and celebrate this important event."

Kylie stepped down from the podium with relief. She made a beeline for the rest rooms, where her reflection in the mirror was every bit as bad as she had expected.

How could anybody consider me a future partner looking like this? Why the hell didn't I get a taxi?

She rifled through her bag, looking for something she could use to tie back her damp hair. Amongst the loose change she spotted the sparkle of a crystal hair-clip. She wound her dark curls into a knot and clasped the clip into place.

The next area of emergency was her face. The downside of her porcelain skin was its propensity for pink cheeks, and the rush through the rain hadn't helped. She patted on some powder and, as a final touch, applied a coat of lip gloss. Then, a deep breath later, she was back in the room of piranhas.

The crowd had segregated into tidy knots in the few minutes she had been gone, a High Potential contender at the centre of most groups. She scanned the room, trying to decide where her efforts would be best spent. She set her sights on a group of less prominent partners who were talking amongst themselves.

"Kylie!" Tim Costello's lips smacked her cheek as she slipped in next to him. "Well done!"

Tim, Isobel's boss, was a warm-hearted, convivial man who didn't seem to be as money-oriented as the other partners. Once a mover-shaker amongst his colleagues, he was now close to retirement and had consequently taken a step back from the coalface.

"Thanks, Tim."

A waiter hovered nearby and Kylie caught his attention. She took a glass of champagne from his tray and downed a healthy gulp.

"You must be happy to see Isobel in the running," she said.

Isobel was Tim's protégée. Ten years ago she had been a raw graduate with a heavy foreign accent. With Tim's encouragement and mentoring, she was now at the top of her field.

Tim lowered his voice to respond. "I'm happy to see all you ladies up there. To tell the truth, I'm fed up of working with crusty old men."

"What's that you're saying, Tim?" Meredith Allen, one of the two female partners, joined their small group. A small harried woman in her early forties, Meredith had worked all the hours on earth to reach partnership level and now she looked totally worn out.

Tim put a friendly arm around Meredith's shoulders. "I'm saying we need a few more women around to shake things up."

"You can say that again."

Meredith had a razor-sharp intellect as well as a pleasant personality. She was always on the sidelines rallying for Kylie and the other female lawyers. The only negative about her was that she sometimes lost her sense of humour beneath her mountain of work.

"Do you know where you're going on your overseas assignment yet?" she asked Kylie.

"No. I think we find out at the residential course."

"It should be exciting – I regret now that I didn't do something like that when I was younger." Meredith's thin lips had an ironic twist to them. "I should say that Neil will miss not having you around."

Kylie flashed a glance to where Neil stood at the far end of the room. He was talking to Carole Matthews, their faces close and smiling. Kylie watched the body language between them.

They're flirting, she thought in surprise.

Meredith followed her eyes. "You should –" she began but seemed to think the better of what she had been about to say. "I have to dash, Kylie. I have a client who is waiting for me in a restaurant up town."

Kylie was wondering if she should interrupt Carole's tête-à-tête with Neil when she heard a deep voice with a distinctive Irish accent whisper in her ear.

"Fixed your hair?"

She turned around and came face to face with Jim Donnelly.

"Did the best I could," she said warily.

"I liked the mermaid look."

"Did you, now!"

She tilted her head back to return his gaze and took the opportunity to study him up close: lightly tanned skin, an uneven nose ridge and thick brown hair that flowed back from a broad brow. Due to the poor lighting, she couldn't tell the exact colour of his eyes but they crinkled at the corners and she realised, with surprise, that this was a man who laughed a lot.

"Brent's being tough on the billable hours," he commented.

"It's outrageous!" Kylie replied. "Getting people to work themselves to death under the guise of career development! I think Brent could do with coming along to our leadership course to explore *his* style of leadership."

Jim's lips widened to reveal slightly uneven teeth. They, along with his imperfect nose, added character to his face.

"I think his style is called 'Master and Slave'," he smiled.

"Is that a derogatory comment I hear from his golden boy?"

"Ah sure now, Kylie, there's no need to be like that," he said in a much stronger brogue.

Kylie had a suspicion that he was trying to make her laugh.

"It's tough at the top, Jim," she quipped with a decent mimicking of Brent's earlier tone.

Jim laughed, a rumbling, unrestrained sound that caused a few heads to turn in their direction.

"I like you, Kylie Horgan."

And with that final statement, he moved his charisma to another group whose faces became instantly more animated with his arrival. Kylie watched, fascinated, only half aware that Isobel had come to stand next to her.

"He looks like JFK Junior, doesn't he?" There was admiration in her beautifully accented voice. "But I'm afraid he is taken, Kylie, and you and I can only admire from a distance."

* * *

Kylie's inner-city apartment was everything that an up-and-coming partner would want: new building, state-of-the-art kitchen, not enough room to swing a cat.

"The space won't become an issue," Geoff had assured her. "Trust me."

She had trusted him about that, just like she had with everything else, and as her penance she was stuck in the awful place for the remainder of the twelve-month lease.

She opened the deadlocks and flicked the light switch just inside the door. The living area was bursting at the seams: books overflowed from the bookshelf to the floor, CDs that didn't fit on the rack were stacked up against the wall, and ornaments and artefacts competed for space on the sideboard. The solution wasn't as simple as having a good clear-out. The apartment was simply too small to accommodate her personality.

She sat on the couch and unzipped her boots. She had worked the entire room before the function wound up. Touching base with every single one of the forty partners was no mean feat and to say she was exhausted was the understatement of the year.

The phone rang and her first inclination was not to answer. However, curiosity got the better of her and she leaned over to check the display panel. It was her parents' phone number.

"Mum?" she said as she picked it up.

"Actually, it's Dad," came back Frankie's gruff voice.

"Oh."

Frankie was not the one who made the phone calls. Rose always did the talking and he was generally content to shout in the odd comment if he happened to have an opinion on what was being said.

"It's about the tickets, love."

"Yes," she said guardedly. Something told her that he was still not over the moon about them.

"Is there any way you can get your money back?"

There was an awkward pause before she asked, "Why would I do that?"

"It's a waste of your money, love. There's nothing for us in Ireland after forty years. Our life is here."

"I'm not asking you to go and live there," she said with a calmness she wasn't feeling. "It's only a holiday."

"I know . . . I know . . . but can you get your money back?"

Kylie knew that the travel agent would at least allow a credit against something else. But she didn't tell him that.

"Let me see what I can do."

"Sorry, love. Goodnight."

"Night, Dad."

Too tired to analyse what it all meant, Kylie went to the bedroom to finish undressing.

Chapter 4

Kylie was jolted from her sleep by a horrible familiar beeping: her alarm clock. She struggled to a vertical position and stumbled across the room. Over on the windowsill the alarm continued to beep until she viciously stabbed the stop button. It was Neil's suggestion to keep the alarm clock out of reach of the bed. He had taken her aside only a few weeks after she joined his team.

"It's clear that you are not by nature a morning person, Kylie. However, if you're serious about being a partner you need to be in the office by 7 a.m. – latest. That's the only way you'll clock up enough billable hours to be the top fee-earner." He had handed her a small box. "Here's a little gift to help you – an alarm clock. *Do not put this where you can reach it.*"

Kylie had obediently put the annoying little clock on the sill, promising herself that when she became a partner she would fling it out the window.

With the beeping still resounding in her head, she stepped into the diminutive shower cubicle. She raised her face to the cascading hot water and mentally went through her schedule for the day.

9 a.m.: Briefing with Neil
11 a.m.: Meeting at SDS regarding workplace agreement
1 p.m.: Lunch with SDS counsel and trade union officials
3 p.m.: Meeting at Citibank to discuss changes to the draft executive contract

The real work happened before 9 a.m. and after 5 p.m.. With fewer meetings and a quieter phone, it was at these times she drafted contracts, dictated letters of advice and undertook complex research that couldn't be trusted to graduates.

Once out of the shower, she put on her make-up: a light foundation, a generous coat of mascara and rose-pink lip gloss. She tipped her head over and worked some gel into her black curls. Once her hair was thoroughly gelled, she allowed it to dry natu

Her wardrobe was crammed with business
of navy, black and grey: dark colours in keeping
the serious image MFJ liked to portray to its clie
Kylie chose a grey trouser suit and teamed it wit
pistachio shirt. Then she laced up a pair of runn
and put her high-heeled shoes into her backpack. S
was ready to start the brisk-paced, half-hour walk
work.

Her apartment block was on one of Glebe'
quieter streets but, due to its proximity to the city
centre, cars were crammed along every inch of the
kerb. The morning air had a bite that wasn't thawed
by the weak winter sun and Kylie's cheeks were pink
by the time she reached the heart of Glebe's urban
village. The cafés were still shut; in another hour they
would be full of sun-glassed mobile-talking patrons.
Similarly, the shops selling books, clothes and home
wares had shutters over their doorways, but Kylie
could still admire their quirky window displays as she
passed.

Once she reached George Street, the surge of
pedestrian commuters carried her past the Asian
food stores, second-hand bookshops and glass-
fronted cinemas. Slightly out of breath, she crossed
at Town Hall. She could have taken a shorter route
but her goal was a full thirty minutes of exercise. It

was her way of making up for the damage that smoking was doing to her health.

At MFJ, the office hummed industriously as if it was the middle of the day. Kylie greeted only the colleagues who bothered to look up as she passed by. In her office, she swapped her runners for the court shoes in her backpack. Heels included, she stood at almost six-foot tall, a height at which very few could look down on her.

Soon she was absorbed in the enterprise agreement for SDS. The agreement was the culmination of many years of disputes between the company and the trade union. For the last four months Kylie had ping-ponged between the two parties and on the bad days had thought they would never agree on the terms and conditions. But now that the end was in sight, she was extremely proud of the final agreement and her pivotal role in the process. As she massaged and redrafted the clauses, she hoped that this would be the final set of changes and the lunch later on would be celebratory.

At eight thirty she stopped to acknowledge a craving for caffeine.

Where's Claudine this morning? she thought as she stretched her arms over her head. The only constant of Kylie's day was the cup of steaming tea that Claudine brought at 8 a.m. No tea meant there was no Claudine.

Kylie got up and rolled her stiff shoulders before strolling around to her secretary's desk. Claudine's computer was switched off and her chair was pushed neatly against the desk.

"Has she called in sick?" Kylie asked the secretary who sat in the next workstation.

"No – nobody knows where she is. You're not the first to come looking for her."

Frowning, Kylie went to the kitchen to make her tea. Claudine had sounded perfectly OK on the phone last night. Something must have happened afterwards. It had to be serious for Claudine to miss a day and not call in.

Kylie tried her mobile phone when she got back to her office. It rang through to voicemail.

"Claudine, it's me, Kylie. Can you call me, please?"

She sipped her tea as she continued to work on the enterprise agreement, deftly cutting and pasting words and phrases. At eight fifty, she saved the document and gathered what she needed for her meeting with Neil.

She was a few feet from his office when her mobile started to vibrate on her waistband. She quickly checked the number: Claudine. Then the time: eight fifty-seven. She had three minutes: Neil abhorred tardiness.

"Hi, Claudine," she said briskly. "Where are you today?"

"I'm in the hospital."

The pitch of distress in Claudine's voice set off Kylie's alarm bells.

"Are you OK?"

"Something . . . *awful* . . . has happened."

"What?"

"Ethan . . ." Claudine broke down into sobs and could go no further.

Ethan? Who was Ethan? A boyfriend? Kylie realised that it would take too long to extract a coherent account of what "something awful" entailed. She switched to factual questions.

"Which hospital?"

"Royal North Shore."

"Accident and emergency?"

"Yes."

"Have you got anybody with you?"

"No."

Kylie took a moment to take stock. Claudine needed to have someone with her, that much was clear. Surely there was some family member who could come and sit with her?

Obviously not, otherwise she wouldn't be alone. If only I didn't have this meeting with Neil . . .

"I'll be there as soon as I can. Give me half an hour."

Kylie hooked her mobile back onto her waistband. She pictured Neil's thin, begrudging face. No matter what the circumstances, putting a mere secretary before his needs wouldn't sit well.

She barged ahead into his office. He was waiting at his meeting table, tapping a pen as if counting the exact number of seconds she was late.

"So sorry, Neil," she said in her most confident tone. "The union have pulled a surprise this morning and I have to rush off to see their official. I hope we can reschedule our briefing for tomorrow morning."

It was the perfect excuse. A client was the only thing that could legitimately come in front of a partner.

The pen stopped tapping and he said, "Make sure SDS pay for this last-minute hiccup."

"Thanks, Neil. Will keep you updated."

She strode from his office as if she was about to strangle the wayward union official with her bare hands.

She was racing towards the lift foyer when she met Jim.

"Kylie Horgan!"

She liked the way he said her name, how he included her surname as if it was an important part of who she was. It was nice, teasing and more than a little flirtatious.

"Jim Donnelly!" she said in return.

Her eyes, of their own volition, started to savour the detail of him: the way his white shirt accentuated the broad sweep of his shoulders; the narrow hips at the waist of his charcoal trousers; the fact there was no excess flesh beneath his well-fitting clothes.

They're grey, she thought, having a clear look at his eyes.

The lift arrived. She had to go.

"Have to fly." She flashed him a smile. "Bye."

* * *

She found Claudine in the waiting room, sitting on a hard plastic chair, staring into space. Her eyes were puffed and bloodshot, her usually immaculate bob in total disarray.

The seats on either side were taken and Kylie crouched down in front of her.

"Claudine, I'm here." She reached to take a limp hand in hers. "What's happened?"

Tears brimmed in Claudine's eyes. "He was sleepwalking. He fell . . . down the stairs." Her free hand indicated the ferocity of the fall.

An elderly man vacated the seat to Claudine's left. "Sit here," he said to Kylie as he shuffled away.

"Thank you."

She sat down without letting go her grip on Claudine's hand.

"Who? Who fell down the stairs?"

"Ethan . . . my son . . . my darling son . . . all I have in the world . . . they can't wake him up . . ."

Claudine had never mentioned before that she had a son. Now that Kylie thought about it, she knew very little about her secretary's private life.

Claudine's grief seemed to captivate the other waiting patients and Kylie looked up as she felt the weight of their sympathetic stares.

It was Tuesday morning, a routine day for most, but not for these people with their broken limbs, gashed faces and fevered children. For some of them it wasn't just a bad day: their lives had changed forever.

White-coated doctors and blue-bloused nurses flitted in and out of the waiting area, consulting with the patients in low voices and sometimes extending a hand to help them to their feet.

My job is so insignificant next to them, Kylie realised suddenly. *I sit at my desk, playing with words. They save lives.*

Then one of the white-coated doctors was standing next to them, addressing Claudine.

"Miss Myers, we've finished the CAT scan and X-rays. Unfortunately both legs are broken – in awkward places. But the good news is that his skull and spine seem to be OK."

Claudine put her hand over her mouth and tried to hold her sobs inside. She seemed to be unable to verbalise the questions Kylie was sure she wanted to ask.

"Has he woken up?" Kylie asked on her behalf.

The young woman turned her way. Her gaze had an astonishing clarity. In the face of such competence and compassion, Kylie once again felt the insignificance of her own career.

"No," she replied, "but we're feeling more confident now that we've seen inside his head." She touched Claudine's shoulder. "We're getting ready to move him to a bed now. Come through with me."

Claudine got to her feet. She looked down at Kylie, who was still seated, and took a moment to find her voice. "Thanks for coming."

"Anything I can do –" Kylie started to say.

"Just please make sure they don't fire me while I'm away."

Kylie stared after her and the young doctor until they were swallowed up by the swinging doors to the emergency rooms beyond.

* * *

Kylie wondered if she had brought about a bad omen by saying that the union had some last-minute issues for, in keeping with her lie to Neil, they came up with three more changes, two of which were substantial. The lunch that followed the meeting was tense, with Kylie the only one who tried to keep some semblance of conversation on the go.

There was no time to go back to the office after the lunch and Kylie caught a cab directly to Citibank.

"Not a bad first draft," Pete Wilde remarked as he cupped his hands behind his head. "However, because this executive is coming from overseas, we will need to give some thought to tax equalisation."

Kylie wished he had told her that the executive was a non-resident at the outset. However, she didn't let the slightest sign of annoyance show on her face.

Pete had some other issues he wanted to discuss and it was well after 6 p.m. when Kylie left his harbour-view office. She lit up a cigarette as soon as she got outside. She called herself a social smoker but, if she was honest, she had become much more addicted since splitting with Geoff. Over those bleak weeks, she had reached for her cigarettes far too often, and now she was smoking more than she cared to count.

When the cigarette was gone deep into her lungs, she hailed a taxi. She phoned Claudine from the cab and was very happy to hear that she had good news.

"He opened his eyes about an hour ago. He recognised me straight away – the doctors say that's good."

"I'm so glad," said Kylie. "Can he talk?"

"Only whisper. But he's coherent. They're sure now that his brain isn't damaged."

"And his legs?"

"They're both hanging from traction – he'll be like that for six weeks while the bones mend."

"How old is he, Claudine?"

"Seven – nearly eight."

"You'll need to stay there with him."

"What about my job?" Claudine sounded sick with worry. "You know what they're like, Kylie."

Kylie knew only too well what they were like. Six weeks' leave would cause a major stir, regardless of the circumstances.

"Leave them to me – don't you worry about a thing."

* * *

Kylie made Neil number one on Wednesday's list of priorities. She found him scrunched over his desk, frowning madly as he read through a hefty contract. He looked like he was in one of his nitpicking moods. Her suspicions were confirmed when he gashed his highlighter through an entire page of the document.

"What's happening while you're away on the course?" he asked as she sat down opposite. His tone was narky, as if she was taking an inconvenient holiday rather than partaking in a firm-sponsored programme.

"I've delegated everything – with the exception of the SDS enterprise agreement, which I should be able to keep tabs on while I'm away."

"Delegated to *whom*?" His eyes narrowed behind the oversized glasses.

"Graham, Sandra and Joe – I have the work plan here." Her tone was calm; she was used to dealing with his moods.

"I hope we can contact you if we need to," he sniped as he picked up the work plan.

"Not during the day," she said, "and most of the evening is taken up with assignments. But I'll be available between five and six – we're meant to use that hour to wind down . . ." Her voice faded away to a cynical smile, as if the idea of winding down was a big joke.

Neil made a sound that was close to a snort, his way of letting her know that he still wasn't happy.

"I suppose it will be a trial run for when you're overseas."

"Exactly."

He started to dissect the work plan, and the next fifteen minutes were taken up with his petty criticisms. Kylie sat through it, biting on her tongue. Now was not the time to let two years of frustration show.

She was standing up to leave when she said, "By the way, Claudine will be out for a few weeks. Her son is ill."

"How many weeks?" Neil frowned.

Kylie had to stop herself from saying, *Shouldn't you be asking what is wrong with her son?*

"Four to six," she replied casually, downplaying the fact that six was more likely to be the minimum than the maximum.

"How many weeks' leave does she have outstanding?"

Kylie had her facts prepared. "There are five weeks of combined sick and annual leave on the payroll system."

He snorted again and resumed reading the contract he had been defacing when she walked in.

His reaction to Claudine's unfortunate news was exactly as Kylie had expected. Neil was generally indifferent to those who didn't further his interests in some way, Kylie his one and only anomaly. He had paved the way for her and turned partnership from a dream into a reachable goal. She never dared to analyse why.

* * *

It was a long day, spent mostly at her desk. She called it quits at eight thirty and started the walk home. Park Street was dark and quiet, Town Hall brighter and busier. Passing by the entrance to the train station, she thought of Claudine. She had intended to call her earlier but billing in six-minute units afforded little time to stop and be human. Guiltily, she took out her number and placed the belated call.

"How is he?"

"Bored already," Claudine sighed. "I don't know how he'll last six weeks of this – or how *I'll* last, for that matter!"

Kylie heard herself asking, "Would a new face help relieve the boredom?"

"It's after visiting hours. But tell them you're family."

"It's the children's ward, right?"

"Yes."

* * *

Kylie walked into the ward thirty minutes later

51

and asked the tired-looking staff nurse where she could find Ethan Myers.

"Bottom room – right inside the door."

Kylie followed her instructions, her runners squeaking on the linoleum floor covering. The sounds of beeping machines and crying children echoed down the long, dimly lit corridor. Each bed in the bottom room was sectioned off by an old-fashioned floral curtain.

"Claudine?" Kylie whispered.

A silhouette rose and created a small opening for Kylie to come through.

"Come in," said Claudine. "We're just watching TV."

The child was lying on his back, his legs suspended from two metal tracks.

Six weeks like that, she thought as she looked at the thick spiral of bandages on each leg. *He'll go crazy.*

She became aware that his dark eyes were waiting for her to speak.

"I'm Kylie," she said.

"I know," was his answer. "You're Mum's boss."

"Looks like you're going to be stuck here for a while, mate."

"Six weeks. I'm already going loopy."

"You should be thankful that you're getting out of here at all," Claudine pointed out. "Two nights ago we thought you'd be a vegetable for the rest of your life."

It seemed an unnecessarily harsh reminder of the initial severity of the situation.

Kylie cocked her head. "You'd make a good turnip."

"No, that's boring," Ethan grinned. "I'm more of a broccoli head."

They giggled but Claudine stayed straight-faced, their sense of the ridiculous lost on her.

Kylie turned her eyes to the small TV that had more static than picture.

"At least you can become a couch potato."

He didn't laugh. "All the TVs in here are ancient – and they don't have any DVD players . . ."

"Would a DVD player make this better?" Kylie asked more seriously.

"Yes, a lot better. I could watch movies."

* * *

Even though Kylie hadn't even heard of Ethan Myers until two days before, he somehow managed to occupy her thoughts disproportionately. All through the taxi ride home, her restless sleep and at work the next day, Ethan's plight nagged away at her. He was a bright spark, his sense of humour more like an adult's than a child's. But would his laughter be killed by six long weeks of confinement, eating, sleeping, even *bathing* in that same bed?

Mid-morning, right in the middle of a complex letter of advice, she decided she would buy him the DVD player. Once the decision was made, she was able to concentrate. But by lunchtime she was dragging her heels again because she remembered the ancient TV.

Even if the DVD player worked with it, the picture would still be terrible. I'd need to buy him a new TV.

It was getting expensive but still within her means. Besides, she owed Claudine for her loyalty and hard work. Decision made, Kylie got on with the letter but it wasn't long before she stalled once more. She realised that she couldn't possibly give Ethan a new TV and DVD player while the other kids on the ward looked on with envy.

How many kids in the ward? Forty? Fifty? Assuming a grand for each — that's fifty grand! I'm out of my depth here.

Her phone rang, interrupting the mental calculations. It was Graham, one of the graduates.

"I'm struggling with that research you asked me to do," he said. "Can I come and see you?"

"Yeah, come around."

She and Graham spent the next few hours poring over the relevant legislation and precedents. Ethan was no longer at the front of her mind but he niggled away somewhere at the back.

* * *

Kylie crammed in as much work as possible over the next week, trying to make up for the damage the residential course would do to her billability. The only break she allowed herself was a lunch with Annie and baby Zack.

"We need to go somewhere that has space for the pram," said Annie when Kylie met her outside the building, "and somewhere he can't be heard if he cries."

From the welcoming smile on Zack's cherubic face, it was hard to believe that he ever cried or that he woke almost hourly during the night.

"Hello, gorgeous!" Kylie ruffled his golden hair. "Why don't we grab a sandwich and eat it in the park?" she suggested to Annie. "We can take Zack out of the pram – he'll have a great time on the grass."

Annie was so relieved at the idea that she looked ready to cry. Somehow going to a café had become the most stressful thing in the world.

They bought some sandwiches at a nearby bistro and crossed the road to Hyde Park. Kylie towered over Annie as they walked under the green canopy of trees. At school they had been called Little and Large; however, despite their physical differences, their personalities were very similar. Over the years their curiosity had got them into all sorts of mischief and their fieriness had fuelled the most extreme arguments, with Jean or Rose sometimes having to pull them apart.

Now Annie jadedly lifted Zack out of the pram and Kylie held out her arms.

"Let me play with him while you eat."

Annie handed him over and he gave Kylie another cute smile.

"I think your mother is lying," she said, tickling him under the chin. "You're too gorgeous to be causing all this trouble."

"Street angel, home devil," Annie remarked wryly as she unwrapped her sandwich.

They spent a pleasant hour together in the park and Annie was a little more relaxed when she said goodbye.

"Don't worry about me," she said, knowing that Kylie was concerned. "I'm just a slow learner – sooner or later I'll get the hang of this mothering business."

* * *

The rest of the week flew by and it was Sunday before Kylie knew it.

"Mum? Dad?" she called as she opened the front door of the house.

"We're out the back," called her mother's voice.

Kylie joined them on the deck. They sat side by side on the lounge, both reading different parts of the same newspaper.

"Hard at work, I see," Kylie commented

"It *is* Sunday," Rose pointed out rather tartly. "Some of us relax at the weekend."

"Where's Stephen?" Kylie asked, kicking off her shoes. The wood was deliciously warm under her bare feet, the deck a sun-trap even in the winter.

"He's not coming for lunch this week," Rose replied. "He's got something else on – maybe a new girlfriend."

"Maybe. Finished with that part, Dad?" Kylie asked, nodding towards the business section of the paper.

"Never read it," he said as he handed it over.

Kylie flicked through the pages. It was important to keep up to date with what was happening in the wider world of business. Her clients expected opinions on matters other than the law.

"There's a big match on tonight," Frankie commented from the depths of the sports section.

"The Wallabies versus Ireland."

"Are you staying up to watch it?" asked Kylie.

"Of course I am," he replied as if it was perfectly normal to watch a rugby game at midnight. "Aren't you?"

"No – I've an early start tomorrow."

The Hunter Valley, famous for its wineries, was a two-hour drive from Sydney and she'd have to be on the road by 6 a.m.

Ten minutes were whittled away before Kylie became aware that Frankie was starting to fidget. She knew what he was working up to even before the words came out of his mouth.

"Did you get your money back on those tickets?"

"No," she said casually. "I haven't called the travel agent yet."

She saw him frown out of the corner of her eye. "Surely the sooner you call, the better chance you have?"

She turned over the page before she answered. "I was hoping I could talk you two around."

Rose looked up. "There's no 'talking around'. We don't want to go."

"Why?" Kylie asked, meeting her mother's gaze.

"It's too long a journey . . ."

"Come on, Mum. I know you'd have a ball. All the family, your old friends!"

Rose seemed to be unable to provide a response.

Kylie went into full interrogation mode. "Did something happen there? Is that why you don't want to go back?"

Rose jumped to her feet, her face flushed. "For heaven's sake, Kylie! We don't want to go and that's *that*."

She marched off to the kitchen, where pots and pans clashed as she made an early start on lunch.

Frankie shook his head at his daughter, as if she had sorely disappointed him. "Let it drop, Kylie – go in now and say sorry to her – and cancel the tickets without any more fuss – that's a good girl."

Chapter 5

"Mum, is my nana alive?"

Rose's answer was far from instantaneous. "No, love."

Kylie quite deliberately lulled her into a false sense of security by letting a few seconds pass before asking the next question.

"How about my other nana? Nana Horgan?"

Another pause, then a reluctant reply. "Yes, she's alive — but she's very old."

"We should phone her," Kylie commented as if the idea had just occurred to her that very moment. "She must be lonely."

More seconds ticked by. Rose looked as if she was

scrambling for an answer.

"She has no phone, love."

"No phone?" Kylie's eyes widened in disbelief. However, she was quick on her feet to think of an alternative. "Well, what if we phoned her neighbours and asked them to go get her?"

"She's too old — she can't leave the house."

Kylie thought about it for a while. Then she queried, "Does Dad write to her at all?"

Rose didn't answer.

"Mum?"

"Yes, he does — when he gets the time."

Rose was starting to sound annoyed but Kylie pressed on regardless.

"How about aunties and uncles? Do I have any of those?"

"Don't you have plenty — Uncle Alexander, Auntie Jean —"

"But they aren't real aunties and uncles."

"They'd be very hurt if they heard you say that, Kylie Horgan."

Once again, Kylie didn't heed the warning in her mother's voice.

"I'm going to write to Nana Horgan," she decided. "I'll put my letter in with Dad's. She'd love to hear from me. I'm sure she doesn't have any other grandchildren who live so far away —"

Rose cut her off. "Kylie, set the table for dinner, please."

"But I'm talking to you about something important."

"I don't want to have to tell your father that you were cheeky," said Rose, her tone very sharp by now.

"I'm not being cheeky." Kylie's seven-year-old face flared red at the sheer injustice of the accusation. "And I don't want any stupid dinner."

When Frankie came home from work, she was lying across her bed, sulking.

"You've been upsetting your mother," he said, his expression resigned.

"She's been upsetting me," Kylie declared.

"Let it drop, Kylie," he sighed as he sat on the bed. "Go in now and say sorry to her. That's a good girl."

Chapter 6

Kylie backed her Audi A3 out of the poky garage where it spent most of its time. She much preferred to walk to work than crawl the car through gridlocked traffic. But she liked driving on the open road and she put her foot down when she reached the start of the freeway. The dial of the speedometer quickly climbed to just above the speed limit. She overtook the first rush of cars and then settled back into the left lane.

The Audi effortlessly ate the kilometres as she half listened to the morning show on the radio. Outside, the sky gradually turned a perfect winter blue and the sun glinted off the roofs of the cars up ahead. The freeway forged on through dense bush and dried-up creeks. Eventually the radio lost its reception and Kylie turned it off. Silence filled the car. Her head felt clear and alert. It seemed like the right time to think of Rose and the memories that had started to surface after yesterday's brief altercation.

Kylie had apologised, Rose had forgiven her and the rest of the afternoon had been amicable and uneventful. Much later in the evening, as Kylie packed the clothes she would need while she was away, a light switched on in her head. For the first time she saw a common theme in the blurred memories of her childhood. She realised that many of her apologies and Rose's absolutions had related to the same thing: Ireland. Kylie's curiosity had always clashed with her mother's reluctance to impart information. During her teens she became preoccupied with clothes and boys and the arguments fizzled away. Now, the tickets had brought about their first quarrel in years and inadvertently turned the clock back. With an adult's hindsight, it seemed that Stephen could be right on the mark when he'd said, "Maybe something happened there".

What could be so bad? Some argument with the family? Surely forty years would bury the most bitter of hatchets. Kylie had her best ideas when she was smoking, and her hand fumbled to find her cigarette box on the dash. Keeping her eyes on the road, she lifted the flap, extracted a cigarette and slid it between her lips. Her lighter was next. She glanced down at the positioning of the flame and the cigarette took light. It took only the briefest second, yet when she looked at the road again it was too late.

She had sailed past the first police officer. The second was up ahead and waving her down.

As she braked, she glanced down at the speedometer: 120 and dropping quickly. What had it been two hundred metres back where the first officer had his camera?

Damn. Damn. Damn.

She eventually came to a stop and rolled down the window.

A young freckled face looked in at her. "Good morning, miss. Are you aware of what speed you were doing?"

"A hundred and twenty?" she asked hopefully.

"One hundred and twenty-eight." His expression was grave. "Are you aware of the speed limit?"

"A hundred and ten," she replied and took a despondent drag of her cigarette. It was going to be a hefty fine.

"Can I see your licence?"

"Sure." Kylie looked around for her handbag. It wasn't on the back seat – she must have thrown it in with her other luggage. "My bag must be in the boot. Can I get out?"

He moved away from the door and she opened it cautiously. Cars whizzed by at ferocious speeds and a wild wind billowed in their wake. Holding down her A-line skirt, Kylie walked to the rear of the car. Thankfully, her handbag was in the boot and she had not left it behind. Popping her cigarette into her mouth, she peered into the junk-filled depths of the bag. The exact location of her black leather wallet was not obvious. She moved a few things around but still no joy.

"Sorry about this," she mumbled to the officer and tipped the entire contents out. The wallet landed on top.

The officer was taking down the details from her licence when Kylie became aware that a car had pulled in further ahead. A man got out. Tall, broad, there was something about his physique that was vaguely familiar.

Jim Donnelly. How embarrassing!

He approached, his expression concerned.

"Everything OK, Kylie?"

No, Jim. Everything is not OK. I'm standing on the roadside with my skirt up around me and a cigarette hanging out of my mouth — more like a chain-smoking hooker than a lawyer. And the fine I'll have to pay would buy a TV and DVD for Ethan Myers — who, in my utter selfishness, I had forgotten about until this very moment.

"Yes," was her answer out loud, "all under control."

It seemed that Jim didn't think so because he turned to speak to the officer. "Can I have a private word, please?"

"What –" Kylie started to protest but Jim stared her into silence.

The two men moved away. Kylie agitatedly puffed on her cigarette while she watched them talk.

Who does Jim Donnelly think he is? I can handle this on my own.

Jim was speaking intently, his gesturing hands adding emphasis to his words. The officer cupped his chin and listened. Kylie felt totally superfluous to the proceedings. The officer seemed to have a question when Jim was finished and looked happy with the answer he got. They walked back her way.

The officer addressed her. "I'm letting you off with a warning, Miss Horgan. I'm confident that this offence was a once-off and you'll observe the legal speed limit in the future."

"Thanks," said Kylie, somewhere between happy and annoyed. "I appreciate the lenience you've shown."

"G'day to you both." The officer nodded and returned to his post further down the road.

Kylie pointedly didn't proffer any thanks to Jim. She brazenly smoked the rest of the cigarette, keeping one hand flat against her skirt. Jim didn't seem at all phased by her very obvious annoyance.

"What did you say to him?" she asked eventually, curiosity getting the better of her.

"Sure now, that's for me to know and you to wonder," he replied, clearly enjoying having one over her.

"I can fight my own battles," she said tartly.

He smiled lazily, not even faintly rattled by the sharpness of her voice.

"See you at the hotel, Kylie Horgan. And for God's sake, take it easy for the rest of the journey."

She glared daggers at his back. He had the cheek to turn around and wave. Stamping out her cigarette, she dumped the contents of her handbag back in place and slammed the boot shut.

* * *

"You'll be living in one another's pockets this week so let's invest some time upfront in getting to know each other," said the facilitator of the course, a large woman by the name of Angela Bardman. She smiled at them with lips that were the very same red as her jacket. "First, let's do something fun. I want you to say three things about yourself – two truths and one lie. The group must guess which one is the lie. You have two minutes to think – starting now."

Angela sat her large frame on the edge of one of the free tables as she waited the allotted time. After fifteen years in corporate education, she had met all sorts of people in varying stages of their careers. This was her first group of would-be partners. Dressed casually this morning, they looked no different to the group of insurance clerks she had facilitated last week. But she didn't doubt that the differences would soon show through. There was nothing quite like this exercise to see the group dynamic as well as the individual personalities at play.

The Managing Partner of MFJ, Brent Lavell, had been very clear about what he expected from the week-long course.

"I want you to watch them like a hawk," he had stated, a thread of menace in his voice.

"You're looking for feedback on each participant," she had replied, putting diplomatic words around his expectations.

He raised his hand, spreading his fingers. "Five things: strengths, weaknesses, attitude to risk, tolerance of pressure and timeliness."

Angela realised there was no point in telling him about the sophisticated leadership-tailored feedback system that she usually advocated. Brent obviously had his own ideas on how the course should be run. And he was the client, after all.

Angela looked at her watch. "Isobel, would you like to go first?" she asked in her honey-smooth voice.

Isobel seemed like a gentle soul amongst her hardened colleagues. Angela watched her closely as she spoke.

"Three things. Here goes. I'm one of six children. I graduated top of my school. I run twenty kilometres a week."

The rest of the group immediately broke into debate.

"Don't think she was dux of her school," declared David, rather loudly.

"Why, David? Do you think I'm not clever enough?"

He bristled. "You know that's not what I mean."

Oliver, a lanky fellow with thinning hair and a roguish face, defused the situation by making a joke. "I think she's lazy and it's the running."

Isobel did her best hangdog expression. "So nice to know that everybody thinks so highly of me," she remarked.

"It's the family of six," Kylie stated, having given it careful thought. "Most educated Colombian women have careers, so smaller families would be more common."

Angela turned her gaze to the black-haired woman with the porcelain skin. Kylie Horgan was an interesting package. Determination shone through her sky-blue eyes and it was very evident that she had fought hard to get where she was today.

Kylie is competitive, thought Angela, *and she doesn't like to be in the dark about anything. Even with a fun exercise like this, it's important to her to know the right answer.*

Angela prompted the other two participants for their opinions.

"Carole? Jim? What do you think?"

Angela saw Jim's gesture to Carole to go first.

Ah, we have a gentleman in our midst.

Carole was to the point. "Running."

She flicked her blonde hair, making it evident to all that she found this game rather juvenile.

Angela pegged her straight away. *Superiority complex. Thinks that she's above everything, particularly silly games.*

Jim went next. "Kylie is always right so I'm going with her."

Angela noticed that he shot a mischievous look in Kylie's direction but it wasn't reciprocated.

In the meantime, Isobel was shrugging. "Well, as it happens, Kylie *is* right! There are only two children in my family."

Angela moved on, choosing David next. Once again, Kylie guessed the right answer.

David's transparent – especially to someone like Kylie who would delight in second-guessing him.

"Your turn next, Kylie," she said. "Time for the others to rumble you."

"They can only try." Kylie grinned, her sense of fun engaging. "OK – pick the lie. I was born in Ireland. I love walking. I read an average of three novels a week."

"You walk to work, don't you?" asked Isobel.

"No comment."

"Geoff used to complain about you always having your head stuck in a book," said Oliver.

Angela saw the grin fade from Kylie's face. Geoff was a sore point, whoever he was.

Carole stopped examining her nails. "Who's Geoff?"

Oliver tried to make amends for his insensitivity by fielding the question. "Someone who Kylie would rather forget." He gave Kylie a sheepish smile. "Sorry – trust me to put my foot in it."

There was an uncomfortable silence. Angela looked on, interested to see how it would pan out. It didn't surprise her that the gentleman came to the rescue of the damsel in distress.

"I can't believe that a 'Kylie', such a quintessential Australian name, would be born in Ireland," said Jim. "Am I right?"

Kylie smiled but Angela noticed that it didn't quite reach her eyes. "Yes, you're right. My parents are Irish but I was born here, in Sydney."

* * *

After morning tea, Angela changed gear and became more serious.

"Have no doubt, this will be a gruelling week," she told them, her bright red lipstick freshly reapplied. "The rest of today will be spent discussing different leadership roles. Tomorrow we will do some personality tests and look at our own individual styles . . ."

Kylie listened as Angela did a rundown of the week ahead. She had regained her composure during the tea break. Oliver's unexpected reference to Geoff had caught her totally off guard. Just the mention of his name was enough to start off the old spin of sadness, guilt and anger in her head. It was still a raw hurt, even though six months had passed by since the final showdown.

"On Wednesday and Thursday you will have the opportunity to apply the leadership roles in a complex simulated business environment . . ."

"What does that mean in plain English?" asked Carole, a critical look on her face.

Angela levelled a steady gaze in her direction. "You will be a senior leader in a fictitious organisation. You will have to develop strategies, organise people and resources, and work through a maze of complex business issues. Every decision you make will have an impact on the financial results and share price."

"So all our decisions go into a computer program and it works out how well we've done?" asked Kylie, her interest sparked.

"Yes," answered Angela. "You'll perform the simulation in teams of two."

"What does the winner get?"

"Just the glory of beating the others," Angela smiled.

"Nothing like some healthy competition to make things interesting," said Jim.

Kylie realised that Jim was every bit as competitive as she was. In his white shirt with its rolled-up sleeves, he looked fighting fit for any contest. He had a different energy to the others.

He goes after what he wants, hell for leather, she

thought. *The more obstacles he has to overcome, the more he covets the prize. He's going to throw himself into this programme and he'll be very hard to beat.*

Kylie turned her attention back to what Angela was saying.

"The week will culminate in a series of PowerPoint presentations to the partners on Friday morning. You will choose the subject of your presentation – the only criterion is that it should be something that will bring long-term benefit to MFJ. Your presentation is something you will work on after hours. Now, any questions?"

David raised his hand. "Have the partners given you any clue about what they'd like to see on Friday?"

"No – the subject is totally open, within the overriding guideline of long-term benefit to the firm."

David looked uneasy with her response. "Maybe the group should spend some time deciding a common approach."

Angela shook her head. "No. Your presentation is individual to you – not a group exercise. It is an opportunity for you to show the partners how innovative and persuasive *you* can be. I suggest you keep the content to yourselves until Friday."

* * *

That afternoon Kylie learned that an effective leader has a number of different roles to play: strategist, entrepreneur, change-driver, captivator and talent advocate. She enjoyed Angela's interactive teaching style and didn't feel the time pass.

"That's it for me today," said Angela at 5 p.m. sharp. "You have a free hour before dinner. Considering our location here amidst some of the best wineries in the world, I perfectly understand the temptation to sample their produce, but do try to set some time aside for your presentations. The partners will expect a high standard on Friday."

Kylie had checked in at lunchtime but did nothing more than drop her bags in the room. Now, as she opened the door, she took time to appreciate its old-style décor. The hotel staff had turned down the bed for the night and drawn the heavy curtains across the French doors. Kylie sat on the four-poster bed and ran her hand over its rich brocade cover. She was sorely tempted to rest back into the plush pillows, but her mobile started to vibrate as if it was intercepting her bad intentions.

"I need to talk to you about SDS." It was Neil.

"What's wrong?" she asked, frowning. She had managed to navigate her way through the last set of changes and had sent out another draft of the agreement over the weekend. A new draft usually brought at least a few days' respite.

"Both parties are ready to sign," he replied.

"Great," she sighed with relief. "So why are you calling?"

"They want to make a fuss of the exchange – invite some press, have some drinks. They've expressly asked for you to be present."

"That's impossible – I'm here for the week."

"You can pop down to show your face."

She could hardly believe what he was suggesting. "It's a two-hour drive each way, Neil!"

"You won't need to cut into your classes – the exchange is tomorrow evening at 7 p.m."

"I'm meant to do assignments in the evening," she told him, even though he was already well aware of the schedule.

There was a brief silence. When his voice came back down the line, its tone allowed no room for negotiation. "SDS have paid close to a million dollars in all for your expert advice – they're entitled to have you there. I'm sure you'll work something out with your assignments."

Typical, she thought as she put the phone down. *Neil's not behind this programme – he couldn't care less what I learn here this week. All he cares about is getting a big fat cheque from SDS.*

Annoyed, Kylie rose from the bed and got her

laptop from its case. She connected the modem to the portal on the wall and dialled into MFJ's network. Her inbox was brimming, many of the messages from Neil. As far as he was concerned, she wasn't out of the office at all.

She took her frustration out on the keyboard as she typed responses, her fingers as angry as her thoughts.

Neil, Brent, the whole lot of them are insular. All they think about is money. They're blinkered from real life . . .

It was from this train of thought that Kylie got the idea for Friday's presentation.

* * *

Kylie woke to an unfamiliar beeping. She soon identified her mobile phone as the source of the alarm. Last night she had placed it on the antique desk and now the only way to shut it off was to get out of bed.

Yawning deeply, she padded across the dark room and stopped the head-splitting noise. The screen of the phone glowed the time as 6 a.m. If she mobilised now, she would be able to get two hours of work done before the start of the course.

Ten minutes later she was sitting in front of her laptop in her cotton pyjamas. She raced through her emails, responding, forwarding and deleting as needed. Despite the fact she had worked on her inbox the previous night, it took a further hour before it was clear. She was about to start on her presentation when a new message flashed up on her screen. It was from Neil.

The venue for tonight is the Four Seasons. Don't be late.

The message immediately reignited last night's anger. Her full participation in the leadership course was clearly not a priority for him. The most frustrating thing was that she had no doubt SDS would understand if the situation was explained. Kylie pushed her chair back and did something she could never do in the office: she walked away from Neil's bullying.

She put on her dressing-gown, grabbed her box of cigarettes and opened the French doors to a frosty morning. Winter was a lot chillier in the countryside than it was in the city. The cold quickly cleared the anger from her head, and soon she was able to fully appreciate her spectacular surroundings. Vines came right up to the veranda, bare and stumped in beautifully perfect rows. Overhead, a pale blue sky was starting to form from the greyness of dawn. Kylie smoked her cigarette slowly and refused to think of Neil or the SDS event that she was compelled to attend that night.

She went back inside only when she heard the distinctive ringtone of her mobile. She checked the number on the screen before answering.

"Good morning, Claudine," she said.

"I got your voice message last night," the secretary said in reply.

"Can you do it for me?"

"Yes. Can I ask why?"

"No – you'll only be disappointed if I don't succeed."

"OK. I'll be popping home around lunchtime – I'll get my camera then."

"OK. Tell Ethan I said hi."

Kylie resumed work and didn't stop until after eight. By the time she had showered and dressed, there was no time for breakfast. She was the last to arrive at the conference room and had barely sat down when Angela started to speak.

"Good morning, all. I hope you're settled into the resort by now and that you enjoyed last night's dinner."

They all responded in the positive because the resort and the food were excellent. However, the conversation around the dinner table had been decidedly flat. It transpired that everybody had used the free hour beforehand to log into their email and had inevitably become entangled in a myriad of issues back at the office. After a starter, main course and quick coffee, they had returned to their individual rooms to get back online to combat what issues they could.

"Today we're going to look at our personality preferences. We'll start with some basic questions." As Angela spoke, she moved amongst the tables, distributing booklets. "There are no right or wrong answers to the questions so don't spend too much time thinking – just answer as best you can. When you finish the test, you can go outside and have a coffee."

Kylie opened the booklet and immediately marked "X" as she responded to the first question. She continued on, finding the answers instinctive, not needing to do too much deliberation. Out of the corner of her eye she saw David chew on the top of his pen. Even Oliver looked as if he was thinking very hard before selecting his answers. Forty minutes later Kylie answered the last question and handed her completed booklet to Angela. Morning tea was set up outside the room. Ravenously hungry, Kylie helped herself to a decadent chocolate muffin. She sank into one of the lounge chairs and had just taken an enormous bite when Jim came out.

"You missed breakfast," he commented as he sat

down across from her.

Her mouth full, she could only nod.

"Were you the kid at school who always finished their test first?"

She nodded again. Speedy Horganez had been her nickname but she wasn't going to share that particular piece of trivia with him.

"So was I." He gave a nostalgic smile. "I was a competitive little bastard. Had to be the fastest, and the best – sure God knows how I had any school friends at all."

It was hard to imagine the tall, muscular man sitting across from her as a schoolboy. His eyes seemed darker this morning. In fact, he looked tired. She guessed that he, like her, had worked into the early hours of the morning.

"Those were innocent days," he continued, his smile turning a little cynical.

It was their first time alone since the incident on the freeway. Kylie had been standoffish around him for most of yesterday, still piqued, though not entirely sure of her reasons. Now she realised that she had been rather childish.

She looked at him deadpan as she said, "I think we should bring some of the school ethic into MFJ – our work day could finish at four, we'd have two months' summer holiday, we'd get to play in the yard

84

at lunchtime . . ."

He threw his head back and laughed with the same lack of restraint as the night of the launch. Then he suddenly reached out and she felt his fingers brush the side of her mouth. She met his eyes, very uncertain of herself, of him, of everything.

"Just some muffin," he said quietly. They both heard the door open and looked up to see Carole, the third-fastest kid in the class, come out.

* * *

Kylie got into her car as dusk began to smudge the sky. She hoped there wouldn't be any traffic delays – she was cutting it tight as it was. She didn't turn the car radio on as she drove along the vine-lined roads. Her mind was too busy as it was.

All day long she had felt on edge, painfully conscious of every movement Jim made, every word he said. She had hung onto Angela's words when she described Jim's personality from the results of the test.

"Jim, you base your decisions mostly on values. You're tuned in to the emotions and motivations of others . . ."

Kylie could believe it. Jim seemed to be able to find common ground with everyone. Talkative and interested, he even managed to coax conversation from the awkward David and icy Carole.

Angela then turned her attention to Kylie. "Now, with you we have the extreme opposite. You base your decisions entirely on logic. You tend to have a *very* black and white view . . ."

A few of the others chuckled.

Kylie smiled self-consciously as she said, "I thought there were no right or wrong answers."

Angela returned her smile. "True – but it does help to know your blind spots. And there's a lot of grey in life, Kylie – you need to learn not to get frustrated by that . . ."

Darkness fell quickly as Kylie drove along the country roads. She eventually reached the freeway and eased into the long line of red tail-lights. Soon she started to unwind from the tension that had been there ever since Jim had touched her face.

He could hardly let me go around with chocolate muffin on my face, she reasoned with herself. *Anyway, there's nothing at all wrong with being slightly attracted to him. All it means is that I'm feeling normal again and I'm finally getting over Geoff.*

* * *

Kylie was greeted like a movie star by the SDS

executives, and they whisked her around the room to meet every single one of the thirty-odd distinguished guests. She smiled for the cameras, accepted congratulations and drank mineral water rather than champagne. It was hard to find the appropriate time to take her leave, and she ended up staying far longer than she'd planned. By the time she escaped, her face ached from smiling and she was totally out of small talk.

She checked her phone as she waited for her car to be brought around to the door of the hotel. There were two new messages. The first was from Stephen. She held his loud voice back from her ear.

"Hi, stranger. Sorry I missed you on Sunday – had a Saturday-night date that overran. Might catch you this weekend. Take care."

Kylie was pleased to hear that Stephen had a date. Maybe, just maybe, this time he had found the right girl.

Kylie called up the second message. It was Isobel.

"Hi, Kylie. A few of us have decided to meet in the bar for a drink. Have a look for us when you get back – that's if you're not too tired."

Kylie turned the radio up loud to keep herself alert on the return journey. She knew she shouldn't even consider having a drink in the bar; there would be a horde of new email messages she should attend to, not to mention Friday's presentation. But Jim would be there and she wanted to see him. To understand why she hadn't stopped thinking about him all day.

It was after eleven when she drove up the gravelled driveway of the resort. She entered the bar, but it was immediately evident that she was too late.

"Sorry, we're closed," said the barman as he wiped down the empty tables.

Kylie turned back the way she came and made for her room. She refused to acknowledge that the feeling in the pit of her stomach was disappointment.

* * *

Kylie made sure that she left enough time for breakfast the next morning; no way was she going to eat a chocolate muffin in front of Jim again. Carole and David were sitting together in the breakfast room and she joined their table.

"We missed you last night," said Carole, prodding some rock melon with her fork.

"I checked the bar when I got back – but you were all gone," replied Kylie with a shrug.

"The bar stopped serving drinks at ten thirty," David explained, his sandy hair combed in a side crease. "I think they must be under instructions not to let us have too much fun."

Kylie laughed. "Yeah, that sounds like Brent all right," she agreed just as the waiter came to ask for her order. "Poached eggs and bacon, please."

She noticed that Carole's eyes widened ever so slightly when she heard the order.

"I burn it off," she said defensively.

"I haven't seen you in the gym," was Carole's reply. She looked genuinely puzzled.

"Let's just say I'm lucky with my metabolism."

"I was hoping to spend some time at the gym," David sighed, patting his protruding stomach. "But you know how it is – trying to keep up with work as well as the course. The printer and fax in the suite have made things much easier, though."

"You have a printer and fax machine?" asked Carole and David nodded. She turned her eyes to Kylie. "Do you?"

"No," Kylie answered. "But at least I know where I can print a copy of my presentation now!"

"Have you done much work for it?" asked David, his puffy face anxious.

"No, not really. I have an idea but I haven't pulled it together yet. How about you?"

"I've got the basic slides. It's hard, though, not knowing what they're after –"

"They're not *after* anything, David," Carole interrupted. "Angela was perfectly clear – the partners want you to surprise them. What is it that you don't understand?"

Kylie had thought she'd never see the day when she felt sorry for David Smythe.

He virtually wilted under Carole's open scorn as he mumbled, "Surprises are not my forte."

Carole pushed her chair back from the table and said, "See you there," before Kylie had the chance to tell her that her attitude sucked.

* * *

"Good morning," Angela called out to Kylie and David when they entered the classroom some thirty minutes later. "Don't sit just yet – some of you will be leaving soon. Now that we're all here, I'll let you know the teams for the business simulation."

Kylie glanced discreetly at Jim. He had a dark shadow on his jaw and she liked the rugged effect of the stubble. Her heart quickened at the thought of being paired with him.

"Team 1: Jim and Carole. Team 2: Isobel and Oliver. Team 3: Kylie and David. Now, please stand next to your team mates."

Kylie obediently moved to stand next to David.

They had never been the best of friends, and the thought of working with him exclusively for two days was not at all appealing.

"Here is your data." Angela handed a heavy folder to each team. "Everything you need to know about your organisation, the X Company, is in here, including staff profiles, products and market share. Remember, your aim is to maximise net profit and share price over two years. Jim and Carole, you can stay in this room. Isobel and Oliver, you are in the room next door. Kylie and David – across the hall."

* * *

Working with David was every bit as difficult as Kylie expected. She read the documentation in half an hour, skipping over what looked to be unimportant. However, David insisted on reading every single word, slowly and carefully.

"I wish I could see these chips that X Company are selling," he said when he finally came to the end.

"You don't need to see them to make a decision," replied Kylie, just about hanging onto her patience. "The data in the pack tells us that the chip is technologically ahead of the competitors – it has the highest bandwidth – that's all we need to know."

"I don't understand things I can't see," he said

obstinately.

"For God's sake, David," she snapped. "We'll never get finished if that's the case!"

David seemed to wilt in the same way he had at the breakfast table that morning. "I'm sorry that I'm slowing you down . . ."

Kylie ashamedly realised that she was no better than Carole; she had belittled David just because he worked differently to her.

"I'll draw you one," she said, keen to make amends. She sketched out the chip and did her best to explain in very basic terms how it worked. "OK, you have the processor, the memory and the cache – and data flows between all three – bandwidth is the term used to describe how fast the data travels."

"How do you know this?" David asked, looking at her handiwork with admiration.

"My brother," Kylie explained. "He was always taking our computer apart – seeing what went where. I suppose some of it stuck in my head."

They got on better after that, but progress through the industry and competitor analysis was still very slow. How slow became evident when they broke for lunch. The other teams had already completed their strategic plans, and Angela was sounding them out on a 3 p.m. presentation.

"Sorry, we won't be ready by then," said Kylie. She

refused to look at Carole, knowing she would be wearing her most disdainful expression.

"Will 4.p.m. be OK?" asked Angela.

Kylie doubted it but had to say yes.

She and David decided to eat back in their classroom in order to catch up. David increased his pace, and his earlier attention to detail paid off with some clever ideas.

"That should do it," said Kylie at ten minutes to four. "Now, we just have to decide on who should deliver the presentation."

"You," replied David as if the answer was obvious.

Carole was the first presenter. She brimmed with confidence and authority and was very believable as the CEO of the fictitious X Company. More than once she said "Jim and I" as she explained each strategic initiative.

Why did I get stuck with David? thought Kylie. *If it had been Jim, or any of the others, I'd have a real chance of winning.*

Even though Kylie was somewhat ashamed of her thoughts, she couldn't make them go away. Winning had always been important to her. It helped her hold her head high at university and at MFJ. In the end, it had given her the motivation to walk away from Geoff. It was ingrained in her to win, even when the odds were stacked against her.

Oliver was every bit as good as Carole and it was with a certain degree of despondence that Kylie got to her feet.

"Within two years the X Company will have obtained 60 per cent of the overall market by concentrating our energies on the booming educational sector and by outperforming our competitors on technology and price." Kylie found her rhythm and spoke with conviction about the opportunities in the educational sector. "The X Company is already on the preferred-supplier list for the Department of Education. The new minister is technologically astute and has ambitious plans for the schools across the country. The X Company can make his plans a reality . . ."

By the time she reached the end, Kylie had almost forgotten that the X Company and the Minister for Education weren't for real.

"Well done," whispered David as she sat down.

"Thanks."

Angela told them they were free to leave. "Remember, Year 1 budget allocations are due at 9 p.m.," she warned as they filed out of the room. "I'll collect them at the bar. No rainchecks."

"I think we had better get straight down to it," Kylie said to David. "No free hour tonight."

"I was hoping to catch up on my emails," he replied, looking stressed.

"Do you want to win this or not?" she asked.

"Of course I do."

"Then send your team an email to let them know that your course commitments will make you unavailable for the next two nights," she replied.

"Is that what you're going to do?"

She hesitated. Neil would go ballistic if she went incommunicado, but it just might teach him a lesson.

"Yes."

* * *

They decided to work in David's room. Kylie was impressed when she saw the separate office and lounge area.

"I didn't realise you actually had a suite," she said as she photocopied the budget-allocation sheet. "The rest of us mere mortals have a standard room."

"I think there's been a mix-up somewhere – but I'm not complaining."

He smiled his first smile of the day as he sank into the sofa. She handed him his copy of the allocation sheet and sat down opposite.

"OK – Research and Development budget first," she said. "Obviously, we must invest heavily in the chip in order to stay ahead of the competition."

David didn't quite agree, and that set the tone for the evening. The marketing, training and project budgets each involved intense debate before a reluctant compromise. A few times Kylie had to scrunch up her sheet of paper and start afresh. Once, when she was feeling particularly frustrated, she imagined that it was David's head she was scrunching.

They ground through each item on the budget sheet and somehow had half an hour to spare at the end.

"Let's see if we can get something to eat at the bar while we wait for Angela," said Kylie. "I'm starving."

Much to her surprise, David shook his head. "No, I need to work on my presentation."

"Oh, come on – live a little." Kylie smiled coaxingly.

"I have to work hard to get ahead," he replied. "I'm not like you."

She made a funny face at him. "Are you implying that I don't work hard?"

He was deadly serious as he said, "I'm saying that you have more natural talent than me and consequently it takes you less effort to achieve the same result."

Kylie got serious too. "I think you're being rather

tough on yourself, David."

He didn't reply. When he started up his laptop, Kylie took it as her cue to leave.

"Make sure that you at least order some food in," she told him on her way out.

* * *

Another conference group had arrived at the resort and the bar was full. Two log fires blazed at either end of the room, and Kylie unbuttoned her woollen jacket as she walked through the crowd. She noticed Isobel and Oliver over by the window, a bottle of wine tilted sideways in an ice-bucket at the centre of their table. Oliver saw her and jokingly put his hand over the budget sheet as if it was top secret.

They look as if they've had a lot more fun than David and me, thought Kylie, a little enviously.

Though she had to admit that working with David had become easier as the day progressed. In many ways their working styles were complementary. Her impulsiveness was reigned in by his caution, and her top-level view was substantiated by his detailed analysis. It didn't take long to realise that she had been wrong when she had previously thought of him as arrogant. The truth was that he had very low self-esteem and the little he had was riding on his career.

Kylie ordered a beer and a bowl of hot chips at the bar. She was paying the barman when she heard Jim's voice.

"All finished?"

She turned and noticed that his jaw-line was now smooth instead of stubbled. She knew if she went close enough she would be able to smell his aftershave.

Carole pushed forward and Kylie jerked back to reality.

"Where's David?"

Kylie found her voice. "Doing his homework for Friday's presentation."

"Slogging is no substitute for aptitude," remarked the other woman.

Kylie stared straight at her. "What exactly do you mean by that?"

Carole shrugged. "He's not the brightest, is he?"

"I beg to differ," stated Kylie, her face colouring with anger. "David tends to undersell himself – unlike some people around here."

She took her beer and bowl of chips and walked away. However, she soon realised there were no free tables and she had no option but to gatecrash Oliver and Isobel.

"Sorry – I know you are still finishing up but I'm seeking asylum," she said sotto voce.

Oliver smirked. "From the Ice Maiden?"

"Ssshh – she's not deaf!" hissed Isobel. "Sit down, Kylie. You can help us decide what to do with the $2,000 we have left over in our budget."

"Invest it in the education market," declared Kylie, blowing on one of the hot chips before popping it in her mouth.

"You mean the Educom contact list?" asked Oliver.

Educom was a fictitious agency that published a pricey *Who's Who in Education*.

She nodded and swallowed before saying, "It will pay off – I guarantee it."

Oliver agreed. "Slot it in, Isobel. Kylie is always right."

Kylie made a mock swing for him and he ducked.

Isobel saw Angela come in and said, "Just in time."

Angela was dressed for the cold evening in a red ankle-length coat.

"She really likes red, doesn't she?" remarked Oliver.

Angela stopped by Jim and Carole at the bar before making her way to their table.

"Like a drink, Angela?" asked Oliver.

"No – got a lot of work to do tonight."

"Maybe tomorrow night?" he asked, a mischievous

glint in his eye.

"Maybe."

She put their allocation sheets in her tote bag before she bade them goodnight.

Isobel sighed deeply. "I'm afraid that I must also go. I promised a client that I would call tonight."

"I've made a pact with David not to check email or voice messages for the next two days," said Kylie as Isobel gathered her things.

"I'm not that brave," Isobel answered with a grimace. "See you tomorrow."

"Neil won't like not being able to contact you," commented Oliver when they were alone.

Kylie reached for her beer. "I've had enough of Neil lately," she admitted. "To be honest, I'm looking forward to my overseas assignment."

"Me too," said Oliver. "I've heard that Brent will be making the announcement on Friday – I hope I'm sent somewhere exciting."

"Crystelle doesn't mind?" asked Kylie. Crystelle was Oliver's wife of four months. A pretty blonde with a loud laugh, Kylie had liked her right from the start. Unlike Geoff.

"She's an airhead," Geoff had declared when he heard of his friend's engagement.

Kylie had instantly objected. "Just because Crystelle likes to have fun doesn't mean she's an airhead."

Geoff wasn't listening. "I didn't think Oliver was the kind to go for a trophy wife."

"I think she's good for Oliver," Kylie insisted. "He's not as reserved as he used to be."

"There was nothing wrong with the way he was."

"You're just jealous of her," Kylie laughed. "You're used to being the life and soul of the party and now Crystelle has pushed you off your perch."

Geoff didn't find it funny, and they had split up by the time the wedding came around. Kylie received an invitation but sent her regrets. She didn't know if Geoff had gone or not.

Kylie came back to the present when she heard Oliver ask, "Where's the Ice Maiden?"

He was talking to Jim who had come over to their table. Her throat tightened at the sight of him, just as it had earlier.

Jim sat down in Isobel's vacant seat. "Carole's gone to her room to catch up on some work," he said in answer to Oliver's question. He then made a half-hearted attempt to defend his team mate. "She's not that bad. She just takes her work a little too seriously."

"More like a *lot* too seriously," said Kylie and was relieved to hear that her voice sounded normal.

"Don't you?" Jim turned his dark grey eyes her way, the intensity of his gaze unsettling. "Aren't you here because you want to become a partner?"

"Yes," Kylie met his gaze head on, "and so are you. And Oliver. But that doesn't excuse Carole's bad manners."

"Kylie's always right," declared Oliver, getting to his feet. "And I happen to agree with her in this instance. Carole needs to come down from her high horse. Now, I'm going to order another bottle of wine. Any preference for red or white?"

"White," Kylie and Jim answered in unison.

"We've something in common," said Jim when Oliver was out of earshot.

She grinned. "White wine! Great – we can get drunk together."

He laughed and she laughed too, happy that he thought her amusing.

I want more chances to make him laugh, she was surprised to realise. *I want to ask him a thousand questions about himself. I want Oliver to get lost at the bar and never return.*

"You seem to know Oliver fairly well," he said, thankfully unaware of what was going through her head.

"We were friends –" Kylie stumbled as she realised that she had subconsciously placed her friendship with Oliver in the past tense. She had regarded it as something that was lost along with

Geoff. In that moment she saw that Geoff and Oliver didn't have to come as a package. "I mean, we *are* friends outside of work."

If Jim noticed something odd about her stumbled response, he didn't say. "What time did you get back last night?" he asked next.

"Eleven," she said out loud, while thinking, *Too late. You were gone from the bar.*

"You must be tired today."

"Yes – but it's my own fault – I need to learn how to say no to Neil. I say the word but it doesn't sink in with him. I still can't believe that I drove for *four hours* last night!"

"Four hours would almost get you from one end of Ireland to the other," he said conversationally. "What part are your parents from?"

"Somewhere outside Dublin." She shrugged, feeling helplessly uninformed about her family history. "I don't know the exact town – they don't talk about it a lot."

"Ask the next time you see them." He smiled. "Maybe I'll know it."

"I will," she promised.

Conversation between them was easy. She could have talked to him all night, told him everything about herself, her family, maybe even Geoff. But Oliver came back. The wine was poured. The conversation resumed and, while it was just as easy, it was much less personal.

It was some time later that Oliver's phone beeped with an incoming message. He picked it up from the table and read the text message on his screen. "Bloody great – a meeting in the city on Friday evening. Crystelle will kill me when I tell her I won't be coming straight home . . . it's at times like these that I wonder why I ever became a lawyer."

"Why *did* you become a lawyer?" asked Kylie as she swirled the last of the tawny-coloured Chardonnay in her glass.

"My dad suggested it. He saw how much money they made and thought it would be a good career for me." Oliver paused before delivering his punch line. "He apologises profusely every time he sees me now."

Relaxed from the wine, his story seemed hilariously funny, and their loud laughter drew the attention of the remaining patrons. When the laughter died down, Kylie asked the same question of Jim.

"Why did you choose law?"

He shrugged his broad shoulders. "I wanted to do medicine rather than law but I didn't get in. I was devastated at the time . . . but now that I know myself better, I'm not so sure I would have made a good doctor."

Kylie added his response to the limited knowledge she had from the "two truths and one lie" game on their first morning. Jim Donnelly had three sisters, he loved rhythm and blues and he was a mad football fan. His lie had been about the football. He'd said that he loved rugby more than soccer when the opposite was marginally true.

So far, he'd made no mention of a girlfriend.

"I'm afraid he is taken, Kylie," Isobel had said on the night of the launch, "and you and I can only admire from a distance."

Kylie was desperately wishing that Isobel had got it wrong when Jim asked, "And you, Kylie? What made you want to become a lawyer?"

"I never wanted to be a lawyer," she told him. "Right from the outset I wanted to be a *partner*."

"Oh, excuse me!" exclaimed Oliver, throwing his eyes to heaven.

"It's not like that." She grinned.

"Well, how is it?" asked Jim.

"It goes back to school," she explained. "One girl's father was a partner in a law firm. Let's say it set the standard for me."

They talked their way through a second bottle of wine. At ten thirty the bar staff began to collect glasses and wipe down tables.

"Time to call it a night," Oliver declared,

stretching as he got to his feet.

Kylie also stood up – reluctantly, for she still hadn't asked Jim a fraction of what she wanted to know about him.

"Goodnight," she said. "See you in the morning."

Outside, she buttoned up her jacket against the cold wind and scrunched her way across the yard to the residential block. Her thoughts were so fiercely focused on Jim that she didn't realise the voice calling, "Kylie, Kylie!" was for real. But the hand that caught her arm was real and she stopped dead in her tracks.

"You forgot these," said Jim, holding out her packet of Dunhills.

"Thanks," she mumbled, disappointed that her cigarettes were the only reason he had come dashing after her.

In the following silence, Kylie felt her eyes drawn to him until they locked into his stare.

"You're a very talented lawyer, Kylie Horgan," he said softly. "*You* set the standard – don't ever forget that."

Kylie was so taken aback that she didn't set him straight. The girl in school, Lindy, had been her friend. Her father was a lovely man who had given Kylie holiday work while she was at university. Her first mentor, he'd shown her how satisfying it was to build your own practice and balance quality service with financial success. Over a few summers, he'd channelled Kylie's unbridled competitiveness and talent into a specific goal: to reach partner by the time she was thirty-two years old. The family lived in Melbourne now but Kylie still kept in touch with both Lindy and her dad. She hadn't told them yet how close she was to becoming partner and achieving the goal.

Kylie should have lost no time in assuring Jim that she didn't have a chip on her shoulder, but his eyes were holding her in a weird kind of spell. She quite simply couldn't speak while he was looking at her like that.

"Goodnight," he said, "again."

She watched him go.

You set the standard.

What a lovely thing to say even though he had got the wrong end of the stick entirely.

*   *   *

Kylie looked at her reflection as she waited for her call to be answered. Her cheeks were flushed, her eyes bright. Rose would have known instantly that something was different had she been face-to-face with her daughter.

"Hello?" Rose's voice sounded wary when she eventually answered the phone.

"Mum, it's me."

"Kylie! What are you doing calling at this hour?" she scolded, and then asked, "Is everything all right, love?"

"It's fine. Just wanted to say hello."

"How's the course going?"

"It's good – interesting – but hard work."

"Has anyone been fired yet?" asked Rose.

"It's not *The Apprentice*, Mum," replied Kylie with a laugh. "But to answer your question, no. Nobody will be eliminated until the end of the year."

"Right," Rose gave a muffled yawn. "Well, it's late . . . I should be going to bed . . . and so should you . . . I suppose we'll see you at the weekend . . ."

"Hold on, Mum," Kylie cut in. "What's the name of the place you come from in Ireland?"

Not surprisingly, Rose didn't answer.

"Mum? Are you there?"

"Yes."

Rose wasn't making it easy. She never did. However, this time Kylie wasn't going to give up.

She repeated the question slowly. "What's the name of the place where you grew up?"

Rose answered with another question. "Why do you need to know that at eleven o'clock at night?"

"Because somebody asked me . . . Jim Donnelly
. . . he's on the course . . . he's Irish . . ."

She knew she had Rose in a corner. There was no
way she could avoid answering, other than to hang
up. If they had been at home she would have rushed
off to attend to some minor but suddenly urgent
task.

"Portmarnock," was the grudging response that
came down the line.

"Portmarnock," Kylie echoed. "Thanks, Mum, I'll
ask Jim if he knows of it."

Chapter 7

"And the winning team is," Angela made the sound of a drum roll, "Team 1, Jim and Carole – with $5m profit and $8 share price. Team 2, you had an OK result … Team 3, well …"

There was nothing positive that Angela could say about the results of Team 3. Both the profit and share price had fallen. Kylie tried to look as though she didn't care.

David was very despondent when they returned to the room across the hall.

"Maybe we shouldn't bother doing anything today," he said. "We would have done better had we spent all day yesterday down at the bar."

His despondency made Kylie feel even more weary than she already was. She had got up at five to work on her presentation. It had taken ages to download Claudine's pictures and put the right text around them.

She rubbed the furrows on her forehead and muttered, "Our investment in the education market made a big dent in our results."

"Well, let's not throw good money after bad in our Year 2 budget," was David's answer.

"No – it's important to stay true to our strategic plan," Kylie argued. "The education market is our long-term strategy . . ."

David chewed the top of his pen. He seemed to need to do that in order to think. "OK – I'm with you. Let's continue to pour money into education – either we fall flat on our faces again or our profits will go through the roof."

"OK." Kylie was relieved that they seemed to be getting faster at making decisions. "Now, is there anything we can learn from the results of the other teams?"

David ran his finger down through the summary page. "Team 1 pumped all their money into training. I think we could do with being more people-focused this year."

"Good point."

They spent the rest of the morning planning a restructure for the X Company: reviewing staff profiles, promoting, hiring and firing. It was fun and they made very good progress.

"Thanks for that tip on the education market," Oliver commented sardonically when they sat down at the lunch table.

"Oh ye of little faith!" retorted Kylie.

"Planning a strong gallop towards the finish line?" asked Jim, a smile playing on his lips.

She smiled back. "Yes. Prepare to be flattened."

The connection with him seemed to get stronger with every smile, every word. She was longing for the time when she would be able to talk with him alone again.

Kylie was distracted from her thoughts by another one of Oliver's smart alec remarks. The competitive banter went on right through the meal.

* * *

"What training courses are we going to sponsor?" asked David, settling back into his seat after lunch. "I like the sound of this project management one."

Kylie wasn't ready to put her nose to the grindstone just yet.

"David," she said, remembering the discussion from the previous night, "why did you do law?"

His face reddened, as if she had caught him with his hand in the cookie jar. "Because it was expected of me."

"By whom?"

"My father's a Queen's Counsel: Kenneth Smythe – you may have heard of him."

"Of course I've heard of him – he's a legend in constitutional law – but I never guessed that he was your father."

David, however, didn't seem all that proud of his old man.

"I'm an embarrassment to him," he said, his voice hoarsened by bitterness. "Ten years as a senior associate – a rather mediocre performance by his only child, wouldn't you say?"

"No, I wouldn't say," she replied. She was about to add that there was nothing wrong with being a senior associate but stopped herself just in time; something told her that David was sick of being patronised.

"He gets frustrated by me," said David. "Even when I was a child he used to try to have these highbrow conversations with me – then he would get irritated when I just didn't get it. Unfortunately, I didn't inherit his brilliant genes . . ." His voice faded away.

For the second time in as many days, Kylie felt sorry for him.

"Why don't we go down to the bar," she suggested. "Find a table next to the fire and work through this budget over a glass of wine."

"Sounds like a good idea to me," he said and gathered up the paperwork. "Oliver and Isobel did it yesterday and still managed to outperform us in Year 1."

* * *

Angela collected the budget allocations at six and said she would announce the results by eight.

"Two hours free," said Isobel, clapping her hands with girlish glee. "It's our last night – let's make it one to remember!"

They boycotted their unread emails, unanswered voicemails and the all-important partner presentations and went straight to the restaurant. Kylie and Jim gravitated to the same side of the table.

"After you," he said and pulled out a seat for her.

"Thanks."

"I asked my mum," she said when he sat down. "She grew up in a place called Portmarnock. Do you know it?"

"Yes – it's an outer suburb of Dublin city," said Jim. "It's very nice – has a lovely beach and one of the best golf courses in the country."

Kylie wanted to know more. "Do you know anyone that lives there?"

"No," was his disappointing answer.

"What's Dublin city like?" she asked next.

"Jam-packed with character: paperboys, buskers, jaywalkers, winos, cobblestone laneways, modern shops in old buildings, Guinness signs outside pubs, live music inside . . ."

His words were so vivid that she had no problem picturing it. Just listening to him speak about his country seemed to go some way to satiating the nagging curiosity that she had. She realised then that part of Jim's attractiveness was that he was Irish. He was willing to answer her questions. Unlike Rose and Frankie.

"Do you miss living there?" she asked when he paused.

"Yes and no . . ." His face took on a more serious expression. "It sounds funny, but one of the things I miss most is the sing-along at the end of a night out. And of course I miss the family, not just the immediate family but the extended aunts, uncles and cousins. I'd never have to go to the *Yellow Pages* to look up a plumber or an electrician. Somebody always knew somebody who knew somebody."

The waiter came around with the wine.

"Red or white, madam?"

"White."

"Sir?"

"White, please."

"Cheers," said Jim so quietly that the others couldn't hear.

"Cheers," she whispered back.

She searched for something to say. Something safe. She remembered where they had dropped the conversation before the waiter came. "What *don't* you miss about Ireland?"

He smiled at her crookedly. "The weather. The bad roads. The fact that in Ireland people's curiosity comes ahead of their sensitivity. Everything is up for discussion, nothing is sacred."

She gave a little laugh. "That certainly makes me Irish, then. My nosiness drives my mother insane . . . "

"I can certainly see that you have the capacity to drive someone insane, Kylie Horgan," was his reply.

This time it was in his tone as well as his eyes. There was no mistaking it: Jim Donnelly was flirting with her.

* * *

They were still at the dinner table when Angela arrived at eight.

"Angela!" Oliver exclaimed and jumped to his feet as if she was a long-lost friend. "You've been working too hard. Sit down. Have some of this excellent wine."

Angela, nonplussed by the attention, unwound her red scarf from her neck. "Yes, well, a glass of Shiraz would be nice."

Oliver got her a seat and asked the waiter for a clean glass.

Crystelle has certainly changed him, thought Kylie. *The old Oliver would never have willingly placed himself in the spotlight.*

"Teacher's pet," she said under her breath as he passed by. Rediscovering their friendship had been the best thing about this week away. Bar Jim.

Angela waited for her well-deserved glass of Shiraz before announcing the winner.

"Well, the results of Year 2 were rather unexpected. But there is a clear overall winner . . . and that is Team 3."

"Yes!" shouted David and banged his fist triumphantly on the table. "Yes, yes, *yes!*"

Kylie had never seen him so excited about anything. She was feeling pretty damned pleased herself.

Carole, looking decidedly pissed off, asked, "Did Team 3 win the whole thing or just Year 2?"

"The whole thing," answered Angela. "Their results in Year 2 surpassed your performance over both years. The education market took off big-time."

"I knew it," said Kylie, giving Oliver an I-told-you-so look as Angela handed the result sheets down the table.

"Look at the profit you made in education," Jim remarked as he studied the results. "And it returned nothing in Year 1. What made you decide to invest in it again?"

Kylie hesitated in her reply, unsure whether she should be fully honest or not. Jim was looking at her intently, waiting for a response. She lowered her voice so only he could hear.

"If there's one thing I learned from my ex-fiancé, it was not to gamble in half measures."

Angela stayed for only one glass of wine and left them with a reminder of the presentations the next morning.

"All of the partners will be present," she told them. "You'll need your wits about you – try not to stay up too late."

Angela knew that her warning fell on deaf ears. It was always the same. In fifteen years of facilitating courses like these, she had observed that it was human nature to throw caution to the wind on the final night. She left them to it and hoped there wouldn't be any casualties in the morning.

*   *   *

They were shooed from the restaurant at ten.

"Where to now?" Oliver asked the group as they stood outside.

"Only thirty minutes left before the bar closes," David pointed out. "Why don't we have a night-cap in my *deluxe* suite instead?"

Laughing and making far too much noise, they crossed the gravelled yard with its ghostly white pebbles.

Carole was noticeably piqued when she saw David's room. "This is double the size of mine."

Kylie couldn't resist saying, "It's not all about size, Carole."

Carole smiled icily while everybody else cracked up laughing.

Jim crouched down and scanned the contents of the bar fridge. "Shiraz . . . Chardonnay . . . four bottles of beer . . . something tells me this lot won't go far."

"Just don't land me with the bill," David complained.

Jim caught Kylie's eye and they shared a secret smile.

"Glass of white, Kylie?" he asked.

She felt as if he was asking her something totally different. "Yes, please."

Kylie watched him pour, anticipating the moment he would hand it to her. But David intervened, belatedly remembering that he was the host.

Kylie took her glass out to the balcony; she needed a cigarette. Setting her glass down on the railing, she searched her bag for her lighter. She located one amidst all the junk, and the orange flame flickered for the instant it took to light the cigarette.

She leaned over the railing and stared down on the darkened vineyards below.

"Jim Donnelly." She whispered his name into the anonymous dark. Everything about him set her nerves on edge. Kylie wished that Isobel was wrong. For if Jim was taken, and there was a girlfriend in his life, then he shouldn't be flirting with other women.

He shouldn't be flirting with me.

She knew Jim would follow her out, and it was only a few minutes later that she heard the balcony door slide open. A glass of wine in his hand, he came to stand next to her. Together they looked out at the peacefully dark vineyard.

She took a drag of her cigarette.

"How many of those do you go through a day?" he asked.

"Somewhere between five and ten," she shrugged and then added, "Before you say it, I know it's a filthy habit."

"I wasn't going to say that," he laughed, "but you put it so well."

A long silence followed. Kylie finished the cigarette and reached for her glass of wine, her next prop.

Jim straightened up and she felt the full force of his gaze. His face was shadowed, his eyes dark wells in which she could drown.

"So, this ex-fiancé of yours," he said slowly. "How long has it been since you broke up with him?"

"Six months."

She took a nervous swig of the wine.

Ask him. Ask if he has a girlfriend. Make it sound casual.

She practised the words in her head, adding, deleting, just like she would do to some problematic sentence in a contract.

"So, what's your girlfriend doing while you're away this week?" she asked eventually.

Her question hung between them. She could tell that the answer wasn't straightforward for him.

Oh, no, there is someone. Why else would he flounder?

The balcony door slid back and they both turned around at the sound. "What are you two doing out here alone?" asked Carole, her voice loud and intruding.

"Giving myself lung cancer," quipped Kylie. "Come on, Jim, let's go inside. It's freezing out here."

The rest of the group was gathered around the coffee table, ten-dollar bills thrown carelessly in the centre. David, the top of his shirt unbuttoned, was shuffling a deck of cards.

"Poker, ante up ten dollars," he said.

Kylie stared at the blue cluster of ten-dollar bills, then at Oliver, the only one who understood. His sympathetic eyes flashed a message.

There was nothing I could do to stop it – other than tell the truth.

Jim reached in his pocket, presumably for his wallet.

I could join in with them. It's not as if they're committing a sin, Kylie tried to reason with herself.

David started to deal, his hands deft: Isobel, Carole, Jim, Oliver.

Kylie's vision blurred and she could see Geoff, the obsessed look in his eyes, the tremor of excitement in his hands.

"Kylie, are you in or not?" David asked impatiently.

I can't, she realised. *I know it's just a game of poker and I'm being melodramatic. But I just can't do it.*

"No," she shook her head, her voice strained, "I think I'll call it a night."

She ignored the questioning look on Jim's face and let herself out.

* * *

Back in her room, she couldn't stop the memories. For three years she had lived with a compulsive gambler. After what she had gone through, it was no wonder she couldn't participate in a simple game of poker.

For the first eighteen months, she was blissfully unaware of what was going on. They lived separately and Geoff had plenty of opportunity to go to the bookies or the casino without having to explain himself. Yes, she had noticed small things but never realised that they formed part of a big, big problem. One day, at the racetrack, Geoff went to place a bet but didn't return. Two hours later, wondering what on earth had happened to him, she went to seek him out. She found him inside, staring intently at a race on one of the TVs, the form guide gripped tightly in his hand.

He's betting on the races at the other tracks as well as here, she realised.

She pulled him away from the TV. "We've come here with our friends and you've totally ignored them – and me."

He kissed her nose. "Sorry, my sweet. I got caught up in the adrenalin of it all."

He didn't leave her side for the rest of the day, and by the time they went home she had forgotten about the incident.

Another time, at a city pub, she had gone searching for him when he didn't return from the ATM. It was a large establishment with various levels. She pushed her way through the crowds. He should have stood out, his red hair quite a distinguishing feature. But there was no sign of him anywhere.

The slot machines were the last place she checked. She saw him straight away as he frantically pressed the buttons, a glazed look on his face.

"What the hell are you doing, Geoff? I've been waiting for you upstairs for the last hour."

He looked at her vacantly. It took a few moments for him to come back from wherever he was in his head.

"I'm sorry, sweet. I got delayed talking to a guy I know. I just had a minute on the machine, I swear."

She sensed he was telling a lie. "What guy? Who

was it you met?"

"An old school friend. Nobody for you to be jealous of."

He had been more careful after that, and their relationship got deeper, more serious. Geoff was smart, sexy and fun. She was really happy when they got engaged. Shortly afterwards they bought a house together. And that was the start of the end.

*　*　*

A thumping noise infiltrated Kylie's sleep. She turned in the bed, hoping it would go away. But it didn't, it only got louder.

"Kylie! Kylie! Are you in there? Are you OK?"

Teetering between consciousness and unconsciousness, Kylie recognised the voice: Isobel.

Why is Isobel calling me?

The answer was slow to come to her sleep-clogged mind but it eventually registered.

I've slept in.

She staggered out of bed, still half asleep, and opened the door.

"Sorry – I forgot to set the alarm clock," she mumbled sheepishly.

"You're going to have to think up something better than that for Brent Lavell," was Isobel's retort.

"The presentations have already started."

"I'll be there in ten minutes," sighed Kylie, running a hand through her tangled hair.

"No," Isobel shook her head, "I'll wait for you. If we arrive separately, it will be two disruptions rather than one."

"Sorry," Kylie said again as Isobel followed her inside.

"Don't worry about it – just hurry."

With no time for a shower, Kylie slipped on a pair of chocolate-brown pants. Flat at the waist and flared at the ankles, they complemented her long legs. A tight-fitting white top and her trustworthy boots finished the outfit. Wetting her hands, she untangled her knotted curls. There was no time for make-up, just a dash of rust-coloured lipstick.

"Not bad for six minutes," declared Isobel as the door slammed shut behind them.

* * *

David was making his presentation when Kylie and Isobel opened the back door to the room. Discreetly, they made their way down the side aisle to the front row. However, it was inevitable that forty pairs of partners' eyes should track their progress.

"OK?" whispered Jim as Kylie sat down on the

free seat next to him.

He looked concerned.

"Yes," she nodded.

David paused to give her a disapproving glance before he moved to the next slide with a click of the mouse. Kylie read the bullet points. It seemed that his proposal related to an expansion of MFJ's tax division.

"Over the last few years there has been a steady divergence between supply and demand for taxation lawyers," he declared. "With the increased audit activity by the taxation office and the continuing complexity of the legislation, a gap has come about in the market. I'm proposing that we boost our investment in the tax division by hiring an extra ten lawyers. We would then have enough manpower to capture and service a significant number of new accounts. If we hire actively over the next three months, we could mobilise before our competitors, who are also very aware of this market gap."

Kylie felt a tangible resistance emanate from the partners behind her. Ten extra heads. Ten more salaries. They would need some serious convincing.

The next few slides didn't add any further substance to his proposal.

Wide open for criticism, he asked, "Any questions?"

Neil was the first to air his derision. "You have a lot more work to do with this, David. All I see is some wishy-washy statements about a market gap. I can't see any concrete evidence of who the clients are – or if they are viable."

David flushed as he defended himself. "I didn't think it appropriate to include names at this forum."

Kylie heard Brent's cold tones next. "You're not likely to get a better forum. This isn't some playact – we want a real pitch – no holds barred."

David looked gutted. Despite all his forethought, he had still underestimated the detail the partners were looking for.

Angela got to her feet and rescued him from the harsh limelight.

"Any further questions?" She scanned the room. "No? Well, thanks, David. It looks like you have some extra homework to do. And thanks to Neil and Brent for your – honest feedback. Now, next we have Jim."

Jim's arm brushed against Kylie as he got to his feet, and the brief touch felt like a bolt of lightning. He stood up on the podium, casual and confident, as *Soccer Australia*, the title of his presentation, flashed across the screen. In the background there was a picture of Brent Lavell heading a soccer ball. The room erupted into hearty laughter and Jim had the partners in the palm of his hand right from that moment.

"Brent, I hope you forgive me for superimposing your head on this player's body, but I took some artistic licence," he said as he smiled down at his audience.

He has the nicest smile. Warm. Sexy, thought Kylie.

As if he could read her thoughts, Jim's smile singled her out. It was only for a few seconds but she felt that the whole room could see. Some colour had started to creep into her cheeks by the time he turned his head away. However, the next words from his mouth made her go cold all over.

"My proposal regards a sponsorship deal with Soccer Australia."

No, Jim! I'm the one asking for sponsorship. You can't ask for it too — they'll never give it to both of us.

"We have a rare opportunity here," said Jim, totally unaware of the turmoil his opening statement had caused for Kylie. "A sporting body that needs financial support — not just any old sporting body but the fastest growing sport of Australia's youth. Think of the executive fathers and mothers who see our name on the shirt of their kid's favourite player — our name would be broadcast to the millions of TV viewers who watch the international matches. The exposure we would get from this sponsorship is massive and would put us in a completely different league to our competitors."

Jim was a natural presenter, with his relaxed stance, easy eye contact and perfectly timed humour.

Kylie turned around once and saw a few nods of approval from the partners.

They're going to agree, she thought desperately. *That means I don't have a chance.*

Oliver talked about designing joint websites with the federal government, and Carole suggested a new MFJ branch for India. Isobel made a pitch for a comprehensive training programme to give the firm a competitive edge in mergers and acquisitions. The partners put challenging questions to all the presenters but Kylie hardly paid any heed to what was being said. She was frantically revising her own presentation so she could make her request different to Jim's.

By the time Angela called her name, she had a loose plan. She got to her feet and, instead of calling up her presentation, she shut down the projector. She had decided that going solo was her best chance.

"Apologies for my late arrival this morning. Those who know me well are aware that I have a dependency on alarm clocks. It's a little problem that I'm seeking help for."

Her joke earned a laugh. A good start.

"Now, I'm going to ask some questions and I'd appreciate if you could raise your hand if they apply to you."

Best to involve them right from the start. Get them to participate before they realise what I'm after. Make it damned hard to back away.

"Hands up if you broke a bone when you were a kid."

There was a healthy show of hands, maybe 25 per cent.

"OK, show your hand if you know some kid who's got cancer," she said next. Hands crept up more slowly this time. After a few moments, she had a show of about 50 per cent.

"Isn't it sobering – frightening – horrifying – that so many kids are stuck in hospital beds for weeks on end?"

Nobody answered. She didn't expect them to.

"It's even worse when you realise that many of the kids don't even have a decent TV to help the long days pass by."

She saw their faces change as they realised that this was another request for sponsorship. She barged on before they fully closed down on her.

"I'm not asking you to solve the whole problem: just one part – an easy, achievable part. Royal North Shore Hospital has fifty kids on average in the ward

– $2,000 will buy a 'fun machine', which is a mobile unit that will enable the children to watch DVDs, play computer games, email their friends and listen to music. That's $100,000 for the whole ward – not a big sum by our standards."

It was Claudine who had unknowingly given Kylie the idea about the fun machines.

"One of the nurses here used to work in Westmead Hospital," she had said on Kylie's first visit. "They have machines there – the kids can get on the internet and watch movies. The nurse said they're like a lifeline for the seriously ill children. Pity they don't have any in this hospital."

Kylie had phoned Westmead to check the cost and the manufacturer of the machines. Now she had her facts and figures and, from the sour look on Brent's face, it was time to fight her corner.

"Have the guidelines not been made clear?" he snapped. "We asked for ideas that would be of long-term benefit *to the firm*. Don't get me wrong, charities are good – but this isn't the time or place."

"The guidelines were made very clear," replied Kylie, holding Brent's mean little eyes in her stare. "I believe that making social conscience part of our culture *will be of benefit to our firm*. We would relearn empathy, broaden our horizons and ultimately provide a significantly better service to our clients."

She finished to a silence. She continued to stare defiantly at Brent.

"Very passionate."

She recognised Neil's sarcastic tones and turned her head his way.

"But interesting that you haven't bothered with slides. I thought that a PowerPoint presentation was part of the guidelines."

She had slides, twelve of them. Pictures of Ethan with his legs hanging from traction. Pictures of bald children, tired parents and smiling nurses.

"Jim was a hard act to follow," she said, "and I decided to try something different."

One of the partners, who she had seen nodding through Jim's presentation, spoke next. "I see far too many similarities between your proposal and Jim's." His tone made it very evident that Jim's was far more appealing.

"Let me help you with the distinction," said Kylie with a tight-lipped smile. Over the last hour, she had mentally rehearsed her answer to this very predictable question. "Firstly, I am not suggesting a contribution by the firm. I'm advocating individual contributions, deductions from the monthly salary run. Social conscience is an individual thing and the individuals must make the gesture. I intend to distribute salary deduction forms to all partners and senior associates. Donations would be at their discretion but the form will provide a guideline of what is needed by an individual to make the target. Secondly, with all respect to Jim, Soccer Australia is blessed with mostly healthy players and members. Nobody is confined to bed for weeks on end. *Nobody is dying.*"

There were no more questions, and Kylie returned to her seat. She risked a glance at Jim as she sat down next to him. Frowning, he spurned her gaze. She had a sinking feeling that he didn't understand.

* * *

A buffet lunch followed the presentations. Kylie was scooping some salad onto her plate when Neil sought her out.

"Given the time you've supposedly put into your presentation, I was expecting it to be spectacular."

She bristled at his tone. "I think it will be very spectacular if I manage to raise $100,000 from the personal pockets of our professional staff for children in need."

She moved on to the cold meat. Neil followed, his plate empty, food apparently not on his agenda.

"And you can hardly justify that it is for the long-term benefit of the company," was his next caustic remark.

She put her plate down – it clattered as it hit the granite ledge. "Do you really believe that insular thinking will benefit the firm in the long run? Money is the only value we teach our staff to understand – yet we have clients with a *full range* of values. We must find a way to relate to them, Neil. Money alone won't do it."

Her passionate outburst had no effect at all on him. His eyes were cold as they stared back at her. "Don't ever turn your phone off again, Kylie."

So that's why you're pissed off: because you couldn't get hold of me for a few days. Well, you can get stuffed!

Her thoughts very nearly vocalised themselves. She picked her plate back up and walked away before she said something she would regret.

Isobel was lined up in the hot-food area.

"Sit with me," Kylie whispered in her ear before continuing on to an empty table.

Isobel obediently followed a few moments later. "No friends, Kylie?" she asked, smiling.

"Feel as if I've been in the wars." Kylie grimaced. "Neil just had a go."

Isobel buttered her bread. "Something tells me you're not in Jim's good books either."

Kylie shrugged as if she didn't care. "There was nothing I could do to avoid it – my cause is more worthy than his and I had to fight for it."

Isobel chewed a mouthful before saying, "I think this programme is hard enough without shooting each other down."

"I didn't shoot him down," Kylie objected.

"That's not how it sounded to me," said Isobel in her gentle way.

Kylie mulled it over as she ate her salad.

Was I over the top? Could I have done it differently?

Jim was sitting a few tables away in a clear line of view. She tried to catch his eye. Smile an apology. But he refused to look her way. Carole was sitting next to him. Her cheeks flushed, she looked more animated than she had all week. They were talking intensely and their closeness made Kylie feel irrationally jealous.

"Have you noticed how Carole seems to specialise in deep one-on-one conversations?" she muttered, half to herself. Her cheeks coloured a little when she realised how catty she sounded.

Isobel made a purring sound. "Maybe she's a soccer fan and they're talking about their mutual love of the sport."

Some others joined their table, and there was no further opportunity to discuss Jim or Carole. The conversation was superficial, mainly about the wonderful facilities of the resort and the drive back home. Kylie contributed to the discussion but still kept a close eye on Jim. Not once did he look her way.

About a half hour later, Brent clinked a spoon against his wineglass and an expectant silence fell over the white-clothed tables. He stood up and put on his most pompous expression.

"This first week in your eight-month-long journey is about to draw to a close. There is just one further item to which we must attend – the overseas postings. I'm sure the suspense is killing you all so I'll make no further delay in announcing your individual assignments." He took a sheet of paper from his shirt pocket, his voice inexpressive as he read its contents. "David, you're off to Edinburgh. Carole, it's Singapore for you. Kylie – Dublin. Jim – Auckland. Isobel – Barcelona. Oliver – New York. You'll fly four weeks from today. Expect an orientation email from your new boss sometime over the next week."

Kylie was in a daze as she watched him sit down. *Dublin,* she thought. *Of all cities!*

"Pleased?" asked Isobel.

"Yes," she replied, her thoughts still going at nineteen to the dozen.

It must be fate. Surely Mum and Dad will go to Ireland now that I'll be there too?

"How about you, Isobel? Barcelona's meant to be

a great city."

Isobel's dark eyes were excited. "Barcelona is almost as good as being sent to Colombia. It'll be so nice to be able to speak Spanish."

"Do you think everybody is happy?" asked Kylie, doing a quick check around the room. They all looked quite pleased. All but Jim who was staring ahead, his mouth in a rigid line. Carole looked slightly uncomfortable by his side.

I suppose he got the short straw, thought Kylie. *Auckland is the closest to home.*

Then suddenly it seemed that everybody was ready to leave. Napkins dabbed against mouths and chairs scraped back on the varnished floor. Kylie looked at her watch: 2 p.m., still a decent chunk of billing time left in the day, even after the two-hour drive back to the city. She had a lot of catching up to do.

She pushed her own chair back from the table. "See you next week, Isobel. Let's try to break away for lunch some day."

"Yes, that would be a good," Isobel agreed.

They exchanged a kiss on the cheek before Kylie turned to go. She headed towards Jim's table, determined to catch him, to explain. But she was too late. The seat next to Carole was empty. He was already gone.

Chapter 8

"Mum, when can we go to Ireland on our holidays?"

Rose, sewing one of Stephen's football jerseys, finished her stitch before replying.

"We don't have that kind of money, love."

"Casey Ryan from school is going to Ireland on an aeroplane," Kylie told her. "She's going to be away from school for a whole month."

Rose seemed rather disinterested. "Her family must be very wealthy," was all she said.

"No, they're poorer than us," Kylie stated with childish certainty.

Rose looked up with a bemused smile. "How do you know

that?"

"They rent their house," Kylie shrugged. "They don't own it like us. So they must be poorer, right?"

Rose was gob-smacked at her daughter's simple but indisputable logic. Kylie saw her silence as acquiescence and became even more persuasive.

"If we can't afford an aeroplane, then why don't we take the boat there?"

Rose shot the suggestion straight down. "The boat takes weeks — your father would be off work for too long. I told you, we don't have that kind of money."

"Does that mean we'll never have the money to go to Ireland?" Kylie pouted.

"I didn't say that, child." Rose sighed and went back to her sewing.

But they both knew that was exactly what she was saying.

Chapter 9

"I have an announcement to make," said Kylie as soon as Rose sat down at the dinner table.

"You're back with Geoff?" Rose looked worried at the prospect.

"I'm not that stupid, Mum."

"You're pregnant!" was Stephen's guess.

Rose took the bait and became sheet white. "You're not, are you?"

"Don't be so gullible, Mum," said Kylie, throwing her eyes to heaven. "I've found out where my overseas assignment will be."

"Where?" asked Frankie, his fork suspended mid-air.

"Dublin."

Even Stephen looked stunned.

"Did you ask for it deliberately?" asked Rose weakly.

Kylie shrugged. "No. I could have been sent anywhere – New York, Barcelona, Singapore – but, for some reason, Brent is sending me to Dublin."

Stephen opened his mouth to say something but Kylie stared him into silence. She didn't want to apply any more pressure about the tickets to Ireland. Once Rose and Frankie had time to think it through, she was sure that they would decide of their own accord to come and visit her in Dublin.

Everybody started to eat, but in a slow, distracted kind of way. A few minutes later, Rose said, "That fellow on the course . . . Jim, you said . . . is he from Dublin?"

"Yes." Kylie felt a hint of colour hit her cheeks at the unexpected mention of Jim's name.

"I suppose he'll give you some phone numbers . . . so that you'll know somebody . . ."

He might have if he was talking to me, thought Kylie.

All the way back on the freeway she had kept an eye out for Jim's car. More than once she had caught herself daydreaming. Coming across his broken-down car and giving him a lift back to the city, or getting a text asking her to meet him for a drink somewhere along the route.

He doesn't even have my phone number, she had reminded herself exasperatedly after that particular fantasy.

She hated being on bad terms with him. Hated having to wait until Monday before she could apologise.

I could ring him, she had thought as she exited the freeway and stopped at the lights. *Say I'm sorry. Ask him out for a drink. Ask him if he likes me . . . because I like him a lot.*

Two seconds later she was talking some sense into herself. Her impulsiveness was her own worst enemy when it came to the cat-and-mouse game of relationships.

Kylie came back to the present and decided it was time to move the conversation away from Dublin and Jim Donnelly.

"So," she drawled looking across at her brother, "tell us about this new girlfriend of yours."

* * *

As soon as Kylie returned to the office it became evident that Neil was determined to extract his pound of flesh before she left for Dublin. He piled the work on, deaf to her protests. Claudine's absence became more noticeable with each passing day, with things that had previously run like clockwork starting to unravel at the seams. The contractor filling the position didn't have anywhere near Claudine's efficiency and couldn't juggle the conflicting demands of her bosses. More than once, Kylie had to talk her out of quitting.

Despite being busy, Kylie still kept an eye out for Jim, but there was no sign of him on the floor and his office was empty whenever she passed by. Her apology burning a hole in her chest, she eventually asked one of the other litigation lawyers where he was.

"He's gone to Auckland. A New Zealand food distributor is suing their Australian supplier – Jim's gone over to try and mediate."

Kylie realised it was no coincidence that Brent had chosen Auckland for Jim. It looked like there was a ready-made job for him over there and it couldn't wait the four weeks until his assignment was due to start.

As the week went on, she became more engrossed in her work and stopped daydreaming about Jim. Late on Saturday evening, she put her work temporarily to one side so she could make a start on the fun-machine project. Brent had given his begrudging go-ahead and Kylie needed to distribute a company-wide communication before the monthly pay run.

She deliberated on the wording of the communication for over an hour. She eventually realised that Claudine's photos would be far more powerful than anything she could write.

She chose three of the best: a young girl with an oxygen mask, a bald-headed boy and Ethan, smiling bravely. Once she had arranged the photos, the caption came easily.

Seen any good movies lately?

Kylie called up the company-wide address list and pressed the SEND button. Happy with her work, she opened a bottle of Chardonnay.

Glass in one hand, remote control in the other, she flicked through the TV channels and ignored the gnawing loneliness that was starting to make its presence felt now that she didn't have anything substantial to distract her. She always missed Geoff most at the weekends. At the start the loneliness had been so bad that she'd go as far as dialling his number. There were so many good things about him – why did his addiction to gambling have to win out? But she would force herself to remember the ultimate humiliation of selling their house to pay the debts. Then, more often than not crying, she would phone Annie instead. Annie would pour a glass of wine on her end and they would talk about Geoff and Zack until they both felt better.

Kylie hadn't cried for months now. However, the lonesomeness, although much diminished, was still there. Her eyes glanced to her laptop, open on the coffee table, to check the time: 10 p.m., far too late to call Annie, who went to bed early in order to get as much sleep as possible before Zack's nocturnal theatrics.

Kylie sipped her wine and continued to gaze absently at the laptop. A string of automatic "out of office" messages were at the top of her inbox. But one message stood out. It wasn't an automatic message; someone else was working this late on Saturday night. She quickly snapped out of her daze when she saw who the message was from.

Hi Kylie,
Count me in for the salary deduction. Sorry about my sour grapes (bad pun, I know) at the Hunter. I've since realised that you were perfectly right and this is a much worthier cause.
Jim 😊

She set the glass down and typed a response.

No – I should be sorry. I got carried away –

one of my many faults.

It took only a few moments before his reply came through.

When I'm back in town, let's go for a drink and put it behind us.

A date! Well, sort of. No specific details of when or where but a clear intention. She kept her answer simple.

You're on.

There were no more emails, but she was crazily happy for the rest of the weekend. She refused to dwell on the fact that he had not yet answered her question about his girlfriend.

* * *

"Hey, mate," Kylie greeted Ethan with a grin, "you've grown since I last saw you!"

"Have I?" he asked, stretching his neck.

"Yes – must be the delicious food they're giving you here."

Ethan stuck his tongue out, making it clear that he

didn't think much of the hospital dinners.

"Is everything OK, Kylie?" asked Claudine quietly. She looked pale and drawn; the last few weeks had taken their toll. "Shouldn't you be at work?"

Kylie smiled. "Yes, I should. But I sneaked out because I have some fabulous news."

Claudine frowned, as was her natural inclination. "Is it something to do with those photos I took?"

"It certainly is," Kylie declared, sitting down on the hard plastic visitor's seat, "and that passing comment you made about those fun machines. The good news is that very soon *every* kid in this ward will have one."

Kylie had come straight from the payroll manager's office. The professional staff of MFJ had risen splendidly to the occasion, with a total of $102,000 collected.

Claudine's mouth dropped open. "How did you do that?"

Kylie shrugged. "Let's say I did a little fundraising at work."

Claudine was still struggling to believe it. "But it must have cost . . ." she paused to do some mental calculations, "thousands of dollars."

"See, Mum," said Ethan, his dark eyes shining, "not all the people you work with are horrible."

* * *

The fun machines were delivered to the ward over the weekend. Kylie knew she didn't have to be there but couldn't keep away. She walked up and down the ward, like a junkie getting her high from the happiness of the kids.

"Why don't you go home for a few hours, Claudine," she said in the afternoon when some of the younger children were napping. "I can stay here with Ethan."

Claudine became flustered at the suggestion. "No . . . no … you've been good enough."

"I'm at a loose end today," said Kylie persuasively. "You'd be doing me a favour."

In truth, she had tons of things to organise before her departure for Dublin, but it all seemed trivial next to the upheaval in Claudine's life.

Ethan added his reassurances and Claudine eventually relented.

As soon as she left, Ethan said, "I didn't mean *you* yesterday when I said that Mum worked with horrible people."

It was obvious that his off-the-cuff comment had got him into trouble with his mother.

"That's OK," replied Kylie and resisted the

temptation to ask specifically whom he had meant.

"I'm glad my mum's got some time off," he said next. "She's here all the time. She doesn't realise that I'd be OK on my own every now and then. I'm nearly eight, you know."

"Mothers can be a little overprotective," explained Kylie. "It's only because they love us so much."

"Yes. And I'm all Mum has," he sighed, sounding much older than his years.

"How about your grandparents?" asked Kylie. "Do they come and sit with you?"

"No, I don't have any grandparents." His voice had a thread of uncertainty. He was clearly at an age where he was starting to question the status quo. "It's just me and Mum."

* * *

"Have you got your passport?" asked Rose for the umpteenth time.

Kylie saw Stephen smirking as she answered, "Yes, Mum. It hasn't gone missing in the last ten minutes."

Her sarcasm was lost on Rose, who continued to fuss. "Did that fellow give you phone numbers? People you can call when you get there?"

"You mean Jim?" asked Kylie with as much

casualness as she could fake.

"How many other Irishmen do you know?" was Rose's terse reply.

"Take it easy, Mum." Kylie put a calming hand on her mother's arm. "No, Jim didn't give me any numbers. He's been in New Zealand these last few weeks."

She was pleased to hear that the disappointment she felt inside wasn't at all evident in her voice. Jim had emailed last week to say he would be staying on in Auckland.

We'll have to take a raincheck on that drink, he had typed.

No worries, she had responded as if it didn't bother her in the slightest. **See you in October.**

He hadn't offered any contact numbers for Dublin and she hadn't asked.

"What about your car?" asked Frankie. "Do you want me to go round and start it up every now and then?"

She shook her head. "I've given it to Annie while I'm away."

Annie's husband needed their car for work and she'd often commented that the days would be shorter if she could strap Zack in the back of a car and drive somewhere. She'd been delighted when Kylie suggested that she take the Audi.

Kylie slung her cabin bag over her shoulder. "I'm going to go through – I want to get some duty free." She kissed Stephen's cheek. "See ya. Be good to that phantom girlfriend of yours."

Despite the family pressure, the new girl in his life had yet to make an appearance.

Frankie stepped up to give her a gruff hug. "Take care of yourself, love."

Frankie and Rose had still made no commitment to go to Ireland and, resisting her natural instincts, Kylie hadn't pushed. She was sure that they would eventually come round to the idea.

She turned to embrace her mother.

"You will come back, won't you?" Rose whispered in her ear.

Kylie laughed. "Mum, what's wrong with you today? I'm only going away for four months!"

"Ireland is a funny place," said Rose, her eyes bright with tears. "Don't be surprised if it casts a spell on you."

Chapter 10

"We're having a real heatwave, luv," said the taxi driver as he pulled away from Dublin airport. His freckled elbow jutted out the open window and gusts of wind blew back towards Kylie as he picked up speed.

"Really?" she asked dubiously. She had been waiting at the taxi rank for twenty minutes, enough time to guess the air temperature to be twenty degrees or so. Hardly a heatwave.

"Yep," he looked over his shoulder at her to make his point. "I told the missus I'd head home early to bring the kids to the beach. Jaysus, they love the sea more than they love Christmas!"

His enthusiasm was contagious and Kylie asked, "Is the coast far from here?"

"Only fifteen minutes from here to Portmarnock," he informed her. "That's where I bring them – Malahide is too busy."

Kylie felt a shiver run down her back. "My parents are from Portmarnock," she said warily. She knew there was no way that Rose could hear, but she nevertheless felt her mother's disapproval as if she was sitting right next to her in the backseat of the taxi.

"I knew you looked as if you had the Irish genes in you," he said, darting another look around. "Only thing is that you don't sound it – where's that twang from?"

"Sydney – Australia."

"Even an eejit like me knows that Sydney is in Australia," was his dry response.

She wasn't too sure what an "eejit" was but apologised to him for underestimating his geographic knowledge.

Judging by the traffic on the road, it seemed that the whole city had decided to take an early mark from work. The taxi edged its way along streets lined with redbrick terraces, their brightly painted doors gleaming under the sunshine. Kylie wound down her window and the medley of car radios and revving engines became louder. The cars were an assortment of old and new models with some of the young male drivers bare-chested. As she sat in the taxi, Kylie felt the vibe of Dublin city take hold of her.

I'm finally here, she thought excitedly. *And just fifteen minutes away is Portmarnock, the answer to all my questions.*

* * *

The taxi eventually pulled up outside Kylie's accommodation, a modern apartment block on the quays of the River Liffey. The driver got her bags from the boot and pointed out some basic directions.

"If you keep walking along the river, you'll pass Temple Bar on the right. Keep on straight and you'll reach O'Connell Bridge. Turn left if you want to go to O'Connell Street or Henry Street. Turn right to go up towards Grafton Street and the Green. Back this way, you have the Guinness Brewery. Now, have you got all that?"

"Yes, thanks."

She tipped him well, thinking that with the traffic it was unlikely he would be home in time to take his kids to the beach.

The one-bedroom apartment was sparkling new, not unlike the one she had left behind in Sydney. She set her bags down inside the door and, cigarette packet in hand, walked over to the large window. The double-glazed glass was heavy to lift and when the bottom panel was pushed as high as it could go, she stuck her head out into the hazy summer's evening. Down below, the murky-green river looked flat and lifeless. Further along, an old-fashioned footbridge arched high over the still water and beyond that was the smooth grey stone of what she now knew to be O'Connell bridge. The stale odour from the river and the malt from the brewery combined to create a distinctive musty smell. Kylie smoked the cigarette slowly. By the time she stubbed it out, the cramped streets, quaint bridges and funny smell felt strangely familiar.

* * *

Kylie didn't intend to sleep away most of her first day in Ireland. She had grand plans to have a leisurely walk around the city, a modest night's sleep and then an early rise to catch the bus to Portmarnock. However, in the middle of unpacking, she started to feel extraordinarily tired and decided to put her head down for a few minutes.

She woke, alert yet disoriented, and was completely horrified when she realised that it was mid-morning, *the next day*. It seemed wise to re-instate the dratted alarm clock on the windowsill and to put Portmarnock on the long finger until next weekend.

The city centre was a ten-minute walk from the apartment and was exactly how Jim had described: "Paperboys, buskers, jaywalkers, winos, cobblestone laneways, modern shops in old buildings, Guinness signs outside pubs, live music inside . . ."

Kylie spent hours meandering around the heart of Dublin city. She stopped to listen to the buskers who ranged from children to whiskered old men. When she walked along the laneways of Temple Bar, she imagined Rose and Frankie walking over the same uneven cobblestones many years before. And inside one of the century-old pubs, whilst listening to a group of traditional Irish musicians, she had her first glass of Guinness.

* * *

MFJ's Dublin office was a much smaller operation than Sydney, with four partners and a mere twenty-eight staff. Kylie's new boss was a portly man by the name of Ted Guerin, and she liked him from the very first moment they met. There was something very warming about his round face with its criss-cross of laughter lines and shiny bald top.

"Welcome to Ireland, Kylie," he said with a handshake so vigorous that it hurt.

He introduced her around the office and everybody else was just as welcoming. Her office, as small as the one back in Sydney, had lots of character, with its high ornate ceiling and large battened window. Her eyes focused on the manila files on the desk.

"Some letters of advice," he said, almost apologetically, "but no rush."

He left her to her own devices and she began to read one of the files. About ten minutes later she had her first visitor.

"Mags Kiely," said the short, skinny girl with spiky blonde hair. Then she added, as an after thought, "I'm the pro bono lawyer – the conscience of the place."

She didn't look like any other lawyer that Kylie knew. In fact, with her cheeky freckles and girlish dimples, she looked like more like a schoolgirl than anything.

Kylie shook the bony outstretched hand, saying, "Kylie Horgan. I'm the assignee from Australia."

Mags nodded impatiently, as if she was well aware of who Kylie was. "I missed you when they showed you around – I was late this morning – or rather,

Seamus, my boyfriend, was late, and he made me late
– he was in Australia last year – went all around the
country – had a great time – didn't want to come
home at all. We met the week he came back – he
couldn't stop talking about the place – I eventually
had to ask him to shut up – we got on great after that
– you're about the same age as me, aren't you?"

Kylie had never heard anyone talk as fast as her
new colleague and didn't realise at first that she'd
been asked a question.

"Your age?" Mags prompted.

"Thirty-one."

"Aha!" Mags looked triumphant. "I'm a year
younger – but I still live at home – saving for a
mortgage – property is so bloody expensive here
now – but, you never know, if things work out with
Seamus . . ."

* * *

"Look – those people there are leaving," said
Mags and quickly darted off.

Kylie followed her to what seemed to be the only
available patch of grass in the whole of Stephen's
Green. All around flesh was brazenly bared with
seemingly little worry of sunburn. The atmosphere
was so intensely summery that even she was

beginning to believe that this was indeed a heatwave like no other.

"You must be used to this kind of weather," said Mags as she stretched out on the grass.

"I don't usually sit out in it," Kylie admitted. "I burn – it's my Irish complexion."

"You'd sit out in it if you only got a few days like this the whole year around," Mags declared. "That's why we all go a little mad when we see the sun – I suppose you take it for granted in Australia –"

Kylie closed her eyes as Mags chattered on at a hundred miles an hour. She felt like she had been in Ireland for much longer than a week. Work-wise, it had been pretty unremarkable; plenty of straight-forward letters of advice to keep her busy but nothing that provided any kind of challenge. Ireland's legislation, trade unions and dispute-resolution mechanisms were going to take time to learn, and in the meantime anything more complex than the simplest query was out of her league.

Work aside, everything else was wonderful: Mags, Ted and the city that she already loved.

The sun hot on her face, she slowly tuned back into Mags' chatter.

"I'm meeting Seamus down at Café en Seine at six – his work crowd will be there too – one of them might take your fancy – they're all accountants – bit serious, but you could do worse – they'll be all over you when they hear you're from Australia – even better when they realise you'll be going back in a few months – scared shitless of any kind of commitment, the lot of them –"

After listening carefully, Kylie concluded that Mags was expecting that she join her friends for drinks after work. It sounded like there would be a big crowd of them.

"OK. I'm on for a night on the town." She lifted her sunglasses to give Mags an unfiltered stare. "And I can't wait to meet Seamus – who must be some man to put up with your good self."

"The cheek of you!" Mags gave her a shove and she fell back on the grass.

Suddenly the two of them were in fits of giggles. None of the amused onlookers would have ever guessed that they were lawyers.

* * *

It had occurred to Kylie that Seamus would have to be Mags's opposite, and he was. Seamus Sheehan was tall, conservatively dressed and listened more than he talked. But he had a droll sense of humour and something about Mags appealed to it because his lips twitched into a smile every time he looked her way.

"Kylie's fitted straight in," Mags told him. "Everyone in the office has said so – you'd hardly even know she's Aussie – I suppose it's because her parents are Irish – on some subconscious level she must understand our funny ways –"

"You give me too much credit," Kylie cut in, with a serious look on her face. "I just nod and make the right noises. Truth is, I haven't the foggiest idea what is being said half of the time."

Seamus's belly rumbled with an alarming sound. It took Kylie a moment to realise it was a laugh. "Mmm, that could get you into trouble, Kylie from Australia. I can see it now. 'Kylie, would you like some black pudding?'" He stopped to nod furiously. "'Kylie, would you buy me and my ten friends a round?'" He bobbed his head for the second time.

One of the ten friends got in on the joke. "Kylie, would you like a shag?"

Kylie turned to him. "Ha, ha. I'd understand that *particular* question in any accent. And the answer is no."

It was hard to remember the names of all Seamus's colleagues. One was John, another Joe, someone else Mick. Actually, there were two Micks. Within minutes she found herself at the centre of an interrogation like none other she had experienced in her life, and it didn't seem to matter at all that she couldn't match the faces to the names.

"How long are you here for?"

"Is this your first time in Ireland?"

"What do you think of Dublin?"

"Do you miss Sydney?"

"Do you live near the beach?"

"Can you surf?"

"Rugby is huge over there, isn't it?"

"Did you see the Lions when they played last year?"

She answered the questions as best she could. Even the personal ones.

"Do you have a boyfriend?"

She told them that she'd recently finished a long-term relationship. A big mistake, because of course they wanted to know all the gory details.

"What happened?"

"How long were you with him?"

"Do you see him now?"

"What you need is an Irishman – and you're very lucky that I'm free at the moment."

"Don't mind him, Kylie, my darling. I'd show you a much better time."

"Don't mind those two culchie yobbos. You need a sophisticated city man like myself –"

Luckily, Mags rescued her from the onslaught.

"Ye're a disgrace, the lot of ye!" she said sternly as

she pulled Kylie in the direction of the Ladies'. "Ye've no idea how to treat a visitor."

Kylie groaned when she saw her reflection in the mirror. "Look at my red face – I can't believe I got sunburnt in Ireland."

Mags squinted her already tiny eyes. "It looks kind of cute – as if you're blushing – but that's no excuse for Seamus's friends to mob you."

"Are you sure they're accountants and not journalists?" asked Kylie as she rummaged through her shoulder bag for her face powder.

"We're a very nosy race of people, us Irish," said Mags. "We all have a budding journalist somewhere in our personality make-up."

"You're telling me!"

"You're just a novelty to them, that's all. Every week it's the same old crowd so it's understandable that they would go a bit mad when an exotic creature from the Southern Hemisphere comes along."

"Oh, well," Kylie dabbed the powder over her glowing face, "at least you saved me from them."

"I'll need to do a better job the next time," was Mags's reply, "or Jim will be on my case."

"What?" Kylie startled, the powder sponge mid-air.

"You know – Jim." Mags threw her a funny little glance. "He asked me to take good care of you during your stay in our fair city."

* * *

Kylie slid the fare under the plastic window and the driver checked it before issuing her ticket. All the seats were taken on the bus and she had to stand along with many of the other commuters. She sighed. If there was ever a day she needed a seat, it was today.

Last night she, Mags, Seamus and his wannabe-journalist friends had progressed from the pub to a nearby nightclub. When the bar at the club shut down, a sing-song started off. Kylie had an awful feeling that she'd been coerced into singing "Waltzing Matilda" but she wasn't entirely sure. At 4 a.m. she had finally bid everyone a very intoxicated goodnight.

Great, she'd thought when she saw a taxi rank right outside the nightclub. *Hop into a taxi and straight home.*

However, she soon realised that people were joining the queue at triple the rate of those leaving in taxis. Resigned to a long wait, she lit a cigarette to pass the time.

"Can I have a light?" a girl behind her asked.

Kylie handed her the lighter and they struck up a

conversation. After a long wait, Kylie's turn finally came around and she gave the girl a wave as she got into the back of the taxi. It was only then she realised that she had talked to her for a whole hour without exchanging names.

I know that she has two brothers, her grandmother is a demon, she rents a house in Rathmines and she works in the Green Shopping Centre. But I don't know her name. How bizarre!

Kylie came back to the present just as the bus driver, possibly a hobbyist rally driver, swung around another merciless corner.

"I'm so sorry," she said as she fell on top of one of the seated passengers for the second time in as many minutes.

"Yer all right," the old man assured her.

The clanging in her head worsened as she straightened up. She was very hung-over and being jostled around in the stifling heat of the No. 32 bus was about the last thing she needed.

"Are yer visiting for long?" the old man asked. Evidently he had been able to tell that she was a foreigner just from the few words of apology she had uttered.

"Four months," she answered. "I'm on assignment with one of the law firms in the city – MFJ, they're called. I'm just visiting Portmarnock for the day – my parents came from around here – they moved to Australia about forty years ago –"

God, she thought as she heard herself chattering nineteen-to-the-dozen just like the girl at the taxi rank last night, *talking to strangers is like a hobby in this country*.

"Jaysus!" he exclaimed. "That was a long time ago. Portmarnock was nothing but countryside back then. What are the names of yer old folk?"

His shaggy eyebrows frowned in anticipative concentration as he waited for her answer.

"Horgan – my dad is Frankie Horgan."

He shook his head slowly. "Don't know him . . . Would ya press that bell there for me, girl? This is me stop coming up."

She did as he asked and a bell rang out to alert the driver.

The old man gripped the pole, his knuckles white as he pulled himself to his feet. He tutted, "Jaysus – me ol' knees are knackered."

Kylie nodded as if in perfect agreement. The old man made his way unsteadily down the aisle as the bus came to a stop.

The backdoors had opened when Kylie called after him, "How about the Careys? Would you know them?"

He paused. Slowly his head turned around. Was

that a flicker of recognition she saw in his eyes?

"Are ya right back there?" called the bus driver impatiently.

The old man yielded under pressure and, with Kylie's question unanswered, he descended the steps as fast as his old knackered knees would allow.

* * *

Kylie walked up and down the main street of Portmarnock village a number of times. She stopped to read the Mass times at the church, the menu at the Golf Links Inn and the notices outside the primary school. But she was really studying the people, looking for someone like the old man, someone who had lived in the area for a lifetime. However, it was mostly children and teenagers that she saw. She eventually wandered into one of the shops. The boy behind the counter looked to be in his mid-teens.

Maybe it would be more productive if I came back here on a school day, she thought as she looked through the postcards on display. *That must be when all the retirees come out of the woodwork.*

She picked out some postcards and handed the cash to the young assistant.

"Are you a local around here?"

"Naw," he replied, a nail-bitten finger pressing the

buttons on the till, "I come from Baldoyle."

Down on the beach, Kylie slipped off her sandals and walked through the sun-warmed sand until she reached the tidemark. From there, it was a long soggy stretch down to the water's edge. Children zoomed past on either side of her, their short skinny legs racing towards the sea. Water splashed high as their bare feet charged through the shallow puddles.

"Come on, last is a loser!" she heard their young voices carry with the wind.

Kylie sat down where the sand was soft and admired the magnificence of the beach as it swept around the bay. To her left there was an old tower, rather like a child's sandcastle, and out on the horizon there were two craggy islands. And yachts, lots of them, as many as you would see in Sydney Harbour on a fine day.

Kylie took her postcards from her bag. Her pen poised, the right words were very slow to come.

Dear Mum and Dad,

This is a beautiful place. I'm sitting on the beach as I write and I'm thinking of how lucky you were to grow up here. I'm told it has changed a lot in forty years but I imagine that the beach and the tower are timeless.

Love, Kylie

It didn't take much to fill the compact space on the back of the postcard. It was probably for the best that there was no room to say all the things that were running through her head at that moment in time.

The wind picked up and Kylie lifted her face to catch its rip. It brought a taste of salt and the smell of the sea. She felt happy. Very happy. She didn't know if she was being fanciful or not, but there was something about this place that felt like home. And it wasn't the Sydney-like yachts.

* * *

"What did you do for the rest of the weekend?" asked Mags on the following Monday morning. She perched herself on Kylie's desk and swung her bare legs to and fro. More than ever, she reminded Kylie of a schoolgirl.

"I went to the beach," Kylie replied but should have known that she wouldn't get away with being so vague.

"What beach?"

"Portmarnock."

"Why didn't you go to Malahide?"

"It's too busy." Kylie used the same reason as the taxi driver on her first day.

Mags seemed to accept her explanation and proceeded to give a blow-by-blow account of her own weekend. "Was comatose for most of Saturday

– even missed my hip-hop dance class – just watched a movie that night – went to see the in-laws yesterday – had different kind of headache from that – still, all the same, Seamus's mother made a lovely apple-tart – my mother can't bake for crap and neither can I – have you looked up your relatives yet?"

Kylie still wasn't used to Mags' peculiar way of asking questions. Invariably they came at the end of a monologue, were related to a completely different topic and were not even distinguishable by a change in her tone. Often the ensuing silence was the only clue that an answer was expected.

"No," Kylie lied. She regretted that she had ever told Mags that she had relatives living around Dublin for it meant that Mags would enquire about them on an intermittent basis at the very least.

I don't want to answer questions about them, she thought. *Not yet, anyway. God – maybe I'll turn out to be as secretive as my mother.*

Mags squinted her eyes; it was clear that she found it very strange that Kylie had not made contact with her extended family. But whatever she was thinking, she didn't voice it and Kylie felt inordinately relieved.

"Good morning, young ladies!"

The well-timed interruption came from Ted. He ambled into Kylie's office, caught hold of a chair and dragged it on its two hind legs towards her desk.

"How convenient to find you together." He smiled as he sat down. "I have the perfect job for both of you."

Kylie sat up straighter when she heard him refer to a "job". The Dublin office was a busy little firm and she had more than enough work to keep her going. However, she was starting to miss certain aspects of her old job, particularly the client contact.

"I'm very excited to say that MFJ are partnering with The Simon Community to provide a new legal advice clinic for the city's underprivileged," he said. "The initiative will be called *Just Ask*. In order to get the programme off the ground, I'm going to dedicate you both full-time over the next few months."

"No problem," said Mags, who was still perched on Kylie's desk. "Now that the Red Cross work has slowed down, I'm looking forward to something new."

Kylie was doubtful that she could be of any help. "I'm not exactly an expert on Irish law. It's OK when I have the time to look something up here in the office, but face-to-face . . ."

Ted redirected his gaze so it was fully focused on her. "You'll find that a lot of questions you'll be asked aren't matters of the law – the poor sods just want somebody to talk to them, to listen. The questions that *are* law-related are mostly black and white: letters of offer, termination, discrimination. More often than not, you'll be able to respond without referring to the specific legislation."

Kylie had one other concern, and she felt embarrassed to even voice it. "I don't mean to be calculating, but I won't meet my annual billability target if I work full-time on pro bono . . . You see, my billability is being tracked while I'm on this assignment."

Ted's amiable voice adopted an edge. "This is *my* practice and we follow *my* rules – you're billable if I say you're billable."

"Well, if you think I'm capable, I'm very happy to be involved," said Kylie, thinking that her work in Dublin was going to be worlds different to Sydney. She recalled the last contract of employment she had worked on: the Citibank executive.

The next contract I'll see is likely to be that of an ex-con on a minimum wage.

Rather suddenly, she felt relieved that she wouldn't have to deal with any overpaid nit-picking executives while she was in Dublin.

* * *

Thirty or so people squashed into the new clinic to celebrate its opening. The facilities consisted of a dungeon-like basement room with freshly painted magnolia walls and a neutral-coloured carpet. The only window was encased in a grille of black metal bars and centred in front of it was an old table that had seen better days. An array of multi-coloured plastic chairs provided seating.

The heavens opened shortly before the 7 p.m. start and the guests left their dripping umbrellas inside the door. Several posters were pinned around the room with the words "*Just Ask*" scribed in red on a plain white background. The catering budget, as meagre as the printing budget, had stretched to a case of sparkling wine and two Simon volunteers manned a make-shift bar. They poured the wine generously and it wasn't long before the conversation amongst the guests soared above the background music.

"I'm Mary." A slight woman in her fifties with laughing eyes proffered her hand to Mags and then Kylie. "I'm the receptionist at the main desk. If you need anything, just holler."

"Is there anywhere our clients can wait until they're seen?" Mags asked her.

Mary shook her head. "The premises are fully used up and, as you know, there's hardly room to swing a cat in the reception area."

"They'll have to wait in the hall," Kylie concluded.

The dark narrow hallway would make a rather depressing waiting area but it seemed that there was no alternative.

Mary started to chat to a bald old man about the sudden change in the weather and Mags pointed out the more distinguished guests to Kylie.

"That's Dick Roche, the Minister for the Environment . . . and there's Mary Murphy – she's the chairperson of the Housing, Social and Community Affairs Committee – a very busy woman. No points for guessing the Lord Mayor – nice necklace, isn't it?"

"What's her name?" asked Kylie, looking across at the grey-haired woman with the kindly face.

"Catherine Byrne," replied Mags. She threw back the last of her wine and grabbed Kylie's arm. "Come on. Let's get our picture taken with Dublin's first lady."

* * *

The next day Kylie and Mags returned to the basement room with their supplies: reference books, journals and some basic stationery. Kylie noticed a new piece of furniture: a bookcase, just what they needed.

"Do you think anyone will turn up?" she asked as she unpacked the textbooks. She was having trouble visualising what the clinic would be like when it was up and running. The plan for the initial few weeks was to man the office from nine to five. Then, depending on demand, they would consider extending the hours.

"Who knows, we may even need to open shop on Saturdays," Ted had said to one of the politicians at the opening.

Kylie had been doubtful when she overheard him.

It seemed that Mags had no such doubts. "Wait till the word gets out on the street. Some of them will be trying to see if they can sue someone, anyone really, just to make a few easy euros. Others, the genuine cases, will break your heart."

They were unpacked in no time and sat on either end of the old desk. Outside, rain streaked down the window and it seemed that Dublin's heatwave had died a death.

Mary stuck her head around the door.

"All settled in?" she asked. "Here, I brought you down *The Herald*. You're on page four."

A phone started to ring in the distance and Mary tutted before darting back to her post.

"We didn't make the front page," complained Mags as she looked at the grainy photograph on page four.

"We're obviously not good-looking enough," Kylie joked. "Still, I'm going to cut it out and send it home."

"Ugly or not, you can always rely on your mammy to be proud," retorted Mags.

She resumed reading the paper while Kylie doodled on her notepad. She wished she had her laptop. Neil and the rest of the team were still emailing queries on a regular basis and she could have cleared a few of the messages. However, the new clinic was to be technology free.

"For two reasons," Mags had stated when Kylie questioned her. "Firstly, computers alienate our clients – remember, some of them can't even *read*. Secondly, and probably more likely, they might try to rob the place if they see any high-tech stuff lying around."

Lunchtime crawled slowly around without a single client, and they braved the deluge to get lunch in Temple Bar.

"Welcome to the real Dublin," said Mags sardonically as she took off her sodden jacket.

Kylie looked around the dark pub with its roaring midsummer fire.

"I like the real Dublin," she replied.

Mags' good humour was soon restored with a calorie-laden burger, and Kylie asked a question that she'd wanted to ask for some time.

"How did you get into full-time pro bono work?"

When Mags answered there was no sign of her usual mischievous smile. "A few years ago we had a tragedy in the office. One of our lawyers died – a car accident – straight into a wall – boom – life over. It hit us all hard – we're a small office – we all knew her – loved her . . ."

Her voice trailed off: she was obviously still very cut up about it.

"I'm sorry," said Kylie.

Tears glittered in her new friend's eyes. "It was a horrible time at work. We all reacted in different ways. Jim had to get away – two months later he went to Australia and hasn't been back since. The partners were also shook up – they saw that life was short and stopped working themselves to the bone. And me, well, I felt compelled to do something more meaningful with my life. I resigned but they talked me into staying as a full-time pro bono lawyer."

Kylie was dying to ask more. Who was the girl? What age had she been when she died? Who was she to Jim, to say he had to "get away"? But Mags discarded her half-eaten burger and reached for her coat. It was very clear that she didn't want to talk about it any more.

Chapter 11

"Mum, we're doing family trees at school."

Rose's hands slowed as they scrubbed the dishes in the sink.

"That's nice, love."

Kylie took her heavy schoolbag from her back and rested it on the linoleum floor. "I need to know everybody's name," she stated importantly. "In Dad's family too."

She shot a look in Frankie's direction. He sat at the kitchen table, the newspaper spread out in front of him. He was only ever home at this time of the day when it was raining and the house he was building didn't yet have a roof.

"My parents have passed away, remember?" said Rose in a strangled voice.

"But it doesn't matter if they are alive or dead." Kylie turned to Frankie for support. "Tell her, Dad. It doesn't matter."

Frankie looked towards Rose but he said nothing.

"And it's not just about grandparents," said Kylie. "I need the names of aunts, uncles, cousins . . ."

She became aware that Rose had removed her hands from the sink and was drying the suds with a tea towel.

"I'll give you the names, love," said Frankie.

"Why not Mum?"

"Sure, she's too busy."

Rose left the room and a few moments later Kylie heard the bedroom door click shut.

"I need to go back at least three generations, Dad — my teacher rolled up this big sheet of paper for me so I could fit everyone in."

Kylie removed the elastic band and placed the A3 sheet over her father's newspaper.

"No such thing as waiting until your dad is finished reading, is there?" Frankie sighed.

"You're the one who's always saying that homework should be done before everything else."

He had no comeback to that and they commenced the project straight away.

Chapter 12

The A3 sheet of paper was now in front of Kylie, its curling sides held down with paperweights. Her childish handwriting, in silver pencil, was faded but legible. Just looking at it reminded Kylie of that rainy afternoon with her dad.

Rose Carey was the eldest of three children and Frankie Horgan the eldest of five. The names of their siblings spaced across the bottom of the sheet: Rose, Carmel and Elizabeth; Frank, Peter, Johnny, Hannah and Molly.

I have four aunts and two uncles. Not one of whom I have ever met.

On the screen of her laptop, the Eircom online phonebook waited for her search details. It was obvious that she should start with her dad's brothers, as a marriage would not have resulted in a change to their surname.

Horgan, Peter, she typed into the search tool. *Dublin.*

The search came back with no hits.

Horgan, P, she tried the second time.

It returned with three possible phone numbers.

Kylie dialled the first.

"Hello," said the brusque voice at the other end.

"Hello. I'm looking for a Peter Horgan –"

"It's Paddy here – no Peter in this house."

The phone was hung up before she had even the chance to thank him for his time.

She tried the second number.

"Hello, I'm looking for Peter Horgan," she began, fully expecting to be cut off again.

But the woman who had answered seemed to be waiting for her to continue.

"He would be fifty-eight years old and have a brother Frank who went to Australia –"

She was just starting to get her hopes up when the woman unknowingly dashed them.

"My husband is Peter – but he's ten years younger than the Peter you're looking for. And there's no

Frank in his family. Sorry, love. Good luck to you with it."

Kylie thanked her and moved on to the next number. The phone rang unanswered and eventually diverted to a message bank.

"You've reached Patricia Horgan –"

Another dead end. She put the phone back in its cradle and chided herself for feeling disappointed.

I can't expect to find him in five minutes – it's been forty years without contact. Peter may not live in Dublin – for that matter, he may not even live in Ireland.

* * *

"Do most people here have silent numbers?" she asked Mags the following Monday.

Mags looked up from her crossword puzzle. "Silent numbers?"

"Not in the book."

"Oh, at least half, I would say."

It was not the response that Kylie wanted to hear, but it certainly explained why she had failed to find her uncles in the phone directory. She had searched the entire country for Peter and Johnny Horgan. After sixty-odd phone calls, she had reluctantly called it quits. It was time for Plan B: her aunts. Maybe one of them hadn't got married. And maybe, if she was lucky, that same one had her phone number listed.

"Are you trying to contact your relatives?" asked Mags.

Kylie nodded cautiously. She preferred for Mags to know as little as possible about her mission. However, she had asked her a question and that allowed Mags one question in return.

"Why don't you just ask your parents for the phone number?"

Kylie should have known that Mags was incapable of stopping at one question. But she was saved by the bell. Or rather by a tentative knock on the door.

"Welcome," Mags beamed at the tall gangly youth. "Take a seat, please."

He did as he was told, the chair much too low for his long legs.

"I'm Mark," he said awkwardly, his denim-clad knees jutting forward.

"I'm Mags. This here is Kylie. How can we help you today?"

The dull red acne on his face brightened with colour. "I've got this new job, see. They've sent me a letter. Don't get me wrong – I can read it – but I just wanted to check it out, you know, the small print."

Kylie smiled at him. "That sounds right up my alley. Have you got a copy with you?"

He unzipped his denim jacket and took a brown

envelope from the inside pocket. Kylie extracted the letter of offer. It was a simple document, only three pages long. The position it was offering was that of a store hand.

"It looks OK, Mark," said Kylie when she got to the end. "They'll pay you weekly – directly into your bank account. You start at nine and finish at five thirty. Overtime will be paid at time and a half. You'll need a doctor's note if you're sick for more than three days."

"Does that mean they'll pay me?"

"Yes, once you have the doctor's note and don't use up more than ten sick days in the year."

He looked happy with her answer.

"How about if it gets quiet there?" he asked next. "Can they just lay me off?"

"Yes," she replied, "if it's within the first thirteen weeks. After that they have to give you a week's notice."

He looked less happy with that answer. Something told Kylie that he'd been laid off many times in his young life.

"Thanks," he mumbled as he stuffed the letter back into his pocket.

Mags waited until he was well gone before she remarked, "Illiterate! Sad how these kids fall through the cracks, isn't it?"

* * *

Kylie raised her hands behind her head and yawned. She had spent the last hour searching for Carmel and Elizabeth Carey. Before that she had tried for Hannah and Molly Horgan. One of her phone calls had been promising to start off with.

"Hello. Is that Elizabeth Carey?"

"Yes, this is Liz," the woman had confirmed.

"My name is Kylie Horgan. I'm from Sydney. Liz, do you have a sister called Rose?"

"Yes, I did."

Kylie was so excited that she didn't pick up that the woman had used the past tense. "She went to Australia –"

"No, Rose died when we were young."

"Oh." Kylie was embarrassed and disappointed all at once. "I'm sorry."

The woman was philosophical. "Ah, sure, how were you to know?"

"OK . . . well, thanks . . ."

"Right, so," said Liz, "I hope you find who you're looking for. Bye bye, now."

Kylie yawned again and closed down the phone directory. The clock on the bottom right of the screen reported the time as eight thirty. Back in

Sydney she'd still be working, be it at the office or home. Now she spent her evenings calling up strangers asking if they knew of Rose Carey or Frank Horgan. It seemed that some of the energy she had previously focused on work was being redirected to the search for her family.

Kylie turned on the TV. A short while later her mobile phone started to ring. She had set up international roaming in order to be contactable while she was away, and she assumed that it would be Neil or Graham with one of their queries.

"Hello?"

"Kylie – it's Claudine."

The secretary's voice was clipped but there was nothing unusual in that.

"Hi, Claudine," she said. "How are you? And how's Ethan?"

"They've fired me," was the shocking reply. "The *bastards* have fired me!"

Kylie went cold. Surely they wouldn't dare fire Claudine?

"Just tell me what happened," she said as she muted the volume of the television, "tell me *every single thing* that happened."

She heard Claudine take an unsteady breath.

"Well, Ethan finally came out of the traction. I was so excited about it – I had this naïve image of us walking out of the hospital hand-in-hand – nobody told me that his muscles would be wasted away, that he'd need a few weeks of physiotherapy. Of course, as soon as I saw him trying to sit up, his head hanging like a puppet, I realised that I'd been on cloud nine."

"Poor Ethan," said Kylie, picturing the brave young boy who now had yet another hurdle to get over.

"So I called Neil," Claudine continued. "I told him that I had to take another few weeks off. I explained about the physiotherapy and how Ethan still needed me. Neil wasn't over the moon about it – but he seemed OK. Then I get this letter today. It says . . ." she paused before quoting, "*Due to the fact you have not made yourself available for work as we requested in our letter of June 16, we regret that we must terminate your employment.*"

"What's this other letter?" asked Kylie.

"They've enclosed a copy of it," Claudine told her. "It said that I had used up all my annual and sick leave and that I had to make myself available for work within fourteen days. But I swear to you I never set eyes on it until today."

Kylie's heart sank. "OK – let's not panic," she said, not letting on how concerned she was. "I'll draft a response for you – but please, Claudine, please don't tell a soul."

"You know you can trust me." Claudine sounded relieved.

Kylie was keenly aware that, regardless of Claudine's trustworthiness, she was putting her own job on the line by helping her. She shuddered to think what Neil would do if he ever found out.

She stopped thinking about the dire consequences of what she was about to do and said, "OK, Claudine. Listen carefully. I want you to write down the dates, times and details of every discussion you've had with Neil, and me, since Ethan had his accident —"

"But I don't want to drag your name into it," she objected.

Kylie reassured her. "Fact is that I, one of your bosses, told you not to return to work until Ethan was well. It is grossly unfair for Neil to come along and say it is suddenly *not* OK. Even worse that he fabricated a letter of warning."

"Thanks, Kylie," said Claudine, her voice very weary. "I'm not sure how I can ever repay you for these last few weeks."

"Don't worry about it. Just email me the details and I'll take it from there . . . OK, better get my beauty sleep . . . say hi to Ethan for me."

*   *   *

The clinic was gradually becoming busier. On the Thursday morning, a week after their grand opening, they had four people come in: a woman who needed advice in relation to a dispute with her landlord, a man who wanted compensation for a drunken fall, a young girl who needed assistance with her contract of employment and an elderly lady who believed she was a victim of workplace discrimination. Kylie and Mags were kept occupied right up to lunchtime.

"Word is spreading on the street," said Mags when the last client left. "Come on, let's go for lunch. I'm starving."

"I've got something that I need to work on," Kylie replied. "Can you bring me back a sandwich?"

"What –" Mags started to ask.

Kylie headed her off at the pass. "It's something for the office back in Sydney. Now, get out of here – and don't be so damned nosy."

Mags laughed as she headed out the door.

As soon as she was alone, Kylie took her laptop from the bag she usually used to carry files. She felt a pang of guilt as she plugged it into the socket.

I just want to look at Claudine's letter in the cold light of day, she justified to herself as she opened up the document.

It was one of the hardest letters she had ever written. Not only did she have to contest the grounds of termination, she also had to disguise her usual writing style so that Neil wouldn't cotton on.

She was deep in thought when she heard the door swing open.

Damn, Mags must have forgotten to put up the "closed" sign.

The man who stood in the doorway was hard to put an age on. Grime coated the top half of his face and a grey scraggy beard the bottom half. His heavy anorak, totally inappropriate for the time of year, had rips in the vinyl and his pants were nothing more than filthy rags. His boots, split open at the toes, revealed muddied socks, and a black toenail protruded through the frayed wool.

Homeless, she thought. *Maybe one of the curled-up bodies I've seen sleeping in the big arched doorways of O'Connell Street.*

He finally moved, the sour stench of alcohol reaching her before he did. She tried not to flinch at the smell.

"Can I help you?"

He pointed to an old wound above his eyebrow.

"They cracked a bottle off me head."

"Who?"

"The bloody winos."

In some bizarre way it seemed that he thought himself superior to the "winos", as if the alcohol that warmed him from the coldness of street life was of a much better quality.

"When did it happen?" she asked.

He shrugged. It was clear that days, months and years were blurred in his mind.

"What's your name?"

"Jerry," he mumbled and came a step closer. The stench got even stronger.

"Jerry, my name is Kylie," she looked directly into his coal-black eyes, "and I'm going to be honest with you. That wound is a few months old. There's nothing we can do now to get you compensation."

His leg shot out in sudden vicious anger and kicked over one of the plastic chairs.

"Fuck you!"

There was so much venom in those two words that they frightened Kylie much more than his kicking the chair.

"Why don't you go home now, Jerry, and come back sometime when you're a little bit calmer?"

She heard the waver in her voice and could only assume that he did too.

I don't want him to know how scared I am.

"Yer all the fucking same!" he shouted in response and kicked the chair a second time. It boomeranged off the wall and Kylie gripped the edge of the old table, the only thing that separated her from his violence.

"Stop, Jerry."

He ignored her, his head turning frantically from side to side as he tried to locate something else that he could use to take out his frustration.

OK, being calm isn't doing it.

She stood up behind the table, her knees knocking.

"Go home, Jerry!" she yelled at the top of her voice. "Go on, get out of here!"

Who knows what would have happened next had they not heard footsteps rushing down the hall. Mary, the receptionist, ran into the room.

"What's all the commotion about?"

"A misunderstanding," said Kylie, relieved to have back-up, regardless of the fact that Mary was frail enough to knock over with a feather. "Jerry is just leaving now."

Seconds ticked by. Jerry looked from one woman to the other, as if weighing something up. Thankfully, he decided to take his leave.

"What were you doing here on your own?" asked Mary. "Don't you know how dangerous it is?"

"Sorry for causing you such a fright," Kylie apologised and noticed that her hands were shaking. "Mags and I got our wires crossed. She didn't put up the 'closed' sign and I didn't lock the door."

Mary stared at the laptop. "You're asking for trouble with that. You're lucky he didn't swipe it."

"I know," said Kylie, feeling very stupid and out of depth with this ugly side to pro bono work. "I won't bring it here again. And please don't tell Mags what happened."

Mary replied with something that sounded like "harrumph". Kylie wasn't sure if it was a promise to keep quiet or not.

Chapter 13

"It's hard to believe that I've been here six weeks already," said Kylie.

"Time flies when you're having fun," Stephen bellowed down the line.

She held the phone back from her ear. "Do you shout at your girlfriend the same way you shout at everyone else?"

"Piss off," he retorted.

"Still in love?"

"Met any poor sucker Irishman yet?" he countered.

"No – I'm more of a curiosity than an object of desire to them."

"No news there."

When he had finished chortling at his own wit, Kylie asked, "Any give with Mum and Dad yet?"

"Not an inch," he replied. "Ireland is taboo — a no-go zone."

Kylie sighed at his response. Truth be told, she was beginning to feel less confident that her parents would come around.

"I've started to search for the family here," she said quietly.

"How?"

"Just the phone directory so far — nothing very sophisticated. I haven't had much luck, though."

"Tread carefully, Kylie," he warned. "Something tells me that Mum would be mighty upset if she knew what you were up to."

"I know," she closed her eyes, picturing Rose's face, "I know."

Kylie was pensive when she hung up the phone. She truly didn't want to upset her mother in any way but she couldn't stop what she was doing. She needed to find the rest of her family. It was something she couldn't deny herself. Like an addiction. Like how Geoff had felt about gambling.

Sleep was slow to come that night as Rose and Geoff flitted in and out of her head. Rose had been wary of him right from the start.

"That's an expensive car," she had said when she first saw his Jaguar.

"No point in waiting until you're fifty to get one," Kylie had answered airily.

There had been a similar reaction when she saw their new house.

"Are you sure that you and Geoff can afford this?"

It turned out that Rose was right to be wary of Geoff's cavalier attitude to money. For Geoff saw no problem with extending himself to the very limits of his income, even beyond. It was only a matter of time before he had gambled himself into a huge hole.

"What?" Kylie had been utterly shocked when he finally owned up. "Our house? The bank is going to foreclose on our house?"

He nodded, his eyes cast downwards to his clasped hands.

"But we had money in redraw. We're ahead with our repayments. Our last statement –" She stopped, trying to remember when she had last seen a bank statement. She groaned when she realised it was months ago.

"I'm sorry, Kylie – that money is gone."

Distraught, she had run to her mother for comfort.

"He was hiding the mail from me – I never had an inkling the mortgage was in arrears. Had I known I could have done something about it!"

"It will be OK, pet." Rose squeezed her hand. "It's just bricks and mortar at the end of the day."

But Kylie wasn't quite so philosophical about it. Through no fault of her own, she had lost her house and gained a bad credit rating. Her career would be over if anyone at work found out.

"I'll never forgive him, Mum!"

Rose's reply was not what she was expecting. "If you don't forgive him, Kylie, then who can he turn to? Who will save him from himself? What about 'for better or for worse'?"

"We're not married yet, Mum," Kylie pointed out.

"You're as good as married – you made the promise to him when you accepted the engagement ring."

Kylie knew that a big part of Rose wanted her daughter as far away from Geoff Kemp as possible. However, she was a strong believer in right and wrong. And evidently it was wrong for Kylie not to give Geoff another chance.

So she did give him a second chance. And a third. And a fourth.

* * *

An uneventful week passed by with still no word from Claudine. Kylie resisted the urge to call her. She knew Claudine would make contact as soon as she had a response from MFJ. Knowing Neil, he was deliberately dragging his heels and trying to psych her out.

On the Thursday, Kylie received an email from Angela, the facilitator of the High Potential programme.

Trying to organise a teleconference for the group to see how everyone is doing. Thinking of Southern hemisphere a.m., Northern hemisphere p.m. Would you be able to link up at 10 p.m. tomorrow night?

Kylie responded in the affirmative. She was looking forward to hearing what the others were up to. She tried not to dwell on the fact that Jim would be there. She wasn't at all successful.

* * *

Kylie arrived home just before ten. The usual Friday-night drinks with the gang had given her all the Dutch courage she needed. She dialled the conference number and stated her name. It echoed back at her.

There was silence.

I must be the first on.

"Hello, Kylie Horgan."

She nearly jumped out of her skin when she heard Jim's voice say her name. Her courage instantly deserted her and left her with an awkwardness that was akin to what you would feel after running into an ex-boyfriend unexpectedly: that hopeless feeling of what might have been. Only thing was that she and Jim had never even got as far as dating.

"Come straight from the pub?" he asked before she had the chance to return his greeting.

"How did you know?"

"I know the scene too well over there. Was Mags with you?"

"Yeah. And Seamus, her boyfriend. And all his friends."

A small silence followed.

"Are any of those friends someone special?" he asked, his voice serious.

"No."

The tension that had been building all day reached an unbearable climax. Hardly daring to breathe, she waited for what he would say next. However, the moment was cruelly shattered with an incoming beep and the words, "David Smythe." They were no longer alone.

Damn it, David. Ten out of ten for bad timing!

The rest of the callers were not long after David. Angela allowed a few minutes of general chit-chat before she called for some structure to the conversation.

"Let's do an update one by one. Isobel, how is sunny Madrid?"

"Great," Isobel replied enthusiastically. "I'm doing work for one of the largest conglomerates in Spain – speaking the language has given me a huge advantage. I'm going to find it hard to leave here – I can tell already."

Carole, sounding as disdainful as ever, gave her update next. "I didn't realise that the Singapore office was so small – there is little opportunity to use the full extent of my talents here. I would be bored out of my mind if it wasn't for the fact that I'm helping Jim remotely with the case in Auckland."

Kylie knew it was perfectly reasonable for Jim and Carole to be in professional contact, but she couldn't help feeling a little jealous.

"Carole's been a big help on some of the international aspects of the case," said Jim. "I've almost got the parties to agree to an out-of-court settlement. I may be back in Sydney sooner than the rest of you."

Oliver was next to speak. "It's dog eat dog over here – the New Yorkers are tough on each other, not

to talk about strangers. Crystelle loves it, though –
she's got the agro attitude down pat – and I don't
want to even talk about how she's abused our credit
card in Fifth Avenue."

When Kylie's turn came round she told them
about *Just Ask* and the new legal clinic.

"It looks like I'll be dedicated to it for the next
few months. It's an interesting experience – I'm
learning lots. Not about the law, about life: the
homeless, destitute and illiterate. Let's say I've well
and truly fallen out of my ivory tower."

She included the incident with Jerry, making it
sound funny when it had been far from that.

"It was lucky that Mary heard all the commotion,"
she recounted. "I now know why it's important to
have two of us there at all times."

David, the last to speak, was very down in the
dumps. "The sooner this assignment is over, the
better. The tax system is totally different here – it
would take months to become competent enough to
offer even basic advice. And Edinburgh is cold, even
in summer – I'll never take Sydney for granted
again."

Angela consoled him. "I'm sure it will get better,
David. You'll find your niche and won't want to go
home when the time comes."

Angela then finished up with the promise she

would organise a similar conference call at the end of the next six-week milestone.

* * *

When Kylie logged into her email the next day there was a new message: from Jim. It had no subject. She had a peculiar feeling in the pit of her stomach as she double-clicked to open it up.

Hi Kylie,
It was great to talk to you last night. It's been a while since I've thought of Dublin in a nostalgic way but speaking to you made me long for a Guinness and a good night out in Dublin town. You've probably forgotten, but we still have a raincheck on that drink. It's looking possible that it may be in an Irish pub rather than an Aussie one – I'm thinking of coming home for a brief visit.
Take care until then,
Jim

Feeling rather strange, Kylie read the message again. It was straightforward, really. Jim was sounding out if she was interested in a date in Dublin. His tone was relaxed, and she realised that the pressure she felt didn't originate from anything he had written. It came from inside herself.

She shut down her email a few minutes later without sending a response. Suddenly the apartment was claustrophobic and she needed to get out, go somewhere she could unravel her feelings.

Outside the sky was an angry grey, and Kylie fleetingly considered if she should turn back to get an umbrella.

Oh, what the hell if I get wet, she thought defiantly and walked briskly towards the city.

On her left, the Liffey was sunk down low, a solid line of green slime showing the level it had reached at high tide.

I'm not sure if I want Jim to come here, she admitted to herself after a while.

Why? asked a voice in her head.

Because something will happen between us. I know it.

Isn't that what you want?

Yes ... no ... I like him ... But I don't know anything about him ... I still don't know for sure that he's single. The last thing I need is to make another big mistake.

The voice had no answers. Clearly, there was merit in her doubts.

Kylie crossed the river at the Ha'penny Bridge and kept on walking until she reached the Moore Street markets. The atmosphere drew her there most weekends: the citrus smell wafting from prams packed with fruit, the broad accents of the traders and the feeling that this market could be the one part of Dublin that hadn't changed much in forty years.

Kylie bought some fruit and other knick-knacks and wasted an hour or so bargaining with the stallholders over a few cents. The sun made a tentative appearance as she headed home. Her feet ached when she got back to her apartment but the walk had cleared her head. She was ready to answer Jim.

It was nice to talk to you too, Jim, she typed. **I hadn't forgotten about the drink and I rather like the idea of having it in Dublin. Let me know when you make a decision so I can tell Mags to organise the welcome-back party.**

Kylie read the message out loud. It was friendly and warm, just like his. She sent it on its way to Auckland.

Trying not to watch the clock, she started to make dinner. She cubed the vegetables and meat while her ears stayed on alert for an incoming-message beep from her laptop. Her nerves were so on edge that she nearly chopped her fingers off when the phone shrilled through the silent apartment.

"Hello?"

"Hi!" It was only Mags. "Fancy going out tonight?"

Kylie hesitated. She could hardly tell Mags that she was waiting for an email from Jim.

"I'm all settled down for a lazy night in front of the TV," she said instead.

"OK," replied Mags. "No problem."

Despite Mags's assurance, Kylie could tell that her friend wasn't her usual chirpy self.

"Everything OK?"

"Had a fight with Seamus, that's all."

Mags would normally give chapter and verse. Just by her silence it was clear that this was no run-of-the-mill argument.

"Why don't you come over here?" Kylie offered. "I have dinner half ready."

"OK. I'll bring some vino."

* * *

"Where do you keep your wineglasses?" asked Mags, looking around the compact kitchen.

"Top left," Kylie replied as she added some cashew nuts to the stir fry.

Mags poured the dark red Shiraz into two large bulbous glasses.

"Cheers," she said in a brittle voice. "Thanks for letting me gatecrash."

"No worries," Kylie replied lightly. "Are you OK

with sitting at the kitchen bar?"

Mags nodded in a way that said she couldn't care less where they sat. Her eyes were dull and her pale face was even more wan than usual.

The conversation through dinner was sparse. Mags didn't open up until she had topped up her glass for the second time.

"Ever had your heart broken, Kylie?" she asked.

"Doesn't everyone?"

"Maybe that's true," her tone was dark, "and at the grand old age of thirty, I'm obviously a latecomer."

Kylie shot her a wry smile. "Well, then, I must have been a latecomer too – I was the same age when I broke up with my fiancé."

Mags swirled the wine around in her glass. "Tell me about him – your fiancé."

Her broken engagement was the last thing that Kylie wanted to discuss. Particularly not on this night when she was hoping that something new would start with Jim. She side-stepped the question and said, "Time for me to indulge my nicotine habit."

Her ashtray and cigarettes sat over on the windowsill. As she came closer, she noticed rain drops glistening on the glass pane.

"Oh, it's raining!"

"Why do you sound so surprised?" Mags was

sardonic.

"The sun was trying so hard to break through the clouds all day," she said, flicking the lighter. "But it seems that the rain won out in the end."

Mags cast a derisive look her way. "Christ – it's just the weather. You sound like you've done nothing but think about it all day – you must be spending too much time on your own."

Kylie laughed as she pushed up the window and puffed a mouthful of smoke into the darkness. Down below, the city lights reflected fuzzily on the river, and traffic clogged the quays. The footpaths were unusually deserted; nobody wanted to walk in the rain.

After a few minutes she asked, "What happened with Seamus?"

From the reflection in the window, she saw her friend's shoulders droop. "He got arrested last night," her voice was uneven, "for drunken driving."

Kylie tried to think back to the previous night. She had left the pub early due to the conference call. She could recall Seamus with a beer in his hand when she said goodbye, and she remembered buying him one earlier on in the night as well.

"He wasn't much over the limit," said Mags. "But that doesn't matter – he was still stupid enough to get behind the wheel. Now he's lost his licence and he has to go to court. I'm so mortified – I don't think I'll ever forgive him for this."

Kylie stubbed out her unfinished cigarette and closed the window. She sat down on the coffee table so that she and Mags were eye to eye.

"You have to forgive him, Mags. For if you don't, then who else can he turn to?"

* * *

The soft rain still lingered on the next morning. Kylie threw back the covers and shivered when her warm body encountered the damp cold. She wrapped a towelling robe over her light pyjamas and went to make a warming cup of coffee.

The kitchen was not a pretty sight with the unwashed dishes and empty bottles. Mags had gone home in the early hours of the morning. Kylie had no idea if she would forgive Seamus or not. In the cold light of day, she wasn't at all sure that she'd given her the right advice. Just because Rose had said the same thing when Geoff lost the house – that was nothing to go by. Nothing at all.

With her coffee in hand, she sat down in front of the laptop, which was still switched on since yesterday. She re-established the connection to the MFJ network and refreshed her inbox. It took only a few seconds in all, during which she felt sweet anticipation at the thought of a message from Jim. The anticipation wasn't long deflating. There was nothing in her inbox, no new message from Jim, or anyone else for that matter.

Is this thing between me and Jim totally in my head? Am I making too much of this drink? Maybe he just wants to be friends and a date is the last thing on his mind.

She abruptly shut down the frustratingly empty inbox and opened up the internet. It was time for another wild goose chase, which was exactly what the search for her family had become.

Desperate for some progress, illogically angry with Jim, she hit the keys with unnecessary force as she typed in a search for "**births deaths marriages Ireland**".

She scrolled down the first page of results. Towards the end she found a website for the General Register Office and she double-clicked on the link.

She sighed loudly when she read **"we do not engage in genealogical family history research"** in the very first paragraph. However, with nowhere else to look, she stayed on the website in the hope that she would get some ideas from it.

It turned out that she did get an idea. Further down on the home page she read, **"Roman Catholic parish registers are normally still held**

by the parish priest."

Now that she stopped to think, it was very obvious. Why bother with the phone directory when the local priest should be able to tell her what she needed to know?

* * *

"I'm taking Friday off," said Mags when they were having lunch the next day. In the harsh light of the Temple Bar café, she still looked dreadfully wan.

"Going somewhere for the weekend?" asked Kylie.

"To Galway. Seamus and I have some talking to do. Obviously, I'll be doing the driving."

A young waitress, who sounded East European, delivered their food and asked if they needed anything else.

"No, thanks," said Kylie.

She started to eat. Halfway through her sandwich, she said, "Do you think Ted would mind if I took Friday off too?"

It was high time for a second visit to Portmarnock and a weekday would be so much more suitable than a busy weekend.

"Ted won't mind if we close shop for one day," Mags replied confidently. "It's not as if we're rushed off our feet."

* * *

As if to prove her wrong, the afternoon was extraordinarily busy.

"It's a pity we can't squeeze another table in here and run parallel consultations," said Kylie as she packed up for the night.

"We'd still have a problem with confidentiality," Mags replied. "What we really need is another room. But that's not in the budget so we have to make do with what we have. Anyway, this afternoon was probably just an anomaly."

Mags had just turned the key in the lock when Kylie's mobile started to ring.

"Hello?"

"You had no right to give Claudine unlimited time off!"

Kylie flinched at the sound of Neil's snarling voice.

"Neil, this isn't a good time."

Not only was she too tired, she didn't want to have a conversation like this standing in the hallway with Mags looking on. She needed her full wits about her.

"I'll give you an hour," he snapped. "I'll expect your call."

Kylie put her phone back in her bag. She and Mags said goodbye out on the street and went their separate ways. Kylie was so preoccupied that she hardly noticed the huddled body in the doorway of the building next door. It rose from its slouch and dark eyes watched her every step until she was out of sight.

* * *

"I didn't give her unlimited time, Neil," said Kylie as she paced her apartment the allotted hour later. "I said she didn't have to return until Ethan was well."

"It's the same thing," he said dismissively.

"No, it's quite different," she argued.

"Well, regardless of your empty promises, she's not going to get a dollar out of us. She's a foolish woman for even thinking that she can take on MFJ and win."

Kylie had to bite down hard on her lip. She was suddenly overwhelmed with the extent of her dislike for Neil. She didn't care any more how much he had done for her career: he was totally insufferable. However, it was imperative that she tread very carefully; he could not know where her loyalties lay.

"Look, Neil, why don't you consider her request?" she said in her most reasonable tone. "It's only a few grand – if you pay her now, you may save yourself a lot of time and bother down the line."

Her suggestion did not go down well. Neil ranted and raved for the next five minutes. By the time she hung up, Kylie had the sinking feeling that she had made things worse than they already were for Claudine.

Chapter 14

Kylie heard a lone voice sing out as she approached the modern church. The voice was answered by a reverent murmur. Friday morning Mass sounded to be well underway at St Anne's church. She stood and listened to the rhythm of the voices for a few moments before she went inside.

The congregation were mostly gathered at the front of the church. Their heads bent, they appeared to be praying fervently. She slid as inconspicuously as possible into the last pew as the young red-haired priest, with his deep baritone voice and flowing green robes, began to read the gospel.

Kylie couldn't remember the last time she had been in a church. Even as a child, Sunday Mass had never been a constant like it was for other families. Given the hundreds and thousands of questions she had asked her parents over the years, she was somewhat surprised to realise that she had never asked them about religion. Now, looking at a congregation that was largely the same age as Rose and Frankie, she understood just how lapsed her parents were. Had it always been so, or was it something that had come about when they moved to Australia?

The service was finished in less than half an hour. In a flurry of genuflections, the congregation started to leave. Kylie met their curious stares one by one. Soon she was alone.

What now?

As if to answer her question, the white-robed attendant came back out to the altar. Kylie got up from her seat.

"Excuse me – I was wondering if it is possible to see the priest," she said.

"He's back in the sacristy," he replied.

When Kylie looked blank, he added, "Through that doorway – first room on the right. Make sure you knock."

"Thanks."

She followed his directions. The door to the room was closed and she gave a gentle knock on the varnished wood.

"Come in!"

The green robes had been removed and the young priest wore black with the conventional white collar.

"Kylie Horgan," she said, extending her hand.

"Dermot Flanagan," he offered in return. "Have a seat, Kylie. I apologise, but I have only a few minutes to spare this morning. One of the parishioners is going down hill . . . I promised the family I would go there straight after Mass . . . Well, how can I help you?"

"I'm searching for my extended family," she explained, very conscious of the ill parishioner who had a much more legitimate claim to the priest's time than she did. "My mother, Rose Carey, and my father, Frankie Horgan, emigrated to Australia in the sixties. Their parents are dead now . . . it's their siblings I'm trying to find . . ."

He looked thoughtful. "Horgan is a popular enough name around here – there are a few of them in the parish. Now, Carey would be less common and I can't say I know of any . . ."

"I'll write down the full names for you if I may, Father," she suggested. "Perhaps you could ask around . . . ?"

"That's a sound idea. Here," he handed her a notepad and pen from the desk, "jot your phone number down as well, would you?"

Kylie left shortly afterwards. She felt pleased with her morning's efforts. The parish priest would know somebody who knew the family. It had to be so.

It wasn't yet 11 a.m. and she still had the best part of the day at her disposal. She was drawn back to the beach. She had since discovered that it was called the Velvet Strand, a most appropriate name for the luxuriously fine sand under her bare feet. She looked out to the horizon to see if the yachts were out in their droves again. But other than a few triangles of white, it seemed to be a lot quieter than the last time.

Closer, just at the water's edge, two racehorses trotted along with their straight-backed jockeys. The horses, their heads hung and front knees high, moved with a beautiful elegance through the shallow water. Kylie watched their progress to the very end of the beach where they were nothing more than two indecipherable dots.

Sometime later, she left the beach and headed towards the Country Club Hotel. On the way she caught sight of an overgrown cemetery and, before she knew it, she was in the middle of the ancient tombstones. Trees, bushes and wild grass grew in the untended graves. A gabled wall of a ruined church presided over the souls buried in its sacred grounds. Brambles scratched Kylie's bare legs as she checked the etchings on the mottled grey tombstones: *Murphy, Kennedy, Lowry, O'Neill, 1854, 1890, 1924, 1792.* It seemed that nobody had been buried in the cemetery in recent years. Her grandparents' graves were somewhere else.

* * *

She was coming back on the bus when her mobile rang. Neil was the first person who came to mind and, as result, she answered it warily.

"Kylie, it's Jim."

"Jim?"

"Jim Donnelly – have you forgotten me already?"

"No," it was a good thing he couldn't see the colour flooding to her face, "I just didn't expect it to be you, that's all."

"Well, it *is* me," he sounded amused, "and I was wondering what you're doing tonight?"

"Why?" She gave a nervous laugh. "Are you planning on buying me a virtual drink on the internet?"

"No," he chuckled back, "I'm planning on buying you a *real* drink. I'm not in Auckland – I'm here in Dublin."

"Dublin?" she squeaked.

"Yes," he answered. "Dublin – the same place as you."

The rest of the journey to the city was a blur. Jim was in Dublin. She had agreed to meet him. Not tonight or tomorrow but right away.

We have a date. He's going to meet me off the bus.

There was no chance to prepare, look her best. Yet she didn't care that she was wearing old cut-off jeans and no make-up. She just wanted to see him. It was that simple.

It took an age to reach the city centre, the Friday-afternoon traffic dense. Finally she got off the bus and looked around so zealously that she didn't see him right in front of her. But there he was: tall, smiling, black polo shirt and tanned muscular arms that hugged her to him with a force that took her breath away.

"You look great." He smiled down at her. "Dublin suits you."

"Thanks."

He took her hand in his and led her through the commuters who were gathered at the bus stop. "Come on, let's go somewhere."

"Somewhere" was the Gresham Hotel. Despite the hotel's old stone façade, the bar was surprisingly modern. They sat on two of the high-backed barstools.

"What would you like?" Jim asked, with one elbow resting on the bar.

"A Guinness, please."

He ordered two and the barman half-filled the pint glasses from the tap.

"Well, Kylie Horgan," Jim turned his gaze to her, "how have you been?"

"Great."

He laughed. "I come all the way from the other side of the world to see you and that's all you have to say for yourself?"

In that moment she realised another thing about Jim that attracted her: absolutely nothing was an obstacle to this man. Who else would have jumped on a plane without giving it more than a few days' thought? It was exciting just to sit this close to him and let his energy envelop her. To believe, be it only for one afternoon, that anything in life was possible.

She called his bluff. "Come on, now – I don't think you came all the way here just to see me."

His hand reached out and touched her face. "Not that I would *ever* admit it to my family, a big part of me did come here just to see you."

She smiled at him. This thing with Jim wasn't in her head. It was real. The barman topped off the pints of Guinness and set them down carefully on the counter. Some of the smooth cream trickled down the sides of the glasses.

"Cheers," said Kylie.

"Cheers," he echoed.

"How long are you here for?" she asked.

"A week."

Seven days, full of possibility, stretched out in front of them, and from the look in Jim's eyes it seemed that he had the same hopes as her.

* * *

Kylie woke with a smile the next morning. She stretched out in bed and allowed herself the luxury of recalling every special detail of the day before.

Goodness knows how many glasses of Guinness she'd drunk. All she knew was that she and Jim stayed in the Gresham right into the evening. The bar got busier with the after-work crowd – however, they were in their own private cocoon. They were laughing most of the time: at the prams of fruit in Moore Street, how normal it was to tell your life history to a total stranger and the "heatwave" on Kylie's arrival.

But at one point, Kylie got serious.

"I feel I know so little about you, Jim."

"What do you want to know?" he asked.

"Lots of things – I'm a curious individual."

He grinned. "OK. Let's do Angela's two truths and one lie game."

"OK – go on."

"Right," his eyes twinkled at her, "I once broke my nose playing second division rugby. I can play the guitar. And the place in the world I'd most like to visit is Cairo."

"Mmm . . . let's see. You have the physique for rugby, and I already know that you're a big fan of the sport, so I think it's very possible that you've played at a senior level." She pretended to study his nose. "It does look a little crooked. Now, Cairo is a place I'd also like to see so I can understand the appeal . . . I think I'll go for the guitar."

He shook his head. "Wrong, Kylie Horgan."

"Your nose?" she tried next.

"Nope."

"You mean you don't want to go to Cairo?"

"No – it's just that I've already been there."

"That was a trick one – that's not allowed."

"Says who?"

She pouted her lower lip in mock sulkiness. "Me."

When they stopped laughing he said, "I'm sorry, Kylie. I have to go soon – I need to catch up with the family."

"But I haven't had my turn. I had a great lie – you

would have never guessed it."

"Tomorrow." He smiled.

He walked her back to her apartment, pointing out the not-so-famous landmarks and giving her some trivia on the city that was temporarily her home. It was still daylight; the long summer evening had not yet yielded to nightfall. Despite the fact that they strolled rather than walked, they still reached the apartment far sooner than Kylie would have liked.

"Thanks for a lovely afternoon," she said.

"My pleasure."

They both moved to close the distance between them. A hug. He tilted her head back. A kiss. Brief. But then a second one. Deeper. Her hands clasped around his neck and his spanned the small of her back as their bodies pressed together. Kylie was oblivious to everything but his kiss and it was some time before the teasing hoots of the passing cars pierced her consciousness. Her face flushed and her knees slightly weak, she stepped back.

"I'll see you tomorrow," he said, his voice hoarse.

"OK."

She didn't go inside straight away. She watched him walk back along the quays, his long legs making little of the distance. He stopped once and turned around. They waved at each other. Then he was off again, striding back towards his family and everything else that she didn't yet know about him.

Now, Kylie glanced across at her trustworthy alarm clock over on the window sill: 9 a.m.. It wasn't too late to put a call through to Sydney.

"Hi, Mum."

"Hello, stranger."

"Sorry," she was sheepish, "the time difference is so awkward – whenever I remember to call, it's usually too late or too early for you."

It was partly true. However, guilt also made it hard to pick up the phone.

"You can call anytime, love," said Rose quietly. "I don't mind being woken up."

"Did you get the photo from *The Herald*?"

"Yes – you looked very well."

"And my postcard?"

"Yes."

An awkward pause followed.

"It's a lovely place, Portmarnock," Kylie said carefully. "Was the golf course there in your time?"

"Yes." Rose sounded rather tired, as if she was weary of battling the inevitable. "Golf was always a big thing – your grandfather was a handy player."

Kylie didn't stop to analyse the first voluntary piece of information that Rose had ever offered on her family.

"And the beach, it's so impressive . . ."

"Do the kids still play aeroplane pilots?" asked Rose.

"I didn't notice – why?"

"The beach has a long aviation history," Rose told her. "Kingsford-Smith did the last leg of his round-the-world trip from the Velvet Strand. In the early thirties many pioneer aviators arrived or took off from there. It all caused great excitement and our parents told us about it so many times it was as if we were there ourselves. Carmel, Liz and I never tired of playing pilot – we'd be out there till nine o'clock on the summer nights."

Her words conjured up the most vivid picture of three fair-haired little girls, racing up the beach, arms spread, their imagination soaring them across the Atlantic.

However, it seemed Rose had finished with her reminiscing, as her next question was about the weather. They then lapsed into their routine conversation about work and Stephen's elusive girlfriend. They hung up without any mention of the unused tickets to Ireland. However, Kylie was pleased.

She's starting to soften and there's still enough time left for her to change her mind.

Kylie yawned and wondered when Jim would ring. Through the parting in the curtains she saw a slice of dull grey sky. There seemed to be no reason to hurry out of bed and she closed her eyes. It was midday when she opened them again. She knew she would have heard her mobile ring had he called, but she still checked to see if there were any missed calls. The screen on her phone was disappointingly clear.

Might as well shower and get dressed, she thought.

She had her breakfast, checked her emails and read two chapters of her book. 3 p.m., still no call. She vacuumed the apartment, cleaned the bathrooms and put on a wash. 6 p.m., it looked like she would be having dinner alone.

At 10 p.m., when she was on the last chapter of her book, the door buzzer sounded.

Probably a neighbour who has forgotten his key, she thought, putting the novel down.

"Yes?" she spoke into the intercom.

"Kylie! It's me."

Jim. As far as she was concerned, it wasn't a case of better late than never. Did he know that she had waited all day? Did he think she was someone he could call at the end of the day when those who clearly mattered more to him were no longer around?

"I don't want to talk to you, Jim."

She walked away from the intercom. The buzzer went off again. She ignored it. She finished reading the novel and went to bed.

* * *

The next morning she was woken by a beep from her phone. Groggy, she reached over to the bedside unit. She squinted at the screen: there was a message.

I'm downstairs. Please let me explain.

She got out of bed and tried to sort out her muddled head with a shower. She raised her face to the hot water while her mind battled with itself.

He stood me up, said the unforgiving side.

No, he didn't, answered the voice of reason. *He never said what time he'd see you. And he did turn up — eventually.*

She shook her head under the gushing water. *If he had any respect for me, he wouldn't put me after everyone else.*

But there was a ready reply of, *He's only home for a week — he must have lots of people to catch up with.*

She brushed her teeth and dressed in a pair of combat pants with a tight-fitting khaki T-shirt. A half hour had passed since his message. If he was still downstairs, then she supposed that he deserved a hearing.

OK, she texted him back.

The buzzer sounded just a few moments after she pressed the SEND button.

"Second floor, number 22," she said and let him

into the building.

She checked her reflection while she waited for him to come up. Her dark curls were damp and her cheeks had a pinch of pink. She was putting on some lip gloss when he knocked.

She opened the door and was met head on by his steel-grey eyes. They exchanged a wary greeting before he followed her inside.

"Sit down," she told him for the living room was suffocating with him standing in the centre of it.

"Come and sit next to me," he said from the couch.

She was about to refuse when he added, "Please."

So, against her better judgement, she sat next to him.

"I did the wrong thing on Friday," he began. "It was incredibly selfish of me to spend the entire afternoon with you when there are people who I haven't seen for the past two years – people who I left in the lurch when I ran off to Australia."

He paused. He seemed to be struggling to find the right words to continue on. Kylie waited, her face impassive.

"Has anyone in the Dublin office mentioned Laura to you?" he asked, rather abruptly.

She shook her head. She was good with names; she would have remembered.

He frowned, as if he found that unbelievable. "Nobody mentioned the girl who died? Who ran her car into a brick wall?"

He seemed so disturbed that she reached out to reassure him. "Yes, Mags mentioned her. She just didn't tell me her name."

He sighed raggedly. "God – for a minute there I thought they had forgotten her."

"Was she your girlfriend?" asked Kylie with trepidation.

"Yes." His voice was very low. "In fact, we lived together. The night of the accident was like any other. At 8 p.m. she called by my office and said she was heading home. I told her I'd be another hour or so – not to wait up for me –"

His voice faded away as emotion took over. Even though Kylie didn't know Laura, she still felt the devastating sadness at the waste of a young life.

A few seconds passed before Jim continued. "The coroner concluded that the accident was caused by over-tiredness." Then he quoted, *"The young lady worked a thirteen-hour day before she lost control of her car. I seriously recommend that her employers look at their part in this terrible tragedy."*

Kylie tried to offer him some consolation. "They did take a serious look at themselves, Jim. Nobody works crazy hours any more, and they do an enormous amount of pro bono . . ."

His mouth twisted into a cynical line. "And all it took was Laura's life."

A sad silence followed. Kylie didn't move a muscle, her hand still on his arm. It ached from the awkwardness of the angle but she didn't dare move it.

"I'm sorry. I had no idea that you left Dublin under such terrible circumstances."

"Australia was my haven," he replied, running a hand through his thick brown hair. "Nobody there knew anything about Laura. I implied early on that I had a girlfriend back home, and everybody accepted that at face value. It enabled me to heal at my own pace, without the pressure to date."

Kylie nodded. It explained why Isobel thought he was attached.

He released her hand from his arm and clasped it in his. "I was with Laura's family yesterday," he said. "It wasn't a visit that I could cut short – I had to stay until their grief ran its course. And I could hardly tell them that I had to leave to meet another woman."

* * *

Mags had some of her old sparkle back when Kylie saw her the next day.

"Good weekend?" she enquired as Mags unlocked the door to the clinic.

"As good as can be expected," was her airy response.

Kylie followed her into the room.

Mags hung her jacket on the back of her chair. "How about you?"

"Yeah, good," Kylie replied and added casually, "Jim Donnelly is back in town."

Mags turned around, her eyes wide with shock. "Have you seen him?"

"Yes."

Kylie thought it best not to mention that she had seen him more than once. She didn't know what kind of reaction she would get. After all, Mags had been Laura's friend first.

"Well, is he going to call in to see us?" asked Mags impatiently.

"Yes. He mentioned something about lunch today."

The first visitor of the morning was Mary from the main reception.

"I meant to catch you on the way in," she said, her face flustered. "There was an attempted break-in last night. They broke the lock on the outer door. The alarm went off, of course, and from what I can see they didn't take anything. Is everything all right down here?"

"Yes," Kylie answered. "The door was still locked this morning – nobody's been in here."

"Disgraceful, it is!" Mary was clearly upset. "How can they rob the very people who are trying to help them?"

Mags crossed the room to put her arm around the older woman's slim shoulders. "Logic doesn't come into it – not if they're out of their heads on drink or drugs."

"I know," Mary had tears in her eyes, "I know all that. But I feel let down all the same."

The mood was sober after she left. Even more sober when the first client came in, a homeless young woman with a red-cheeked baby.

"I get nothing from him," she stated bitterly. "He drives around in his brand new Renault while we're on the streets. All his money is off the books, no trace can be put on it. But I need to get some – I can't have the baby growing up in shelters."

Mags went into action. She admired the baby, sympathised with the mother and then, only when she had her trust, she asked the detailed questions.

"You'll get your maintenance," she promised at the end. "We'll get a hearing –"

"He won't go to no court," the young woman interrupted.

Mags gave her a quietly confident smile. "Oh, yes,

he will. He might do a 'no show' the first time but I can guarantee you that *I will* get him there and *he will* pay you maintenance."

She was so convincing that even Kylie believed her.

Kylie kept a keen eye on the clock as the morning passed by. It had just edged past twelve thirty when Jim arrived.

Mags jumped up from her seat and ran around the desk. "Jim Donnelly!"

He caught her in a bear hug. "How the hell are you, Mags Kiely?"

She grinned. "Life is mostly good. And you?"

His wry smile told that the last two years had been difficult and not easy for him to summarise. He settled for, "I'm good, too," and then looked over at Kylie who was still sitting at the desk. "Come on, Kylie Horgan, woman about town – take me to one of your haunts!"

They went to Fitzsimon's in Temple Bar. The restaurant was full and they were lucky that a window seat was vacated just as they walked in.

Mags ordered a bottle of wine and the waiter poured it into three long-stemmed glasses.

Jim raised his glass. "To old friends!"

"And those who are no longer with us," returned Mags.

Kylie clinked her glass along with theirs, but she felt a little like an impostor.

The food was superb but the conversation painfully awkward. Jim and Mags skirted around the subject of Laura, and it soon became evident that they needed time alone to talk freely about her.

"Coffee?" asked the waiter as he cleared the plates.

Kylie had been waiting for the opportunity to excuse herself. When the other two nodded at the waiter, she said, "Not for me, thanks." She stood up and smiled at her companions. "I think you two need some time alone."

Her stomach churned with emotions as she walked back towards the office. Did Laura, presuming she could somehow see what was going on, feel animosity towards the woman who had stolen both her friend and her partner? Kylie would have understood perfectly if she did. It was so sad to be robbed of her life, even worse to have to relinquish her rights on the people she loved.

The first drops of rain started to fall as Kylie reached Cope Street. She ran the rest of the way, past an unkempt figure who seemed to be standing aimlessly on the footpath. His face was hardly visible behind the drooping hood of his anorak, but she caught a fleeting glimpse of a dirty grey beard. Was it Jerry?

She was soon distracted by Mary, who had come running in the opposite direction.

"Fine summer this is," the older woman muttered as she stuck the key in the lock.

* * *

Later that night, while Kylie was watching TV, the phone rang. She muted the volume before taking the call.

"Kylie, this is Father Dermot Flanagan."

She had almost totally forgotten about the priest, what with everything that was happening with Jim.

"Hello, Father Flanagan."

"I've been making enquiries on your behalf," he began, sounding very prim and proper.

Kylie was glad that she had met him in person because it would have been easy to be put off by the formality of his phone manner.

"It seems that your mother's family have been gone from Portmarnock a long time."

"Oh," she said, feeling the bitter taste of defeat in her mouth.

"It took me quite a while to find anyone who knew them at all," he continued. "The parents, God rest their souls, died twenty or so years ago. Carmel,

I believe, is over in England and Liz, the youngest daughter, moved down to Cork. Whether she is still there or not, I don't know."

"How about the Horgans?" asked Kylie.

"I'm sorry," he said, his tone softening. "Even though we have a number of Horgans in the parish, I haven't been able to find any trace of your father's family. I'll pray for you all – God takes special care of families."

Kylie lit a cigarette and agitatedly puffed her frustration out the window. In Dublin for almost two months now, she had absolutely nothing to show for her efforts. In two more months she'd be back in Sydney and, the way things were going, she wouldn't have satisfied the aching need to know her family roots.

The cigarette extinguished, she went back to the sofa and stretched out along the length of it. She watched ten minutes of the evening news before something registered in her head.

"*Liz moved down to Cork,*" Father Flanagan had said.

Was it a coincidence that Kylie had talked to a Liz Carey in Cork? She remembered the call very clearly. It had been so very promising to start off with; the woman had a sister called Rose. However, she had quite definitely said that her sister was dead.

But what if her sister is not dead? The very thought propelled Kylie into an upright position. *Could Liz Carey be wrong?*

* * *

The crazy thought would not go away. All night long, through disturbed sleep, and the next morning, when there was more than one occasion that Mags had to repeat herself, it played havoc with her mind.

Could Liz Carey be wrong? Could her sister, Rose, be alive?

"What is wrong with you today?" Mags asked in exasperation when Kylie didn't respond to yet another question. "You're away with the fairies."

Kylie apologised. "I'm sorry." Then added, "It's just a family thing," for fear that Mags might think she was daydreaming about Jim.

Should I phone Liz Carey again? Or would it be better to see her face to face?

As the morning progressed the clinic got busier and Kylie found it impossible to reach a decision. There was such a backlog that shutting shop for lunch hour was out of the question.

Mary, on her way out, bustled into the room. "I'll bring ye back some sandwiches," she offered. "The queue is all the way down the hall – ye'll need three of ye at this rate."

"She's not far wrong," said Mags when she was gone. "Though, I can't figure out if this is a short-term boom or a more permanent trend."

Much later in the afternoon, when Kylie was finishing off a consultation, her phone beeped with an incoming text. The client, a woman who liked the sound of her own voice, was hard to shake off.

"I'll make him sorry – not that I'm vindictive, mind – it's just that I don't let anyone get away with doing me wrong – when I was younger, I did – but I'm older and wiser now –"

"Thank you, Mrs Connelly. I'll let you know the outcome of our enquiries," said Kylie pointedly.

But she still lingered on. "You never know with people, do you – he seemed so nice at the start – but it was all put on – a right con-artist, he was –"

"Yes, it certainly seems so. Have a nice evening, Mrs Connelly."

She finally took the hint and Kylie had a few free moments to check her phone.

Dinner tonight?

Jim. She smiled. Other than the awkward lunch in Fitzsimon's, she hadn't seen him since Sunday. But he had sent a number of text messages, and she knew that he was thinking of her. As she was of him.

Take me to one of your haunts, she texted him back.

Then the next client came in, and it wasn't long before she was caught up in another sad story.

* * *

Mary had gone home by the time they finished, and Mags did all the locking up.

"I'm going your way tonight," said Kylie and the two of them started off down the street, neither one aware of the hooded figure that followed some distance behind.

At first there was an awkward silence. Their friendship wasn't the same these last few days. Kylie was unsure if it was to do with Jim's arrival or the upset with Seamus. Maybe it was a combination of both.

"What's the best way to get to Cork?" asked Kylie as they approached O'Connell bridge.

"Depends what part you want to go to," replied Mags, and she turned her face away from the force of the wind that blew up the river.

"Ballincollig."

"I think that's outside the city centre – you'd be better off driving there, I'd say," was her advice. "Is that what's been distracting you today?"

"Yeah," Kylie confessed. She had decided that she wanted to go to see Liz Carey. A two-minute phone conversation might not be enough to determine if it was possible for her dead sister to be alive. "I just wish the weekend wasn't so far away . . ."

They came off the bridge and waited at the pedestrian crossing.

"Take a day off if you need to," Mags suggested.

Kylie frowned. "But that would mean we'd have to shut for the day – and it's been so busy this week . . ."

"I'll call Ted tonight and ask him to send over one of the graduates," was her solution.

Behind, the hooded figure stood motionless as he watched the two women blend into the sea of people crossing the road. He thought to himself that there would be a better time and place. He turned back the way he came.

"I have to cross again for my bus," said Mags, stopping on the corner. "Unless I hear otherwise, I'll assume that I won't see you till Thursday. Bye!"

Kylie continued on to the General Post Office. With its granite façade, complete with bullet holes from the 1916 Rising, it was a popular meeting spot. Dozens of pairs of eyes glanced her way to see if she was their tardy sister, colleague or friend. Jim was already there, and he claimed her for his by lifting her up in a tight hug.

When he set her down she noted that his eyes

were hollowed and his face drawn. Dublin held a lot of personal baggage for him, and the strain was taking its toll.

Hand in hand, he led her down a maze of back streets until they came to an Italian restaurant with a rather nondescript front.

"One of my old haunts," he said as he opened the door to let her through.

Small square tables squashed up against each other in the poorly lit interior, yet the patrons didn't seem to mind the lack of space, their loud conversation, laughter and scraping cutlery indicating they were all having a good time.

The only free table was down the back of the restaurant, almost in the kitchen itself.

"I used to know all the staff here," said Jim when the waitress had taken their order, "but none of the faces here tonight look familiar – I guess it has been two years."

The wine came quickly, a sure sign that the food wouldn't be quite so prompt.

"Cheers!" Jim raised his glass.

She followed suit. Their glasses clinked. In the ensuing silence Kylie tried to banish Liz Carey from her thoughts.

"Penny for them," she heard Jim say.

"Sorry." She looked up apologetically. "I was just

wondering where I can hire a car around here."

"Why?" he asked.

"Because I need to go to Cork tomorrow."

"I'll drive you there," he offered unexpectedly.

"That's very kind of you, but –" she started to protest.

"Let me do it. Please."

"What about your family?"

"I think I've earned some time out."

"OK." She took an uneasy sip of her wine. "I guess I should explain why."

He seemed to understand that she was on edge and gave her an opening. "Well, it is your turn at two truths and one lie."

"So it is." She suddenly wanted to tell him all her dark secrets. "OK. Pick the lie . . . Patience is not one of my virtues . . . My ex-fiancé gambled away our house and left me up to my eyes in debt . . . I think that I have an aunt in Cork to whom my mother hasn't spoken in thirty years."

Was Jim going to jump up and run while he still could? It didn't seem so. He appeared to be weighing it all up.

"From what I've observed, patience is certainly not one of your strengths. I also recall that you went all funny when we started to play poker at the Hunter Valley – your experience with your fiancé would explain that reaction. So," he raised an eyebrow, "is the lie about your mother and aunt?"

She smiled cynically. "Correct. They haven't spoken in *forty-three* years. In fact, my aunt thinks that my mother is dead – that's if I have the right woman."

Their starters arrived, and she was just about to begin eating when Jim said, "If you're trying to scare me off, Kylie Horgan, you'll have to try a lot harder than a gambling ex-fiancé and some family skeletons down in Cork."

The wine, plus Jim's charm, eventually lightened Kylie's mood. By the end of the meal, the laughter and sexual tension of the afternoon in the Gresham were back in full force. Every time their hands touched or their eyes met, there was a promise of something more . . . later on, when they were alone.

Jim had asked for the bill when the waitress arrived with two glasses of port.

"We didn't order these," he said.

She jerked her head towards the bar. "Compliments of the manager."

A bald-headed man raised his hand in recognition as soon as Jim looked his way.

"That was nice of him," Kylie commented. "He must have remembered your face."

She really didn't want another drink: she was

intoxicated enough as it was. However, neither did she want to insult the spirit in which it had been given, so she drank back its heavy sweetness in one gulp.

On the way out, Jim stopped by the bar to thank the manager. Their voices were low and Kylie's head fuzzy, but she did catch the manager saying, "It's good to see you happy," at the end of their conversation.

Outside was cold in comparison to the cosy warmth of the restaurant. Kylie left Jim to his thoughts as he led her through unfamiliar streets. They eventually came out at the Ha'penny Bridge and crossed over its dainty arch, the black Liffey underneath.

The fresh air had cleared Kylie's head by the time they reached her apartment. She didn't ask Jim if he would like to come in – there was no need.

She closed the door behind them and turned into his waiting embrace. He cupped her face and her last impression was of his smouldering eyes before she got lost in his kiss. His lips were demanding and she kissed him back with just as much passion.

They somehow made their way to the bedroom – she wasn't too sure how. He scooped her legs from underneath and lifted her onto the bed. He paused, his face lined with the light that filtered through the blinds. "OK?"

She realised that she had been waiting for this moment ever since his first touch, the day in the Hunter Valley when he'd brushed the chocolate muffin from her face. Three long months had passed since that first spark of attraction, and now she wanted him so much that her whole body was on fire.

"Yes."

He surprised her with the gentlest kiss, a mere peck on her lips, then a succession of kisses down the length of her neck to the collar of her shirt. Patiently, his deft fingers dealt with the inhibiting buttons and soon after, her bra. The little butterfly kisses continued their perfect line downwards. She clasped his shoulders just as his mouth reached her slightly rounded tummy.

"I'm feeling decidedly underdressed in comparison to you," she pointed out in a husky voice that didn't sound like her own.

He looked up, a mischievous glint in his eye. "Please, Miss Horgan, feel free to address the imbalance as you see fit."

She slid her hands under his T-shirt, his torso smooth and taut to her touch, and she lifted the brushed cotton up over his head. It fell to join her bra on the floor. Keeping his gaze, she undid the heavy buckle on his belt and the metal studs on his fly. She inched the denim downwards. He began to do the same with her pants.

There were a few moments of mutual admiration before the full force of his naked body came to lie on hers. He pinned her arms over her head as his mouth, demanding once again, met hers. The kiss went on and on, the skin-on-skin sensation providing fuel for its passion. His hands explored her, and hers him, but their mouths didn't part.

The kiss eased only when he moved inside her. Her body rose to meet him, wanting to let him in. Their lips still touched, but only just, and their hands clasped together above her head. It seemed that they were joined in every possible way.

* * *

Despite the early start, the traffic heading south was bumper-to-bumper. Kylie didn't care. She could have quite happily sat in the car for the whole day, once she was with Jim.

This morning he was wearing his customary casual wear, T-shirt and jeans. She was getting used to this Jim, the dark-suited litigator a foggy memory. However, both were as sexy as hell.

"What are you smiling to yourself about?" he

asked, shooting her an amused glance.

Her cheeks blushed with colour. "Nothing."

Last night, in the afterglow of their lovemaking, they had cuddled up in bed and talked about life: their families, friends and careers. As they talked into the early hours of the morning, it became clear to Kylie that their hopes and dreams were on the same wavelength. Along with the physical chemistry between them, it all combined to make something very special; something good enough to last.

Once they got past Kildare, the traffic unclogged and Jim put his foot down. Kylie looked out the window at the rich green fields and grazing livestock.

"I can see why songs are written about the green fields of Ireland," she commented.

For the next few hours, the sun played hide and seek in the patchy blue sky. However, just after they crossed the Cork border, the windscreen speckled with drops of rain and she couldn't help but think it was a bad omen.

"Do you know how to get to Ballincollig?" she asked.

He nodded. "I once handled a case for a plastic manufacturer out there. It's been a few years, though."

Kylie felt a knot of nervousness form in her chest as he drove through the bustling centre of Cork City.

Her brief impression of Patrick Street consisted of old buildings, wide pavements and colourful umbrellas.

"UCC – University College of Cork," Jim pointed out a short while later when the people walking the pavements were mostly late-teens with backpacks.

"Cork County Hall," was the next landmark he pointed out. "The tallest building in Ireland – all sixteen stories of it."

Then the city was over and they were driving through green fields.

"Ballincollig is Cork's biggest satellite town," Jim informed her, "or at least it used to be."

It wasn't long before suburbia started up again as housing estates reclaimed the green countryside. Soon Jim was driving down the main street of a village that looked to be quite modern. Up ahead, a car reversed out and he turned into the vacant parking spot it left behind.

"Time to get a bite to eat," he said, "and discuss strategy."

They were parked almost directly outside a pub called *Darby Arms,* and it seemed obvious that they should go in there to eat.

"I'm starting to think that this wasn't such a good idea," Kylie admitted as she sat down. "This woman will think I'm a nutter for coming all the way down from Dublin without calling ahead. She probably won't even be home. I'm so sorry for dragging you into this . . . Once again, I've let my impatience get in the way of my common sense."

Jim grasped her hands with his and she felt an instant steadying effect.

"Don't be apologetic, Kylie. You're following a hunch, that's all. You aren't committing a crime."

She gave him a wry smile. "I think my mother, if she could see what I'm doing, would think it's a crime."

"Maybe you don't know your mother as well as you think."

"That's precisely the problem," she told him.

"Now you're being stubborn."

"Funny, that's exactly what my mother says about me."

Some of the tension eased away with their laughter.

The food was good but Kylie couldn't do it justice. Jim asked the waitress for directions to the housing estate and left her a generous tip as thanks for her detailed instructions.

"Number 64," muttered Kylie a few minutes later. The estate was a loop of red-bricked semi-detached houses with an oval green in its centre. "That was Number 30 just there. Keep going."

He came to a stop outside a house with a freshly varnished door and well-tended garden. Unlike some of the other houses, there was no car in the driveway.

"There's no one home," said Kylie, suddenly relieved beyond description.

"Go and knock," was Jim's patient response.

The drive was puddled from the earlier rain. Kylie knocked. So sure that no one was home, she jumped when the door opened inwards.

"Hello." The woman looked to be somewhere in her fifties. She was nicely dressed in beige trousers and a black scoop-necked top. Her short hair was fair, her face petite and her blue eyes inquisitive as they looked at the stranger who obviously wasn't a door-to-door salesperson or charity-collector, the usual kind of callers for this time of the day.

"My name is Kylie Horgan . . ." she began awkwardly.

The woman clearly had a sharp memory, for she immediately said, "The girl who phoned a few weeks ago?"

"Yes."

The blue eyes shifted from Kylie to the car parked at the end of the driveway. "Is that your husband waiting?"

"No, a friend."

"Does he want to come in?"

"I think he's OK there for a while."

Liz Carey led the way down a narrow hallway into the neatest kitchen Kylie had ever seen. Everything was so precisely in its place that she could instantly tell Liz lived on her own. There was no way she could have maintained this level of order with a family.

Liz took the kettle from its stand and filled it with fresh water. While it boiled, she arranged some sweet biscuits on a plate. Kylie had lived in Ireland long enough to understand the routine, and she sipped the boiling tea and ate one of the biscuits.

She had already rehearsed what she would say – after all, there had been ample opportunity in the car. She had decided that it would be totally outrageous to directly suggest that Liz's sister might not be dead. Her parents, possibly Kylie's grandparents, were a better place to start.

"Liz," she began, "were your parents called Seán and Maureen by any chance?"

Liz replied slowly, "Yes, they were."

"And do you have another sister called Carmel?"

"Yes."

Kylie's heart thudded. "I think my mother, Rose, must be your sister."

Liz looked utterly shocked. "But they told us Rose was dead . . . Mam and Dad . . ."

"She's lived in Sydney the last forty years," said

Kylie. "She's married to Frankie. He's Irish too. Did you know him?"

Liz shook her head in a bewildered kind of way. "No. Ours wasn't the kind of house that you'd bring a boyfriend home to. Our parents were very strict."

It became clear to them both at once. It was Liz who voiced it first.

"She must have eloped. And they were so furious they told us she was dead." Tears glittered in her eyes. "How cruel of them!"

Kylie was taken aback at the sheer bitterness on Liz's face. She reached for her hand.

"Maybe they were cruel to be kind . . ." she said, not quite believing it herself.

"No," Liz was vehement. "Your grandparents were cruel, Kylie. And pious. A lethal combination that made life miserable for Carmel and me. As soon as we had the means, we lost no time in getting out of there. It seems that Rose was just faster off the mark than we were."

A long emotional silence followed. Liz cried tears of shock, and Kylie felt terribly guilty for landing on her with no warning.

"Did you have no idea that Rose might be alive?" she asked eventually.

"Sure, I was only twelve and Carmel thirteen," was her reply. "We weren't brought up to question what we were told. Looking back, we were so naïve that we bordered on stupid."

* * *

"OK?" asked Jim when Kylie slid in next to him.

She answered with a nod. She didn't have the energy to speak. After two hours and three cups of tea, there was only one thing that was clear to her: she had not just found her aunt, but also Stephen's aunt, Rose's sister and Frankie's sister-in-law. Not to mention Carmel in England, her husband, her three children, two grandchildren and the criss-cross of relationships that they brought too.

How can I tell Mum?

Of course, Liz had wanted Rose's phone number there and then. Kylie had no option but to be honest.

"I haven't told her that I was coming here," she confessed. "She's always been so secretive about Ireland. And the more secretive she was, the more curious I became . . ."

Liz didn't seem too bothered. In fact, she smiled. "You must take after your Aunt Carmel. She's always been a nosy bat!"

The silence in the car restored Kylie's equilibrium, and eventually she told Jim what had transpired in the modest semi-detached house. She imparted the information in a drib-drab manner. She'd tell him something, then be exhausted from the vast implications of that one thing and revert back to silence. A few miles on, she'd tell him something else. He didn't ask questions and she, for once in her life, didn't analyse.

"Enough about me and my screwed-up family," she yawned when they were about an hour outside Dublin. "Let's play a game."

"I spy?" he laughed.

"No. Two truths, one lie. And it's your turn."

He waited to speak until he had overtaken a car that was going about twenty miles less than the speed limit.

"Country drivers," he muttered before asking, "Where were we? Oh, yes, the game . . . I've wanted to kiss you ever since that night you walked into the function room in Darling Harbour. You were soaked through but you still looked so – defiant – as if you were saying, 'Stuff the lot of you!'"

"Mmm," she leaned back in her seat, "I hope that one is true."

He continued with, "When we are both back in Sydney, I'm going to take you for a drink in The Oyster Bar, right on Circular Quay, where we can look at the ferries come and go and spend a lazy afternoon mulling over the differences between

Dublin and Sydney."

"I like that one too," she smiled.

"I'm going to spend another wonderful night with you tonight."

Her smile faded. His tone was a give-away.

"That's the lie, isn't it?"

"I'm sorry, Kylie," he said quietly. "I'd like nothing better than to spend the night with you – but I promised Laura's family that I'd call around."

"It's OK. I understand," she replied as disappointment mingled with her tiredness.

Sometime later her curiosity got the better of her exhaustion and she asked, "Do you mind me asking what Laura was like?"

"No – I know how nosy you are." He cast an affectionate sideways look at her. "Laura was lots of fun, a child at heart."

Kylie needed to know more. "What did she look like?"

"Pretty. Long straight brown hair. Medium height."

"Was she possessive?"

He read where she was going straight away. "You're worried that she'd disapprove of us? No, Kylie, she wasn't overly possessive. I'm quite certain that she'd be happy I've found someone – I wouldn't be doing this otherwise."

They encountered green lights all the way into the city centre, as if someone was wishing Jim away from her. It seemed no time at all before he pulled up outside her apartment.

"I'm not going to see you again, am I?" she said, her voice flat.

He shook his head. "Tomorrow is my last day – my flight is at six in the evening. I wish I could say that I'll call into Cope Street, but it's unlikely . . ." He undid his seat-belt and leaned across to circle his arm around her shoulders. His face was sincere as he promised, "Seven more weeks, then you and I will finally be in the same city."

He was right. Seven weeks was nothing in the scheme of things. So why was she hugging him as if this would be the last time?

Chapter 15

Deep down, Kylie still held out some hope that Jim's family commitments would miraculously disappear and he would drop into the clinic the next day. Just to say hello. Or goodbye. She didn't care what. But no matter how many times she looked at the door, or how hard she tried to will him to walk through it, he didn't show.

All in all the day wasn't very busy, mainly because Ted had given his permission for the graduate to stay on a trial basis. Her name was Sarah. Just twenty-two years old and naïvely eager, the dynamics of the office were totally changed by her presence.

"I'll research that for you, Kylie."

"I can write that letter for you if you like, Mags."

"Anyone for a tea, coffee?"

As soon as Sarah left the room, Mags took advantage of their first moment alone to ask, "How did you get down to Cork in the end?"

Kylie decided to be honest. "Jim drove me."

Mags went back to the matter she was researching without commenting. However, her disapproval was very clear from her stony expression. In the following minutes the atmosphere became so frosty that it was a relief when Sarah burst into the room carrying a tray of steaming coffees.

There was no need to work late that evening – everything was smack up-to-date with Sarah's extra pair of hands. It was five thirty when Kylie opened the door of her apartment. She put down her briefcase and walked to the bedroom, where she changed into her most comfortable old jeans. At five forty-five she went to the kitchen and defrosted some bolognese. At six fifteen she loaded the dirty dishes into the dishwasher. Just ten minutes later she switched on the television and at the same time opened her novel at the marked page. Never had she felt at such a loose end. For the first time in a week there would be no texts or phone calls from Jim, and somehow her book or the TV didn't seem enough to fill the hours before she went to bed.

Then, as if someone understood her dilemma, the phone rang. She pounced on it.

"Kylie, it's Liz here."

"Oh, hello," she said in surprise.

"Is this a good time to call?"

"Yes, it's fine."

"I just thought – I'd call for a – chat." Liz sounded a little breathless, as if she was nervous. "I got such a shock yesterday – when you left I realised there was so much that I didn't know, that I hadn't thought to ask you."

"Ask anything you want," said Kylie as she took the phone over to the sofa and leaned back into the cushions.

Liz's first question was astonishingly simple. "Is Rose happy?"

"Yes," Kylie assured her. "She and Dad have a good marriage and a wide circle of friends. I think the first years in Australia were financially tough for them – but they're comfortable now. And, of course, they dote on Stephen and me."

"Who is the eldest, you or Stephen?"

"Stephen – he's five years older."

"Married?"

"No," Kylie laughed, "despite all our best efforts."

"What does he work at?"

"He works with Dad – he's an engineer."

"And you're a lawyer." Liz was impressed. "You must be a very brainy family."

Kylie laughed again as she asked, "Does that come from the Carey side of the family or the Horgans?"

"The Careys, of course," replied Liz, without missing a beat. She had a nice laugh, a girlish giggle that made it impossible not to join in.

Afterwards, there was a brief silence and Kylie took it that Liz's curiosity was at least temporarily satiated.

"Do you work, Liz?" she asked.

"I retired earlier this year," was her response. "I was with Bank of Ireland for thirty-seven years – I enjoyed it. I wasn't at all sure about taking early retirement when it was offered – but it was a generous offer and I thought I could use the money to travel. I'm a bit long in the tooth to see the world but I suppose it's better late than never. I'm going to France in October and who knows where after that."

"That sounds great," said Kylie. "I've never been to Europe – you're so lucky to have it practically on your doorstep."

Liz sounded regretful as she admitted, "I never took advantage of the proximity before now. I went from Dublin to Cork and no further. Of course, I asked the bank for the transfer down here. Carmel had gone to England years before and I thought I'd better get away from my father while I still had the nerve."

A quiet descended and the mood became markedly more sober.

"Was it that bad at home?" asked Kylie.

"You know, I've questioned myself many times over the years," said Liz, her voice thoughtful. "I've gone over my memories one by one, trying to be objective, trying to account for the fact that they were different times. But no amount of reasoning can justify their actions . . ."

"Like what?" Kylie couldn't help prompting.

It took Liz a few moments to respond.

"The sixties were a revolutionary time in Ireland. Women were starting to think for themselves – become independent. In the summertime the village was full of girls wearing miniskirts – some smoked, others would kiss their boyfriends in full public view. Your grandfather felt the world was changing for the worst. He was determined that *his* daughters wouldn't flaunt themselves like those brazen girls in the village. He made our house a prison – we weren't allowed to see our friends after school or go to parties, and we didn't dare wear lipstick. When we left school and went out to work, we'd always have to be on the six o'clock bus home."

Kylie couldn't help but notice that Liz called him "your grandfather" rather than "Dad". It was as if she had totally disassociated herself from the man.

"Why didn't you leave home sooner?" she asked.

"A number of reasons," Liz sighed on the other end of the line. "When you live with a tyrant you doubt yourself and your ability to survive without him. But money was also a factor. Our wages were poor and, after we paid board at home, there wasn't much left to save. It was easier for Carmel – they were crying out for nurses over in London and the hospital paid her fare. I was twenty-five before I got the money together. I only just had enough to pay four weeks' rent on a tiny bed-sit in Cork. I can clearly remember that first night away from home. I cooked myself a chop and potato for dinner, then I lay on the bed reading until midnight – I wasn't one bit lonely."

Listening to Liz, Kylie was at last starting to understand her mother's reluctance to talk about her family in Ireland. But, regardless of the tyranny of her father, what about her mother, Maureen? Surely, some kind of long-distance relationship could have been salvaged with her before she died?

"Your grandmother never once disagreed with him," said Liz as if reading her thoughts. "She was a cold woman – very detached. The only time I remember her saying anything of significance was when Rose 'died'. 'You're not to mention her,' she warned Carmel and me. 'She's gone. No amount of crying will bring her back.'"

"That *was* cruel," Kylie exclaimed.

"Yes," Liz said bitterly, "I told you they were cruel."

In the end it was after nine when Kylie hung up the phone. She felt exhausted in the very same way she had when she left Liz's house. There was so much to take in, the implications so far-reaching that they were downright daunting.

I know I should call Mum. But I'm too tired now. Tomorrow.

She closed the novel that she hadn't read, turned off the television that she hadn't watched and went to bed.

* * *

She knew it was cowardice, but she tried Stephen first. She thought that by answering his questions she would be better prepared for Rose. Still in her pyjamas, she sat cross-legged on the bed as she waited for him to answer. His phone rang through to his voicemail. She didn't leave a message.

OK, looks like I have to jump in cold, she thought and dialled the number for home.

Rose answered straight away. "Hello, love. You're up early today."

She had worked out the time difference and established that it was just after 6 a.m. in Dublin.

Kylie could have made small talk. She could have told Rose that the sky outside was a curious mix of grey and white as dawn crept across the city or that the sound of traffic on the quay had woken her before the alarm clock. However, she said only what was relevant.

"I've met Liz Carey."

Not surprisingly, the announcement was met with stunned silence.

"Mum?" she prompted a few moments later when there was still no reaction from Rose.

"Mum?"

A stifled sob came down the line.

"Mum? Are you OK?"

Even while she was asking the question her conscience was screaming, *"She's not OK, you idiot! She's crying!"*

"I told Frankie . . ." Rose was crying so hard that Kylie could hardly make out what she was saying, "I told him this would happen . . . that you'd go digging around . . ."

"But I've found your sister," Kylie reminded her. "That's good, isn't it?"

"No, it's *not* good!" Rose shrieked. "How many times must I tell you? *Everything is not for you to know!*"

Never had she heard her mother so upset. Or so angry. She had no option but to defend her actions.

"Liz is *my aunt*, Mum. I think I have every *right* to know her."

Her logic seemed to make Rose even more angry.

"You don't care who you hurt, do you?" she accused. "Once you get what *you* want."

"That's not fair, Mum." Kylie tried to restore some calm. "I understand how you feel – Liz told me about your parents, how cruel they were. But they're dead now – and Liz, Carmel and Carmel's family are alive –"

She was cut off by the sound of the dial tone. Rose had hung up. It seemed that the most caring and loving of mothers didn't want to know about her sisters. It just didn't make sense.

* * *

That day was another quiet one at the office. It wasn't just Sarah's contribution that made the difference: there were noticeably fewer clients.

"It's so hard to predict," Mags remarked in the

afternoon. She tapped her pen as she spoke, her face flushed. The afternoon sun streamed through the metal grilles on the window and the room was unusually suffocating.

"From what I've seen, we seem to be busier early on in the week," said Kylie. Today, of all days, she needed the distraction of being busy. However, they had only two people come in so far, and there was nothing to stop those awful words with Rose from replaying in her head.

"Maybe you could introduce appointments for the quiet days," Sarah suggested. "It might help spread the load."

Kylie nodded. "That sounds like a good idea."

Mags, however, didn't comment. It occurred to Kylie that Mags didn't consider it a good idea only because she did.

Sarah also seemed to sense something. Her eyes glanced from Kylie to Mags and back again. However, no matter how bright Sarah was, there was no way she could guess that the tension between the two women was caused by a man called Jim Donnelly. And a girl called Laura, who had run her car into a brick wall two years before.

The discord in the room was eased only when Kylie's mobile phone started to vibrate with an incoming call.

She picked it up.

"Is Liz happy?" asked the ragged voice at the end of the line. Rose.

"Excuse me," said Kylie to Sarah and Mags. "I need to take this outside."

As she walked down the narrow hallway, she registered that Rose and Liz had asked the same question. Happiness was the summation of everything, the fastest way to bridge forty years apart.

"Yes," said Kylie as she walked out into the late afternoon sunshine. "She seems happy. She has a nice home. She worked in a bank until early this year, and she's planning on travelling the world in her retirement."

"Is she married?" Rose asked next.

"No, she lives on her own." Then she added, because Rose would probably not know, "In Cork."

"And Carmel?"

"Carmel lives in London," Kylie answered as she sat down on the smooth granite steps at the front of the building. "She's been there since she was twenty-one. She's a nurse – but I'm not sure if she still works. She's married – three children, two grandchildren – I don't know any of their names yet. Liz sees her a couple of times a year – now that she's retired, she's hoping to get over to London more often."

Kylie didn't say outright that Liz and Carmel had a close relationship, but she knew it could be read between the lines. The sad thing was that it seemed very unlikely that Rose could resurrect herself from the dead to share in that closeness.

Rose started to cry softly. This time there was no anger, just the grief of forty years of loss. Kylie bowed her head to hide her own tears from the passers-by.

"They were told you were . . . dead," she said by way of explanation. That was the most terrible part but it needed to be said. It was rock solid evidence of the cruelty.

They cried together for another few minutes before Rose sniffed, "I'd better go back to bed – before your father comes looking for me."

Kylie didn't persuade her to stay. "Sleep will give it perspective, Mum. Talk soon."

She stayed on the steps and took deep breaths as she tried to regain her composure. Underneath all the sadness she was inordinately relieved that she and Rose had made up.

I never want to upset her like that again, she thought, thinking of how they had parted that morning. *Whatever she wants to do from here is up to her. I won't pressure her.*

Eventually Kylie stood up. As she turned to go

back inside, her eyes glanced at a stooped figure across the road. It was hard to tell for certain with the distance, but the man looked like Jerry: grey beard, dark anorak and toe-less boots. Despite the sunshine, a cold feeling came over her. Jerry was homeless and disadvantaged. He deserved her compassion. But something about him frightened her, and she wished he would find some other street to make his home.

Back inside the office, she didn't offer any explanation for her red eyes.

"I don't know about you two, but I'm going to call it a day. I need a drink."

* * *

The cobbled streets of Temple Bar were full of suited people who had been lured from their offices by a perfect blue sky. They gathered outside the pubs, their faces flushed and happy with a mix of alcohol and sunshine. The vibe reminded Kylie of her first week in Dublin. However, two months had passed since then and the leaves gathered in the gutters were a sign that autumn wasn't too far away.

Sarah knew a place that had a small courtyard out the back. She and Mags found sitting space on a brick wall while Kylie went to the bar.

"What's the occasion?" asked Mags when Kylie returned with three martinis.

"To celebrate Sarah's first week," replied Kylie.

They clinked their glasses and Mags seemed to relax a little.

"Do you have a boyfriend, Sarah?" she asked.

"Sort of," Sarah answered with a grin. "How about you?"

"Sort of." Mags smiled. "Seamus is on thin ice."

"How about you, Kylie?" asked Sarah.

Kylie wasn't going to deny Jim just to make Mags happy. "Sort of," seemed like the right response for her too.

When Sarah had gone off to get her round, Kylie tried to mend the rift with Mags by confiding in her.

"I'm sorry I had to dart out like that earlier," she said. "It was my Mum – she was upset."

"Something to do with your trip down to Cork?" asked Mags.

"Yes." Kylie threw back the last of her Martini. "I went to see my aunt – she and my mum haven't spoken in forty years –"

"Wow!" Mags's eyes widened. "That's some squabble they must have had."

"No, the argument wasn't between them," Kylie explained with a sigh. "It was their parents who caused it all. From what I can figure out, they disapproved of my dad so Mum eloped with him. They were so angry that they told her sisters she was dead."

Mags's jaw dropped open. "Gosh, that was a bit extreme, wasn't it?"

"Yes."

"Are the parents, your grandparents, alive?"

"No. They died a long time ago."

"And your mother never made contact with her sisters even then?"

"No," Kylie shook her head, "I think that maybe she associated them and Ireland with a very unhappy period of her life. It was much less painful to blot it all out than to try to salvage something from the wreck."

The truth was that Kylie didn't fully understand her mother's logic. It could have been too painful. Or maybe it was guilt that she had, in effect, chosen Frankie over her sisters. Whatever it was, it was strong enough for Rose to hold out for forty years.

Many martinis later, Kylie fell into bed. She felt much happier. Things were on the mend with both Rose and Mags. And Jim would be back in Sydney by the time she woke. She would be able to talk to him on the phone. Life was looking up on all fronts.

* * *

The next day Kylie purposely didn't wait at home for Jim's phone call. She wasn't good at waiting around and it was not how she wanted to spend the next seven weeks. Better to keep busy than watch the clock. So she went to Grafton Street and, for the first time in weeks, she did some serious retail therapy. It was one of those days where everything appealed, and soon she had quite a collection of carrier bags. She was buying some perfume when her mobile rang.

"Kylie Horgan!"

"Jim Donnelly!" Her face lit up with a smile. "How was the flight?"

She could only just make out his response. "Long and boring. Where are you? It sounds noisy."

"I'm in Brown Thomas," she said as the assistant handed back her credit card. "Just give me a minute and I'll go outside."

Out on the street it was just as noisy and she walked down one of the paved laneways, away from the main thoroughfare.

"OK, this is better." She sat down on one end of a wrought-iron bench, and the old woman on the other end flashed her a toothless smile.

"So," he said, "what have you been doing with yourself these last few days?"

"Creating family havoc." She grimaced. "I told Mum about Liz."

"How did she take it?"

"Not well. She hung up on me – but she rang back later on. We were both rather emotional."

"Are you OK now?" he asked, concern in his voice.

"I think so."

"You know, many families would love the excitement of some new faces to liven things up."

He was trying to make her smile and he succeeded.

"Were your family OK when you left?" she asked.

"Yes," he replied. "I promised them that next time I wouldn't leave it as long . . . I rather like the idea of Christmas in Dublin. There's nothing as uplifting as the street decorations on the cold dark evenings – or as intense as Moore Street on Christmas Eve. What do you think?"

She was unsure how to answer him. Was he asking her to spend Christmas with him? Or was he simply asking if she agreed that Christmas in Dublin would be rather special?

"Sounds good," she said lightly and moved the conversation back to safer ground. "A graduate has started with us at the clinic. Her name is Sarah. She's bright – eager. In fact, she's a lot like I was at that age – before I became cynical."

He laughed. "Cynicism is like an extra-curricular

course for lawyers."

The talked for another ten minutes. More than once he made her laugh loud enough for the old woman to cast a curious glance her way. Kylie didn't care.

"I'd better go," said Jim eventually.

"OK."

"I'll call again . . . soon."

"Bye, Jim . . ." She paused. It felt as if she should be adding something else. Had they been in love, this would have been the point where she would have said, "*Love you*".

"Bye, Kylie."

There was no pause on his end. She put her phone back in her bag and, rather than dwell on the strange feeling in the pit of her stomach, she lost herself back in the shops of Grafton Street.

Chapter 16

The dust got caught in Kylie's nose and she couldn't stop the sneeze. She lay very still, hoping her mother hadn't heard. The radio was on in the kitchen. Surely a small sneeze wouldn't be heard over the crackling music.

But moments later the door flung open and a cross voice asked, "What are you doing down there?"

Kylie came out, her face a guilty red.

"Cleaning."

Rose didn't buy it. "Under my bed?"

"It's very dusty," said Kylie, putting on a most disapproving tone.

"I hope you weren't prying."

"No, Mum."

Rose gave her a hard stare before she crouched down to verify her daughter's response.

"Why is the top off the shoebox?"

Kylie quickly realised there was no point in perpetuating the lie. She had been found out.

"I just wanted to see the old photos . . . to see where you and Dad grew up . . . what your brothers and sisters look like . . . if I'm like them."

Rose reached in for the box with its black and yellowed-white photographs. At the top there was a picture of a young woman, her long fair hair blowing wildly in the wind.

"That's you, isn't it?" said Kylie.

"Yes."

"How old were you then?"

"Seventeen."

"It's taken on the boat."

"Yes. The trip here took five weeks."

"Did you have lots of fun?"

A shadow came over Rose's face. "Yes." There was absolutely no conviction in her response.

Kylie looked at the girl in the photograph more closely. Her smile didn't reach her eyes.

"You need to learn to respect people's privacy," said Rose sternly as she put the top back on the box. "You shouldn't be going through my things."

"But I need to know —"

Rose cut her off mid-sentence. "*Everything is not for you to know, Kylie Horgan.*"

The old shoebox was gone the next time Kylie dared to look under her mother's bed.

Chapter 17

The next few weeks went by quickly. They adopted Sarah's suggestion, and Thursday and Friday afternoons at the clinic became by appointment only. The appointments attracted a different body of clients. They were usually employed and, more often than not, their problems were related to their workplace: wages, conditions, benefits and termination. A few of the more serious cases progressed as far as the Labour Relations Commission, and a series of conciliation conferences took Kylie away from the clinic. Sarah took her place at the coalface. She was helpful and resourceful with the clients. She lived quite close to Kylie and they often walked home together. Sometimes they went for a drink and talked about Sarah's on-and-off relationship with her boyfriend. They became good friends.

*   *   *

Claudine finally got a letter from MFJ stating that they believed her termination was fair and that they did not accept any further liability.

"I can't believe that Neil kept you waiting this long," said Kylie when Claudine phoned with the news.

"I can well believe it," was the resigned reply.

"Look, you're going to need a lawyer," Kylie told her. "I know this woman —"

Claudine cut her off. "I don't want a lawyer."

"You can't progress it any further —"

"I don't want to progress it, Kylie," Claudine stated stubbornly. "I've decided that I'm going to drop it and get on with my life."

"But you must be running out of money," Kylie objected.

Claudine was instantly offended. "Look, Kylie, I know you mean well — but my money is my business. Yes, the last few weeks have been tough. However,

Ethan's physiotherapy is nearly finished now and I'm already looking for a job."

"But you're entitled –"

"I'm entitled to make up my own mind. And I have decided that I want to put everything about MFJ behind me and move on."

It was very evident that "everything about MFJ" encompassed Kylie. They said goodbye in such a way that it was clear they didn't expect to see or hear from each other again.

*   *   *

Annie called to say that she'd dinged the Audi but it had been fixed and was as good as new.

"I was coming out of the shopping centre when it happened. The woman in front of me moved to join the main traffic but changed her mind at the last minute. Of course, Zack was screaming his head off in the back while I was trying to write down my details . . ."

Kylie listened sympathetically, told her that the car didn't matter once she and Zack were OK and thought to herself that Annie still sounded totally stressed out.

"I'm going back to work part-time," said Annie as if reading her thoughts. "I think a little time apart will be good for both me and Zack."

* * *

Kylie kept in constant contact with Jim, talking to him by phone or email on most evenings. The settlement with the food distributor in Auckland ruptured and Jim had to fly back there to start negotiations afresh.

"Both parties broke the terms of the settlement agreement," he sighed when he called from his hotel. "It seems that what we agreed is not workable – I just wish they had said so at the time. Carole is coming over from Singapore to help draft the new agreement."

Kylie felt fiercely jealous that Carole was in the same city as Jim. Possibly even in the same hotel.

I have to trust him, she told herself. *Otherwise we'll never get through these last few weeks.*

However, it was easier said than done as Carole popped up more and more often in their conversation.

"Carole and I met with them today," he would say casually, or "Carole went through her strategy over dinner tonight."

Kylie would change the subject or make a joke, anything to clear the horrible haze of jealousy that overcame her at the mention of the other woman's name.

Other than Carole, she could talk to him about anything, and often they were on the phone for more than an hour at a time. Was love the correct label for the dizzy happiness when she heard his voice, their long deep discussions and the fact that she would sell her soul for just one touch? She noticed that now Jim paused too before saying goodbye at the end of their calls. If it was love, neither of them was ready to say it yet.

* * *

Liz phoned regularly, and she was a welcome distraction from the thought of Jim and Carole having candle-lit dinners together.

"I thought I might come up to Dublin for a visit," she said one night.

"That would be great," Kylie exclaimed. "When?"

"Next week, if that's OK with you," she replied. "I could get the train up on the Thursday evening . . ."

"You must stay with me," said Kylie.

"Are you sure? I could book into a hotel . . ."

"It's no problem," Kylie assured her.

Rose was the opposite extreme to Liz; she didn't initiate phone calls and was distant when Kylie rang her. She even remained tight-lipped when Kylie told her that Liz was coming to stay.

"Tell her I said hello," was all she said.

You could tell her that yourself, Mum, Kylie thought with frustration. *All you have to do is pick up the phone.*

But she didn't voice her thoughts. The last thing she needed was for Rose to retreat even further into herself.

* * *

The Cork train, running fifteen minutes late, trundled into Heuston Station. Kylie leaned over the railing and scanned the hundreds of faces that descended onto the platform. She waved furiously when she saw Liz disembark from one of the back carriages. Her aunt looked a million dollars. Her fair hair was beautifully styled and she wore a chic striped top with tailored black trousers. Kylie felt proud that this gorgeous woman was related to her and waved even more vigorously. Liz stood still as the other commuters milled around her in their hurry towards the gate. Her searching eyes finally saw Kylie and her face broke into a relieved smile.

"I can't put you out of your bed," she said when she saw that the apartment had only one bedroom.

"There's a sofa bed in the living room," Kylie told

her. "It's not exactly as if I'll be sleeping on the floor."

"Let me sleep on the sofa bed."

"Honestly, Liz, don't worry." Kylie put her bag in the bedroom and the dispute was thereby settled. "Now, would you like to go out anywhere? For a walk? Or maybe a drink?"

Liz glanced at her watch. "You know, Kylie, we have the whole weekend to go out. I'd much rather stay here tonight and have a nice cup of tea."

Kylie went to the kitchen and ransacked the cupboards in search of a teapot.

"You look as if you read a lot," Liz commented from the living room.

"Those are just the books I've acquired since I got here," Kylie replied, no teapot in sight. "You should see my apartment back in Sydney! I should sell them, because I never read anything twice, but I can't bring myself."

"Oh, you must get your love of books from me," Liz sounded gleeful. "Carmel and Rose had no interest in them."

Kylie smiled as she poured the boiling water into two mugs. "So we've established that I get my nosiness from Carmel and my bookworm tendencies from you. What about my untidiness? And my inability to get out of bed in the morning?"

"Your father must be responsible for those particular personality traits!" Liz's infectious giggle sailed into the kitchen.

The mood was set for the night and it was many a time that the conversation dissolved into giggles. However, they couldn't avoid the serious indefinitely.

"Mum said hello," Kylie told Liz when they were on their second mug of tea.

"That's nice," was her reply.

"I feel like a medium," Kylie sighed, "connecting the dead to the living."

"She'll come around," Liz said with a gentle certainty. "As a child, Rose cried the most and scared the easiest – even though she was the eldest. It took her time to gather up courage to do the smallest of things. I'm not worried, Kylie – I know she'll call me when she's ready."

Kylie sipped her tea thoughtfully. "If she was such a scaredy cat, how come she plucked up the courage to elope with Dad?"

Liz shrugged as if the answer was simple. "She must have loved him an awful lot."

"How about you? Have you ever been in love?" Kylie immediately apologised when she realised the audacity of her question. "I'm sorry. That was very rude of me."

"Don't be silly," chided Liz. "We're family –

there's no such thing as rude. Yes, to answer your question, I have been in love. More than once, as a matter of fact."

"Oh."

"The first time I was very young – just eighteen years old." Liz stared into her mug as if the tea therein reflected the image of the man in question. "I was a trainee at the bank when Philip came in to make a deposit. He was a cadet in the army and, oh, Kylie, he was so handsome that I blushed bright red as I filled in his bank book. When he leaned across the counter to ask me out to dinner, I told him I couldn't possibly go. I had to get that six o'clock bus home – I was sure that your grandfather would come into the city to look for me if I wasn't on it. So Philip suggested lunch instead – and I fell for him straight away. I was no match for his sophistication and chivalry. He was only twenty but I was so innocent for my age that it could have been ten years between us and not two. He was always off somewhere or other with the army, but I couldn't allow him to write to me while he was away – your grandfather opened all the letters that came to our house, no matter who they were addressed to. Philip and I continued with our luncheon dates for about five months. Then a neighbour spotted me with him and asked your grandfather the name of the young man I was courting." Liz's mouth pursed together as she recalled the unpleasant confrontation that had followed. "Of course, that was the end of Philip and me."

Kylie was sympathetic. "How very sad for you both!"

Liz set her mug down on the coffee table. Her tone matter-of-fact, she answered, "Oh, I'm sure I remember it as much more romantic than it actually was. I was eighteen, very innocent, and ripe for falling in love. Had your grandfather allowed me to court Philip, I might have eventually realised that he wasn't the man for me. Who knows how it would have turned out?"

Kylie took another mouthful of tea before she asked, "Who was the other love of your life?"

"Conor," her face contorted as she said the name, "I was more mature – thirty – so I should have known better. I did love him – but we fought like cat and dog right from the start. We moved in together –"

"You lived with him?" Kylie interrupted with surprise.

"Yes," she confirmed with a certain degree of nonchalance. "I could do as I pleased down in Cork. As it turned out, Conor and I didn't need your grandfather to break us up – we eventually saw how incompatible we were and parted ways. Thank goodness we weren't stupid enough to get married."

Then Liz yawned and Kylie asked if she wanted to call it a night.

"Yes, I think that would be a good idea. All this talking has exhausted me."

"You're so different to Mum," said Kylie as she cleared the cups from the coffee table. "You're so open – you just wouldn't believe how *secretive* she is."

Liz chuckled. "I would believe it. I've told you how nosy Carmel is . . . well, I would just simply answer her questions. But not Rose – she kept her cards close to her chest – it was just the way she was. It used to drive poor Carmel mad . . ."

Rather suddenly, Liz's merriment became emotional.

"Thank you for finding me . . ." She kissed Kylie's cheek. "You're a lovely girl and I'm so happy to have this – *miraculous* – opportunity to get to know you."

Kylie was moved to tears. "Me too," she replied.

"Well, goodnight, Kylie. And thanks for the lovely chat."

* * *

Over the next few days, Kylie and Liz experienced Dublin at its best. The sun shone benevolently as, arms linked, they strolled in and out of shops, revisited the tourist attractions and posed for lots and lots of photos.

In fact, it soon became evident that Liz was rather fanatical about capturing every precious moment on film.

"We should take a snap here," she would say at regular intervals. Then she would look around to establish if there was anyone close by who was worthy to be entrusted with her ancient camera.

"She doesn't look as if she'd be much good . . . He's eighty, if he's a day . . . That young one would probably run off with it."

After much deliberation, she would eventually approach someone who met her high standards.

"Just press the large button on the right," she would tell them, her face already smiling in anticipation of the shot.

But half the time the shutter wouldn't release and Liz would have to leave Kylie's side to try to resolve the problem. After much pressing and winding on, the shutter would eventually release, the outcome an out-of-focus photograph of the footpath or someone's feet.

It was on one of these occasions, outside Trinity College, that Kylie's mobile started to ring.

"Hello," she answered as, with affectionate exasperation, she watched Liz fiddling with the camera.

"This is Carmel here," said a breathy voice. "Liz gave me your number." Kylie found herself momentarily caught for words. It would have been helpful if she'd at least seen a photo of her aunt in London so she could put a face to the voice on the phone.

"Yes, Liz said that you might call," she replied after a pause.

"Are you having a nice time together?"

"It's been wonderful," Kylie told her. "I only wish you could be here too."

It was obviously something that Carmel had already considered because she said, "I was thinking that maybe I could organise a trip over before you go back to Sydney. I'll talk to my daughter, Lucy. She would need to come with me, you see. This blasted wheelchair makes it very hard to travel on my own."

"Oh," Kylie's smile froze on her face, "I didn't realise . . ."

Why on earth didn't Liz mention that Carmel had a wheelchair? What was she thinking?

"Liz didn't tell you, did she?" Carmel asked but she didn't wait for an answer. "She has this thing about me being stigmatised. I had the riding accident ten years ago – I've had plenty of time to get used to being a cripple, and I'm not worried at all about being stigmatised. But once Liz gets an idea into her head, you just can't get it out."

From Carmel's remark about Liz, Kylie was able to gain a sharper sense of the individual personalities of the three Carey sisters.

Liz was headstrong, Carmel curious and Rose sensitive.

"Maybe it would be a better idea if I came to London to see you instead?" Kylie suggested.

"Let me talk to Lucy first," said Carmel. "She has two little ones – she would love the break – and I can't think of anything more fun than the four of us having a weekend in Dublin together. Gosh, I wonder if there's any chance that Rose could come too?"

For the first time ever, Kylie felt ashamed of her mother. Here was Carmel pulling out all the stops to get to Dublin while Rose, who had a prepaid ticket and perfect health, had evidently no intention of making the journey.

At that point Liz came bustling over. "Who's that on the phone?"

"Carmel."

Liz took the phone. "Carmel, we're tied up here. Yes. That does sound good. OK, dear, I'll call you when I get back to Cork."

She hung up briskly. Then she put an arm of steel around Kylie's shoulders.

"Smile for the camera, dear!"

When the shot was taken and the camera returned, at least temporarily, to Liz's bag, Kylie asked, "Why didn't you tell me about Carmel's wheelchair?"

Liz's lips tightened into a stubborn line. "Because she never sat still until she fell off that damned horse. She could run much faster than me and Rose, and she always won the long-jump contest down on the strand. That chair is at odds with the very essence of Carmel and I'll *never* use it to describe what she's like."

* * *

Liz caught the last train to Cork on the Sunday evening.

"I'll come again soon," she promised. "It was so nice to be back in Dublin – I shouldn't have allowed my bad memories to cloud out all the good. And maybe next time there'll be Carmel and Lucy too – it would be quite a crowd of us let loose on the city!"

Then, with one of her infectious giggles, she was off down the platform.

Kylie smoked a cigarette on the walk back from the train station. She and Liz had got on like a house on fire and it had been a great weekend. The only niggle was in relation to Carmel and the wheelchair. Should she tell Rose? Would Liz be angry if she did?

Did Rose deserve to know?

Back at the apartment, she put on the kettle and opened one of the kitchen cupboards to get a mug. Right at the front of the cupboard, where she couldn't miss it, was a beautiful ceramic teapot.

For next time, Liz had written on the gift card.

Kylie smiled and, instead of making a cup of tea, she made a pot. She drank the tea and mulled over Carmel's injuries. Was it her back that was injured? Or had her legs been crushed? Could she move her arms? These were the questions Rose would ask – if she told her.

I'll ask Jim what he thinks, Kylie thought after a while.

However, Jim's phone was switched off and she was put straight through to his voicemail.

"Hi, Jim, it's me. I guess it's still early over there and you're in bed. Well, if you happen to rise in the next hour or two, give me a call. Talk to you soon . . . Bye."

She and Jim hadn't talked for a few days. She supposed it was more due to her than him, as she had been so preoccupied with Liz. All of a sudden she really missed him and wished she could be zapped over to Auckland. All she needed was enough time to see him, touch him and remind herself that their relationship was real.

Chapter 18

The next morning Kylie checked her phone and her email but Jim hadn't sent a message.

He must be busy.

She focused her thoughts on the conciliation conference that she was due to attend at 9 a.m. Her client, a young woman called Amy Harris, was an administration officer for a company that manufactured fitness equipment. Amy's only colleague had resigned a few months ago but had not been replaced.

"The work is still there," Amy had explained on her first visit to the clinic, "but now there's only me to do it. I have to work sixty plus hours a week. The boss refuses to pay me overtime – he says it's a salaried job, not a pay-by-the-hour."

Amy's boss, Barry Dowling, was tight-fisted, self-important and totally impossible to reason with. Kylie couldn't see the most talented of conciliation officers being able to convince him to give ground. As a result, she didn't hold high hopes for a successful outcome to the conference.

She surveyed her wardrobe. She needed something with clout, something to show Barry Dowling she could be every bit as stubborn as him. She chose a pinstripe trouser suit and, for the first time in months, she put on full make-up. As a last touch, she tamed her long black curls into a no-nonsense French knot. Looking at her reflection in the mirror, she was inevitably reminded of the job she had left behind in Sydney, the one where she had to power-dress every single day. In less than four weeks she would be back in that job with all its pressures, impossible deadlines and long hours. She would eat lunch at her desk rather than try out new cafés with Mags and Sarah. She would have to work with Neil's tense greediness rather than Ted's affable generosity.

But there's one big positive to going back, she told her reflection. *Jim.*

* * *

Kylie had agreed to meet Amy in the reception area of the Labour Court. Half afraid that she would back out, Kylie was relieved to see her waiting.

"I must have been mad to go up against Barry," she said, her haggard face pale with nerves. "I have no chance of winning."

Amy was in her mid-twenties but a drug-addicted youth had added ten years to her appearance.

"Don't worry," Kylie told her. "The idea of this conference is to see if you can come to a mutual agreement – there are no winners or losers."

The receptionist gave them directions on where to go. Joe Green, the conciliation officer, and Christopher Murray, Barry Dowling's lawyer, were already seated in the small room with its basic furnishings. Kylie shook their hands firmly and Amy followed with a more timid handshake.

"Where's Barry?" asked Kylie.

"Answering nature's call," Christopher replied.

Barry arrived a few minutes later. It was hard to believe that fitness was his area of business. His shirt strained against his overhanging belly, his jowls sagged and greasy black hair flopped over his eyes. He greeted Kylie with the slightest of nods. He didn't even look at Amy.

Joe started the proceedings with a brief introduction. He then asked Amy to give a verbal statement.

"I joined Sportsquip four years ago," she began. "There were two of us handling the administration for the company – the other girl's name was Sandra. We had to answer the phones, type letters, do the banking and handle the mail – we were always kept busy. Sandra resigned last June. Barry put some ads in the paper for a replacement – but when nobody suitable applied, he changed his mind about recruiting and decided that one person, me, was all that was needed. The only way for me to do Sandra's job is to work late, and I'm here today because I want to get paid overtime for all those extra hours."

Kylie gave her an encouraging smile when she finished. Amy had delivered her statement perfectly, with exactly the right amount of inflection in her voice for it not to sound as if she had learnt it off by heart.

Barry Dowling was next to give his side of the story and he went straight on the attack.

"Amy has never been the sharpest tool in the shed – yet, I've supported her and kept her in a job these last few years. I can guarantee you that other employers would not have been as patient as me. The problem is that Amy is too slow," he cast a derisive glance in his employee's direction, "and I don't see why I should have to pay extra because of her snail's pace . . ."

Kylie let him go on insulting Amy until he was finished with his statement. When Joe asked if she had anything to add, she was more than ready to say her piece.

"Amy is far from *slow*, as you have so unkindly put it," she said to Barry, her voice icy cold. "She's doing the job of two people – something to be commended, not sneered at. Sandra was a full-time employee – there has been no reduction in the productivity of your company to support the redundancy of Sandra's old position. Therefore, not only is it unfair of you to expect Amy to do Sandra's job, but it is utterly outrageous that you are not prepared to pay her overtime."

"Sandra was as slow as Amy," was Barry's cutting response. "They were two of a kind."

Kylie stared him in the eye. "My written submission to Joe includes statements from other employees who testify that Amy is prompt and efficient – nobody describes her as *slow*."

"How dare you involve my staff in this!" Barry thundered across the table.

"I didn't approach them," Kylie delighted in

telling him. "*They came to me.*"

"Who is it?" he asked, sardonic now. "The people on the factory floor? Fat lot they would know about administration."

Kylie played her trump card. "My written submission also includes an analysis of the incoming phone calls and outgoing correspondence of your company. The analysis supports a staff of *two point five people.*"

"Well, you know what I think of your analysis –"

"Barry!" Christopher Murray stepped in to caution his client.

"Stuff it!" Barry stood up, his face puce. "Sportsquip is *my* company and I'll have as many people in administration as *I* see fit. If Amy doesn't like her lot, then she is free to go. And good riddance, I say. Now, you can take your conciliation and stick it up your arse!"

He stormed out of the room.

Christopher was apologetic in his wake. "I'm sorry – Barry has a short fuse."

"I can see that," said Joe wryly.

"I guess I'll see you in court." Christopher got to his feet. "And, once again, apologies to all for wasting your time today."

Kylie wondered if Christopher would still be Barry's lawyer when the Labour Court hearing came around.

* * *

Amy wasn't keen on going straight back to the office so Kylie suggested a coffee. Rain drizzled down in the old army barracks where the Labour Court was situated.

"Ready to run for it?" Kylie asked.

Amy nodded and they scuttled through the grounds and out the arched gateway.

"Part of me feels so guilty," Amy confessed, taking off her damp jacket in the café across the road. "You see, Barry gave me a job when I was at my lowest. I know he had selfish reasons – I was so desperate that he knew he could get away with paying me shit money – but the job helped me crawl my way back to a normal – drug-free – life."

"Four years of slave labour is more than enough to repay any debt you might have to Barry Dowling," Kylie told her.

"I suppose so," she said but didn't sound totally convinced.

The waitress came to take their orders. "Miserable day," she commented as she gazed woefully out the window. "Now, what would you like?"

They ordered and the waitress returned to the counter. Soon the hiss of the coffee machine could be heard. "The overtime money is not for me," Amy said. "It's for my dad. He's on the streets, you see. If I could pay rent for him, he would at least have a bed to sleep in at night. No matter what state he was in, he could find his way home and safely sleep it off."

Amy left a lot unsaid. She didn't say outright that her father was an alcoholic. Neither she did she say that she had given up on him becoming rehabilitated. And she didn't say that her own drug problems were born from a horribly rough childhood. Kylie's heart went out to her.

"You must think I'm awfully selfish not to let him stay in my own place," Amy continued, "but he'd drag me down, Kylie – I'd be back on the drugs within a week. And he's dirty. I know my flat is nothing special, but at least it's clean. And if everything around me is clean, then I stay clean too – from drugs, that is."

Kylie listened as she continued justifying her stand against Barry Dowling and did her best to be supportive.

"I'd better get back," Amy sighed when her coffee cup was empty. "Otherwise, he *will* have reason to fire me."

Kylie paid the waitress and agreed with her, once again, that the weather was miserable.

Outside, taxis were scarce. Amy spotted one

letting off a passenger up the street and waved madly to get the driver's attention.

"I'll be in touch when the Labour Court sets the date for the hearing," said Kylie as Amy sat into the back.

"Are you sure you don't want to get in?" she asked. "I could go to the city first and drop you off."

"It would only make you later than you already are," Kylie replied. "Here, it's on me." She put the taxi fare into Amy's hand.

She waited on in the steady drizzle for a second taxi. Twenty minutes later, soaked through, she gave up and started the long walk back to the city. With every step in her sodden shoes, she became more and more determined that Amy would get her father's rent money.

* * *

The next day was just as wet, and Kylie accessorised for the weather with a large golf umbrella. She felt despondent as she negotiated her way past other umbrella-bearing pedestrians on the way to work. Jim still hadn't called. Nor had he sent a message. She knew he was busy but how long did it take to say a quick hello?

It was a quiet day at the clinic, the rain always

seemed to have that effect, but it gave them a chance to catch up on the filing and other outstanding paperwork. At morning tea, Mary arrived down from reception with some home-made scones.

"I always eat like a horse when I'm depressed," said Sarah, putting a thick gooey layer of strawberry jam on her scone. "Ben and I had another big row last night."

"Not again!" Mags threw her eyes to heaven.

"That's what I said too – when I calmed down." Sarah bit into her scone. When she had chewed her first mouthful she added, "We've split up so many times that everyone thinks it's a big joke – but it's far from that – I'm crying my eyes out every second week – it's like being on an emotional roller-coaster – so I've told him that this is it – it's over and I don't want to see or hear from him again."

There was not a lot anyone could say in response because she was right: they had all thought of it as a joke. Yet, Sarah was obviously hurting so that didn't make it funny.

They ate silently until Mary asked, "How's your young man, Mags?"

"Fine," was the offhand reply. "He's a bit preoccupied – there's some tax deadline coming up. Don't ask me what – I tune out when he talks about work."

Kylie had missed Seamus at the pub these last few weeks. She had assumed that the DUI charge was the reason, but it sounded like work also had something to do with it.

Mary turned her attention to Kylie. "And how about you? Anyone special on the scene?"

But Mags butted in before Kylie could respond. "Anyone for another cup of tea?"

She had an odd expression on her face, as if she was well aware that her question would cause everyone to realise they should be getting back to work.

* * *

Kylie ordered pizza that night and checked her email while she waited for the delivery. There was still no message from Jim. An old familiar anxiety, which had been threatening all day, tightened the muscles of her stomach. The kind of feeling she used to get when Geoff was late home and she knew he had betrayed her trust by going to the casino. Had Jim betrayed her too?

As she stared at the ominously empty inbox, a new message came in.

From: Angela Bardman
Subject: Conference call

Kylie double-clicked to read the content.

**Brent Lavell will be addressing the group at
7 a.m. AEST today. Apologies to all for the short
notice but please make your best efforts to be
present. Phone number and access code are
detailed below.**

The pizza arrived. It was cold, bland and very
cardboard-like. But maybe the pizza was perfectly
OK and the problem was with her. She had lost
interest in food for weeks after she had broken up
with Geoff. Were her tastebuds telling her that the
same thing was about to happen with Jim?

* * *

At two minutes to ten, Kylie dialled the
conference number and announced her name.

"Kylie!" Isobel was already on the line. "How are
you? I keep meaning to drop a line but I've been so
busy."

"I'm great," Kylie lied and was instantly amazed at
how believable she sounded. "And how are you?"

"Fabulous," was the unqualified response. "I love the job and I've met this man! Oh, he's wonderful, just wonderful!"

"Does that mean you might be staying on in Madrid?" asked Kylie.

"Maybe," Isobel replied coyly, "but don't say a word, OK? How about you? Any man in your life?"

It was the perfect opening for Kylie to tell her about Jim. She hesitated only because she wasn't sure if there was anything to mention any more.

She forced a laugh. "No, all's quiet on that front."

Oliver was next to come on the line and there was only time for a quick hello before Brent and Angela announced their names.

Angela did a roll call.

"OK, we're waiting on David, Carole and Jim. I expect Carole and Jim will be together."

Her prediction was true. Five minutes later the line beeped and Jim's voice said, "Jim and Carole here. Sorry we're a tad late."

Kylie squeezed her eyes shut but couldn't stop the image of Carole's blonde head next to Jim's as they shared the speaker phone. They had been holed up in Auckland together for three weeks now, and it made Kylie's time with him seem paltry in comparison. Her jealousy simmered up inside her, and it was all she could do not to yell down the phone, '*It's Jim and Kylie*

— we're the couple — not Jim and Carole!"

"It looks like we'll have to go ahead without David," said Angela. "He must not have seen the message. Now, I did intend to have a conference call later on this week just to see how everyone was doing. However, there have been some changes in MFJ and we brought the call forward so Brent could update you in advance . . ."

Brent cleared his throat, the horrible phlegmy sound magnified by the speaker.

"I want to take this opportunity to announce my resignation as managing partner of MFJ. After five years, I think it's time for me to move way and give someone else a chance at the helm."

Kylie was shocked and, from the silence on the line, it seemed that so was everyone else. It didn't ring true. Brent simply wasn't the type to "give someone else a chance". There had to be another reason.

"Who's the new managing partner?" she asked.

"Neil Gatwood."

The dynamics of the High Potential programme changed irrevocably with his answer. Those who had formed allegiance with Brent realised that they had wasted their time and Kylie, Neil's protégée, became the front runner. One of the three partnerships was hers for the taking. She should have felt happy.

"Are you staying on in the partnership, Brent?" asked Carole.

"No," was his reply. "I don't want to shadow Neil – he deserves the chance to make his mark. I'll be moving across to mainstream commerce – in fact, I'm talking to a major conglomerate at the moment."

It seemed that Brent had resigned without a firm job offer from the "major conglomerate". Kylie was even more certain that there was something else behind his resignation.

"Does your departure mean that there's an extra partnership available for the High Potential team?" asked Oliver.

Brent gave a nasty laugh, as if Oliver was trying it on. "No free rides, mate. There are still only three partnerships on offer to this group."

Oliver had asked a valid question and there was really no need for Brent to imply that he was looking for a free ride. Kylie was glad that Brent was going. She only wished that Neil, ally or not, was going too. His obsession with control would not make him a good managing partner.

Brent signed off shortly afterwards and Angela stayed on the line to do a quick check on how everyone was. Oliver had earned the respect of his co-workers and was now enjoying New York as much as his wife. Isobel was as enthusiastic as ever about Madrid. Jim said that the negotiations in Auckland were the toughest of his career and, with one failed agreement hanging over the parties, it was uphill work to convince them to try again. Carole agreed; however, she said that she was much happier to be in Auckland than Singapore. She didn't specify why.

"Kylie?" Angela prompted.

"The clinic has expanded to a staff of three," she replied. "I've had a number of conciliation conferences and Labour Court hearings. I guess that must mean we're making a mark."

"Who's paying for it all?" asked Carole in a disparaging tone of voice. "It must cost a fortune to have three of you there . . ."

Red flashed before Kylie's eyes. "It's not about the money — although that may be hard for *you* to understand."

"Thanks, everyone." Angela's dulcet voice came back on the line. "Neil has decided that the final residential for the programme will be held in Fiji in December. I'll provide you with more details when I see you all back in Sydney in a few weeks' time."

Kylie was too angry to be happy about going to Fiji and she hung up without saying goodbye. She was about to light a cigarette when the phone rang minutes later.

"Yes," she snapped.

"That was an unnecessary attack on Carole," said Jim.

She gritted her teeth. "You two are obviously the best of buddies by now – but that doesn't mean I have to like her. She's rude –"

"Funny," he interrupted, "the only person I heard being rude was you."

"Hang on a minute," Kylie said heatedly. "She was implying that the work the clinic is doing isn't worth the cost."

"She implied nothing of the sort," he said, sounding deadly calm. "It's in Carole's nature to question, that's all."

"Good for you that you are so well acquainted with her *nature*," Kylie shot back.

He sighed. It was an impatient kind of sigh that said he would rather be somewhere else. "Look, why don't I call back another time when you're in a more receptive mood?"

Part of Kylie knew that what he was suggesting made sense. But the stubborn part of her wouldn't let it go at that.

"If this is all getting too hard for you, then just say it, Jim."

"What do you mean by that?"

"I left you a message on Sunday –"

"Christ, Kylie," now he was angry, "so I missed calling you last night – is that such a crime?"

"You could have emailed!" She sounded petulant, even to her own ears.

"I'm at a critical stage with these negotiations – *I have other things on my mind.*"

"Well, I'll let you get back to it," she said smartly and hung up the phone.

*　　*　　*

Their first argument. Had they been in the same city they could have kissed and made up. Kylie could have reached out her hand and said, "I'm sorry."

For she knew that she was in the wrong. There was no rule that said Jim had to call or email every day.

If he was here she could have admitted, "It's more to do with Carole than anything. It's killing me that you two are sharing breakfasts, strategies, in-jokes . . . Laura may not have been the possessive type, *but I am.*"

She crawled into bed and fell into a fitful sleep. All night long, the argument replayed over and over without reprieve. It was a relief when her alarm clock called an end to it. She got ready for work, her limbs heavy as she forced them into clothes. She was having her breakfast, a solitary cup of coffee, when her mobile rang.

Her heart jumped for nothing; it was only Mags.

"I've got a bad flu – I won't be in today."

Kylie said that she and Sarah would be fine on their own. However, as if to prove her a liar, it turned out to be a very difficult day. For some reason, all of the queries were complicated and the waiting time got longer and longer. Most clients had a good crib about how long they had to wait before getting on with their business. One woman, unhappy with the answer to her question, screamed a string of abuse at Sarah. The chaos climaxed when a feverish-looking toddler vomited on the floor.

"You walking home tonight?" Kylie asked Sarah when the time finally came to turn the key in the clinic door.

"I've a date." Something about Sarah's blush told Kylie that the date wasn't with her on-and-off boyfriend. "I was going to go home to get ready but, considering the time, I think I should go straight there."

"OK," Kylie waved her off, "have fun."

She locked the outer door and set off home. Her legs still felt heavy – in fact, she was leaden all over. It seemed that the only way she could lighten her body was to say sorry to Jim. She stopped to get her phone from her bag.

Sorry, she typed.

There, that felt better. But before she could press the SEND button, a shadow fell across her. She looked up to find herself face to face with Jerry. She instinctively took a step backwards. He came further forward, his eyes glittering on his dirty face. As if they were doing some kind of macabre dance, he responded with a step forward every time she took a step back. Nothing was said. Then his hands spread in a wide semicircle and she was trapped. She tried to look past him to see if there was anyone close enough to call for help, but he was taller than her and she could see nothing other than his putrid anorak. She had to make a decision. Stay where she was and let those filthy hands encircle her neck. Or step back over the kerb and into the traffic. He came forward again. It was a shock when he spoke.

"Sorry," he said.

She teetered on the kerb. How ironic that he had uttered the same word that was displayed on her phone. Could he read it from there?

She meant to ask him but she lost her balance. The phone flew from her hand as she fell under the oncoming four-wheel drive.

Chapter 19

"Kylie," a hand grasped hers, "it's me, Liz. I didn't think I'd be back in Dublin quite so soon – this was a pretty drastic thing to do to get me back here . . ."

Kylie waited for her girlish giggle but was rather surprised to hear a sob. "They've fixed up your leg – the surgeon said it was broken in a number of places. He seems very good at his job, Kylie – I think you were lucky that he was the one on call . . ."

I'm in hospital, Kylie thought. *Yes, I fell in front of that four-wheel drive.*

She tried to open her eyes but they were glued shut. Her mouth wouldn't work either.

"That was two days ago," Liz continued. "We've been waiting for you to wake up."

Ah, I'm asleep.

Kylie was happy that there was such a simple explanation for her inability to talk or see.

"This room they've put you in is very nice. The girls from your work sent a big bunch of flowers and I put them over by the window. The card says, *We miss you. Get well soon, from Mags and Sarah.* They wanted to see you but the surgeon said that it's family only for now. I've been staying in your apartment – I hope you don't mind. It's just a bed at night – I'm here all throughout the day. I'm not a busybody so don't worry about me looking through any of your private things . . ."

Kylie could see Liz being so very careful with everything in the apartment. It made her want to smile. But, of course, she couldn't.

Liz talked some more before her voice drifted away and Kylie went back to a deeper sleep.

* * *

"Oh, my God, look at her!"

It was Rose. She sounded quite hysterical.

"Frank, look at her! Dear God, help us all . . ."

Mum, you're here . . . please don't cry . . . Dad, tell her

320

not to cry!

Kylie heard a heaving sound that was quite distinct from Rose's high-pitched sobs.

What's that? Dad? No, you can't be crying too. Oh, please, stop it the two of you!

Her hand was lifted from the bed and she felt a familiar coldness. "Bad circulation," Rose used to say about her icy cold hands.

"You'll be OK . . . my love," she said now in a broken whisper. "We're here for as long as it takes . . . for you to be OK."

"Here, Rose, a seat for you."

A chair scraped across the floor and Rose's grasp loosened a little as she sat down. Frankie must have come around the other side of the bed for Kylie felt him take her other hand. His had a sandpaper feel to it.

Hands are important. Very important. I must remember to appreciate them more when I wake up.

"Qantas were very good to us, Kylie," said Rose, her voice more even now. "They got us on the first flight out of Sydney . . . We had to change over in Singapore and Heathrow . . ." Frank, usually one to leave the talking to his wife, continued on with the details of their journey. "Dublin looks so different . . . well, at least from the little we saw from the taxi . . . we came straight here, bags and all . . ."

"I wonder where Liz is?" Rose suddenly remembered her sister. "She must have gone for a cup of tea . . . we're a little bit earlier than we expected . . ."

Kylie tried hard to open her eyes. She so wanted to be able to see the reunion between Rose and Liz.

"Did she flutter her eyes just there?" asked Rose urgently.

"I didn't notice," said Frank.

I did, Kylie thought in frustration. *I did flutter them – but they won't open.*

"She did it again," said Rose.

Frankie must have noticed the second time but he wasn't convinced the movement was intentional. "Maybe it's normal for them to do that when they're unconscious."

"Come on, Kylie." Rose's grip tightened on Kylie's hand. "Wake up, darling!"

Kylie tried. She really tried.

Then she heard the door open and, from the sudden limpness in Rose's hand, she knew that it was Liz who had come in.

Two sisters reuniting after forty-three years apart, and all Kylie had to go on was sound: soft footsteps, the rustle of an embrace, heart-wrenching sobs. Not a word was uttered, but Kylie knew that everything would be there on their faces if only she could see.

She tried again to open her eyes. She used every ounce of her willpower until she became exhausted from the sheer effort. The sobs faded to a point where she could no longer distinguish Rose from Liz. Then there was nothing at all.

* * *

This time the hand was a bony one and it had a slight quiver.

"Your mother said I could come in even though I'm not family."

It was Mags.

"She said it would be good for you if I talked out loud. So, even though I feel like a bit of an eejit, I'm going to pretend that we're at work and we're chatting like normal – or at least how we used to chat before things became . . . strained . . ."

Kylie heard a muffled sound. It seemed that Mags was crying into a handkerchief or tissue. She wanted to reach out, comfort her, but her arms could not lift of their own accord.

"You see, Seamus and I broke up a few weeks ago . . . I was too upset to tell you so I let you believe that we had patched things up . . . then, I suppose, the right time had well and truly passed and it got harder and harder to say it. The split wasn't amicable – we're not on talking terms. I've been so miserable about it all – and I took it out on you. I'm sorry, so sorry." Her bony hand clutched tighter. "Then I was so silly about Jim driving you down to Cork. I was jealous. Not for me, for Laura. She got the short straw – dying so young – missing out on so much. I didn't want Jim to make new friends – I wanted to keep him intact for Laura – so that she could still recognise him – silly of me – for heaven's sake, he's been in Australia these last two years and the life he lives there would be totally foreign to her."

I forgot all about Jim. Does that mean he's not important? Or is my brain only able to process one thing at a time? I never sent that message – I never said sorry to him. Does he know that I'm here? Did you tell him, Mags?

Mags didn't answer the silent question. She changed the subject and started to talk about the clinic.

"The Lord Mayor called in to see us – she'd heard about your accident – she was very concerned about you. And this man called Jerry came in. He said he was sorry for getting angry – he shouldn't have shouted abuse at you – the drink brings out the demon in him – he claimed that he saw the accident – I don't think he's right in the head, though . . ."

Mags chattered on and on until her voice became a drone, quite similar to the sound emanating from the machines around Kylie's bed.

* * *

A loud voice boomed its way through Kylie's slumber. The hand that matched the voice was big and meaty. Stephen.

"Hi, Kyls. How are you doing, kiddo? Yes, I'm here too and we have a full family quorum in Dublin now. I couldn't come with Mum and Dad – I had to put some arrangements in place to keep the wheels going round on the business. You know Dad – he thinks all his customers will disappear the very instant he turns his back."

Kylie was so happy to hear Stephen's droll humour. She knew without trying that her eyes wouldn't open so she concentrated her energy on her fingers.

He seemed to feel the movement. "Can you hear me, Kyls?"

She did it again.

"Good girl, Kyls . . . Do you want to know what happened? What am I saying? This is Kylie Horgan we have here – of course you want to know every little detail. Well, here are the facts and figures: it started with your dive in front of the four-wheel drive – I won't ask what you were thinking – the driver was in a total state of shock – she fainted when she saw you underneath the vehicle – a passer-by, a homeless fellow, got you out . . ."

Jerry, Kylie realised. *I remember him holding my hand – telling me that he was sorry he had frightened me – that it would be OK – help was coming . . .*

"Your leg had multiple fractures – but, on the positive side, you were damned lucky that your chest and head didn't go under the wheels. You were conscious when they brought you into accident and emergency but they put you under in order to operate on your fractures. You should have woken up after the operation – but you didn't. A CAT scan found a spot on your brain – it's called a fat embolism – it's a complication of traumatic long-bone fractures. According to both the surgeon and the internet – I've looked it up – we just need to wait until it dissolves. In another few days you should be bright-eyed and bushy-tailed."

As children, Stephen had taken his responsibilities as older brother very seriously. The first stop for Kylie's endless questions, he had never lost patience and always explained things in the appropriate level of detail for her age.

"I'll come back to you on that, kiddo," he'd say if he didn't know the answer. Then he'd research it at the library or ask his teacher.

It was so typical of him to double-check the surgeon's advice by looking on the internet. She wanted to thank him for that, and for all the other times he had been there with the answers to her questions. She willed her fingers to move again.

He grasped them tight. "Good girl, Kyls."

* * *

When the time was right, Kylie's eyes opened easily and there was no evidence at all of the glue that had kept them so firmly shut. It was night-time, the only light in the room stolen from the corridor outside. Her eyes moved slowly in an anti-clockwise direction. To the left, the door. Straight ahead, her broken leg stretched rigid. Next was the jagged outline of a flower arrangement on the table in front of the curtained window. And there, immediately to her right, was Rose, asleep in the armchair.

"Mum?" Her voice was nothing more than a breath.

"Mum?" Now it was stronger, a croak.

To her amazement, Rose heard and her eyes flew open.

"Kylie?"

"Mum," she repeated, overjoyed that her voice was working.

Rose staggered up from the armchair.

"Oh, darling!" Her cold hands cupped Kylie's face. "Are you in pain?"

Kylie shook her head. There was no pain.

"I thought I'd lost you . . . I love you very much . . . I don't tell you that often enough."

"Me too," Kylie rasped, her dry lips stretching to a smile.

Rose's hands left Kylie's face and pressed together. She lowered her head. "Dear God, thank you for giving her back to me . . . I'll try to make good my sins . . . thank you, *thank you* . . ."

Kylie, befuddled, watched her mother pray. Rose wasn't religious. What was going on?

"Mum, what are you –?"

"I've got to call the nurse," Rose remembered suddenly and jabbed at the buzzer next to the bed. "There!"

Kylie's head was incapable of holding any thought for very long and she forgot her question.

"You saw Liz?" she said instead.

"Yes." Rose's face collapsed and she started to cry.

"How was it?"

"The same . . . different . . . confusing . . ."

"But good?" Kylie needed reassurance.

Her face streaming with tears, Rose nodded, "Yes, good."

Kylie had a thousand questions to ask but the nurse charged into the room, brandishing her torch like a weapon.

"You're back with us," she stated matter-of-factly. "Can you remember what happened?"

"Yes." Kylie could remember quite clearly. Somebody had explained it all, but she wasn't too sure who.

The nurse continued to speak as she grasped Kylie's wrist to take her pulse. "My name is Maura. No doubt we'll get to know each other very well over the next few weeks."

Kylie was confused. Nice as Maura seemed to be, it wasn't obvious why they would be getting to know one another. "What?"

Maura inclined her head towards Kylie's injured leg. "You'll be going nowhere soon with that."

* * *

"Hi, kiddo," said Stephen the next morning. "How are you feeling?"

"I was great at the start," she told him, "but now it's beginning to sink in."

She looked at the two pins protruding from the side of her thigh, joined by a long bar. A skeletal traction, Maura had called it. In addition to her injured leg, Kylie had a sprained wrist and bruising along the side of her torso.

"It seems I'm going to be stuck here for quite a while," she sighed.

He answered her straight. "At least six weeks – and add another few on for physiotherapy."

"Just like Ethan," she said, her tone ironic.

"Who's Ethan?"

"Remember the kid who inspired me to raise the money for the fun machines?"

"Yeah," he bobbed his head, "that seems like a lifetime ago now. How is he?"

Kylie grimaced – she was still smarting from her last conversation with Claudine. "I don't know – his mother and I aren't in contact."

"You could do with one of those fun machines yourself now," Stephen commented.

"Yeah," Kylie sighed again. "Well, looking on the bright side, at least I have medical insurance that covers the cost of all this."

Stephen sat his towering bulk into one of the miniature visitor chairs.

"Mum is so relieved – I don't think she believed the doctors when they said you'd wake up –"

"Did she get home OK?" Kylie asked. Rose had still been teary when she'd left the hospital in the early hours of the morning. She, Frankie and

Stephen were staying in an apartment a stone's throw from the hospital.

"Yeah – but she was weird – saying strange things . . ."

"Like what?"

"Like she didn't deserve you," he shrugged his broad shoulders, "and that your accident was some kind of payback for her sins."

Kylie remembered Rose's prayer the night before; she had said something about sins then too.

"She's overwrought, that's all," said Kylie. "Her sins are all in her head – she doesn't have a bad bone in her body."

Just then there was a knock on the door. A woman in a blue uniform bearing the most delicious-smelling breakfast tray came in.

"It smells divine," said Kylie. It felt like a very long time since she had last eaten.

"Cathy is my name, love," said the woman as she set the tray down on the bedside table. "We'll get to know each other very well over the coming weeks."

Kylie recalled Maura's turn of phrase from last night. "Yes, I know, I'm going nowhere soon."

* * *

Later on in the day, when Maura was back on duty

and doing a keen examination of Kylie's toes, there was a knock on the door.

"Delivery for Kylie Horgan."

It was a beautiful boxed arrangement of brightly coloured chrysanthemums. Just looking at them lifted Kylie's spirits.

"An admirer?" Maura enquired as she updated the chart at the end of the bed.

"I don't know," said Kylie but her heart was thumping at the thought that they could be from Jim. "Is there a card?"

Maura searched the foliage. "Yes, there's one tucked away here."

She handed it over. "Now, don't forget to keep wiggling those toes – your circulation is very important – the physio will tell you the same –"

"When will I see the physiotherapist?"

"Tomorrow."

Then Maura was off on her rounds and Kylie was alone. She opened the card.

Dear Kylie,
My name is Karen Woods and I'm the driver who ran you over. I'm so very sorry – I didn't see you until it was too late. I know you have a long recovery in front of you but I am so happy that you are conscious and doing well – I've been ringing the hospital regularly to check on you. I wish I could apologise

*in person but my solicitor says that I'm not to contact you —
he'd have a fit if he knew about this note. Solicitors, they have
no hearts!*

I'm praying for your speedy recovery,
Best wishes,
Karen

There was an address at the top of the note and
Kylie immediately penned a response.

Dear Karen,
*The fault was all mine and I'm so sorry for giving you such
a fright. You're right: solicitors have no hearts — I should
know, I'm one of them — but I hope I'm the exception to the
rule.*

Thank you for your prayers,
Kylie

When Maura returned with her painkillers, she
gave her the note to post. Then she fell into a deep
sleep where she dreamed that the flowers were from
Jim.

Chapter 20

The physiotherapist looked the part with her capable face, muscular arms and shiny hair pulled back in a swishy ponytail.

"I'm Jane." Even her name sounded right for the job. "I've come to see what we can do to prevent your muscles from getting stiff while you're resting in bed."

"I wouldn't exactly call it *resting*." Kylie smiled cynically.

Jane gave her an efficient smile in return and said, "OK, let's start with your feet and work up."

She asked Kylie to do a number of straight lifts

with her good leg. Then she strapped a weight to her ankle.

"OK, do another ten lifts now."

"What about my injured leg?" Kylie asked. "Will we be doing any exercises with that?"

"No – all that hard work will have to wait until you're out of traction."

"The surgeon said six weeks." Kylie watched the physiotherapist for her reaction. "Any chance that it might be sooner than that?"

Jane was cautious in her response. "It depends on how fast the healing takes place . . . You have some nasty fractures . . . I wouldn't watch the clock too much, if I were you . . ."

"Force of habit – I'm a lawyer."

Jane laughed and asked Kylie more about her job. After hearing about six-minute billing units, the High Potential programme and the *Just Ask* clinic, she started on Kylie's upper body.

"We'll take it easy with your sprained wrist for now, but you can start on some lateral raises with the other arm . . ."

* * *

"I need to go back to Cork soon," Liz said a few days later. She had a guilty look on her face.

"Of course you should go home," Kylie agreed.

"I left in rather a hurry, you see. I made no arrangements —"

Kylie cut her off. "Honestly, Liz, you don't need to explain — I've plenty of people here. In fact, sometimes I wouldn't mind some time on my own."

Everybody would have to go back to their real lives at some point: Rose, Frankie and Stephen too.

Maybe when I'm on my own I'll be sorry that I didn't appreciate their company as much as I should have.

"Will we watch some telly?" asked Liz.

"Yeah, I haven't had it on for a whole hour."

Just three days into a very long road to recovery, Kylie already felt like smashing her hand through the TV.

What is wrong with me? I should be happy to be alive.

The television sparked to life and they watched the travel programme in silence. Liz was happy not to talk if there was nothing to be said. Kylie liked that about her. Everyone else tried to keep the conversation going at all costs, as if Kylie was likely to drop back into a coma if there was the slightest lull.

"How are you and Mum getting along?" she asked Liz during the ads.

"OK," was her guarded response. Then she elaborated, "These have been difficult circumstances

. . . and with our shifts here at the hospital, we haven't had much opportunity to talk – I mean, *really* talk."

"I'm gone past the stage where I need to have somebody by my bedside 24/7," said Kylie. "I'd much rather you two spend some quality time together."

Liz opened up. "I know it sounds selfish, but I'm dying for the chance to have Rose all to myself. I'd love to talk with her about times gone by – it was like my childhood ended when she went away –"

"It doesn't sound selfish at all."

"And I could find out who she is now. What makes her happy, what makes her tick . . ."

The travel programme came back on with a feature on Paris.

"You'll be able to get some tips for your visit next month," said Kylie.

However, Liz wasn't paying any attention to the enthusiastic travel presenter as he broadcast from outside Notre Dame. Her forehead creased with thought; her mind seemed to be far from her upcoming holiday. The presenter viewed Paris from the top of the Eiffel Tower, sailed down the Seine and admired the *Mona Lisa* before Liz spoke again.

"I wonder if Rose would like to go down to Cork with me for a few days?"

Kylie thought it was a wonderful suggestion.

* * *

"Please, Mum."

Rose tutted. "I can't be dashing off down the country and leaving you here on your own."

"I have Dad and Stephen."

Rose picked an imaginary piece of fluff from the bedclothes. "I'm here for you – you need your mother right now."

Kylie resorted to emotional blackmail. "Liz needs you too."

Rose didn't answer but Kylie could tell that she really wanted to go.

"Please, Mum," she said beseechingly. "It would make me very happy if you spent some time with Liz."

* * *

With Stephen and Frankie on board, it was another two days before Rose was swayed.

"Your mother took an awful lot of convincing," said Frankie when he popped in on his way back from the train station. "I almost had to shove her through the gate."

"I can imagine," Kylie replied and they shared a look of mutual fond exasperation.

"Here," he put a carrier bag on her bed, "I bought you some books – I know you must be sick of the television by now."

Kylie turned the brown paper bag upside down and the books tumbled onto the white covers of the bed. There were five in all: big, thick novels that promised to engross and take her far away from her hospital bed. She was touched that he had gone to so much trouble.

"Thanks, Dad."

He grasped her hand in his. "I hate seeing you confined like this," he said, his eyes watering.

"I think it's some divine plan to teach me the virtue of patience," she joked, blinking back her own tears.

"Some chance," he came back and they laughed tremulously together.

Frankie sat in the armchair and opened up his newspaper. Kylie started one of the novels. The afternoon passed by companionably, like many an afternoon where they had read alongside each other on the deck at home. However, there was no scent of warm wood or potted flowers here, only the distinct detergent-like hospital smell.

"Dad . . ." said Kylie when she came to the end of

a chapter.

"Mmm," was his distracted reply.

"Have you looked up your family at all?"

"No." His eyes were downcast but Kylie could tell that he had stopped reading.

"Why?"

"They're not from round here — it's not as convenient as you might think."

"Where are they from?" she asked.

"Belfast."

"Oh."

That certainly explained why she wasn't able to find any trace of them in Portmarnock.

Frank's eyes started to move again, doggedly across the page.

"Life is short, Dad," said Kylie quietly. "If there's any lesson to be learnt from this accident, then it must be that. This is your chance — here and now — don't use convenience as an excuse because even I know that Belfast is only a few hours' drive from here."

Frankie's eyes became still again. Then, slowly, the newspaper came down and revealed his face. The daylight coming in from the window was unkind to his wrinkles and made his hair look more white than grey.

He's aged over the last few months, she realised, and even though she knew that aging was part and parcel of life, she felt sad.

"It's complicated," he sighed. "I didn't just leave, I was *told* to go. My family refused to accept your mother . . . she was a Catholic . . ."

"Oh." Kylie absorbed this significant piece of information. It didn't take long at all for some things to click into place. "That's why we never went to Mass like other families."

"Yes." He nodded. "Your mother and I felt that religion was used as a cover for many acts of cruelty – the warring North of Ireland, Rose's father and his narrow-minded, unforgiving piety ... We were burned by religion in more than one way and, whether right or wrong, we steered clear of it in Australia."

Frankie looked vulnerable and Kylie decided to chance one more question.

"Do you think your family would still bear Mum a grudge after forty years?"

She saw his eyes water up again and she became desperately afraid that her big, strong, indestructible father would break down in tears.

"The grudge is centuries old, love. Forty years isn't a drop in the ocean."

* * *

"I really like Dublin," said Stephen a few days

later. "I love the oldness of it, the vibe on the street, the way you get potatoes of some description with every meal, even pizza . . . You know, I'm starting to realise that I've seen very little of the world."

"Well, you should spread your wings, my dear brother," said Kylie, and added mischievously, "before you settle down with your phantom girlfriend."

He smiled sheepishly. "Her name's Tamsin . . . She'd like to travel too . . . but it's hard for her right now . . ."

"Don't tell me she's in prison?"

Stephen didn't laugh at her joke. "She has a child, a two-year-old girl called Emily."

The atmosphere shifted gears and became deadly serious.

"Were you afraid that we'd disapprove?" asked Kylie. "Is that why you didn't tell us about her?"

He folded his long, gangly arms. "I didn't want you all to judge her . . ."

"But *I* wouldn't have judged her," Kylie protested.

From the look on Stephen's face, it seemed that he disagreed.

"Tamsin is a stay-at-home single mother," he said. "She's from a different orbit to you . . . She lives off State Welfare . . . She would think I was lying if I told her how much money a partner earns —"

"But I'm not a partner."

"It's just a matter of time."

"Just because I'll earn a lot of money one day doesn't mean I can't relate to people who don't."

"It's not just money," he said. "It's ambition. You're the most ambitious person I know, Kylie."

"You've always said that's a good thing," she pointed out, perplexed by him.

"Yes, I did," he shrugged, "but now I'm not so sure. Tamsin is the kind of person who stops to smell the roses . . . She enjoys what each day has to offer . . . She doesn't force deadlines or goals on herself. It's made me see that there's another way to live life."

Kylie stared him straight in the eye. "She sounds lovely and I'm very sure, regardless of what you say, that I'm really going to like her. To be honest, I don't care if your girlfriend is a pole dancer with *six* kids – I'm just glad that you've found someone to be happy with. Now, quit labelling me as a money-hungry ambition freak and hand me the remote control – *You're a Star* is coming on."

* * *

Kylie was halfway through the last of Frankie's novels when someone rapped on her door. She could tell from the sound of the knock that it wasn't one of her usual visitors.

"Come in," she called.

It was Mags. She tiptoed inside and glanced surreptitiously down the hallway before closing the door behind her.

"I know it's not visiting hours – why they can't coincide with lunch hour, I don't know – I had to sneak past the main desk – I didn't want them to catch me and kick me out!"

"They don't enforce visiting hours for private patients," Kylie told her and Mags looked mildly disappointed that her subterfuge had been for nothing.

She put some glossy magazines on the bedside locker. "Something for you to flick through – I know you must be bored to death – Sarah says hello – she's got a new boyfriend – oh, and I have something here from Mary . . ."

She took a small envelope from her shoulder bag and handed it to Kylie who placed it, unopened, next to the magazines on the locker.

"Sit down, Mags," said Kylie and gestured towards the armchair.

Mags perched on the very edge of it, as if there was some unwritten rule that visitors outside the official hours were not permitted to make themselves comfortable.

"How's the clinic going without me?" asked Kylie.

"Ted's sent us someone new – his name is John – he's a bit green – Ted sends his regards, by the way."

The question answered, an awkward silence descended on the room. Kylie looked at her friend objectively. She seemed even skinnier than before, the cheeky look had gone from her eyes and her chatter was nervy rather than natural. Then, somehow, Kylie knew what had caused the change.

"You've broken up with Seamus, haven't you?"

The expression on Mags's face confirmed it was true. Kylie reached out to clasp her hand with its long thin fingers and protruding knuckles. The feel of it was very familiar.

"Were you here when I was in a coma?" she asked suddenly.

"Yes – I told you about Seamus – a bit late, I know – and you weren't even conscious –"

"I remember your hands, Mags. I must have been conscious on some level."

"Spooky," said Mags with an exaggerated shudder. "If I had known that I wouldn't have gone and told you my deepest and darkest secrets."

Kylie laughed. Over the last few weeks she had missed the quirky, effervescent girl who had given her such a unique welcome to Dublin. She should have guessed about Seamus; in hindsight, all the signs had been there.

They continued to hold hands and Kylie worked up the courage to ask about Jim.

"Mags, did you tell MFJ in Sydney about my accident?"

"Yes," she replied. "I spoke to Neil, your boss."

"What about Jim? Did you tell him?" she asked, looking at her friend closely.

Mags's face was clear of its usual reticence regarding Jim. "I asked Neil to put me through but he told me that Jim was out of the country. He promised to pass on the message – and then he asked me not to speak to anyone but him about the accident – he personally wanted to handle all of the internal communication."

Jim must know. Neil would have told him.

Kylie, more from habit than anything else, didn't let Mags see how crushed she was.

"It's just like Neil to be so controlling," she remarked and changed the topic of conversation back to the clinic.

She cried and cried after Mags left. Much later on, when the long evening had dwindled away the last of the daylight, she opened Mary's envelope. There was a prayer card inside. She read the beautiful words and was so touched by them that she started crying again. It was her darkest day by far.

Chapter 21

Rose's stay in Cork extended to a week, and she was markedly different when she came back. Kylie felt it from the moment she walked in the door, but she couldn't put her finger on what it was. She looked the same, talked the same, yet Kylie knew that something very fundamental had changed in her mother — whether it was for better or worse she wasn't yet sure.

Rose didn't tell her straight away. Instead she talked about Liz and what a lovely time they'd had together.

"It felt wrong to be giggling and laughing with her when you're here laid up on a hospital bed," said

Rose, looking a little shamefaced.

"Don't be silly, Mum. Being a misery guts isn't going to make me feel better. I'm glad you two had fun together."

Then Rose became nostalgic. "When we were children, Liz could always make me laugh – sometimes at the most inopportune times, like the middle of Mass, and we'd both get a clip around the ear as result –"

Kylie smiled at the thought of two giggling fair-haired girls in the church pew. "Did you like Cork? Did Liz take you sightseeing and torment you with constant photographs?"

"Yes," a shadow came across Rose's face, "we saw some of the sights." She paused and wetted her parched-looking lips. "Actually, Kylie, there's something I need to tell you – something I should have told you a long time ago, but I was too ashamed . . ."

"What?"

Rose looked down at her hands and examined them as if she had never seen them before in her life. Seconds ticked by. Whatever it was she wanted to say, it seemed to be taking every ounce of her will to muster up the words.

"My memories of Cork aren't very happy. I was in a home down there . . ." Her voice trailed away.

"What kind of home?" asked Kylie and then suggested the first thing that came into her head, "Was it a mental institution?"

"No." Rose directed a vague smile her way before dropping her eyes again. "It was a home for unmarried mothers."

Kylie's jaw dropped open. "Does that mean you had a baby . . ."

Now, she was the one who couldn't finish sentences.

"Yes." There was force behind Rose's affirmation, as if she was sick of the denial. Then, she raised her head and looked Kylie head on. "Stephen was not my first child. I had a little girl, Ellen, in the early hours of June the eleventh, 1962."

Her staggering confession brought about a toxic range of feelings in Kylie: a searing curiosity to know more detail, a wariness towards Rose because she felt that she must hardly know this woman at all and a terrible fear about the fate of the baby, Ellen.

All those emotions threaded through her voice when she asked, "What happened to Ellen?"

Rose sighed. The sound was soft yet ridden with guilt. "That's what I'm trying to find out."

Kylie looked at her in total confusion.

You gave birth to Ellen; you're her mother. How could you not know what happened to your own baby?

"Ellen was with me in the home for the first three months of her life," Rose started to explain. "She was beautiful – a shock of black hair on her head, big blue eyes, bonny cheeks. She thrived despite the grim surroundings. The home was run by the nuns – and I'll never, to my dying day, forget the cruelty of the sister in charge."

Rose paused, as if she needed to recharge her batteries before providing any further description of the home.

When she continued, her sadness had drawn the strength from her voice and it was much weaker. "Heavily pregnant girls and sleep-deprived new mothers scrubbed floors and tended the gardens, but the worst job of all was the steaming hot laundry – your hands would be red raw from there. We weren't allowed to use our real names – I was called Pauline – and we were not allowed to speak to each other. The only time the silence was broken was for prayer or when some poor girl was being berated by the sister."

Kylie tried to visualise what her mother was describing. It sounded like something out of the Dickens' era rather than the sixties.

Bewilderedly, she asked, "Why did you stay there if it was so bad?"

"Because I saw what happened to the girls who

ran away." Rose's eyes were defeated as she relived the hopelessness of it. "They never got far – the locals knew not to pick them up from the road. Even the ones who made it home were usually sent straight back by their families. Of course, the sister made sure that they suffered even more because of the transgression."

"I can't believe that there was no way out of the place," said Kylie.

"There was one way," Rose conceded. "You could pay the council the boarding-out fee for the baby. That meant the baby could be sent on to the orphanage and the mother was free to leave the home. My mother came with the money after three months. I left Ellen behind and went with her – but only as far as the bus station. I refused to get on the bus – there was no way I could go back home and substitute my father's oppression for the sister's. I knew Carmel and Liz would be devastated – they thought I was at hospital with some mysterious illness – but I still couldn't get on that bus. Mother slapped me across the face, called me an ungrateful slut and said I wasn't worth the money she'd spent on the boarding-out fee. I can still see her bitter face staring out at me as the bus took off . . . It was as if I was something come up from the gutter rather than her own daughter . . ."

Rose paused once again but Kylie couldn't bear for her to stop at this critical point. She leaned forward in the bed to urge her mother on. "What happened then?"

"I rang Frankie at work . . . God love him, he didn't know what had become of me. He knew about the baby, of course – we were going to get married – but my mother guessed that I was pregnant and shipped me down to Cork. I never had the chance to tell Frankie where I was going . . ."

"Gosh," was all Kylie could say.

"I was in an awful state on the phone . . . but he was able to decipher where I was and he got the first bus down . . . I waited in the bus station until he came – it was seven or eight hours later. I sat, all huddled up, as silent as I had been in the home . . . I remember people coming up to ask if I was OK . . ."

Rose seemed to be running out of steam. Her shoulders drooped and her head hung, possibly not unlike the girl in the bus station all those years ago.

"So you went straight from Cork to Australia?" Kylie concluded.

"Yes." Her voice was only a whisper now. Where was all the affirmation gone? "We left poor little Ellen behind . . ." Her face crumpled. "It seemed impossible to get her out of the orphanage. That's my shame, Kylie – we should have got her out – by hook or by crook —"

"Oh, Mum!" Kylie held her cold hand tightly in hers.

Rose cried, softly at first, but her sobs gained strength until she was almost hysterical.

Many times she repeated, "We should never have left her behind!"

Kylie said nothing, just held her hand.

* * *

Kylie knew she wouldn't sleep that night. How could she? Rose's revelation changed everything, absolutely everything.

Many times when she was young she had wished for a sister. Stephen had been a great older brother, but he didn't do dress-up, dolls or make-believe tea parties.

Maybe Ellen wouldn't have either. After all, she's twelve years older than me.

But a twelve-year age gap, whilst significant in young children, would be nothing now; Ellen would be the same age as many of Kylie's friends and colleagues.

Is her hair still black, like mine? Is she married? Will I like her? Will she like me?

Kylie lay in the semi-darkness, her head racing as

it checked over Rose's story for gaps or cracks, in the same way it would check a client's affidavit.

"I told Liz everything," Rose had said when she could cry no more. "It was such a relief to tell someone after all these years – and she was so supportive and understanding . . ."

Therein was the clue to the change in Rose that Kylie had noticed from the moment she walked into the room. The secret was finally out and the sheer relief had lightened her whole demeanour.

"Liz knew where the home was," Rose had continued. "We went there together. It's still open for business – but it's been totally modernised. All the girls have their own rooms now – they're counselled and given all sorts of options. Their lives aren't over because of one mistake . . ."

Rose always gave people a second chance. Now Kylie was able to understand why. There had been dire consequences for Rose's "mistake": a horrific few months in the home while Frankie had no idea where she was, separation from her baby and estrangement from the entire family.

"The sister who's responsible now was so lovely to me. She recommended that I have some counselling before proceeding with the trace – and I took her advice: that's why I stayed on a few extra days . . ."

"What kind of things did they counsel you on?" Kylie asked.

"My legal rights, Ellen's legal rights – that's the first step. The second step is who to tell and when. Family and friends, even though they mean well, can apply pressure to what's already a difficult situation. Step three is dealing with feelings: guilt, grief or how I might feel if Ellen isn't alive or has problems . . ."

Kylie hadn't thought of the possibility of Ellen having problems. She had assumed that they would find a normal forty-three-year-old woman. The thought of it not being so was very frightening.

"So what happens now?"

"Now, I wait," said Rose in a resigned way. After all, she had been waiting for over forty years: what was another few days or weeks? "The sister needs to check the Baptismal Register to see if she can find an entry for the adoption or, if we're very lucky, a marriage. If the last known address was in a rural area, they'll make enquiries at the local post office to see if the family still lives in the area."

"Maybe Ellen emigrated," said Kylie.

"Maybe," fresh tears welled in Rose's indigo eyes, "or maybe she doesn't want anything to do with me. My only defence is that I truly believed I had no right to march into her life and turn it upside down. But your accident, and talking to Liz, changed my perspective. Now I just want to see her – to tell her I never *ever* forgot her and that I'm sorry for leaving her behind ..."

Chapter 22

Kylie burst into the bedroom.

"Mum, I can't find the sticky-tape."

"I thought you were playing next door," said Rose, looking startled.

"I am. I need that wide roll of sticky tape — Annie just has the narrow stuff."

"Try the second drawer in the kitchen."

"I already did."

"Look harder," Rose told her.

It was only then that Kylie noticed one of her mother's hands hiding behind her back.

"What have you got there?"

"Nothing."

The reflection from the mirror on the dresser said otherwise.

"It's not nothing," said Kylie in a stern adult-like voice. "I can see it in the mirror. You shouldn't lie, Mum."

Rose sighed. "No, I shouldn't lie. I'm sorry."

"Can I see it?"

Rose was on the back foot after being caught out lying. "You can have a quick look."

She took her hand from behind her back for a moment.

"It's such a lovely pink," said Kylie in admiration. "Can I keep it?"

"What would you want with it, Kylie?"

"Mindy needs a hat."

Mindy was her dolly.

"It's not a hat — it's just an old rag."

"It is a hat — I saw it."

The doorbell rang in the middle of their debate. They both went to answer it. Annie stood outside.

"My mum said to tell you that she has the kettle on," she announced.

"Well, I'd better go right there," smiled Rose. "Come on, Kylie."

"I have to get the sticky tape," Kylie replied. "I'll follow you."

She found it in the second drawer, just as Rose had said. She stole back into her parents' room and picked up the soft pink cotton from the bed. There was no question but that it was a baby's bonnet. Kylie's eight-year-old mind couldn't fathom why her mother had lied.

Chapter 23

Seeing Stephen seemed to manifest everything that had changed. He was no longer the eldest and Kylie was no longer the only girl. They were three, not two.

"It's weird, isn't it?" he said.

"Yes."

His big face set in a frown. "I hope that Ellen isn't hostile towards Mum – that's assuming they find her, of course."

"I know." Kylie had the same worry. "It would be too cruel if she rejected her."

Stephen drummed his calloused fingers on his jeans. He wasn't usually one for fidgeting. "Tamsin

361

says that there's still a lot of stigma attached to being a single mother," he commented.

Kylie nodded. "We can only imagine what it was like back in the sixties . . ."

The conversation ebbed away as the stark images of the home took over. Neither had been there to experience it for themselves, but Rose's description had made her misery and despair their own.

"Not everyone was sent off to a home to have their baby," said Kylie after a while. "Things were starting to change in Ireland, and Mum said that some girls, the ones with supportive families, kept their babies. But her parents didn't care about the changes in society – having a baby out of wedlock was the worst sin imaginable to them; it was irrelevant that Mum and Dad were planning to get married."

"It's so stupid." Stephen's voice was uncharacteristically quiet. "Ellen was lost for no reason other than the pig-headedness of our grandparents."

There was another brief silence before Kylie confessed, "I can't get her out of my head. What's her life like now? What was it like when she was a kid? Did she stay in the orphanage or did someone adopt her? What does she do as her job? Does she have a husband, partner, children? Does she look like me?"

There was a spark of Stephen's usual humour as he remarked, "She'd be as ugly as sin if she's anything like you."

"Thanks a bunch."

They shared a grin, then he quickly became serious again.

"I won't see Ellen, Kyls. Well, at least not as soon as the rest of you. I'm flying home on Friday."

"Oh."

Of course she knew that he would have to go home at some stage. He couldn't stay here for months on end. He had a life, and a girlfriend, to get back to.

"Dad is staying on here with Mum," he explained, "which means I have to go back to keep the business running –"

Kylie was flippant as she said, "Yeah, someone around here has to work."

She was going to miss him. Terribly. "Steve, can you do me a favour before you go?"

He raised a sandy eyebrow. "You want me to smuggle in your cigarettes?"

She hadn't smoked since the accident.

"No," she smiled, "it seems that going cold turkey has cured me of that particular vice. It's my laptop that I want – it's in my apartment on the counter."

"Consider it done."

* * *

He came with the laptop the next day.

"It's a good machine, this," he said as he carefully extracted it from its black case.

She shook her head in mock despair. "Please don't tell me that you've taken it apart."

"I just cleared up some space on your disk drive," he defended himself, "and I downloaded some software upgrades."

He clicked the modem into the portal on the wall and pushed the ON button. The laptop whirred to life and he watched it load up with critical eyes.

"Yes, it's much faster now," he said with satisfaction.

He placed it on her lap.

"It's OK," she said. "I'll check my messages later on."

"I want to make sure your dial-up is working before I go," he insisted.

With Stephen looking intently over her shoulder, she clicked on the dial-up icon and typed in her password. The modem sounded as it dialled the phone number.

Connected to MFJ server, flashed up on the screen.

"There," she said, "I'm in – it's working."

He looked pleased with himself. "Was the connection faster than usual?"

She really couldn't tell if there was a difference but said yes anyway.

"Is there anything else you need before I go?" he asked.

There was no rush for him to leave, only that neither of them liked prolonged goodbyes.

"No, Stephen. Thanks for everything."

"Take care of yourself, kiddo." He gave her an awkward hug. "I'll be in touch."

"Safe home," she choked and pulled him back for another clumsy hug.

The door closed behind him and she stared blankly at it until the heat emitting from the bottom of the laptop reminded her that it was there.

She opened her inbox and the screen filled up with the bolded text of unread messages. Most of them were from Jim. She started at the oldest and worked her way up.

12/09 Our first fight. Wish I was there to make-up. Sorry.

15/9 Still mad at me?

17/9 Earth to Kylie Horgan?

20/9 If you're trying to get me back for not

**calling, then you've made your point. Now, stop
ignoring me.**

Kylie's heart was thumping painfully when she got
to the last message.

**22/9   These kinds of games do nothing for
me, Kylie. We obviously don't have as much in
common as I thought.**

As she stared at the angry words, the door flew
open and Maura came in with her usual hustle and
bustle.

"How's the patient today?" she asked.

"OK," Kylie answered distractedly.

She knew the routine only too well and didn't pay
any heed while Maura felt for a pulse on her foot.

"How does the leg feel?" she asked as she
scribbled on the chart.

"Fine."

"That's good." She nodded with approval.
"Before you know it you'll be dancing a jig for us."

She hooked the chart back onto the end of the
bed.

"Don't leave that laptop on for too long," she
instructed on her way out. "It can interfere with the
electricity supply and medical equipment around
here."

*Jim doesn't know about the accident. Neil didn't pass on
the message.*

366

She was euphoric that there was such a logical, sturdy explanation for why Jim hadn't been in contact. However, there was no denying that the relevance of the explanation had diminished significantly with the passage of time. It was three weeks since their argument. It would be bizarre to ring him now, when he thought it was over between them, to say, "Guess what? I've been in a major accident – that's why you haven't heard from me."

Would it change how he felt about her? Or would he just say, "Sorry to hear that" as he would to any other ex-girlfriend?

The old Kylie, the one with the high-flying job and energetic lifestyle, would have called him in an instant. The new Kylie, the one who lay day-in-day-out on a hospital bed, didn't seem to have the self-confidence.

"You seem rather down today," said Rose when she came in later on in the afternoon.

"I'm missing Stephen already," Kylie replied, but it was only one of the reasons that she felt so low.

"He's not flying out until the morning," said Rose. "I could ask him to come around now, if you'd like."

Kylie was firm. "No, we've already said goodbye."

She let the conversation fall into a lull. This was one of those times where she would have preferred to be on her own, but she didn't have the heart to ask

Rose to go away.

"I expect that Stephen's keen to get back to Tamsin," Rose commented after a while.

"Yes," Kylie gave a wry smile, "he seems to be rather smitten."

"Now, if I could get *you* settled, I'd be completely happy," said Rose.

On any other day Kylie could have laughed it off. But not today. Tears welled in her eyes.

Rose was totally taken aback. "What it is, darling? Is it your leg? Is it hurting?"

Kylie shook her head, her hand rough as it wiped the tears away before they had the chance to fall.

"Is it something I said? I didn't mean to be insensitive."

Rose looked so distraught that Kylie tried to tell her. She wanted to keep it simple and just talk about Jim, but she inevitably got tangled up in Laura, Mags, Carole and Neil, and their pivotal roles in the whole sorry saga.

"It was never meant to be," she said wearily at the end. "It's too complicated."

"It's only as complicated as you want it to be," replied Rose authoritatively. "Your defences are down, Kylie, and everything looks bleak and impossible to you right now. I felt the same when I was trapped in the home. Don't make the same mistake as me – *nothing* is impossible."

Rose said goodbye soon after and left Kylie to mull over her words of wisdom. After much deliberation, Kylie eventually picked up the phone and called Jim's number. It rang on for some time before it was answered. She recognised Carole's clipped voice straight away and quietly returned the receiver to its handset. It was very early in the morning in Auckland and there could be only one reason that Carole was answering Jim's mobile phone.

That night was another one where she cried herself to sleep.

* * *

A few days later Maura turned Kylie's bed so it was facing the window. "It can't stay like this permanently," she warned. "I'll have to turn it back at dinnertime."

"I don't mind," said Kylie. "I'm happy once I can face something other than the wall every now and then."

The view constituted a narrow pavement along a terrace of red-bricked houses. Kylie watched people walk along the pavement and go in and out of the houses like she was watching some reality TV show.

Over the last few weeks, summer had transformed into a windy autumn that had stolen the leaves from the trees.

She stared out the window and didn't notice when the door opened quietly behind her. She nearly jumped out of her skin when she heard a voice say, "Hello."

It was Amy and she was carrying a bunch of flowers that would have made a sizeable dent in her meagre income.

"I'm sorry I frightened you. It's a habit I have – Barry kills me for 'sneaking around'."

"Thanks for the flowers," said Kylie. "They're beautiful. Can I smell them?"

Amy brought them closer and Kylie inhaled their beautiful fragrance. It was such a pleasure to smell something other than hospital-grade detergent.

"Do you have a vase?" asked Amy.

"There should be one in the bathroom."

Amy opened the door of the bathroom with the same trepidation as one might open the door of a furnace. Even when she turned on the tap, Kylie heard the sound of a soft trickle rather than the usual gush. Everything about Amy was gentle, and it was frustratingly easy for Barry to treat her like a doormat.

The vase filled with water, Amy started to arrange

the flowers. She looked awkward as she adjusted the angle of the stems. It was obvious that flower arranging wasn't something she did very often.

"Has the Labour Court set a date?" asked Kylie.

"Yes. The middle of next month – Mags, your colleague, said that she will be attending in your place."

"Barry will meet his match with Mags," Kylie assured her.

Amy gave the flowers one last critical look before coming to sit down.

"Actually, I didn't come here to talk about the Labour Court – I came with a message from my father."

Kylie frowned with confusion. What had Amy's father to do with anything?

"Jerry," said Amy. "Jerry is my father."

Kylie was knocked sideways. It had absolutely never entered her head that Amy's alcoholic father was Jerry: the man who had shouted abuse at her in the clinic, the man who had terrified her to the point where she had lost her balance on the kerb, the man who had pulled her out from under the vehicle and held her hand until the ambulance came.

"It's a small world," was all she managed to say.

"Not as small as you think," replied Amy. "It was Dad who told me about the clinic. He said you girls knew what you were doing and would tell me straight if I had a case or not."

While Kylie took in the unexpected connection, Amy undid the clasp of her PVC handbag and took out a folded sheet of paper.

"He wrote you a message. He asked me to bring it to you – they'd never let his sort inside the doors here."

Kylie unfolded the sheet with its rough perforated edge. The spidery handwriting spilled over the pale blue lines.

"I hope you can read it," said Amy. "He has terrible shakes in his hands after so many years on the turps."

I'm deeply sorry about your accident. I'd been following you for weeks but I couldn't get you alone – you were always with someone. All I wanted to do was say sorry for shouting at you that day in the clinic and to thank you for helping Amy. Of course, you wouldn't have known that I meant you no harm – the look of me is enough to scare anyone. The drink has made me into a filthy, foul-mouthed shell – but inside I'm just like any other man who loves his daughter beyond anything else.

My sincerest apologies,
Jerry

Kylie clutched the piece of paper long after she

had finished reading it. She was incredibly sad: sad for Jerry and his unquenchable thirst, sad for Amy and her rotten childhood, sad that had she the tiniest ounce of faith in the homeless man, her accident would have been avoidable.

* * *

On Sunday Kylie was determined to be more upbeat. Shit happened. She had lost Jim, smashed her leg, but life went on. She had many blessings to count: a wonderful family, great friends and a promising career. She was done with the dark, dogged despair – she was going to force herself to be positive.

Frankie came in mid-morning and she was happy to see him.

"Where's Mum?"

"At Mass," he replied.

She thought she had misheard and checked again. "*Mass?*"

"Yes." Newspaper under his arm, he ambled over to the armchair. "She prayed a lot when you were unconscious – she said it gave her strength –"

"But I didn't think Mum did the whole religion thing . . ."

"She was always very spiritual," Frankie told her

as he spread the newspaper out across his knees, "but her father's extremism and the cruelty of the sister in the home pushed her away from the church . . . It took your accident to push her back."

Kylie thought he would start reading but he delayed.

"It seems that your mother's prayers have been answered on all fronts," he said slowly. "We've heard from the home. They've made contact with Ellen and she's interested in a reunion."

Kylie sat up straighter in the bed. Ellen was the big unknown – she felt nervous even hearing her name mentioned.

Frankie was nervous too; apprehension cloaked his whole face. "Ellen's been having counselling too – that's why it's taken a while . . ."

"When? Where?"

"Tuesday – at the home. They say a neutral place is best and there will be counsellors on hand if it doesn't go well . . ."

"How's Mum?"

"She's a knot of nerves." Frankie shrugged as if the answer was obvious. "We're both trying to keep our expectations low."

"Did they say anything about Ellen? Is she –"

Frankie cut her off. "They said nothing other than the time and place of the reunion."

He raised the newspaper with a certain amount of defensiveness and began to read. Kylie felt fiercely protective of him and Rose and hoped for all their sakes that Ellen would not be vengeful or have serious problems.

* * *

The next forty-eight hours were the slowest of Kylie's entire life. On the day of the reunion, she couldn't stop herself from second-guessing every move that Rose and Frankie made.

7 a.m: Getting into their rented Toyota Corolla to start the drive down to Cork

9 a.m: Halfway there, having a quick cup of tea to break the journey.

11 a.m: Driving through Cork's busy streets.

12 a.m: Seeing Ellen, the baby they had left behind, now a grown woman. Finding out her life story. Telling her theirs. Crying? Hugging? Forgiving?

3 p.m: Heading back up the main Dublin Road, maybe talking, maybe not.

7pm: Home.

Kylie had made Frankie promise to come straight to the hospital. In the end it was after eight when they arrived. Their faces were tired, a little on the pale side, but other than that they seemed OK.

"Well?" she asked.

"We met her," was Rose's frustratingly simple response.

"What was she like?"

"She was nice."

"Mum!" Kylie exclaimed in exasperation.

"Give me a minute to catch my breath, Kylie!" Rose wearily rubbed her forehead. "It's been a long day."

"Sorry."

Frankie pulled up one of the straight-backed chairs and Rose sank into it. Then she unzipped her bag and took out a photograph.

"Ellen gave me this. Her husband's name is Paul – they've been married twelve years. James is nine – football mad. Ciara is five – she's just started school."

Kylie looked down at the family photograph with the cheeky looking boy, cute button-nosed girl and two smiling adults. The man, Paul, had a receding hairline and an intelligent face. His arm was draped around his wife's, Ellen's, shoulders.

"She does look like me," Kylie said as she studied her sister's short dark hair and sky-blue eyes.

"I told her that," said Rose, a proud smile forming on her lips. "It's only the hairstyle that's different."

Kylie searched Ellen's face for clues to her personality. "Was she angry that you left her behind in the orphanage?"

Rose looked utterly relieved to be able to answer in the negative. "No, not at all. She was adopted when she was five months old and all her memories are of a happy family environment."

"Did she know she was adopted?"

"Yes." Rose nodded. "Her adoptive parents told her when she was twelve."

"Did she understand why you had to give her up?"

Frankie answered, "She didn't think about it until she had children of her own." He was still standing, his hands awkwardly shoved in his trouser pockets. "Shortly after James was born she saw an RTÉ documentary about unmarried mothers in the fifties and sixties. There was a lot of public outrage when the documentary aired how badly the girls were treated in the homes. Ellen discussed it with her adoptive parents and they gave her every support when she said she wanted to try to find her birth mother. She wrote to the home but, not surprisingly, they weren't able to trace Rose. She was disappointed at the time, but she put it behind her and got on with life."

Ellen clearly bore no animosity, and by all

accounts the reunion had gone as well as could be expected. For some strange reason it felt like an anticlimax to Kylie.

"When will I see her?" she asked.

"I don't know if you will." Again it was Frankie who fielded the question. "On the counsellors' recommendation, we didn't exchange addresses or phone numbers. We're all having a cooling-off period, as it were."

The notion of "cooling off" after forty wasted years was totally baffling to Kylie.

"Why?"

"So that we take it slow." From the tone of Frankie's voice, it seemed that he agreed fully with the recommendation. "We can arrange a second meeting through the home – and because we're not in direct contact, there's no pressure on Ellen to agree. It's not our intention to force our family on her. She has her own life and it wouldn't be fair to invade it."

"But what if she *wants* to be part of our family?" asked Kylie.

"Then we'd be delighted to have her," Rose replied softly.

Chapter 24

A huge rush of circulation surged into Kylie's leg, and it felt like it was about to explode. She looked at the swollen, mottled skin and burst into tears.

"Now, now," said Maura, squeezing her shoulders, "this is a happy occasion, not sad."

Coming out of traction was a huge milestone, but instead of feeling jubilant, Kylie felt dizzy and disoriented.

"I feel that I'll never be the same again."

"Of course, you will. You'll be dancing a jig in no time."

Fond as she was of Maura, Kylie thought that if

she heard her talk about dancing a jig one more time she would surely throttle her.

For the following few days, Jane, the physio, continued to visit her in the room. Kylie started to realise what she'd meant when she'd said that the hard work would start once she came down from traction.

"This machine is called a CPM," she said, putting the contraption on the bed. "The letters stand for Continuous Passive Motion. Now, we strap your leg in like this, then I select the range of movement – start small – and off it goes, up and down, nice and slow."

More like, nice and excruciating.

After that first encounter with the CPM machine, Kylie made sure that she had her painkillers before Jane's visits.

Four days later, Jane announced that Kylie was ready for her first visit to the gymnasium. This involved an exciting ride in a wheelchair. While the orderly pushed the chair down the long corridors, Kylie smiled self-consciously at the people they met along the way. She knew she was incapable of walking, but it still felt like the height of laziness to be pushed around by someone else.

In the gymnasium Kylie saw the real Jane at work.

"Now, flex back this way, slowly."

"I don't think my leg is ready for what you're doing to it," Kylie told her through gritted teeth.

"Your leg just wants an easy life – don't we all?"

When she finished with the range of movement exercises, she helped Kylie across to the parallel bars.

"This is hopeless," said Kylie when she couldn't bear any weight at all.

"Nothing is hopeless – just think of how far you've come on since last week –"

"I was still in traction last week," Kylie pointed out.

"Exactly."

Kylie thought the session would never reach an end. Jane kept on massaging, pushing, hurting and Kylie was on the verge of tears when the orderly finally showed up with her chair.

"Jane says you have to get into bed without my help," he announced when they were back in her room.

"So you're in cahoots with her," Kylie complained and mustered up the last of her strength to pull herself out of the chair. She sat on the bed and, just as Jane had showed her, she carefully used her good leg to lift the injured one onto the mattress.

"Well done," said the orderly and then added, as if it was something to look forward to, "See you same time tomorrow."

* * *

In the long week that followed, Kylie was bombarded with unqualified advice regarding her recovery.

"Swimming is meant to be a great way to improve mobility," Mags commented on one of her regular visits.

"I'm eons away from getting into a pool," Kylie informed her.

Mags had the grace to look a little sheepish. "Maybe it's something to keep in mind for later on, then. By the way, the clinic is moving to new premises — same street, but lots of space — you'll have to come and visit when you get out of here."

Shortly afterwards, Stephen sent an email suggesting that she join a gym.

I can only just about get in and out of bed, she typed back. **A workout, even a light one, is a long way off. But it sounds like a good idea for you. I thought you looked a little podgy when you were here — you shouldn't let yourself go just because you're in love.**

He sent a characteristic smart-assed response and the gym wasn't mentioned again.

Liz was the next to jump on the bandwagon.

"I got this stuff from a naturopath in Cork," she said, unscrewing the top of a clinical-looking tub. "It returns vitality to the skin."

She massaged the thick cream onto Kylie's leg.

"There," she said with immense satisfaction. "It will look as good as the other one in no time."

However, Kylie developed an allergic rash to the cream and Liz was justifiably outraged.

"But it's meant to be all natural ingredients – or so the woman told me –"

It seemed that Carmel was the only one who had sound advice to offer.

"Just listen to the physiotherapist," she said at the outset. "Do everything she says – plus more."

Kylie liked talking to Carmel because she was the only one who had any idea of what she was going through. She took her advice and practised Jane's exercises over and over in her room.

She did her best to stay focused on the here and now but couldn't stop her thoughts from veering occasionally to Sydney, where the High Potential team were settling back into their old jobs.

Will anyone wonder where I am? Will they care? What about Isobel? Has she stayed on in Barcelona? David will be ecstatic to be back on familiar ground and I bet Oliver had to drag Crystelle home. Jim and Carole . . . no, I don't want to go there.

Kylie tried to imagine herself back in Sydney, picking up the reins of her old job. However, she could hardly picture herself sitting at her desk, not to talk about competing for a partnership. Since the accident, all her energies had been concentrated on one immediate goal: to be able to walk again. Being a partner by age thirty-two seemed rather unimportant in comparison.

The phone rang on Thursday night. Kylie expected that it would be Carmel, who called every few days. She answered with a breezy hello but tensed up straight away when she heard Neil's voice.

"I hear your recovery is going well," he remarked.

She forced a false brightness into her tone. "Yes. I'm out of traction and the physiotherapy has started in earnest – it's slow and painful, but I'm managing to bear some weight now –"

Neil cut in before she was finished, making it clear that he was disinterested in any kind of detail. "I've told the others that you've been detained on some urgent business and won't be joining us until the final conference in Fiji."

The conference in Fiji was in December, only six weeks away, and Kylie had no idea if she would be able to travel by then.

"Why didn't you tell them that I'd been in an accident?" she asked. "Why the need for all this cover-up?"

His reply was as controlled and measured as ever. "Isobel and David have pulled out of the programme. I don't want everybody thinking that you're out of the race too –"

Kylie had an inkling about Isobel but David was a total surprise. He had wanted the partnership more than anybody else.

"Why did David pull out?"

"He fell apart," was Neil's scathing response. "Angela contacted the Edinburgh office after he missed the last conference call. She found out that he hadn't been in work that week – nobody knew where he was. She was concerned so she asked them to call around to his apartment to see if he was OK. They found him cowering in a corner. He was having some kind of mental breakdown – seems that he couldn't handle working out of his comfort zone."

"Where is he now?"

"Back in Australia – in some institution or other."

Guilt punched Kylie in the chest.

I didn't contact him once over the last few months. Edinburgh is so close to Dublin – I should have gone there. A friendly face might have made all the difference . . .

David didn't deserve this to happen to him; he had worked too hard. Now his career at MFJ was over. It wasn't the sort of organisation to accommodate even a minor psychiatric illness. All his slogging had been for nothing.

"You're still a front runner for a partnership, Kylie," said Neil. "I don't want any doubt with the team or with the selection committee. Angela Bardman knows of the accident only because you've missed some of the coursework – the others don't need to know until they can see for themselves that you are well over your injuries."

She was very disturbed when she hung up the phone. Why hadn't Neil concocted a cover-up for David to protect his place on the programme? Why did he give her special treatment?

What does Neil see in me?

The question had always been there at the back of her mind. She would have liked to think it was down to talent, but she was not so sure. This cover-up, totally unnecessary in her mind, made Neil seem rather obsessed, and it made her very uneasy.

* * *

"That's good," said Jane encouragingly as Kylie took a rigid step. "Just another now . . ."

Kylie smiled with satisfaction and forced another step from her reluctant leg. After three weeks of intensive therapy, pain was no longer a deterrent: it was her motivation.

"Well done," said Jane.

Kylie used the rails to rest for a moment.

"I think we might let you go home soon."

Kylie did a double-take. "Really?" she asked. She was hesitant only because she had learned not to press Jane for timeframes regarding her recovery.

"Yes – I think you're ready."

"Great." Kylie grinned delightedly. "My parents will be thrilled."

"Don't go planning your return flight to Sydney just yet," Jane warned. "You'll still have to come in to outpatients every second day for therapy. Now, back to work . . ."

Kylie took her hands off the rails and managed a few more heavy steps under Jane's critical eye.

"To be honest, I didn't expect you to have this much functionality by now – the bone had so many breaks, and the tissue damage was so severe . . ."

Kylie had no idea that Jane had harboured doubts. Ironically, it was her unfailing certainty that had helped Kylie transcend the pain.

"But you've exceeded even my most optimistic expectations," Jane continued.

Kylie knew her well enough by now to tell that she was pleased. Maybe even a little proud.

*　*　*

Kylie's apartment seemed vast in comparison to the hospital room. She used her crutches to limp from room to room: kitchenette, bathroom, bedroom and living room. It felt good, although more than a little peculiar, to be back.

She hopped over to the window and looked down at the murky green of the Liffey.

"Mum, can you help me open this?"

Rose pushed the stiff aluminium frame upwards and Kylie leaned out over the sill. She inhaled the mingled smell of the river and the brewery malt as if it was an exotic perfume.

"Would you like a cup of tea?" asked Rose from behind.

"Yes, please."

It was just the two of them; Frankie had been despatched to the supermarket to buy some essentials. Frankie and grocery shopping were not on familiar terms and Kylie didn't expect him back for quite some time.

Rose went into the kitchen and soon Kylie heard the hum of the kettle. Even that everyday sound made her happy.

Stale smells and boiling kettles — I'm easy to please these days.

It was only when Kylie hopped across to the couch that she noticed her black holdall on the floor. She manoeuvred herself onto the soft cushions and rested the crutches next to her. The bag looked as if it had been through the wars, its black leather torn and scuffed, the handle hanging off. Feeling like she was prying through someone else's belongings, she looked at its jumbled contents: scrunched receipts, various make-up items, purse, novel and the shattered remains of her mobile phone.

Rose came out with the tea.

"How did my bag get back here?" asked Kylie.

"A police officer gave it to Liz shortly after the accident," she replied. "Is everything there?"

"Seems to be."

They drank the tea in a thoughtful silence.

"You know, I didn't miss it," said Kylie after a while. "I didn't wonder where it was, not once. Yet, I couldn't go anywhere without it before the accident. Strange, isn't it?"

Rose was philosophical with her reply. "I guess that whatever you carry in that handbag just wasn't important when it came down to it . . ."

She was right. What had been important were the family and friends who had given her their support and companionship through the long dark days.

"Mum, I haven't thanked you and Dad for coming

here . . ."

"Oh, stop it," said Rose dismissively. "You're our daughter – what else would we do?"

"But you've stayed on – you should have gone home long ago."

"That's what families do." Rose shrugged. "They stick around like glue – whether you want them or not."

She smiled at her little joke and topped up their cups of tea. Kylie smiled too. It felt nice to have Rose to herself and even nicer that all the old barriers had come down. Nothing was taboo now.

"What's it like with Liz and Carmel after all these years?" Kylie asked.

"Wonderful," she replied. "I missed them terribly – there wasn't a day that I didn't think of them. Now it's as if time has frozen – even though age has changed us on the outside, we still feel like teenagers when we talk."

"Watch out, London," Kylie laughed. Liz, after having a wonderful time in Paris, had decided that London was her next stop. Rose was going too. "Somebody should warn them that there's three middle-aged teenagers about to hit the streets – one of them bearing a dangerous camera." Then, more solemnly, she asked, "How do you think you'll feel when you see Carmel's chair, Mum?"

"It'll be hard." Rose lost her smile. "Even harder knowing she went through all that and I wasn't there for her – but she pulled through. She's as strong as an ox, Carmel – not like me."

"Oh, Mum! Don't bash yourself up."

"It's true," said Rose, her voice hardening. "I talked myself out of coming back here so many times. Yes, I felt guilty – ashamed – but had I any backbone at all, I could have risen above those feelings."

"It'll be so nice for the three of you sisters to be finally reunited – I'm kind of jealous!"

Kylie wasn't really jealous – she was only trying to make the conversation positive again.

"You have a sister too, Kylie," Rose pointed out with an odd look on her face.

Kylie wasn't likely to forget. She thought about Ellen all the time.

"Yes," she sighed, "but it's pretty obvious that Ellen doesn't want to be part of our family, isn't it? A whole month has passed by – she's snubbing us."

Rose's reply was unexpected. "As a matter of fact, Ellen has been in touch – a number of times."

Kylie frowned. "Why didn't you say so?"

Rose shrugged. "Because we – that's Frank, Ellen and I – agreed to take it slowly. It's only now that we feel ready to extend our relationship to our wider families."

"Does that mean I'm finally going to meet her?"

"Yes. She's going to try to come up at the weekend."

Kylie frowned harder and her tone was sharp as she asked, "What do you mean '*try*'? Is she coming or is she not?"

Rose gave her a stern look. "Everything in life isn't black and white, Kylie Horgan. Her husband is a doctor – sometimes his schedule changes at short notice. She can only come if Paul is available to look after the children."

Suddenly Kylie felt very apprehensive. What if she and Ellen didn't get on? Even worse, what if Rose preferred Ellen and she was left out in the cold?

Rose must have read her thoughts because she put down her cup of tea and leaned over to take her hand. "Kylie, you and Ellen may look alike, but I can see already that you have very different personalities. She's cautious; you're impetuous. She's restful; you're high energy. I shudder to think of the arguments had you grown up in the same house. But I know you'll like each other – you just have to take it slow. Don't force it."

* * *

Kylie first met Ellen on a bleak winterish day. Pebble-sized hail came down in short angry showers, a steady rain falling in between. Frankie and Rose picked Ellen up from the train station and dropped her to Kylie's apartment. They didn't come in.

Kylie opened the door to the mirror image of her own face: pale, pierced by two startling blue eyes, topped with short dark hair that seemed to have the same untameable curl. They were of similar height and build – they could have shared clothes had they been like normal sisters.

Their greeting was wary and Kylie, without the assistance of her crutches, led Ellen into the living room where she shrugged off her wet jacket.

"Where can I put this?" she asked.

"Let me," said Kylie and hung it on the back of a chair.

"This is a great location," Ellen remarked as she walked to the window to admire the rain-drenched view of the city. "So close to everything."

"Yes," Kylie hobbled towards her, "before the accident I used to walk everywhere – I didn't need any transport at all."

Ellen's eyes glanced down to Kylie's injured leg. "Rose says you've exceeded the expectations of the doctors a hundred-fold."

Kylie smiled conspiratorially. "I think she might

393

be exaggerating just a little – a mother's prerogative, I suppose."

Ellen gave a fleeting smile in return and then the room filled with a horrible awkward silence.

Mum and Dad won't be back for an hour, thought Kylie in despair. *What on earth are we going to talk about until then?*

"Would you like some tea?" she asked.

"No, thanks."

Kylie was scrambling for something else to say when Ellen asked suddenly, "What do you think of all this?"

It was a big question and not one that Kylie could take standing. She gripped the armrest of the couch and carefully lowered herself down.

"It's a bit surreal," she confessed. "But deep down it makes sense – it fits – it answers all the questions I've had over the years. I used to pester Mum about Ireland – her secrecy drove me crazy – then I'd go to Dad, and if he couldn't distract me with something else, he would tell me only enough to keep me quiet. Then there were times I would catch Mum being sad for no reason ... Once I found her holding a baby's bonnet – I knew it wasn't mine: she would have said if it was. I was too young to put two and two together, but still, part of me knew that she and Dad were hiding something."

Ellen left the window and came to sit down next to her. Her back ramrod straight, she sat as if she might need to jump up at a moment's notice.

Her expression inscrutable, she asked, "What was it like growing up in Australia?"

Kylie supposed it was a reasonable question. If Ellen hadn't been left behind, she would have grown up there too.

"Our street was very close-knit," Kylie told her. "Greeks, Italians, Irish, English, a few Aussies for good measure – we all had the same struggles. Summers were the best – running under the hose in the garden, eating outside, the beach only a short bus ride away. Even though we didn't have a lot, we had the sun and the sea – they were free and we took every advantage of them."

Ellen's smooth brow knitted into a frown. "I grew up on a farm," she revealed. "It was isolated . . . lonely. We went to the beach once a year – in the summer. It rained more often than not."

It seemed like she thought she had got the short straw.

"I'm sorry," said Kylie. "I was under the impression that you had a happy childhood."

"I did," Ellen insisted. "My parents doted on me – I was all they had. But our neighbours were a good mile away and their children were much older than me – so it was lonely. Just hearing you describe your childhood made me a little jealous, that's all."

"Belated sibling rivalry," Kylie commented.

Ellen laughed. Kylie felt hugely relieved that there was a sense of humour underneath the seemingly serious exterior. She knew then that Rose was right. Given time, she and Ellen would get along fine.

* * *

Frankie dropped Kylie outside the clinic's new premises, a few doors down from the old place. She was very impressed when she saw that the inside boasted a reception/waiting room and four consultation rooms. It seemed that *Just Ask* had taken off beyond all their expectations.

"Hello," she called out and the receptionist turned around from the photocopier. Kylie was stunned to see it was Amy.

"Oh, hello, Kylie." She smiled brightly. "Look at you – standing, walking – it's great to see you back on your feet."

"Thanks." Kylie returned her smile. "I didn't know you were working here!"

"Barry lost the hearing last week," she explained with a nonchalant shrug that was very unlike the Amy that Kylie knew. "He was so mad that he fired me – there and then – right in the middle of the courtroom. So now he's up for another hearing – unfair dismissal. In the meantime, Mags said she needed some help here . . ."

Kylie could tell from looking at Amy that she was much happier. Her face was less haggard and her eyes less sorrowful. It was as if a light had been switched on inside her former shell.

"How's your dad?" asked Kylie, her voice softening at the thought of Jerry.

"Still bingeing and off his face for half the time," she said, matter-of-fact, "but I got him a place and at least he's out of harm's way."

Kylie nodded and left it at that because nothing, least of all talking about it, would cure Jerry of his addiction.

"Both Mags and Sarah have somebody with them," said Amy. "They shouldn't be long."

Kylie sat down in the waiting area and killed some time with a magazine. Sarah was the first to come out. Wearing a grey suit that looked new, she seemed so much more mature than the graduate who had started a few months earlier.

"Well, what do you think of our fancy new premises?" she asked proudly.

"Fabulous," Kylie replied. "Can I see your office?"

Sarah was only too happy to show her around.

"All the rooms have a computer, printer and fax," she said when Kylie was surprised to see all the latest technology. "We have a state-of-the-art security system," she crouched down and showed Kylie a red button on the underside of the desk, "see – a hidden panic button – security can be here in less than five minutes."

Kylie was impressed; it looked like the security system alone cost a few thousand euro, not to talk about the premises.

"Did Ted pay for all this?" she asked.

Her back was to the door and she didn't see Mags come in.

"It was Laura's parents," she heard her say. "They wanted to do something meaningful with her life-insurance money. She loved the law and loved helping people – so investing in the *Just Ask* clinic seemed like the perfect memorial. I know I should have told you this before now . . ."

She didn't finish the sentence; she could hardly admit that she still saw Kylie as Laura's rival.

Kylie opened her mouth to tell her she was no threat, that it was all off with Jim.

But Sarah got in first. "Come on, we'd better get going."

They ate in Temple Bar for old times' sake.

Chapter 25

Kylie had massive doubts about going to the conference in Fiji. Of course, facing Jim and Carole topped the list. Being back in Neil's controlling vice-grip was a close second. And the fact that she no longer knew if she wanted to be a partner made a very creditable third reason not to go.

As the time came closer, and her leg looked as if it would sustain the journey and not offer a legitimate excuse to stay away, Kylie sought counsel from her immediate support circle.

"It seems that all my ambition just dwindled out of me while I was in hospital," she commented to

Sarah one evening when they were having a drink.

"What do you mean?" asked Sarah and swigged from her bottle of Budweiser.

Kylie tried to explain. "I don't have the same drive – before I could *see* myself as a partner, building a business, managing a team, making a difference. But now when I try to imagine it I see nothing – a big, blank nothing . . ."

"You've been out of work for three months," Sarah pointed out. "Once you're back in the thick of it, you'll feel different – your old zest, and ambition, will return, no doubt about it."

Her voice had all the certainty and confidence of a young lawyer who, other than a few boyfriend problems, had not yet experienced any of life's serious blows.

I was once just like you, Kylie wanted to tell her. *Ambition was the air in my lungs, I didn't understand people who didn't have goals. But the problem is that all my old goals seem to be totally unimportant in the face of what I've gone through these last few months.*

However, Sarah was entitled to her confident outlook on life, and Kylie didn't want to sound like a crusty old woman.

"Let me get another round," she said and shuffled to her feet.

"Why don't I –" Sarah began.

"No, I can manage it – really."

When she came back they talked about Frankie's imminent departure for Sydney.

"He's dying to get back to the business," said Kylie. "He's not been out of work this long in his entire life."

"How about your mum?"

"She's staying on – in fact, something tells me that I'll be leaving here before her. She really wants to get to know her grandchildren."

The conversation drifted onto Sarah's new boyfriend and Fiji wasn't mentioned again.

* * *

Annie was of a similar view to Sarah.

"It's easy to forget who you are when you don't have a job to define you," she stated. "I know it will be hard to go back – but you'll be glad you did. Take me, for example."

Annie had got herself a part-time job and declared it as the smartest move she'd made since Zack's birth.

"At least I can recognise who I am now," she said.

"How's Zack getting on in child care?" asked Kylie.

"Apparently, he's an absolute angel for them."

"That's great."

"He's still a devil at home, though," Annie's tone was ironic, "but at least I'm better able to cope with it now."

* * *

Liz was the next person Kylie asked for advice. They met for lunch in a small café off Grafton Street, and Kylie dutifully admired the stacks of photographs from Paris and London. God only knew how many hapless people Liz had pestered with instructions on how to operate her dysfunctional camera.

"The organisers of the conference in Fiji are pushing me for a commitment," said Kylie when Liz had finished talking about her travels. She'd received a message from Angela Bardman that morning asking if she had any special needs for her accommodation at the resort. "I just don't know –"

"You want to turn down a free trip to paradise?" Liz interrupted in disbelief. "Are you sure you didn't suffer some brain damage as a result of the accident?"

"Maybe I did." Kylie couldn't help giggling.

"So, let me get this straight." Liz searched her memory for everything she knew about the trip to Fiji. "You'll spend a week on an island, in a beach-facing bure, with activities like snorkelling and sailing. What exactly is it that you don't know about? Are you afraid that the hammock outside your bure will be too saggy?"

Sometimes Liz could be extremely funny and Kylie giggled again. "No. The problem isn't with the hammock —"

"Ah, so it's a man," Liz concluded quite correctly.

There were actually two men who were posing a problem, but Kylie didn't want to talk about Jim.

"My boss," she said. "Neil."

"Are you having an affair with him?" asked Liz.

"God, *no!*" Kylie shuddered at the thought. "It's just that I really dislike him. I didn't realise how much until I came here and didn't have to work for him any more. Now, the thought of going back, having him watch my every single move again — make his snide little remarks . . ."

Liz didn't say anything for a few minutes — in fact she seemed to be more interested in eating than offering an opinion. Eventually, she put down her fork and said, "I can tell by your body language that this man really repulses you."

"Yes." Kylie nodded. "'Repulse' is exactly the right word to describe how I feel."

"Has he ever . . ." Liz paused, her mouth pursing with distaste, "has he ever forced himself on you?"

"No," said Kylie. Then she shuddered again because somehow Liz had managed to hit the nail on the head. "Maybe I'm wrong – but I feel that he's biding his time."

It was the first time she had ever admitted that to anyone, even herself.

"Is there someone you can report him to?" asked Liz worriedly.

Kylie shook her head. "He's not just my boss – he's head of the whole firm now. Besides which, he hasn't actually *done* anything – I can't report him just because of the way he makes me *feel*."

Liz looked so troubled that Kylie started to feel bad.

She was full of the joys of her travels at the start of the lunch and now I've ruined it for her.

"Don't worry, Liz," she said brightly. "I'll just keep out of his way. Let's order some tea – and I'll take another look at those photos: there were so many of them that I didn't take it all in the first time."

Liz didn't need to be asked twice about the photos. Kylie found one of the three sisters that she really liked. With Liz and Rose on either side of Carmel's chair, they beamed at the camera, oblivious to the obstruction they were creating for the pedestrians of Oxford Street. Kylie asked Liz if she could get a copy of the photo.

* * *

While uncertainty about her career goals and repulsion at the thought of being back under Neil's thumb were significant enough deterrents in their own right, the thought of seeing Jim overshadowed them. When he was far away she could deny her feelings, but as soon as they were face-to-face she knew that she didn't have a hope. With only four people left on the programme, there was no way that she could avoid him. She'd have to go through classes, team activities and meals in close proximity with him. He would see her ungainly limp, and there would be pity in his eyes as they had a belated discussion about the accident. Then there was Carole; Kylie simply couldn't bear to see him with someone else.

It was Mags who saw through all her humming and hawing and confronted her.

"It's because you and Jim have fallen out," she stated out of the blue. They were watching TV together – they hadn't even been discussing Fiji.

The suddenness of her accusation pulled the carpet right out from under Kylie's feet.

"Excuse me?"

"You and Jim had a fight – that's the real reason you don't want to go."

For a few moments Kylie teetered on the brink of a lie. All of her self-protective instincts wanted to deny it and keep her feelings inside in the hope that they would eventually fizzle away. As soon as she gave them a voice they would be tangible and so much harder to ignore.

However, she acknowledged that she really needed to make a decision about the conference; she still hadn't answered Angela's message about her accommodation needs. Besides, if she and Mags wanted to have a meaningful friendship, they had to get through the impasse and talk about Jim, and Laura, openly.

"Yes." Her voice came out sounding squeaky and unnatural.

Mags's head nodded with the satisfaction of being right. "So was the argument before or after your accident?"

"Before," said Kylie and then added, "He doesn't know about the accident – Neil didn't tell him."

"If Neil didn't tell him, then why didn't *you*?"

It was a very valid question and Kylie had two equally valid reasons.

"Firstly, he thought it was over between us. Secondly, I'm pretty sure that he's seeing this other woman on the programme."

Part of her wished that Mags would exclaim, "Rubbish! That can't be true. You must call him straight away to put it right."

But she didn't. She obviously thought that Kylie's reasons were robust.

"Well, Kylie," she began, her expression earnest, "the fact is that you're going to have to face Jim at some point. It can either be on a tropical island or back in Sydney. It can be in front of a handful of people or the entire office. I know what I'd choose if it was me."

Chapter 26

"Have you got your passport?" asked Rose for the umpteenth time.

"Yes, Mum."

It was a replay of when Kylie had left Sydney but instead of Stephen stirring the pot, it was Mags.

"And you're sure that you don't have any sharp objects in your luggage?"

Rose looked so alarmed that Kylie had to tell her Mags was only joking.

"Flight EI168 to London Heathrow is now boarding."

They all started when they heard the

announcement.

"Well, that's me!" Kylie felt very emotional all of a sudden. She hugged Mags first. "Take care of yourself. And thanks for everything."

For showing me Dublin's pubs and clubs, for teaching me the ropes of pro bono work, for your friendship.

"You too – see you next March." Mags had booked a holiday Down Under and was looking forward to it immensely. "Good luck with Jim."

Kylie appreciated how hard it was for her friend to say that.

She turned to Rose. "Bye, Mum."

Tears seeped from her mother's eyes. She was staying on in Ireland for a few extra weeks to spend time with James and Ciara.

"Come on, Mum, don't cry. I'll see you at Christmas."

But even as she was telling Rose not to cry, Kylie felt tears trickle down her own face. It wasn't about leaving her mother for a few weeks. It was about leaving Dublin, the city that had changed her life in so many ways.

"Goodbye," she said one last time but it was not to Rose or Mags. It was to Liz, Ellen, Sarah, Ted, Amy, Jerry, Father Flanagan, Maura the nurse, Jane the physio, the nameless girl she'd met at the taxi rank and the countless others who were living testament to the warmth of the Irish.

* * *

The boat sliced through the crystal water and left a trail of rich white froth in its wake. Kylie held onto the railing at the bow where the salt water sprayed high into the air and fell to glisten on her face. Every now and then an island would erupt from the otherwise perfect Pacific Ocean. Some of the islands were established holiday resorts, others nothing more than uninhabited lumps of rock.

About ten minutes into the journey, two of the deck hands started to strum guitars and sing in native harmony.

"I love the Fijian music," said a middle-aged woman with a low-cut top. "I feel it right here." She slapped her deeply tanned bosom to indicate the location of her heart. "Which island are you going to?"

"Treasure," Kylie replied.

The woman bobbed her head with approval. "Are you on honeymoon?"

"No." Kylie smiled wryly. "I'm going to a conference."

Just saying it out loud brought back the

nervousness that had temporarily abated with the beautiful scenery and soft melodies. In a few hours, maybe even sooner, she would be face to face with Jim. In her mind she replayed their last kiss, in the car outside her apartment. She saw his face as he promised that soon they'd be together in the same city. He didn't know then that thanks to a petty argument, an unfortunate accident, poor communication and terrible timing, it would be almost four months before they set eyes on each other. Now he was with Carole. At least Kylie thought he was. There had been moments over the last few days when she'd acknowledged that she'd assumed a whole relationship just from the fact that Carole had answered his phone. Granted, it had been very early in the morning, but it was still a big assumption. Truth was, she wasn't sure of anything any more; only that she felt weak at the knees at the thought of seeing Jim after all this time.

The boat, after making a few stops at some of the other islands, eventually pulled up alongside Treasure's jetty.

"Don't work too hard!" the woman called after Kylie as she alighted.

In all, the boat was lighter by nine people when it headed off again. Giant barefooted men with tight curly hair hoisted the luggage onto their wide shoulders and carried it away. Kylie and the honeymooning couples were treated to a warm musical Fijian welcome before commencing the short walk to the resort.

While she waited to check in, Kylie glanced surreptitiously around the reception area. Large bold plants and the absence of any walls brought the outside in. Her eyes scanned the fat-cushioned cane lounges and she breathed a sigh of relief when she didn't see anyone she recognised.

It was a short tree-lined walk to her bure with its traditional thatched roof.

A king-sized bed dominated the bedroom, its covers turned down, an exotic red flower on one of the pillows. Over on the table there was a basket of fruit along with a bottle of champagne and a welcoming note. In Treasure Island everyone was on honeymoon.

White sand, flecked with coral, came right up to the shuttered French doors. Kylie took its silent invitation, slipped off her shoes and followed it down to the water. There, she lifted her sarong and waded in until the clear green-blue sea was up to her knees. Tiny fish in an array of stunning colours darted around her legs as the dropping sun smeared orange across the horizon.

Liz had been dead right when she had said that

this was a free trip to paradise.

Pre-dinner drinks were scheduled for seven. Kylie resisted the urge to climb into the beautifully turned-down bed and started to get ready. The journey was by far the most ambitious thing she'd attempted since the accident. On the plane she had to forsake sleep for regular walks up and down the aisle.

"Don't sit still for longer than thirty minutes," Jane had warned her. "Otherwise you'll cramp up badly."

The wait in LA was long and the seats in the transfer lounge scarce.

Now, Kylie's leg was sending sharp stabs of pain up through her body, telling her it couldn't take much more.

She slipped on her dress, black with a deep V-neck and a wide sweep of material at the end. Mags had been with her in Brown Thomas when she'd forked out an insane amount of money for it.

"Walk towards me again," Mags had said, then, with brutal honesty, remarked, "All that extra material at the end definitely makes your limp less obvious."

Kylie gathered her hair in a loose bunch of curls and, on impulse, she took the red flower from the pillow and pinned it behind her ear. She was as ready as she would ever be. She didn't want to be late: the last thing she needed was a hobbled grand entrance.

She asked one of the staff at the main bar where she should go.

"Ah," his teeth were startling white in his dark face, "drinks for the MFJ party are not in any ordinary place tonight."

He led her across the outdoor restaurant and along a short boardwalk. It ended in a generous balcony that seemed to be suspended in mid-air. Lanterns hung from the canopied roof and Kylie heard the sound of soft waves from below. She leaned over the balustrade and looked down on the water as it lapped gently against the ghostly sand.

"Can I get madam a cocktail, perhaps?" the barman asked.

"Yes, please."

"A menu –" he began.

"No," she looked up to smile, "I'll have whatever you recommend."

He was pleased to get a carte blanche and gave her a beam of his white teeth before heading back to the main bar. As she watched him cross the restaurant, he stopped to speak briefly with a full-figured woman. It was Angela in a splendid but predictably red dress.

Angela was a little puffed when she reached Kylie, but she seemed genuinely delighted to see her.

"It's so good to see you!" She squeezed her plump arms around Kylie in a very surprising hug. "I was so worried when Neil told me about the accident. And don't worry about what you've missed on the course – I've kept all the assignments open for you."

"Thanks," said a bemused Kylie.

"How was the journey?"

"Hard." Kylie's hand unconsciously touched her aching leg. "I'm feeling the strain of it now."

Angela was concerned. "Shall I ask for a seat?"

Kylie shook her head. "This spectacular setting isn't made for sitting down . . ."

She trailed off as she saw the others cross the restaurant. Carole wore an elegant white dress and a sleek hairdo. And there was Jim, head and shoulders over Oliver and Neil, his profile forbidding even in the distance. They came down the boardwalk two abreast, with Neil and Oliver to the front.

"Kylie!" Oliver smacked a kiss on her cheek. "Hello, stranger – like the flower – very Fijian!"

"I stole it from the bed," she admitted.

She felt Neil's beady eyes assessing, and no doubt disapproving of, the flower in her hair.

"Hello, Neil."

"Kylie. You look – well."

He hitched his glasses higher up his nose and the familiar gesture made Kylie even more tense.

She brushed aside his compliment with a vague, "Thanks."

Then, after a quick no-love-lost hello to Carole, there was only Jim left to greet. He looked very handsome in a dark dinner suit and stark white shirt; however, when she looked into his eyes they showed nothing: no sign of their stolen time together in Dublin, the short-lived long-distance relationship that had followed or the way it had all ended.

Even his voice was devoid of any kind of emotion.

"Hello, Kylie."

"Hi."

"How are you?"

Somehow or other she summoned up a half-witty response. "As they say in Dublin, I'm *grand.*"

It was the barman who saved her from the excruciating awkwardness.

"Your cocktail, madam."

Kylie gave him a relieved smile of thanks as she took the flamboyant concoction from his tray. It caught the imagination of the others and the barman left with an order for cocktails all round.

When everyone was armed with a drink, Neil gave them a pep talk on the week ahead.

"The first few days of the conference will be a refresher on the Partnership Act, and we will look at some of the practicalities of running a partnership. An area close to my heart, I will personally deliver the training." He stopped to adjust his glasses. "We will finish at noon on Wednesday, and there will be a team sailing activity in the afternoon. On Thursday, Angela will go back to the core leadership qualities and help you examine your progress since last May. On Friday you will be free to do as you wish."

"When do we find out about the partnership?" asked Oliver, his expression keen.

"The selection committee will meet next week," Neil replied. "Leadership qualities, communication skills, client development and billable hours will be the criteria used to make a recommendation to the board. Anything else you want to ask?"

He seemed taken aback when he got a second question.

"Who is on the selection committee?"

Neil was curt. "I'm afraid that's confidential."

Oliver didn't take the hint. "Will the decision process be documented?"

"Yes," Neil barely contained a sigh of annoyance, "but, again, any documentation will remain confidential and the partners' decision will be final."

Kylie had learned years ago that Neil had a fundamental dislike for questions: they challenged his control. Oliver, who had never worked for him directly, would get the picture soon enough.

The head waiter appeared and told them their meal was ready. Kylie held back as the others moved towards the boardwalk. She followed, a discreet distance behind, her leg dragging. It was killing her by now.

* * *

The game was up much sooner than she expected.

"Why are you limping?" asked Jim before she even had the chance to sit down at the table.

All conversation stopped. Kylie was conscious of Neil's frown, but she was damned if she was going to carry on any further with this silly cover-up.

"I broke it," she said and pulled out her chair. She couldn't help wincing as she sat down.

She was dimly aware of the stunned reaction of the others but it was Jim she focused on. He frowned across at her as if she had committed some heinous crime.

"What happened?"

"I fell under a car – a four-wheel drive, to be more precise."

"Ouch!" Oliver grimaced at the thought. "You must have been laid up for some time."

"Yes," Neil cut in, "but she's almost fully recovered now. Right, who wants to choose the wine?"

For the rest of the meal Neil continued to jump in with a change of subject whenever the conversation veered towards the accident, and Kylie wondered if the others found his behaviour as bizarre as she did.

It seemed so, because as soon as Neil excused himself to go to the Gents', Oliver asked, "What's with him tonight? He's like a cat on hot bricks."

"He's always like that." Kylie shrugged. She caught the eye of the barman and he came straight to her side.

"Yes, madam?" he asked with a flash of his brilliant white teeth.

"Can we have some more wine for the table, please?"

"It will be my pleasure to get a beautiful wine for the beautiful lady."

His flirting was a welcome change to Neil's prickliness and Jim's moody stares. The wine he chose was indeed beautiful and Kylie drank it far too quickly.

When Neil returned, the conversation became strictly business and it was so unriveting that Kylie concentrated her energies on making sure they didn't run out of wine again. It turned out that she and the barman made a good team. He chose and uncorked the bottles; she tasted and complimented him on his choice.

In the end she was the first to call it a night.

"I'm stuffed," she said to no one in particular. "It was a long journey." She gripped the table and forced her reluctant leg to bear her weight. "I'll see you all in the morning."

"Do you need any help to get back to your bure?" asked Angela.

"No, thanks," she said, injecting a chirpiness into her voice to show them she was fine, just fine. Not hurting. Not drunk. And most definitely not broken-hearted. "It's just around the corner. Goodnight."

Once out of the restaurant, the whole façade came crumbling down and tears filled her eyes. How on earth was she going to get through the week? Neil was even more unbearable than she remembered. Jim was colder than she had ever imagined. And her leg . . .

It was all hopeless, just hopeless.

"Kylie!" she heard from behind. "Wait up!"

Oh no! Not now.

She blinked the tears away just as Jim's hand grasped her arm.

"I just want to know one thing," he said, his voice stone hard. "When did the accident happen?"

She focused her eyes on his feet. "It's water under

the bridge –" she began.

But he insisted. "Just tell me when, Kylie."

"September the thirteenth." She kept her eyes steadfastly down.

The significance of the timing softened his voice. "Why didn't you tell me about it?"

Kylie was too drunk and too sore to do justice to an answer. She felt herself sway along with the gentle island breeze.

"Jim, I'm too tired to go into it now. I just need to get back to my bure – go to bed –"

He must have seen that she was at the very end of her endurance because he dropped it.

"Which one is your bure?" he asked.

"Down there," she pointed. "Number two."

Suddenly her feet were swept from under her.

"Jim, put me down! *Put me down!*"

"You're ready to collapse." His eyes stared ahead as he strode down the pathway. "Why did you refuse Angela's offer of help?"

"Because –"

But he cut her off. "Because you're totally and utterly obstinate, that's why."

He deposited her outside the bure and stated, "You owe me one big explanation, Kylie Horgan."

She smoothed her dress down. "Tomorrow," she promised unsteadily.

He stared down at her, his face dark, his eyes fathomless.

Finally he nodded, "Tomorrow."

Then he was gone into the Fijian night with its rustling trees and twinkling stars.

* * *

Jet lag, a vicious hangover and the ins-and-outs of partnership law were a hideous combination. Despite her throbbing head, Kylie sat upright in her seat because she knew that Neil was watching. Closely. The only mercy was that her leg had appreciated the eight hours' rest and was feeling much better.

Neil's attention to detail made him a good teacher. He covered everything from the basic to the complex. He provided relevant examples. His only flaw was that he didn't allow much opportunity for questions.

"Exhausting, isn't it?" commented Oliver on one of the strictly timed coffee breaks.

"Yeah," she grimaced, "and having tasted every white wine on the menu last night doesn't help one little bit."

Her recollection of the night before was a little blurred. She knew Jim had been angry but how angry she wasn't sure. She knew he had cared enough to want an explanation but, again, she wasn't sure how much. Only one thing *was* for sure: a snatched five minutes during one of the breaks would not be enough. Any discussion would have to wait until the end of the day.

Now Oliver beckoned her towards one of the poolside tables. "Let's sit over there."

Bronzed bodies lounged around the stunning aqua pool. Kylie sat down amongst them and ignored the urge to submerge her aching head in the cool water.

"Wouldn't it be great to just jump in?" said Oliver, echoing her thoughts.

"Yeah."

They soaked in the sun and sipped their coffees for a short while.

Then Oliver said, "I was hoping you could give me some pointers with Neil."

She squinted across at him and waited for him to continue.

"I get the distinct feeling that Neil doesn't like me and, with only three partnerships up for grabs, I can't help but feel that I'll be the casualty."

Kylie didn't tell him that she didn't yet know if she wanted a partnership and it was quite possible that there would be no competition for him.

"Neil is hard to work with," she said. "He's a

control freak – he wants to have a say over every little decision. So, all that I can suggest is that you consult with him as much as possible over the next few days – bow to his opinion – and don't ask so many challenging questions."

Oliver looked thoughtful. "I know that Brent was a beast in many ways, but I think I preferred him to Neil."

Kylie was surprised to realise that she did too.

"Obviously, the scandal with Claudine seriously undermined Brent's position as managing partner," Oliver continued, "and he was forced to resign before it became public knowledge."

Kylie spluttered on her coffee. "*What?*"

"You haven't heard?" Oliver raised his eyebrows. "It's meant to be all hush-hush, but it's the secret that everybody knows. Brent resigned because Claudine is suing the ass off him."

"For unfair dismissal?"

He shook his head. "No – for child support."

Kylie nearly fell off her seat. "Are you saying that Brent is Ethan's father?"

"Yes . . . that's, of course, if the rumours are true."

There was no question in Kylie's mind that the rumours were true for suddenly everything made perfect sense. It explained why Claudine disliked

Brent so intensely; for seven years she had continued to work in MFJ while he refused to acknowledge their child. Brent must have *hated* having her around. Ethan's accident would have provided the first decent opportunity to get rid of her, and Neil, his lackey, had facilitated her dismissal.

"It's just me and Mum," Ethan had said that day at the hospital.

Kylie could only conclude that Claudine's family had ostracised her for having a child out of wedlock.

Just then Angela fluttered over to tell them it was time to reconvene.

Claudine didn't want me involved because she knew it would damage my chances on the programme, thought Kylie as she returned to the classroom. *I hope she takes Brent to the cleaners!*

* * *

"This afternoon we're going to do some role-play," Neil announced when they returned to the room.

From the awkward look about him, Kylie guessed that the idea had originated from Angela.

He cleared his throat before he continued. "The scenario is as follows. The four of you are partners in a firm. It has been a difficult year and, as result, there is a question mark over whether you should run this year's graduate recruitment programme. Jim and Carole: you want to run the programme because you feel that to pull out would send a damaging message to the market – maybe with the effect of making business even worse." Neil then turned his bespectacled eyes to Kylie and Oliver. "You two are in fundamental disagreement. You're worried that you won't have enough work to keep the graduates busy and you're concerned about incurring unnecessary costs . . ."

Neil looked over to Angela as if to say, "*What happens now?*" and she smoothly stepped into organisational mode.

"Kylie and Oliver, you can sit over there," she pointed to the far side of the room, "Jim and Carole – this side of the room, please. Now, the object of this exercise is to reach a unanimous decision – that is, you must do your level best to persuade the others to your point of view."

Kylie and Oliver dutifully moved to the other side of the room.

"Thank goodness the afternoon won't be as dreary as the morning," Kylie commented sotto voce.

"You just like to play actress," replied Oliver with a grin.

"You have half an hour," Neil called out once they were seated.

"Time Nazi," muttered Kylie and Oliver laughed. "Better get down to business," she went on, becoming serious under Neil's suspicious glare. "If the other two are worried about the market, then I suggest we address that concern first."

Oliver agreed. "We need to convey a strong message to the universities and to our existing staff. We want them to see that our firm doesn't shy away from difficult decisions, that we are focused on the bottom line and that even though we are not recruiting this year, we expect to have a strong graduate intake next year."

They used the rest of the allotted time to prepare an internal and external communication package. While Oliver played around with the final wording, Kylie secretly studied Jim and Carole. He was the note-taker. Every now and then he would stop writing to consult with Carole. Kylie watched his body language very closely.

They're just colleagues, she realised. *Nothing more – I was wrong.*

She wanted to rush across the room to explain that it had all been a terrible misunderstanding. But even though in her heart it may have been the right time, it most certainly wasn't the right place.

Somehow, she would have to wait.

* * *

That night, dinner was a traditional buffet-style Fijian feast. While they ate, they were entertained by native music and dance. The dancers threw spears of fire through the black starry night as their song, a celebration of battle and life, soared.

Many times throughout the day Kylie's eyes had glanced fleetingly off Jim's. Now, as the music reached a fierce crescendo, her eyes were drawn to him once more. He nodded. It was time for her "big explanation".

She quietly slipped away from the table and he caught up with her at approximately the same place as the night before.

"Let's go down to the beach," he said and they walked past her bure down onto the fine white sand.

Kylie tucked her long flowing skirt around her knees as she sat down. Jim sat next to her. He was close, so very close that it was hard not to reach out to touch him.

"I was saying 'sorry' when it happened," she began, "sorry for that silly argument we had over the phone – sorry for being jealous of Carole –" She stopped. It was all such a mess, it was difficult to find a starting point. She tried again. "I had the word texted on my phone – *sorry* – all ready to send, when I saw Jerry. I was petrified of him ever since that day he terrified me in the clinic – I didn't know that all he wanted was to say 'sorry' too – I thought he was going to attack me – I backed up until I was on the very edge of the kerb – then, I lost my balance ..."

Her voice faded away and the lapping waves took over the conversation. Jim was looking down into the sand, as if it was some kind of TV screen that enabled him to visualise what had happened.

"How long were you in hospital?" he asked after some time.

"Two months in all – I was unconscious for the first week –"

He looked up, shocked. "Did you have head injuries as well?"

"No – it was a fat embolism lodged in my brain – a complication from the broken bone –"

He shook his head as if he couldn't believe what she was telling him. "Why didn't you – or anyone else – tell me what had happened?"

"Neil told Mags that he'd pass on the message," Kylie explained, "but he didn't. Of course, I didn't realise it at first – not until I saw all your email messages in my inbox –"

"But I left you text messages as well," he cut across her, "and voicemails."

"My phone, including the SIM card, was smashed to bits," she told him. "And I did call you when I realised that you didn't know. It was very early in the morning in Auckland – Carole answered –"

"She didn't tell me you called," he said.

"That's because I hung up straight away – I thought that you and her were an item."

He took a moment to think. When he spoke again his voice was very quiet.

"Carole and I had many early starts – some nights we didn't get to bed at all – but it was hard work, nothing else. And, just for the record, I don't find her attractive –"

"I can see that now," said Kylie with an uneven sigh. Inside, she couldn't help berating herself for jumping to the wrong conclusion yet again. Had she any faith in Jim, or in Jerry, things would have turned out very differently.

"You find it hard to take even the smallest gamble, don't you?" Jim remarked rather suddenly.

She looked at him warily. "What do you mean?"

"I mean trust," he said, meeting her eyes with a full-on stare. "Sometimes you have to go out on a limb – take a gamble that someone really does love you –"

Kylie felt her heart miss a beat. Was he talking about love generally or specifically? Was he talking past tense or present?

"Geoff, my ex —" she started to say.

"I'm not your ex, Kylie," he said firmly. "I would never abuse your trust — so don't tar me with the same brush . . ."

He was right, absolutely right, but the real question was whether this was all too late.

"I'm prepared to take a gamble now," she whispered as she bravely held his gaze. "To try again with you . . . that's if you want to . . ."

For a horrible moment she thought he would say no. Not a muscle moved on his face. But then, just as her heart started to plummet, he leaned forward. His lips met hers in a soft kiss.

"Of course I want to."

They were both so caught up in the moment that it didn't occur to them that there might be someone watching. Just as they started to kiss again, a shadowy figure left the dark cover of the coconut trees and returned to the main path.

* * *

The next morning, Kylie was so on air that she couldn't even start to disguise it. She simply couldn't stop sneaking glances in Jim's direction and was equally unable to suppress her smile.

While Neil droned on through case law and precedents, Kylie thought about the night before. Eventually they had left the beach and returned to her bure where Jim had told her, quite specifically, that he loved her.

"Since when?" she asked, coy all of a sudden.

"Since the night you walked in pink-cheeked and scraggily-haired to the programme launch." He looked down on her with teasing eyes, "I knew straight away that you had *High Potential.*"

"Very funny."

"Or maybe it was when you scowled at me so ferociously the day you got pulled over for speeding . . ."

That day on the freeway seemed like a lifetime ago, and Kylie was reminded of a question that she had been meaning to ask for quite some time.

"By the way, you never told me what you said to that police officer to get me off."

"I told him that the Wallabies had already trounced the Irish at the weekend and he was obliged to give me – and you, being of Irish descent – a break."

"You mean you two had a yarn about the rugby while I was left stewing at the car?" she asked incredulously.

"That's right," he said and started to kiss her again.

The time for talking was over.

Much later on, when Kylie's body was curled into his and they were on the verge of falling asleep, she whispered, "I love you too, Jim."

Now, she risked another look in his direction. He winked at her and she beamed him another smile. She felt so happy that she could burst.

In retrospect, she should have known that Neil would notice that something was going on between them. And that he would disapprove.

* * *

Neil, being the sort he was, bided his time. It was Wednesday afternoon, while they were out sailing, that he made his move. After a lazy lunch at sea, washed down with a few glasses of champagne, Kylie's guard was down. Jim was in deep discussion with the skipper and the others were chatting idly amongst themselves when she went below deck.

In the bathroom she reapplied her sunscreen and fixed her windswept hair into a tighter ponytail. When she came out she didn't see Neil lurking to the side.

"Kylie! A word, please."

She stopped dead. She knew at once what he wanted a "word" about.

"This fling you're having with Jim is a big mistake . . ."

Slowly, she turned to face him. "That is absolutely none of your business, Neil."

"I beg to differ." He took a step closer. "I've invested a lot in your career – office romances don't work –"

"I can assure you that this is much more than an office romance," she said haughtily.

"That's what you think."

"That's what I know . . . Jim loves me and I love him."

Neil's face contorted into an ugly scowl. "You don't know the meaning of love."

She caught a strong whiff of alcohol from his breath. Neil, always so carefully in control of himself, seemed to be drunk.

"Let's go back upstairs," she said in a lighter voice. "People will be wondering where we are."

Her suggestion fell on deaf ears.

"All these years I've nurtured your career," he slurred.

"And I very much appreciate all you've done –"

But there was no appeasing him. "If I'd known you were such an easy lay, I would have screwed you early on and not bothered pushing you up the ranks."

His lewdness turned her stomach.

If I stay calm, he'll stay calm, she told herself.

"Don't say that – you don't mean it – now let's go back to the others."

Again, he was deaf to the voice of reason. He took another step closer and, her back right up against the bathroom door, she realised she was in big trouble.

"Let me pass," she ordered.

His thin-lipped mouth descended towards her.

He's going to kiss me, she thought in blind panic. *I'm trapped – I've nowhere to go – no kerb to jump off.*

She turned her face away but his hand gripped her chin and forced it back.

"Stop it," she implored him. "You're drunk – don't do this!"

His mouth came a fraction closer and she could see the pockmarked pores around his jaw.

"No, Neil," she cried, trying to shake herself from his vice-like grip. "*No!*"

Just as she thought it was all over, his head jerked dramatically back.

"What the –" he exclaimed, a pained expression on his face.

"Get away from her!" she heard Jim thunder.

Neil's slim frame was no match for Jim's brawn

and, like a rag-doll, he went flying across the room.

Jim eased Kylie away from the rigid door. "Are you OK?"

She wasn't but nodded dazedly.

"Did he . . ." Jim couldn't bring himself to complete the question.

"No . . . you got here on time . . . just on time."

"You'll pay for this," said Neil, scrambling to his feet. "Both of you."

Jim ignored him as he guided Kylie gently towards the stairwell.

"Go up to the deck," he said. "Put on a brave face and I'll be up in a minute —"

Still in a daze, she ascended the narrow carpeted stairs. At the top she paused and strained to decipher the voices from below.

"You'll pay —" Neil began again.

Jim spoke over him. "No, *you'll* pay, Neil. I want your immediate resignation."

"You're crazy — I'm the boss —"

Jim cut him off once more. "I'll personally drag you through every court in the country — I will not let you get away with this . . ."

Kylie didn't need to hear any more. She never wanted to lay eyes on Neil Gatwood again and she knew she could rely on Jim to make it so.

Chapter 27

"I do!" bellowed Stephen.

"It's not a building site, Stevo," someone shouted from the back and the crowd tittered.

The service was being held down on the beach, and heckling from the guests was part and parcel of the relaxed atmosphere.

Tamsin's affirmation was much softer and Kylie couldn't help but smile. She was the total opposite of Stephen: petite, gentle and more than a little vague. However, no one could deny that they worked wonderfully together and their wedding day was a truly happy event for all.

Kylie's eyes momentarily left the couple to scan the fifty or so guests that formed a semicircle around them. Of course, there was the usual gang of neighbours and friends. Alexander looked very suave and Russian in a black suit. Jean was unashamedly wiping away tears. Annie stood close to her mother, Zack stuck to her leg like some trendy accessory.

Then there was the Irish contingent. Liz, looking totally rapt at the experience of attending such a "bohemian" wedding ceremony, was standing close to Alexander, who she had declared was "a very dashing man". Carmel, the wheels of her chair sunk into the sand, had a look of quiet achievement on her face. It had been a phenomenal journey but she had managed it well enough with Liz's assistance.

"The world suddenly seems very accessible," she had told Kylie on their arrival at Sydney airport.

Last of the Irish delegation was Ellen with Paul, James and Ciara. Ellen's RSVP had surprised Kylie the most.

"I'm not at all adventurous," Ellen had admitted on one of their regular phone calls. "I know my life is boring but I like it that way."

Still, here she was, and Kylie knew her life well enough by now to appreciate the effort it had taken, including Paul's locum, pulling the children out of school and passports all round.

The celebrant declared the couple man and wife, and the guests clapped and cheered as Stephen bent to kiss Tamsin. Kylie felt Jim's hand on the small of her back and she looked up to smile at him. With his white shirt opened at the collar, he looked relaxed and totally at ease. Ten months had passed since she'd first introduced him to the family, and now it was as if he had always been around.

A lot had happened, both personally and professionally, in those ten months. She and Jim had moved to a modest-sized house in Sydney's North Shore. They were so ridiculously happy that Kylie often stopped to do a reality check. Somehow she had found a man who not only didn't mind her mess, but on occasion *cleaned it up*. Who agreed that alarm clocks were evil and insisted that she be woken with a gentle morning kiss. Who had proved to her time and time again that he would not let her down. This all on top of being extraordinarily handsome and clever.

After Neil's sudden resignation, Meredith Allen had been unanimously voted in as managing partner, the first female to hold the position. Meredith had never supported the competitive foundations of the High Potential programme, and she'd made a strong recommendation to the board that all remaining four contestants be offered partnership. Her recommendation was sanctioned. In addition, her strong views on work-life balance and community service were bringing about a very distinct cultural change in the firm and were at the core of Kylie's decision to accept the partnership.

Kylie was back in regular contact with Claudine but wasn't able to convince her to return to her old job.

"You must think I was mad to stay in MFJ all those years with Brent refusing to acknowledge me or Ethan," she'd said when Kylie made the job offer, "but I was terrified to lose my income, even in the short while it would take to find another job. We were hand to mouth – the loss of one week's pay would have put us on the streets. Now that I've finally got that bastard where it hurts the most – his money – I can take some time to find the right job."

Kylie had heard that David was working in a small country practice. She'd made a few unreciprocated attempts at contact but had eventually accepted that he wanted to be left alone.

Life was domestic bliss for Oliver and Isobel, who both had babies on the way. Carole was more condescending than ever now that she was a partner, but Kylie had learned to tolerate her. Only just, though.

Kylie glanced over to Rose, who seemed to be

clapping harder than everyone else. Her mother had every reason to be happy. It was her son's wedding day. Her dearest friends were there to share in her happiness, as were her long-lost sisters, who were at home on this South Sydney beach as much as their own Velvet Strand. And Ellen, the baby she had left behind, was in the midst of everyone, where she belonged. In many ways, this was Rose's day as much as it was Stephen's.

Kylie came back to the present as Jim's arm tightened around her waist.

"OK?" he asked.

She smiled again.

"Yes."

THE END

THE END

If you enjoyed reading *High Potential*, don't miss out on Ber Carroll's other novel *Executive Affair*, also published by Poolbeg.com

Here is a sneak preview of the first chapter . . .

Chapter 1

Executive Affair

It was one of those Friday nights in Dublin where it seemed as if the whole population was seeking solace from the approaching winter in the crowded pubs. The noise inside Maguire's was deafening. People shouted over each other to be heard. Everybody seemed to have so much to say.

Amtech employees were shoulder to shoulder as they packed the limited floor space. Maguire's, only three doors down from their Ballsbridge plant, was a compulsory stop on the way home from work. Claire was jammed into a corner, surrounded by the newly formed Oracle Upgrade Project Team. It seemed like a good idea to come to Maguire's after their first meeting that afternoon. Reality was that very little team bonding could be done with the overwhelming noise.

Claire saw Susan and Margaret come in and waved at them across the bar, using sign language to indicate she would catch up with them later. Michael was having an intense conversation over to her left. His pint of Guinness was hardly touched as he talked through the project plan with another team member. She tried to make eye contact with him to see if he wanted another pint. He seemed to be oblivious to her presence so she squeezed her way to the bar to order a solitary vodka.

On later reflection, she realised that Michael had become more remote and preoccupied as the evening progressed. She remembered trying to engage him in conversation, talking to the others in the group when he gave monosyllabic answers. More images – kissing him, holding his hand – all without registering his lukewarm response. It was all very obvious with the wisdom of hindsight and without the glow of several vodkas.

She had no idea something was wrong until they were walking home. She was babbling about Paris. They were going there for Christmas. He was walking very fast, holding her hand firmly, and she struggled to keep up with him.

"We need to book our tickets . . . we should get up early tomorrow to do it . . ." she said breathlessly. When he stopped suddenly, she bumped into him, giggling.

"I don't think Paris is a good idea . . ." he said quietly.

She giggled again at his serious expression. "Stop being funny . . . we really need to get our act together or all the flights will be booked out . . . Christmas is a very busy time."

"Claire . . . look . . . I don't know how to say this . . ."

"Say what?" she asked with mild curiosity.

"I don't think we should see each other any more . . ."

"Are you joking?" she asked sharply. "Because if you are, I'm not finding it very amusing."

"I'm sorry . . . I'm not joking . . . it's not anything you've done . . . it's just me," he said awkwardly, playing with her fingers as he spoke.

She stared at him in shock, taking a few seconds to absorb the awfulness of what he was saying.

"You want to break up with me?" she asked stupidly, pulling her hand from his grasp, stepping back from his closeness.

"Yes . . . look, we've been together for three years and the writing's on the wall . . . marriage and kids. I'm not ready for that. I want some fun before I settle down . . ." His voice trailed off, his eyes focused downwards, away from the hurt on her face.

Another few seconds of silence.

He's serious. He's leaving me.

"Is there someone else?"

She didn't expect a positive answer to the pathetic question.

3

"I have met someone. Her name is Karen . . . but it's very casual." His voice sounded foreign with insincerity.

More silence, then thankfully anger came to her assistance.

"Well, that's very nice for you. I'd hate to think of you alone without a girlfriend."

"There's no need to be bitchy."

"I think there is . . . I think that I have some excellent reasons to be a bitch."

"I was hoping we could stay friends . . ."

"Oh, for God's sake, don't give me that 'friends' bull-shit!" She was vaguely aware that she was shouting.

"Look, we still work for the same company. I thought it would be easier for both of us if we were on speaking terms . . . but, if this is how you want it . . ."

"Don't you try that . . . it's the way *you* want it, not me . . . you know what?" She glared at him. "I hope you are sure of what you're doing because I really think you're throwing away something special . . . see you around and all that crap!"

Her steps were quick and frantic as she walked away. She turned her ankle, cursed and looked around to see if he was watching. She saw only his back as he strode in the opposite direction. She was at least ten minutes' walk from home and she was suddenly aware that the residential street was deserted and badly lit. She opened her mouth to yell at him to come back but realised he was too far away to hear.

4

She reached the flat and let herself in. She didn't turn on the lights, making her way to the bedroom from the streetlight outside. It was a tiny place; she and Fiona had squeezed themselves into it for three years. Claire hadn't bothered to look for a new flatmate when Fiona went to Sydney last year. It seemed pointless when Michael spent so much time there. She sat on the side of the bed and turned on the lamp. His aftershave was on the dresser. His things were all over the flat. She would have to collect them tomorrow, put them in a box.

It's over . . . it's really over . . . but it can't be . . . not after three years . . . not in ten minutes . . . but he's got a girlfriend . . . Karen. He was meeting her behind my back . . . how could he do that? How could I not know he was doing it? When did he meet her? Does she know about me? Does she know that he slept here last night?

* * *

She couldn't find her swipe card to get in. She stood in the cold, her frozen fingers searching through her handbag. It wasn't in there. She would have to wait until someone else came along. She hoped it wouldn't be someone that she knew, someone that she would have to talk to. It turned out to be Mark, her boss.

"You're a security risk, Claire . . . you're always losing that thing." He was only half joking.

She was glad he wasn't in a good mood. He was too preoccupied to ask her about her weekend.

She took the stairs, knowing she wouldn't be able to stand up to the closer scrutiny she might get from Mark in the lift. Most of the workforce were in transit – hanging coats, making coffee, gossiping. She had no choice but to mumble a response to the numerous cheerful "Good mornings" that were bestowed en route to her desk. Margaret and John were huddled around Susan at her desk. They cupped their coffee mugs fervently with both hands, as if trying to extract some energy that would get them through the long week ahead.

Shrugging off her jacket, she switched on her PC, staring impatiently at the screen as she waited for the machine to start up. She typed her password furiously, ignoring the well-established ritual of having a chat with her colleagues before starting the working day. She saw them looking at each other with raised eyebrows, their conversation dying. She could feel their curious looks turn in her direction. She made sure her face had a look of intense concentration that nobody could dare interrupt.

Susan waited a polite thirty minutes before sitting, uninvited, on Claire's visitor's seat.

"Had a good weekend?" she asked conversationally.

"It was OK. How about you?"

"Yeah, it was good, but it just went too quickly. I can't believe it's Monday again."

Claire kept typing, hoping she would go away.

"You seem extraordinarily busy this morning," Susan commented.

"Yes, I am. I need to put some financials together for a tender response that's due today . . ."

"Anything I can help you with?"

"No, I just need to concentrate . . ."

"OK, I can take a hint – talk to you later." Susan went back to her desk.

Claire wasn't brave enough to go down to Michael's office to see if he was there. Her phone taunted her all morning to call his extension. She even picked it up once but put it back down when she remembered it wasn't possible to have a private conversation in the open-plan office. The memory of his face, the unarguable resolve, the unmistakable lack of emotion, should have been enough to make her accept it was over. But she couldn't help thinking that if he rang today, there was still some hope of forgiving him. She had thought the same all day Saturday and Sunday. The only phone call she had received over the weekend was from her mother. She didn't tell her what had happened.

"Do you want to grab some lunch with me?" Susan was back, determined to find out what was wrong.

Claire was prepared for her. "No, I can't. I still haven't finished this."

"Is everything OK? You don't seem yourself today"

"Everything's fine . . . or at least it would be if I could get this done."

"Do you want me to bring you back some lunch?"

Claire didn't feel like eating. "Yeah, thanks. Just pick

me up a sandwich, anything will do . . ."

It was a relief to leave at six thirty. Her head was throbbing from the harsh glare of the computer screen. Engrossed in her work, she had had an ironically productive day, clearing most of her backlog. She had almost managed to keep thoughts of the weekend at bay. Now, as she left, the piercing cold stung her face and images came crashing into her consciousness. It was dark already, a severe frost glistening on the footpath. A miserable evening, matching her mood perfectly.

* * *

She struggled through the week. Michael didn't call. His only attempt at communication was an email, inviting her to the next project meeting. She didn't answer it. It was Mark who forced the issue.

"Aren't you coming to this meeting?" he asked, stopping by her desk on his way.

"I sort of forgot about it . . ." She reddened when she heard how lame her excuse sounded.

"Well, it's not too late – walk down with me."

She hesitated before getting up.

"I didn't know that you were going," she said.

"I asked Michael to invite me to the first few meetings so I can keep abreast of what's going on. This is the most important step forward that we've had in Finance since I joined Amtech. I want to make sure I can at least bluff about it when I need to."

She couldn't help laughing with him.

All the others were there, chatting while they waited. She was glad she had Mark to walk in with.

"OK, let's start," said Michael. "Thanks to everyone for coming along. We'll try to keep this under an hour – I appreciate how busy you all are." He looked and sounded relaxed. "As you all know, the first stage of the plan is the payables module. We've picked this because our current processes in that area are weak. We've already established, at our meeting last week, that we'll get an immediate benefit from implementing the module. I want to have a go at agreeing the roll-out schedule today." He made comfortable eye contact with each of the team members. Claire looked away when his eyes met with hers.

"I'd like to see Ireland first on the list. The project is being driven from here, after all," Mark said, briefly looking at Claire for her agreement. "How long would it take to get it up and running?"

"My best guess is three months, maybe four," Michael answered confidently. "We'd have a full complement of people on site to work on any glitches."

"Any suggestions for the next country after Ireland?" Mark asked. "Claire?"

"Um . . ." She could see him looking at her suspiciously when she reddened for the second time that day. "I dunno . . . maybe Australia . . . they are a medium-sized subsidiary, not too big or too small. And there's no language barriers."

9

After the meeting, she and Mark walked up the stairs together.

"You seemed preoccupied in there," he remarked.

"Yes, I was."

"Is there something I should know?"

"Can you take me off this project?" she blurted, stopping on the stairs.

"Why? Has something happened between you and Michael?" he asked, his voice suddenly kind.

"It's too close for me to talk about, Mark. I'll tell you at some point – just for now I need to get off the project."

"OK, I'll stand in for you in the interim."

She gave him a grateful smile.

* * *

Friday came with painful slowness and she was faced with being alone with her thoughts for the weekend.

"Are you coming to Maguire's with us?" Susan had her jacket on.

"Thanks, Sue, but I can't. I need to get up early tomorrow morning. I'm going to come to work to catch up on a few things." Working was a better alternative to being alone in the flat, looking at the box she had filled with his things. She had spent too much time already trying to figure out how she was going to return them to him.

"Come on! A drink will do you good. It will cheer you up. You can go home after one . . . that's not such a big deal, is it?" Margaret had joined Susan, bag on shoulder, lipstick gleaming, ready to leave.

"I . . ." Claire tried to resist but relented due to their jointly formidable expressions. "OK so – just one, though."

Just like the previous Friday evening, Maguire's was buzzing with the high-spirited working population. Margaret expertly negotiated their way through the crowds, keeping an experienced eye out until some seats were available.

Claire drank quickly, keeping out of the conversation, anxious to get home before they started to interrogate her. She had her jacket in her hand, ready to leave, when Susan slammed another drink in front of her.

"Susan, I have to go home. I can't drink this . . . have it yourself." She pushed it away, standing up with purpose.

"Relax, for God's sake . . . it's Friday night," Susan said, pushing it back.

Not wanting to appear churlish, Claire sat down again, drinking obediently.

They had trapped her. Like a well-trained relay team, they ran to the bar each time she was ready to leave.

"Michael's dumped me," Claire divulged, several rounds later.

"We guessed. Look, it's an awful thing to happen but you're better off without him."

Claire didn't expect Susan's clumsy hug and spilt some of her drink down her front. When they stopped

11

laughing, she asked, "Why am I better off?"

"He was too . . . well . . . boring." Margaret said and immediately looked as if she regretted being so honest.

"Yeah, he was," Susan agreed. "That would have annoyed the hell out of you if you had got married. There are much more interesting men than Michael out there . . . look around you." She leered at a group of males nearby to prove her point and earned a communal laugh.

"I never knew you thought that about him."

"I know – you'll probably never speak to us again if you get back together with him." Susan made a face.

"I'm never going to get back with him . . . he has a new girlfriend."

"What? Already? Get this girl another drink," Margaret barked at John, the office junior. He jumped up, too scared to question her authority even outside work.

"Do you know her?"

"No, Karen somebody." Claire covered her face with her hands. "How was I so stupid to get involved with somebody I work with?"

Her question was met with damning silence from the group. She became conscious of the roar of voices around them. It occurred to her that Michael might be amongst the crowd.

Margaret saw her looking around and asked, "Have you seen him since last weekend?"

"Just at the project meeting on Wednesday . . . he looked as if he hadn't a bother on him. I've barely moved from my desk in case I bump into him . . . sooner or later I'll run out of luck and I'll meet him . . . if not at work, then at some pub . . . he might even be with her . . ."

"Yeah, Dublin can be a small place and working with him doesn't help. Hopefully he'll have the good grace to keep a low profile."

"I don't think he sees the need to keep a low profile. He was perfectly calm on Wednesday whereas I was a mess. I've asked Mark to take me off the Oracle Upgrade Project. I know it's not very professional of me to let my personal life affect my business life, and Mark must think I'm pathetic, but I really can't face Michael."

"Don't worry about Mark – he'll understand where you're coming from," Susan said, finishing her drink and wondering where on earth John was.

Claire scanned the crowd again. Michael was tall, he would stand out. She only saw John as he returned with the drinks.

"I bet that Karen will dump him after a few weeks anyway, then he'll be a sorry bastard. But you're not to take him back when he comes crawling." This advice was from John, carrying four glasses in his big hands. Working closely with three females had made him an honorary girl and entitled him to give advice.

"I feel like running away." Claire didn't want to be always on edge like this, always looking for Michael in the crowd.

"Go on a holiday – when you come back you'll be able to cope better," Margaret suggested.

"I need more than a holiday . . . I need a permanent solution. There's no way I can continue to work at Amtech while he's there . . . and I'm sick of Dublin anyway."

"Claire, you're young, the world's at your feet – there's nothing stopping you from going to England or America," Margaret said, her voice now serious.

"You're my supervisor – you're not meant to be trying to get rid of me!"

"True, I forgot myself for a minute," Margaret laughed.

They put her in a taxi, their prolonged goodbyes and hugs annoying the impatient taxi-driver. She collected her mail on the way into the flat. Her credit-card statement, her phone bill and a letter from Fiona. From Australia. She hadn't seen Fiona since she moved to Sydney last year. Claire wondered now why she and Susan hadn't gone with her at the time.

She got into bed and opened the letter. It wasn't eloquent; it was basic and blunt, just like Fiona herself. There was a photograph enclosed, Fiona at Ayers Rock. The red earth looked fake. Fiona's brown hair was tied back in a pony-tail that was blowing in the wind. Her freckled face had an underlying tan. She was laughing.

Claire turned out the light, lying on her back, staring into the darkness.

I'll get through this. A few months and I'll feel normal

14

again. It's only been a week. Her eyes became accustomed to the dark. The faint light seeping in from under the blinds outlined the main objects in the room and it felt eerie and lonely. She turned the light back on, feeling foolish.

He's probably out with her tonight. Sooner or later I'm going to meet them together . . . he'll have his arm around her . . . I need to get out of Dublin ...

She had a fitful sleep, images of Fiona, Michael and outback Australia intertwined.

* * *

Whilst other software companies struggled with the harsh challenges that the nineties presented, Amtech Corporation had significantly increased its market share and was placed fifth largest company in the software industry. In the twenty years since its incorporation, there were just three years it had reported a loss. The company attributed its success to an aggressive acquisition policy and an impressive retention programme for its employees. It boasted a board of directors where the newest member had been on the board eight years.

Donald Skates had been the CEO for almost twelve years. He held the record for the longest-standing CEO in Silicon Valley, the fickle IT capital of the world. He had been with the company when it had only one hundred people. It was now the proud employer of ten thousand people across forty-nine countries. In some ways, the real secret of Amtech's success was Donald's conservative streak. It was a differentiating characteristic in an impulsive industry and it went down well with large Government and Financial Sector customers who felt safe in the hands of a risk-adverse company. Amtech resisted pressure to conform to other popular trends in IT, such as casual dress and flexitime, but it still made the grade as an Employer of Choice.

Amtech Ireland, the largest international subsidiary of Amtech Corporation, had a prime location in Ballsbridge, Dublin. It was the only location outside San Jose where software development, manufacturing and user manual translation were all performed on the same site. Reasonable labour costs, generous grants from the Irish government and easy access to Europe were some of the factors that had encouraged the board of directors to open the plant eight years earlier.

It was a modern building, the smooth white walls and black-tinted windows at odds with the old Georgian houses in the district. Most other IT companies in Dublin were located in the outer suburbs and Amtech had the choice of skilled employees due to its convenient location. The current headcount was approximately one thousand but the company expected the number to increase by thirty per cent when it released a significant upgrade to its main product, a human resources information system, at the end of the year.

Claire had been one of two graduate accountants employed in 1997, Susan was the other. In the four years she had progressed from trainee to financial accountant. Amtech Ireland was a fast-moving company and opportunities were frequent, even for those who weren't overly ambitious. Her progress had been easy, cushioned by competent colleagues and 'best practice' standards.

She liked her job and a sizeable portion of her social life was tied up with work. If her world had remained stable, it would never have occurred to her to use Amtech's international presence as a means of travelling overseas. She felt suddenly ashamed that it had taken a personal disaster to make her question the routine of her life.

When she went in on Monday, she turned a blind eye to her brimming in-tray and connected to the *Employee News* section of the Amtech homepage. She got into 'Vacant Positions' and was surprised by the number of roles advertised. There were roles in countries she didn't even recognise. She used the search function to select Finance Management positions only. Her search yielded three hits: two roles in San Jose and one in Sydney, Australia. She skimmed through the role descriptions, skills and qualifications for each. She knew before doing this that she would choose Sydney.

She felt nervous as she knocked on Mark's door. He beckoned her to enter when she opened the door slightly to see if he was free. His phone rang as she sat down and she studied his boyish face as she waited for him to finish. Only thirty years old, he was well-positioned on the corporate ladder but the undoubted stress that came with his position had left no visible marks on his smooth face. He had been Finance Director for two of the four years she had worked at Amtech Ireland. He was a popular boss with his staff, talented and sharp but with a healthy sense of humour.

"Miss Quinlan, what brings you to my office at such an early hour of the morning?" He grinned at her as he put the phone down.

"I've seen an internal advertisement for this role in Sydney that I want to talk to you about . . ." she said bluntly, putting a printout of the ad on his chaotic desk.

"Oh . . ." He seemed taken aback, the grin slipping from his face.

"Sorry, Mark, I should explain myself," she said as she recognised that she had started at the wrong place. "Look, you probably know by now that Michael and I have split up . . ."

He nodded.

"And, much as I try to be professional and not let it interfere with my job, the fact is that my world has turned upside-down and I don't have the ability to act as if nothing has happened when I see Michael at work."

"I understand," he nodded again. He sat back in his chair as he watched a variety of expressions chase across her face.

"So, either I leave Amtech and go to another company . . . or I see if Amtech are willing to transfer me . . . overseas," she concluded, relieved to notice that Mark was looking much more receptive than he was earlier. He picked up the role description to read.

"It's undoubtedly a good career move for you, Claire, a promotion," he stated, his tone matter-of-fact.

"I thought you would approve." She smiled to take the edge off the atmosphere. "What do you know about Amtech Australia?"

"Well, they are quite a bit smaller than Dublin, as it's obviously a sales and marketing subsidiary and not manufacturing like we are. I think they have about three hundred people. I don't know Dan Fielding, the Finance Director, personally but I have heard only positive things about him and the subsidiary."

"Good. So will you support me if I apply for the role?"

"Yes, I will. I don't want to lose you from our team here but this seems like the lesser of two evils. Send Dan your résumé . . . I have a call with Robert Pozos tomorrow and I'll mention it to him then," he answered, looking tired as he picked up his substantial pile of morning mail.

Robert Pozos, based in San Jose, was the Senior Vice-President of Finance and a member of the Board of Directors. Claire knew that he travelled extensively but she had never met him. He and Mark had a good relationship and they spoke weekly. Claire was confident that Mark would pave the way for her as much as he could. The rest would be up to her.

She went back to her desk but found it hard to concentrate so she wasted a few minutes surfing the net. She found a site on Bondi Beach and had difficulty suppressing a smile as she studied the vibrant pictures. Fiona lived close to Bondi.

* * *

She shut the door behind her and sat down before dialling the Sydney number. Her interview with Dan was at eight – she had five minutes to go. The screen came alive with the image of the room in Sydney. There was a long board table. The curtains were drawn to block out the sunlight. Her own image was in a small box on the bottom left of the screen. She self-consciously fixed her hair and when she saw how slow and obvious her movements were on screen, she reminded herself not to fidget throughout the interview. While she waited, she read through a copy of the résumé that she had sent to Dan. She looked up to see a blurred male figure move jerkily across the room until he was seated. It was hard to see his features but his hair was white. He was older than she expected.

"Good morning, Claire." His smile was friendly.

"Good evening, Dan."

"It's nice to meet you at last. Thanks for agreeing to this interview at such short notice."

"It's no problem. I'm very keen to pursue the opportunity and thank you for considering me," she said, making an early pitch to show her enthusiasm for the role.

"Claire, I'll start by giving you some background information on the position. The incumbent is leaving at the end of this week to take on a new role in San Jose, under Robert Pozos. We're looking for a good generalist, with proven operational ability in financial accounting, treasury, taxation and customer proposals." He paused deliberately to allow Claire to respond.

"Dan, I believe I can demonstrate effective skills in each of those areas. Tax may be a bit of a challenge, given that I am not familiar with the local legislation – however, income tax principles tend to be fairly standard in most countries these days."

Dan adjusted his position in his seat before speaking. She could see his lips move but it was a few moments before the sound of his voice reached her end.

"I agree, tax should not be an insurmountable problem. We have advertised the role externally. However, it is our preference to have an internal candidate over an external one. It would be a much smoother transition for us if we found an existing employee who would be familiar with Amtech's policies and procedures."

"Have you had many external applicants?" She hadn't considered the possibility of competition for the role she had set her heart on.

"Yes, but none of them jump out at me . . . Claire, I've

been through your résumé in detail and have talked to Robert Pozos about your role and performance in Dublin. I am not going to make this interview too laborious as I have a lot of positive and reliable information that most interviewers don't have about the candidate they are interviewing. So, why don't we just have a chat . . . you tell me about you and then I'll tell you about me."

Their chat lasted an hour.

When she turned off the video, she sat down to make some notes:

Four Direct Reports – Financial Accountant, Accounts Payable, Payroll, Credit Control.

General Manager – Steve Ryan.

Sales Director – Frank Williams.

HR Director – David Di Gregario.

20% growth in revenue over last year. Increased opportunities in outsourcing of Application Software Support.

External Auditors – average audit report at year end. Concerns with some balance sheet accruals and accounts payable controls.

* * *

Susan was walking along the corridor when Claire opened the door.

"So, that's where you've been all morning . . . Who did you have the video conference with?" she asked, peering into the room and obviously disappointed to find the video switched off.

"I can't really tell you at the moment, but all will be revealed soon. Do you want to come around for dinner and a glass of wine Saturday night?"

"Only if you tell me what's going on."

"With some luck, I'll have something to tell you by then. Prepare to be shocked."

Claire laughed as she left Susan in the agony of her natural nosiness.

* * *

On Saturday night she opened the door to Susan, whose face was red from the icy cold.

"Have I told you that you are a heartless bitch for leaving me in suspense like this?" Susan was bearing a paper-wrapped bottle that was very likely to be white wine.

"Yes, a number of times."

"Stop teasing me. Just tell me, please, before I die of curiosity!"

Claire laughed. "OK, I can't bear to keep it to myself any longer anyway. I'm going to Sydney," she said triumphantly.

"You're what?" Susan was flabbergasted. "How?"

"I applied for a Finance Manager's role there. It was advertised in *Employee News*. I had an interview with Dan Fielding on Wednesday and he called me yesterday to tell me that the job was mine, if I wanted it."

"Really?"

"Yes, really! I'm so *excited!* I'm going to *Sydney!*" She

did a little dance around the kitchen.

"Wow, you've knocked me for six. I didn't think you were serious about leaving Dublin . . . and all this since last week – you haven't wasted any time, I'll say that." Susan hadn't taken off her heavy winter coat. She still hung onto the bottle of wine. She did indeed look stunned.

"I just want to get away from Michael and every-body who knew us as a couple. I know that this might seem a drastic solution but it's perfect. The change will be good for me. It's time for a revolution, Susan!"

"I'm really happy for you but I'm going to be so lonely without you here. And I'll be so jealous of you and Fiona having fun in the sun while I'm stuck at home in the miserable cold . . . where's your damn wine-bottle opener?"

They opened the wine. "Mark and Margaret are going to miss you. We're *all* going to miss you," Susan said, moving cushions to make herself comfortable on the sofa.

"Mark's been great. It's his connections that got me the job. He's pretty close to Robert Pozos and it seems that Robert gave Dan Fielding all the assurances he needed. There was very little for me to do."

"Are they going to pay your relocation costs?"

"They'll pay my airfare and my living expenses for the first four weeks."

"That's a pretty good deal." Susan was looking thoughtful as she swirled the wine in her glass. "You know, I get the impression that Mark might be extending his responsibility outside Ireland and he'll be happy to have you as someone to rely on in Australia."

"What do you mean? Do you know something I don't?"

"Mark's been on a lot of calls with the US lately and he's more involved in the Oracle Upgrade than you would expect. It wouldn't surprise me if they made Ireland some kind of international headquarters for IT and Finance with Mark at the helm. The upgrade will bring a lot of synergies – it would make sense to centralise some of the functions. It would be great if I could somehow wangle a business trip to Sydney . . . I know I'm fantasising, but indulge me."

The wine was an Australian Chardonnay, from the Hunter Valley.

"I'm going to go there," Claire declared, pointing at the wine bottle.

"Where?"

"The Hunter Valley. I remember Fiona saying it's just outside Sydney."

"I bet you and Fiona have been making all sorts of cosy plans for the good times you're going to have without me," Susan retorted with pretend jealousy.

"Actually, I haven't told her yet that I'm coming . . . let's call her now and tell her to start planning my arrival party!"

Grinning, she dialled the number without more ado. It rang and then she heard a muffled "Hello?".

"Fi, it's me, Claire!" she shouted unnecessarily in her excitement.

"Claire?" Fiona sounded disorientated and Claire remembered the time difference. It was early morning in Sydney.

"Oh, sorry, I didn't mean to get you out of bed. Guess what?" she squealed.

"What?" Fiona asked with a loud yawn.

"I'm coming to Sydney! I'm getting a transfer with Amtech! Isn't it great? Can I stay with you when I get there?"

"Of course you can. Hey, that's really great news … even worth waking me up for. When are you coming?" Fiona asked, sounding more sprightly.

"January, provided my business visa comes through by then."

"Hey, that's only a few weeks away!"

"As far as I'm concerned, the sooner the better! I can't wait to get out of here," Claire said, a hint of despair seeping into her tone.

"Why? Has something happened?" Fiona asked with immediate concern.

"Yes, but it's a long story and I don't want to ruin my good mood right now. Susan is here. She wants to talk to you."

Claire handed the phone to Susan who had been hovering impatiently. The three of them had been inseparable through their college years. It would be great to see Fiona again.